Sisters of the Shadows:
The Cagliostro Curse

BY THE SAME AUTHOR

Adaptations:
Judex (by Arthur Bernède & Louis Feuillade)
The Return of Judex (by Arthur Bernède & Louis Feuillade)

Fiction:
Shadows of the Opera: Retribution in Blood

Sisters of the Shadows:
The Cagliostro Curse

by
Rick Lai

A Black Coat Press Book

ISBN 978-1-61227-201-6. First Printing. October 2013. Published by Black
Coat Press, an imprint of Hollywood Comics.com, LLC, P.O. Box 17270, Enci-
no, CA 91416. All rights reserved. Except for review purposes, no part of this
book may be reproduced or transmitted in any form or by any means, electronic
or mechanical, including photocopying, recording, or by any information storage
and retrieval system, without permission in writing from the publisher. The stories and characters depicted in this novel are entirely fictional. Printed in the
United States of America.

Table of Contents

Introduction...7
Dr. Cerral's Patient 9
The Diary of Desolation...25
All Predators Great and Small..39
Urania's Babysitter 59
The Lady in the Black Gloves...63
Corridors of Deceit...89
Cut the Branch 111
Unseen Stratagems...129
Consequences of a Funeral..157
Kingdom of the Blind 173
Incident in the Boer War...209
The Last Vendetta 213
Afterword 229
Cast of Characters 237

Introduction

Rick Lai is bigger on the inside.

Rick first rose to pop culture prominence with his Wold Newton-style essays in pulp fanzines in the 1980s and '90s. He quickly became renowned for displaying an immense degree of knowledge, both deep and broad, in these articles, covering a dizzying array of characters and series from both Victorian literature and the American pulp era. The essays were "Wold Newton-style" in that they reconciled internal inconsistencies, created workable chronologies with reasonable explanations and logical principles, and sometimes drew on other sources, on the premise that the characters existed in a shared continuity.

It's this latter point—shared continuity—that really makes Rick's articles Wold Newtonian creative mythography essays rather than "mere" Sherlockian-like writings. Certainly they follow the Sherlockian tradition of treating their subjects as if they were real people, about whom we the readers are only getting half the story, or perhaps the full story, but distorted. But the scope of Rick's work, and his propensity to look beyond the canonical confines of a particular series to fuel his theories and explanations, demonstrates that he was clearly just as inspired by the universe-expanding work of Philip José Farmer as by the single-character essays to be found in the pages of *The Baker Street Journal* or various Doc Savage or pulp fanzines.

Of course, there have been others who have also followed Farmer's creatively mythological path, but Rick was one of the first, if not the first, both stylistically and substantively. Some of his essays are shared universe works without an explicit connection to Farmer's Wold Newton mythology. Others, such as his landmark "The Secret History of Captain Nemo," are unabashedly Wold Newtonian, expanding on Farmer's foundations, and indeed at times contradicting them, but always with respect for, and acknowledgment of, the inspiration.

Rick's essays have been collected by Altus Press in two volumes: *Rick Lai's Secret Histories: Daring Adventurers* (2008) and *Rick Lai's Secret Histories: Criminal Masterminds* (2009). Both are well worth seeking out.

Not a one trick pony, Rick is also a master fictional chronologist. While he has constructed many series or character chronologies, including Allan Quatermain, Doctor Fu-Manchu, and The Avenger, his masterworks are his *Chronology of Shadows: A Timeline of the Shadow's Exploits* (Altus Press, 2007) and *The Revised Complete Chronology of Bronze* (Altus Press, 2010). The Shadow pulp novels number more than 300, while the Doc Savage canon approaches 200, and Rick has read them all, putting the novels in the context of real historical events and providing logical explanations and speculations to resolve internal contradictions, thus creating realistic timelines for these two pulp heroes.

But lately Rick has not written so many creative mythography essays, or constructed so many timelines.

No, lately Rick has turned his pen to writing fiction. Or, perhaps I should phrase it as a question. Has Rick turned his pen to writing fiction? Or, has he lately discovered some treasure trove of historical documents and files, and made the connections between these and an international assortment of literature and films? Novels, short stories, and movies which are purportedly fiction, but in reality have encoded within them deep secrets and truths?

These tales, the worldwide sources for which are covered in Rick's afterword and cast of characters, are perfectly suited for the pages of the *Tales of the Shadowmen* anthologies edited by Jean-Marc and Randy Lofficier, and now Rick's own single-author collections, from Black Coat Press, a publisher renowned for bringing works of science fiction, fantasy, horror, mystery and pulp from France and other countries to the attention of English-speaking readers. The stories are mysteries within mysteries, connecting various seemingly disparate works, where even the characters themselves can be the conundrum—or the solution to one.

It is because of these connections which Rick concocted—or discovered?—that his tales are bigger than the words it takes to tell them, larger than the pages upon which they are printed.

They are, like Rick himself, bigger on the inside.

And as such, it would only be natural for Rick to next turn his attention to Arnould Galopin's space-and-time-traveling Doctor Omega!

Win Scott Eckert
Denver, Colorado
September 2013

Dr. Cerral's Patient

In his personal laboratory at the Countess Yalta Memorial Hospital, Dr. Anatole Cerral filled a syringe with curare. An injection of this South American poison would bring quick death to the recipient and leave the outward symptoms of heart failure. Dr. Cerral had never before contemplated murder, but a man would soon be arriving who threatened the surgeon's marriage and career. That individual was Victor Chupin, a private detective from Paris.

The Countess Yalta Memorial Hospital was located in Avignon. The institution was named after a wealthy Russian aristocrat celebrated in Parisian society. A decade earlier, the Countess had suffered an accident that resulted in the loss of one of her hands. She had died shortly after that misfortune, and her considerable wealth had been bequeathed to a young Frenchman. Rather than spent the money on selfish pleasures, the heir of the Countess had sought to honor her memory by financing the construction of a hospital. The principal function of this institution was to treat laborers who had lost limbs in industrial accidents.

In a private room at the hospital, a young female patient awoke screaming. Dr. Cerral was summoned from his private laboratory by an orderly. He spent the night calming the distraught girl.

"I dreamed that I was disciplining another student in the boarding school, Papa," murmured the girl. "God then punished me by destroying my hands."

The next afternoon, the disturbed girl was playing the piano in a room in the hospital. Her soft delicate hands swept deftly over the keyboard. As she played, a middle-aged woman with dark hair sang a cabaret song. When the song ended, the older woman motioned her accompanist to sit beside her on a nearby table. On its surface laid *Isis Unveiled* and *The Secret Doctrine*, two books by the occultist Helen Petrovna Blavatsky.

"Your father told me you again had a difficult night, but you have nothing to fear. You now have a new life... a new existence" asserted the middle-aged singer. "Let me show you your destiny."

The older woman took a pack of Tarot cards from her handbag. She proceeded to remove cards from the deck and place them on the table.

It was in June 1890 that Victor Chupin received a telegraph from his sister, Victoire. He had just returned to Paris after a difficult investigation that forced him to spend over three months in London. The message indicated that there was an urgency to discuss the status of her daughter. Chupin immediately settled his affairs in Paris and departed for Normandy.

Chupin was nearly 41 years old. He was a lean, short man with blonde hair. When he arrived at his sister's residence, he was greeted at the door by a slim athletic 16-year old boy.

"Victoire is in the kitchen making dinner," intoned Raoul d'Andresy.

The investigator critically scrutinized his young host. Chupin had always felt a tinge of resentment towards Raoul because of the crucial role that the boy had played in his sister's life. Victoire was five years older than Victor. They were the only children of Polyte Chupin, a pickpocket and a drunkard. Their father's intoxicated rages had caused her to flee the Chupin household when she was 14.

Like his father, young Victor had drifted into a life of crime. At the age of 18, Victor had become a member of the notorious Mascarot blackmail ring. When the gang was smashed by the famous M. Lecoq of the Sûreté in 1867, Victor had surrendered to the police. Rather than prosecute him, Lecoq had arranged for the young miscreant to become a protégé of the wealthy Champdoce family. They sponsored Chupin to become an apprentice to a private inquiry agent. As a reward for his assistance in solving the mystery of the Chalusse heirs in 1868, Chupin received sufficient capital to start his own detective agency.

After 12 years, Victor Chupin was running a sound and profitable business. Nevertheless, he was deeply dissatisfied with his life. He had lofty ambitions of expanding his agency into a nationwide venture that would become the French equivalent of the American Pinkertons. He just needed to solve a case that would give him the enormous publicity needed for his dreams to reach fruition.

Raoul d'Andresy had almost provided the means to achieve Chupin's hopes.

In 1880, Paris had been stunned by the theft of the Queen's Necklace, the property of the Count de Dreux-Soubise. This article of stolen property had enormous significance in French history. It had been purloined in 1785 as part of a complex swindle that severely damaged the reputation of Queen Marie-Antoinette. The original thieves had removed all the diamonds, but the intricate setting of the necklace had survived. The Dreux-Soubise family had arranged for new diamonds to be placed in the setting.

At the time of the robbery, Henriette d'Andresy had been living as a servant at the Dreux-Soubise residence with her six-year old son, Raoul. Due to the loss of the Queen's Necklace, the Dreux-Soubise family fell on financial hardship and discharged Henriette. A police investigation proved that Henriette d'Andresy was incapable of having committed the theft.

In the manner of C. Auguste Dupin in the Marie Roget case, Chupin had devoured the details of the investigation in the newspapers. And like his illustrious predecessor, he had come to a correct solution of the crime: the thief must have been young Raoul.

The question in Chupin's mind was whether the boy had perpetrated the crime as some sort of prank or as the accomplice of an adult. Chupin had located

Henriette and interviewed her. It became apparent to the astute sleuth that she was an honest woman in poor health. She clearly had no suspicion that her son was indeed the architect of this audacious crime. Chupin had thought it wise not to enlighten her about Raoul's thievery.

Chupin had also talked to Raoul, whom he pegged as a rude and obnoxious child. After leaving the apartment, he had continued to watch their dwelling. When Raoul had left the building, Chupin had followed him for a few blocks. The boy had met a woman, whose age was in the mid-thirties. She looked vaguely familiar to Chupin. Raoul had handed her an envelope. Once Chupin overheard her first name, he began to surmise her true identity. Raoul had called her Victoire. She was Chupin's long-lost older sister.

Chupin's subsequent queries had revealed his sister's sordid past. Under the alias of Victoire Tupin, she had once been arrested for transporting stolen goods and had served a year in prison. Victoire had never married, but that did not prevent her from giving birth to a daughter, Irene, in 1870. Four years later, she had been hired as nurse for the infant son of Théophraste Lupin and his wife, Henriette. Théophraste's son was now known as Raoul, but his real name was Arsène.

Chupin had wondered if his niece was the daughter of Théophraste Lupin. After an intense quarrel, rumored to concern an extra-marital affair, Théophraste and Henriette had separated. Henriette had resumed her maiden name of d'Andresy and kept the custody of their young son. Victoire was dismissed as Raoul's nurse. Chupin had concluded that Henriette had learned of a love affair between her husband and Victoire.

Chupin had a difficult choice to make. It became clear that Raoul had stolen the diamonds from the Queen's Necklace and was now passing them to Victoire. There could also be no doubt that Victoire was using her criminal contacts to convert the stones into hard currency. Chupin had a chance to gain national acclaim by solving the celebrated theft. But the only way to achieve this end would be to send his sister to prison.

In order to understand the consequences of his decision, Chupin decided to become reacquainted with his sister. One day, pretending that family ties were his sole motivation, he had knocked on his sister's door. Victoire gave him a cold reception. The investigator had no qualms about sacrificing his sister for his own personal glory, but an unexpected factor stayed his hand.

Chupin had developed a rapport with Irene.

His niece had bridged the gulf between Chupin and Victoire. Consequently, the detective had relinquished the opportunity to secure enormous publicity. Victoire had never realized that her brother knew of her role in the Queen's Necklace affair.

Through observing his sister, Chupin had deduced the true motive behind the robbery. The proceeds from the fencing of the diamonds were anonymously mailed to Raoul's mother. The naïve Henriette presumed that these funds were donations from a philanthropic source and had used the money to secure better lodging for herself.

Her new prosperity had softened Henriette's heart towards Victoire and she soon re-hired her. Both Victoire and Irene had come to live with Henriette and Raoul.

As the years passed, Chupin frequently visited Irene at Henriette's residence. He played the role of an indulgent uncle and often purchased gifts for his niece. She proved to be an excellent student during her elementary education. Irene possessed a love of literature and a gift for foreign languages. At the age of 13, she was already fluent in English. This achievement prompted Chupin to buy her several books by Charles Dickens. By the time she was 15, she was studying Spanish and Italian. She also had some skill as an artist. On the wall of his office, Chupin had framed a sketch that Irene had made when she was only 14. It was a portrait of himself. Her firm strong hands had captured his likeness perfectly.

Chupin's business often took him outside of Paris. One evening, in 1885, he had arrived at the d'Andresy residence. Chupin discovered, to his dismay that Irene had left for the College for Young Women, a boarding school in Provence. Victoire had explained that the school would give her daughter a better opportunity to pursue her interest in the foreign languages.

The following year, Henriette had died from natural causes. Victoire had taken charge of her employer's orphaned son, and the pair of them had moved to Normandy.

Irene had spent five years at the College for Young Women, until a monstrous series of events turned her into a patient at the Countess Yalta Memorial School.

Entering the kitchen, Chupin discovered his sister making a salad. She ceased her labors once Victor entered the room.

"I just returned from Avignon. Dr. Cerral refused to let me see Irene," said Victoire.

"Did he give any reason for this prohibition?"

"He simply stated that she had no wish to see me. He gave no further explanation."

"Cerral can't forbid your visit. Irene is still a minor. In fact, she won't reach her twentieth birthday until next month. You remain her legal guardian, Victoire."

"I tried to make that argument, but he would not listen."

"Did you threaten him to go to the authorities?"

"Such a threat would have been useless, Victor. The Avignon Police will do nothing to disturb Dr. Cerral. They feel indebted to him for his help with the College Girl Murders. I made a far worse threat."

"Which was?"

"I warned Cerral that you would be forced to pay him a visit."

At the *Tivoli* cabaret in Avignon, singer Mathilde Grévin entered the office of the nightclub's manager to discuss her status.

"I'm sorry, Mathilde, but you can longer be a star attraction at the show. We need to give top billing to a younger star. All that notoriety surrounding Teresa's enrollment in that damned boarding school has damaged your career."

"I have a new addition to my act that will change your mind." Mathilde unrolled the draft of a poster advertising her act.

After the manager read the poster, he just had one question for the singer.

"When will your accompanist be ready to start?"

On the train to Avignon, Chupin perused a letter that had been written to him by Irene in late 1885. She had sent it to him only a few months after her arrival at the College. The letter had ended with certain requests:

"When you have time, dearest uncle, you may wish to read Stowe's *Uncle Tom's Cabin* or Dana's *Two Years before the Mast.* You will find them just as enthralling as *Nicholas Nickleby.* I pray for you every night. Please pray for my soul every night, too."

Chupin often wondered if Irene had experienced a premonition of the cruel blow that fate had in store for her. From her letters, it appeared that she had prospered. A select elite of female students functioned as assistants to the headmistress, Madame Fourneau. Irene had joined that exclusive clique in late 1885. In 1889, she had been promoted to Fourneau's chief assistant. A year later, Irene nearly lost her life.

Fourneau had a son who suffered from asthma. His ill health prevented him from being sent to a boarding school for boys. He lived on the premises of the College. At 16, a bizarre idea had come into his head to become a modern Pygmalion. Rather than sculpt his vision of the perfect woman from clay, the boy had opted for a more grotesque ingredient: human flesh.

He had murdered five girls over a period of four months in order to obtain supplies for his ghastly handiwork. He was able to hide his atrocities by creating the impression that the girls had run away from the school. Irene was his sixth victim. The killer had knocked her unconscious and then had mutilated her hands. The headmistress, who had been unaware of her son's butchery, had discovered her murderous offspring and Irene's comatose body in the school's attic. The sudden revelation of her son's abominable crimes had caused her to expire from a fatal heart attack.

Irene surely would have bled to death in the attic if not for a fortuitous coincidence. A doctor had arrived at the College late that night. He had forced the janitor of the school to let his carriage inside the gates. The doctor and the janitor had then searched for the headmistress. Their quest had taken them to the attic. The killer had attacked the janitor with a knife, but the custodian had easily disarmed him. The doctor had found the dying Irene and taken her to his carriage which rushed to the Countess Yalta Memorial Hospital. The doctor was Anatole Cerral.

The newspapers had ruthlessly exploited the horrific events. They dubbed the killings the College Girl Murders. Although journalists had howled for the execution of the youthful maniac, he was eventually judged to be mentally incompetent to stand trial. He would probably spend the rest of his life in an asylum for the criminally insane. Many lurid stories had circulated about the College Girl Murders. It was often claimed that the killer's sixth victim had perished. One popular story was that the butchering youth had completely severed both of Irene's hands.

Chupin knew that the latter story was totally false. He had seen Irene at the hospital twice. The first time was in late January 1890 when she was still comatose. The second was a month later when she was awake, but in a state of delirium due to her terrible ordeal. On both instances, her hands had been wrapped in bandages. Shortly after his last visit, Chupin had embarked on the case that caused him to make a lengthy trip to England.

When the train arrived at Avignon, Chupin took a carriage to the Countess Yalta Memorial Hospital. He was able to secure an interview with Dr. Cerral in his private office.

During his previous visits to the hospital, Chupin had only had brief discussions with Cerral. He was a tall, thin man with black hair and a short beard. His hands were soft and delicate. Cerral had been a talented surgeon who left Avignon to work in Paris in 1871. He eventually secured a position at a medical school, but a controversial proposal concerning surgical procedures had led to his resignation in 1885. Chupin was unaware of the exact circumstances, but he had heard rumors that Cerral's critics had compared him to Moreau, the notorious vivisectionist. Returning to Avignon, Cerral had risen to a position of authority at the Countess Yalta Memorial Hospital. Chupin had only had brief meetings with him during his previous two visits because the surgeon had been occupied with other matters in the hospital.

After thanking Cerral once again for saving his niece's life, Chupin took a chair in front of the doctor's desk.

"You have expected this visit, Doctor, because of your altercation with my sister. Let me assure you that I am not acting in her interests. I am merely concerned with my niece's welfare. My sister and I have never been very close."

"You claim to have no strong bonds to your sister, then why are you so concerned about her daughter?" asked Cerral.

"Doctor, I am over 40 and unmarried. I doubt very much that I will ever be a husband. Bachelorhood suits me. I have always possessed a special kinship for Irene. Perhaps it is because I always harbored a foolish hope."

"I do not understand, Monsieur."

14

The detective noticed a photograph on the doctor's desk. It was of a middle-aged woman, five young girls and a boy. Victor gestured towards the photograph,

"You have a rather large family, doctor."

"The oldest girl is 22. My son is only six years old."

"Do any of them show an interest in becoming a doctor?"

"The girls have no desire to seek a vocation in the medical profession. I hope that young Alexandre may follow in my footsteps, but he is too young to make such a choice now. "

"Yet you would desire that he, too, become a doctor."

"I am conducting a line of research that will probably not reach fruition in my lifetime. The possibility that Alexandre could finish my work is highly attractive."

"I have established a small but profitable detective agency. I harbor the ambition of enlarging it to be a nationwide concern. I have capable assistants, but none of them could function as a possible successor. The thought that Irene might perhaps inherit my business has entered my mind. She is intelligent and perceptive. She may even possess managerial skills. Of course, I recognize that my idea may be naive. Irene had artistic aspirations. Most likely, she might want to be an artist or a writer. In light of her recent trauma, it is now extremely unlikely that she would ever find my line of work appealing."

"If you felt so close to your niece, then why did you concur in the decision to send her to boarding school?"

"I was not involved in that decision at all. If I had been consulted in the matter, I would have opposed it. Of course, I understand the reason for it."

"What is your understanding?"

"My niece wished to study at a school in Southern France because it would be more conducive to her mastering the Italian and Spanish languages."

"You are under a misapprehension, I'm afraid. Your niece was enrolled in that school for a far different reason. She was blamed for a theft."

"Theft? What nonsense are you mouthing, doctor?"

"I assure you that I am being quite serious. Madame Fourneau kept meticulous records. In 1885, she interviewed extensively the two ladies who brought Irene to the school."

"Was my sister one of these ladies?"

"No. The ladies were Henriette d'Andresy and the Countess de Dreux-Soubise. The Countess had visited the d'Andresy residence earlier. On that occasion, she was wearing a diamond brooch. After she left the house, she discovered that it was missing. She returned to the house and insisted that Henriette search the rooms of your sister and your niece. The brooch was found hidden under Irene's mattress. She was accused of stealing it."

"Did my niece offer any explanation as to how the brooch had gotten there?"

"Irene gave a rather intriguing theory: the brooch had been stolen by Raoul, Henriette's son. Your niece argued that he had temporarily hidden the brooch under her mattress planning to retrieve it later. Although Irene was warned that there would be serious consequences if she persisted in her denials, she refused to recant. Your sister declined to defend her. The Countess recommended that your niece be sent to the College as punishment. The headmistress of that institution had gone to convent school with the Countess and Henriette. Your niece was even registered with a false surname, Tupin."

"Did you say Lupin?"

"No, Tupin. I can see by your face that all this information comes as a shock. Do you believe the story that I have outlined?"

"Yes," stated Chupin bitterly.

"Do you feel that your niece was innocent?"

"Yes."

"May I ask your reasons?"

"Because I have a strong belief in my niece's character, and because I know Raoul's all too well."

The investigator reconstructed in his mind the probable significance of Cerral's revelations. Raoul must have hoped to repeat the success of his theft of the Queen's Necklace five years earlier. Victoire knew that the only way to protect Irene would be to expose Raoul. To pursue such a course would have made public both her and Raoul's involvement in the previous crime against the Dreux-Soubise family. Irene had been made a scapegoat in order to protect both her mother and her half-brother. Chupin reasoned that Henriette d'Andresy sincerely championed her son's innocence. He also concluded that Irene had no idea about her mother's role in the theft of the Queen's Necklace.

"I must be honest with you, Doctor. There is one thing that I can't explain." The detective reached into his briefcase and pulled out a packet of letters. "I do not understand why my niece never mentioned these events in any of her letters."

"May I see those letters?"

Chupin handed the letters to Cerral. The doctor untied them and read the letter at the top of the bundle. It was the same missive that Victor had been reading on the train.

"You may be correct, Monsieur Chupin, about your niece's potential as a detective. I wonder if Irene is as talented at discerning clues as she is as deliberately leaving them."

"Clues? Why did Irene leave clues?"

"In order to fool the censor. All of the mail that the students received or sent was read by an assistant of the headmistress. Irene would never have been allowed to write you the truth about her situation at the College. The individual responsible for censoring Irene's mail must have been ignorant of English literature."

"I do not understand, Doctor."

Irene mentioned three books in this letter, *Uncle Tom's Cabin*, *Two Years before the Mast* and *Nicholas Nickleby*. Have you read them?"

"Yes."

"The three books have radically different settings, but they all have something in common. Do you recall what that is?"

Victor paused before answering. "They all deal with physical beatings. Slaves are whipped in *Uncle Tom's Cabin*. Sailors are beaten in *Two Years before the Mast*. *Nicholas Nickleby* involves the flogging of boys in a boarding school."

"Your niece was in a boarding school similar to that portrayed by Dickens. The majority of the pupils were sent there because their families believed them to be guilty of crimes. Fourneau ran her school like a dictatorship. She had a tyrannical personality that must have sparked her son's madness. Corporal punishment was employed to maintain discipline."

"Doctor, you examined Irene. Was she ever beaten?"

"I regret that I must inform you that your niece has permanent scars on her back. She was beaten with a lash during her initial months in the school."

"But Irene accepted a position as one of Fourneau's student assistants!"

"Conformity is a convenient avenue of escape from constant persecution."

"Irene was later promoted to the position of chief student assistant. Did she try to mitigate the oppression?"

"By that time, your niece was a privileged member of the ruling regime. The chief assistant was responsible for censoring the mail and administering the floggings. "

"I can't conceive that Irene would be capable of such acts!"

"Did you ever know an individual who was once a decent person but then was compelled by duress to commit a sinful act? And then became a habitual sinner as a result of that one act."

"I once knew a man named Baptiste Mascarot. He was a blameless teacher of algebra and geometry until those he loved were in danger of perishing from starvation. Mascarot committed an act of extortion to gain money to feed them. He gradually evolved into the most dangerous blackmailer in Paris."

"Your niece embarked on a similar downward path the moment she became one of ruling circle of the College."

"I still find your assertions about Irene's conduct impossible to accept."

"Do you ever hear of a student whose name was Teresa Grévin?"

"Mademoiselle Grévin was the College Girl Murderer's fifth victim. She was slain the night before my niece was attacked." Chupin recalled the grisly details in the newspapers of Teresa's corpse after it was found by the Avignon Police. The throat had been slashed and the hands and feet had been removed. There had been further mutilations as well.

"Teresa was a virtuous girl of 18 years," continued Cerral. "It is my misfortune that I never met her during her lifetime. Unlike most of her fellow pupils, Teresa had never been accused of any crime. Her offense was her mere existence. Her mother, Mathilde Grévin, was a singer at the *Tivoli* cabaret in Avignon. She is now over 40, but she likes to pretend otherwise. The presence of a daughter of Teresa's age called that subterfuge into question. Mathilde simply wished to place Teresa away from prying eyes."

Chupin knew the *Tivoli*. Female entertainers there would generally lose their audience as they grew older unless they were either exceptionally talented or able to develop an unusual gimmick that generated publicity.

"What about Teresa's father? Did he not object to Teresa's enrollment in the College?"

"Mathilde had her daughter out of wedlock. Teresa's father was a former lover who left Avignon before she was born. He was totally unaware of her birth." Cerral paused for a brief moment. "You have probably wondered what prompted me to arrive at the College. Teresa wrote a letter to her mother and arranged for it to be posted outside the normal channels of the school."

"How did she engineer that feat?"

"She befriended a fellow student named Suzanne Noel. Teresa gave the letter to her. There was a workman who delivered firewood to the school. He had arranged a romantic rendezvous with Suzanne. As a favor to her, he posted the letter after he left the school's grounds. The letter revealed that Teresa was being persecuted to join the coterie that functioned as the school's enforcers. Teresa had not been flogged, but she had been warned that constant refusals could result in such a penalty. When Mathilde received the letter, she became distraught. Not only did she decide to remove her daughter from the school immediately, but Mathilde also wanted a doctor to perform an examination. Mathilde wanted to make sure Teresa had not been further abused. My assistance was enlisted to retrieve Teresa."

"Why did Mathilde come to you?"

"I had been a patron of the *Tivoli* early in her career. I hired a carriage and traveled with her to the College. I forced the janitor to open the gates and let us in. You know the rest, how I found your niece in the attic."

"Yes, and I will always be grateful for your heroic actions. What relevance does Teresa's letter have to my niece?"

"You probably assumed that it was Madame Fourneau who was persecuting your niece, but in fact she delegated much authority to her chief assistant. On her own volition, Irene was harassing Teresa."

"I can't believe that!"

Cerral reached into a drawer of his desk and pulled out a letter. "This is the letter, Monsieur Chupin. I will let you read it, but I must warn you that it concerns other unusual practices at the school besides the floggings."

Cerral handed his companion the letter. Chupin read it in silence for several minutes. When the sleuth had finished, he threw the letter on the desk in disgust.

"My Irene... Could she be that corrupt!" moaned Victor.

"Do not be so harsh in judging your niece, Monsieur Chupin. She was accused falsely of a crime and exiled to the equivalent of penitentiary. She was victimized in the same manner as Teresa. If Teresa had not been slain, she could easily have succumbed to the same temptations that ensnared your niece."

"I do not blame my niece. I blame myself."

"How could you be at fault?"

"I failed Irene. I styled myself to be a solver of mysteries, but I couldn't see the cries for help concealed in her letters."

"You had no reason to suspect that the letters had hidden meaning. If anyone failed Irene, it was her mother. Your sister refused to defend your daughter against the accusations made against her, and I suspect there are more complex motivations for her actions. "

"What are you hinting at, doctor?"

"Henriette d'Andresy died in 1886, one year after your daughter was enrolled in the College. The headmistress did not keep her pupils captive for mere spite. She was paid tuition by their relatives or guardians. After Henriette's death, there was nothing to prevent your sister from removing Irene from the College. Nevertheless, tuition to ensure her entrapment in that school continued to be paid for the next four years. I think you may know the man who authorized those payments. You mentioned his name earlier."

"Théophraste Lupin."

"Quite correct. I have been very honest with you, Monsieur Chupin; I expect reciprocity. Who is this Théophraste Lupin?"

"My sister may have told you that she's a widow living under her maiden name. She's lying. I can't prove this, but I have long suspected that Théophraste Lupin is Irene's real father. He is also the father of Raoul d'Andresy."

"Things are becoming clearer now, Monsieur Chupin. The father must have wished to protect his son from being exposed as a thief. Consequently, Théophraste Lupin paid to continue Irene's confinement. Your sister seems to have a stronger affection for her lover's son than for her own daughter."

Chupin wondered exactly what role Théophraste Lupin had played in Raoul's life. Most likely, he had assisted Victoire in disposing of the diamonds. The detective had never heard of any criminal named Lupin. Perhaps Théophraste Lupin was an alias, and Victoire's paramour was a swindler of the caliber of Ballmeyer, Lothaire Stepphun and John Clay.

"Now that we have had a frank discussion, Monsieur Chupin, I can explain my refusal to allow your sister to see Irene. In a physical sense, your niece is in excellent health. The bandages have been removed. With the exception of some

19

surgical scars near her wrists, her hands have healed perfectly. In fact, Irene has even been able to skillfully play a piano. "

"I was unaware that my niece has any musical aptitudes."

"She learned how to play the instrument during her five years at the College. Despite her failings as a human being, Madame Fourneau did have some talent as an educator. It is not your niece's physical state that worries me. It is her mental health. She has nightmares."

"She must be haunted by her memories of the College Girl Murderer."

"It is not the spirit of that deranged youth that troubles Irene. It is the guilt of her conduct as Fourneau's chief assistant. Irene can't live with the knowledge of how she tormented Teresa and other pupils at the College. Your niece views the defilement of her hands as a form of divine retribution. I could not allow a visit by Irene's mother to upset her. At the very least, it would add feelings of betrayal and resentment to her burdens."

"Will you at least permit me to see her?"

"Of course. I recognize that your only priority is Irene's well-being. She is in a therapy room practicing on her piano with Madame Grévin. "

"Teresa's mother? Is it wise for the two of them to be together?"

"Madame Grévin has no desire to revenge herself on Irene. In fact, Mathilde views herself as Irene's benefactor. I must alert you to the fact that Irene has become emotionally dependent on both Mathilde and me. Your niece has adopted us both as substitute parents."

Cerral and Chupin left the office. They went to a room on another floor of the hospital. As the detective entered the room, he heard music. He saw a slender attractive girl with dark hair playing at the piano. It was Irene. Next to her was a middle-aged woman, whom he guessed was Mathilde Grévin. She was singing a ballad. Victor noticed the table with books by Madame Blavatsky. Tarot cards were arranged in a pattern next to the volumes. Irene immediately stopped playing and rose from the piano. Mathilde stopped her singing.

"Uncle Victor!" Irene cried with joy. She then stopped and raised her soft delicate hands. She stared at them and then began to cry. "You had better leave, Monsieur Chupin. Irene no longer exists. She died in the attic of a boarding school." She then rushed towards Mathilde and embraced her. "Mama, have Papa tell this man to leave! I won't be ready for my debut!" she screamed.

Cerral responded by motioning Chupin to leave. The doctor suggested that they confer in his office. When they reach it, Cerral closed the door.

"I am afraid that your visit has only upset your niece further. I don't think your continued presence will benefit her."

"On the contrary, doctor, I must insist that you discharge my niece immediately!"

"On what grounds do you make this demand?"

20

"You have not been totally truthful with me. I may have failed to utilize my deductive powers to help my niece five years ago, but I won't make that mistake now."

"I give you my word that I have not lied to you."

"But you omitted certain key facts. For example, there is the nature of my daughter's operation. You did not simply repair her hands. Irene's slender hands were strong and firm. They are now soft and delicate. Her original hands had been completely severed. You somehow grafted new hands onto her body!"

"Would you rather that I had equipped with ugly appendages like hooks?"

"It would have been better for my niece's sanity if you had. You gave her the hands of Teresa Grévin. Her hands were soft and delicate, like your own. I suspected from your remarks that Teresa was your daughter."

"I swear to you that I did not know that they were Teresa's hands when I performed the operation. I found those hands lying in a darkened corner of the attic. I assumed they were Irene's. That monstrous killer must have severed Teresa's hands in order to practice for his later attack on your niece. I did not realize the truth until I saw Irene's reactions when I removed the bandages. She is an artist with a flair for anatomical detail. She recognized the hands as Teresa's."

"And that knowledge consumed her very being, drove her mad. She came to the absurd conclusion that the spirit of Teresa now lives within her. She must want to expunge her guilt by becoming another person. Mathilde Grévin has fed on that delusion for her own selfish purposes. She has augmented my niece's hallucination with occult paraphernalia such as Tarot cards and the absurd doctrines of Blavatsky. She is an aging cabaret performer who needs a gimmick to revive her act. She intends for my niece to be her accompanist on the stage. Mathilde will present her as the sole surviving victim of the College Girl Murderer. And she will also portray herself as Irene's rescuer, no doubt. I will not allow my niece to be exploited in such a manner!"

"I had no choice but to acquiesce in Mathilde's stratagem. She threatens to reveal my illicit affair with her to my wife. I was foolish enough to write her letters and send her my picture years ago."

"Your domestic problems are your own affair, doctor. You must immediately discharge my niece or I will bring you up on charges to the medical authorities!"

"The operation was a success!"

"It still was an operation not accepted by the medical community. You made my niece the subject of a potentially dangerous operation without the permission of her family. Do you agree to my demand?"

"Yes."

"I have another demand. I want Teresa's letter."

"Why?"

"I intend to burn it in order to prevent it from ever being used to blacken my niece's reputation."

"Please, don't do such a thing. It is the only memento that I have of my deceased daughter."

"I'm afraid that I must insist."

Cerral reached inside his desk and retrieved the letter. He handed it to Chupin, who turned his back on the doctor in order to light a match over an ashtray.

Cerral reached inside one of the side pockets of his jacket. He began to grasp the syringe filled with curare. It would be easy to stab the needle into Chupin's neck. The doctor could then arrange to have the detective's death diagnosed as a heart attack. Cerral had hoped that he would never need to perform this action. It was regrettable that his plan to misdirect Victor without technically lying had failed.

"If you destroy this letter, you are no better than Mascarot," he finally said to Victor.

Chupin then extinguished the match. He turned around to face Cerral. The doctor withdrew his hand from his pocket. It was empty.

"You are correct in your diagnosis, doctor. I return Teresa's letter to you." Victor handed the letter back to Cerral.

"Do you still intend to bring charges before the medical authorities?"

"No. I will use cleaner methods to gain custody of my niece. She is still only 19, and her mother is still her legal guardian. I should be able to gain a court order."

"You can't intend to return Irene to her mother!"

"No. Victoire is unfit to raise her, but I will coerce my sister to make me her guardian. "

"There is no necessity for you to involve your sister. Mathilde will be leaving the hospital in about an hour. I will discharge Irene in your custody afterwards. "

"What will you do to avert Mathilde's threats to tell your wife about your affair?"

"As you said earlier, Monsieur, my domestic bliss is my own concern."
Irene left the hospital in Chupin's carriage. The detective realized that he would need to place his niece in a nursing home to regain her mental health. He thought it best to remove her as far as possible from the rumors surrounding the College Girl Murders. During his recent stay in England, he learned of the recent opening of an excellent nursing home known as the Sanctuary Club. He would secret Irene there.

Chupin recognized that the history of her misdeeds as a disciplinarian at the College could eventually become public knowledge. Besides Teresa's letter, there must be police records. There also were over a score of former pupils at who must have been cognizant of his niece's activities. If his niece ever returned to France, it would have to be under another name.

Chupin also intended to have a stern talk with his sister after enrolling Irene in the Sanctuary Club. Considering his knowledge of the Queen's Necklace affair of 1880, he possessed a powerful tool of persuasion. He would permit Victoire to see Irene on condition that his sister would prevent any contact between her daughter and Raoul. Victor Chupin bitterly blamed Théophraste Lupin's son for all of his niece's problems.

After spending a month with Irene at the Sanctuary Club, Victor returned to Paris. He searched for any news of Dr. Anatole Cerral. He read a report that the surgeon had given evidence at the inquest into the recent death of Mathilde Grévin in Avignon. She had died in the Countess Yalta Memorial Hospital on the day after Irene's departure.

The Coroner's verdict was that she died of a heart attack.

The Diary of Desolation

September 7, 1893: I am known as Sabine Absalom. My mission is about
to begin. This quest of vengeance unites my past and my future. My ancestors
destroyed supernatural monsters. Soon I shall terminate the existence of a monster in human form. No moral qualms can deter me. I must become an executioner. My quarry is a murderess responsible for the death of five innocent girls
in Provence. Her name is Irene Chupin.

This creature is descended from a family of criminals. Her parents were
Victoire Chupin, a common whore, and Lothaire Stepphun, the self-styled
Prince of Thieves. 13 years ago, Lothaire was guilty of a horrible crime. Pretending to be in love with my mother, he treacherously lured her into a fatal ambush. My gallant mother survived long enough to make her way back to our
house in the Rue St. Claude. I was then only 10 years old. My sister Josine, two
years older, has always been stronger than me. As I cried hysterically, my mother asked Leonard, our family servitor, to remove me from the room. My mother
then told Josine the full story of the trap that Lothaire had prepared for her.
When my mother had finished, Leonard brought me back into her presence. My
dying mother insisted Josine swear two oaths, an oath of life and an oath of
death. First, Josine promised to protect me always from all harm. Second, Josine
swore to extinguish the life of Lothaire and all his tribe. Lothaire had two children, a girl, Irene, and a boy, Arsène. As a young child of six years, he had assisted his father in baiting the trap for my mother. Arsène's crimes pale before
the abominations of his decadent sister.

Outsiders know me by the surname of Absalom. This alias is a cloak to
hide my true ancestry. Absalom is an anagram of Balsamo. Like my mother, I
am descended from Joseph Balsamo, the heroic savant called Count Cagliostro.
Many false stories have circulated about my illustrious forebear. In reality, he
courageously protected humanity from the Cult of the Undead. His daughter and
grandson also became hunters of vampires. Cagliostro's great-granddaughter,
my mother, emulated him in a different way. As Alexandre Dumas recorded,
Cagliostro was the secret instigator of the French Revolution. His agents in advancing the cause of liberty were the Masonic secret societies. My mother
joined a different fraternity, the Black Coats. Both my sister and I have imitated
our mother. We are members of the Black Coats.

Our organization is frequently defamed as an association of criminals.
Technically our critics are correct. We frequently violate laws in pursuit of our
goals. We have no choice. The current social order is corrupt. It is ruled by a
hypocritical alliance of aristocrats and factory owners. The Black Coats are dedicated to correcting this great wrong. We will eventually overthrow the ex-

ploitive hierarchy that governs society. Our efforts will lead to a new era of enlightenment.

Due to the Black Coats, I'm pursuing a career in medicine. The Black Coats are strong advocates of feminine equality. Women of great accomplishments swell our ranks. Marguerite Chavain is a celebrated botanist Jillian Blake is a philanthropist who seeks to better the livelihood of impoverished orphans.

My patron in the Black Coats is Urania Caber, a brilliant woman with degrees in medicine and astronomy. Although she prefers to use her mother's maiden name professionally, Dr. Caber's real family name is Moriarty. She's the daughter of the mathematical genius whom Sherlock Holmes murdered in Switzerland.

Urania's late father was the true power behind the Black Coats. The nominal head of our association is a Corsican recluse. Generally this eccentric individual is referred to as the All-Father. Many conflicting rumors circulate about him. It has been said that The All-Father sometimes uses the name of Saladin. Others argue that the All-Father and Saladin are separate people. This Corsican is just a figurehead with little say in the daily operations of the Black Coats. With Professor Moriarty's death, the reins of power have fallen to a retired British army officer, Sebastian Moran. Nevertheless, the Moriarty family has maintained its prominence in the Black Coats. Both Urania and her uncle Noel are influential figures. Noel's wife, Catarina, was responsible for recruiting my sister into the Black Coats.

When my mother perished in 1880, my sister and I became financially dependent on our guardian, a wealthy American named Arthur Gordon. Although he never acknowledged us as his children, Josine and I have long suspected that Gordon was really our father. Together with my sister, I was enrolled in the Marie Gilbert School in Paris under our real names. We were in the care of benevolent nuns, but my transition was difficult. My sister is a natural born leader. She was immediately popular with the other girls at school. Being shy and awkward, I was not so fortunate. The other girls often poked fun at me. My sister ignored my plight until I confronted her. Had not she promised mother to be my protector? Embracing me, my sister apologized for neglecting her oath. I remember her words: "I'll always watch over you, my little sister."

Josine quickly evolved into my protector. If any other girl mistreated me, Josine would retaliate with an appropriate prank. Occasionally Josine was disciplined by the principal, Sister Daphne. My sister weathered all these punishments for the next three years. In 1883, there was a student, Raquel Valencia, the proud niece of the Spanish ambassador. She taunted me by saying I walked like a frog. Josine struck back by hiding such an amphibian in Raquel's bed. The haughty Spaniard screamed in fear.

I have no sympathy for Raquel, but the aftermath of her deserved chastisement led to my separation from Josine. Sister Daphne realized my sister was responsible for the incident. The principal merely lectured my sister and gave her extra chores to do. The matter should have ended there, but Raquel wouldn't let the incident rest. She wrote a letter complaining to her influential uncle. The Spanish envoy was able to unearth the identity of our guardian. When Arthur Gordon was informed of the episode, he overreacted by concluding that the nuns had been too lenient with my sister over the years. Feeling that a stricter environment was necessary, our guardian removed Josine from the Marie Gilbert School. She was sent to a boarding school in Provence.

Madame Fourneau's College for Young Women was located not far from Avignon. It was a sterner institution than the Marie Gilbert School, but no one could deny the College's academic reputation. Both Marguerite Chavain and Catarina Moriarty graduated from the College. Madame Fourneau ran her school with an elite group of senior students. Called prefects, these assistants maintained Madame Fourneau's authority over her charges. Only the best and the brightest of the girls were entrusted with such a position. Catarina Koluchy, the future Mrs. Noel Moriarty, was the head perfect when Josine arrived at the College My talented sister was soon recruited as a prefect by Catarina. Despite the seniority of several older prefects, my 16-year old sister succeeded Catarina as head prefect upon her graduation in 1884.

My sister missed me deeply, but she had made the best of a difficult situation. As Madame Fourneau's right hand, Josine presided benevolently over her fellow students. Unfortunately, a serpent was about to invade Paradise. In 1885, a 15-year old girl was matriculated at the College. She was registered under the false name of Irene Tupin. In reality, she was Irene Chupin. If the true identity of this student had been known, Josine would have been prepared for her acts of treachery

Irene ingratiated herself with both my sister and Madame Fourneau. Soon Irene became a prefect junior to my sister. For the next four years, Irene pretended to be Josine's friend. In early 1889, this viper performed her act of betrayal. She manufactured a quarrel between Josine and Madame Fourneau. There was a lecture in literature class about the works of Dumas. Irene skillfully turned the discussion into a debate about the historical novels concerning our ancestor, Joseph Balsamo. Prompted by Irene, Madame Fourneau dismissed the accurate portrayal of our forebear's true role in the French Revolution as a wild exaggeration. Acknowledging her illustrious heritage, Josine defended the assertions of the great Dumas. Madame Fourneau was offended by Josine's defiance. She ordered Irene to escort Josine from the classroom. Confined in a separate chamber, Josine awaited the judgment of the headmistress.

Madame Fourneau could be a martinet, but she had never been excessively cruel in the past. Irene preyed on Madame Fourneau's insecurities. The young she-devil argued that Josine must receive the sternest form of punishment since she occupied the position of head prefect. At Irene's urging, Josine was flogged. It was the sadistic Irene who held the whip. Stripped of her position, my sister was replaced as head prefect by Irene. Under Irene's domination, Madame

Fourneau transformed the College into a virtual prison. Floggings for the most minor infractions became the norm. Mail was regularly censored. My sister was trapped in a Hell manufactured by the vicious Irene. Catarina luckily intervened. After leaving the College, she had married Professor Moriarty's brother. Residing in Naples with her husband, she was the proud mother of a three-year old son. She wrote the College asking for Madame Fourneau to allow Josine to leave the school early to assume the position of governess to the young child. Since Catarina had already cleared the appointment with our guardian, Madame Fourneau had no choice but to accede to the request.

Before she left the College, my sister repaid Irene for her betrayal. Madame Fourneau had a consumptive son, Louis, 16 years old. Being overly protective, the headmistress kept her offspring isolated from the girls attending the College. Josine suspected that Irene had been secretly flirting with Louis. Before departing for Naples, Josine alerted Madame Fourneau to these suspicions. If the headmistress caught Irene near her son, there was little doubt that the head prefect would suffer a beating even worse than those that she had inflicted on others.

When my sister arrived in Naples, she discovered her most treasured possession missing. Both Josine and I had been given brooches by our mother. These heirlooms were in the shape of pentagrams. My mother always told us to venerate them as a symbol of our sisterly bond. Josine suspected that Irene had stolen the pentagram from her luggage. My sister was devastated by the loss of the brooch. I will always remember how Josine described the pentagram's significance.

"During our long separation, I always looked at the pentagram to remember my little sister. You always remain foremost in my heart."

Under Catarina's tutelage, my sister was inducted into the Black Coats. Abandoning her role as governess, Josine rose quickly to become Catarina's administrative assistant. Catarina and her husband entrusted my sister with a delicate mission to Panama.

Of Josine's ordeal at the Fourneau College, I remained ignorant until 1890. In January of that year, the horrible College Girl Murders in Provence were reported in the press. The perpetrator of these atrocities was Louis Fourneau. He had killed five girls. His motive was to mock his mother by presenting her with an effigy made from their corpses. Upon his incarceration, Louis rambled incoherently that a beautiful siren had prompted him to enact this butchery. Louis only identified this bewitching female as the Muse. The sixth victim of his murder spree was in a coma. The newspapers identified her as Irene Chupin. Shortly thereafter, the papers reported Irene's demise in an Avignon hospital.

When this gruesome tale was publicized, my sister was still in Panama. I asked Josine about the newspaper stories after her return from Central America in the spring. It was only then that Josine confessed the full details of her last days at the College. My sister had even hidden the loss of her brooch until this time. Josine finally told me of the misery inflicted on her by Irene. My sister concluded that Irene Chupin must be the real name of the scheming Mademoiselle Tupin. Josine's former nemesis was the daughter of the miscreant responsible for our mother's murder. When I saw the scars of Irene's lash on my sister's back, I knew every word of Josine's story was true.

My sister skillfully deduced what must have happened at the Fourneau College after her departure. Madame Fourneau must have caught Irene visiting her son. Dethroned from her role of prefect, the young girl must have been flogged at Fourneau's orders. The vindictive schemer must have bided her time. The Muse could only have been Irene. Months after her beating, Irene manipulated Louis into enacting the College Girl Murders. Eventually the homicidal Louis rebelled against Irene and attacked her.

The papers supported my sister's speculations by identifying Irene as a former prefect at the College. The journalistic accounts also cited scars on Irene's back indicting that she had been much earlier chastised with a whip. However, the reporters mangled the facts as usual. They stated that Irene had only been demoted from her position as prefect after the fifth murder in early 1890. Clearly it must have happened before the first murder, which transpired in September 1889. The killings had commenced eight months after Josine had left Provence.

Josine commented that Irene's fate was ironically appropriate. She belonged to a family of thieves. Louis Fourneau reportedly severed Irene's hands. The cutting of a hand was a traditional method to reprimand a thief.

While my sister played no role in punishing Irene, she did fulfill her pledge to my mother regarding Lothaire Stepphun. Tracking Irene's father to New York, Josine engineered his destruction earlier in this year of 1893.

The success of her Panama mission permitted Josine to sponsor me for membership in the Black Coats in 1890. In the subsequent year, I was registered as Sabine Absalom at St. Swithin's Medical School in London. Besides pursuing my studies for the last two years, I have assisted Urania Caber in her scientific research division of the Black Coats.

One of my instructors at St. Swithin's, Dr. Arthur Spratt, gave a dinner party tonight. There he introduced me to Paul Cato, a physician who ran a private sanitarium.

"Miss Absalom, you bear an extraordinary resemblance to a patient of mine. Do you have any relatives in France?"

Could Dr. Cato possibly have met my sister? I bear very little resemblance to her. She's a blonde while I'm a brunette.

"There's a branch of my family in France."

"Are any of your relatives named Chupin?"

I was stunned by Cato's question.

"No, I have no relatives named Chupin."

"Why did that name startle you?"

"I once read a lurid account of a murder case in France. A young woman named Irene Chupin was killed. I have never forgotten the story."

"How extraordinary! Irene Chupin isn't dead. She's my patient."

Cato disclosed that the newspapers had falsely reported Irene's death. After leaving the Avignon hospital three years ago, she had been taken by her uncle to Cato's nursing home. Irene was suffering from hysteria resulting from her experiences at the Fourneau College.

"I have been studying psychological disorders, Dr. Cato. Your description of Irene's case fascinates me. Could I meet her?"

Cato concurred to my request. He would introduce me to Irene two days from now.

My interest in Irene is far from clinical. I could contact my sister in Paris, but I won't. Irene will pay for her crimes against the Cagliostro family. I shall personally extinguish the life of Lothaire Stepphun's whelp.

One of the rules of the Black Coats is that no member should keep a diary. By maintaining this journal, I am violating one of the most fundamental restrictions of our fraternity. Yet I must write down my thoughts in order to strengthen my resolve. Once I complete my mission of vengeance, I will destroy this diary.

My mentor, Urania Caber, once confided in me. She had been consigned to scientific research by her colleagues for a simple reason. They viewed her as insufficiently ruthless. I immediately realized that Josine had convinced Catarina that I was just like Urania. I must demonstrate to my sister that I'm as strong as she. I shall execute Irene Chupin.

September 8, 1893: I have decided to use poison as my weapon to snuff out Irene's existence. Urania had corresponded with Emanuel Medjora, a New York scientist. He developed a virulent form of diphtheria. Urania keeps five vials of the Medjora culture in the storeroom of our laboratory. She gave me the keys to retrieve one of the containers. I was to deliver it to Horace Dorrington, a colleague with offices in Bedford Street. Without Urania's knowledge, I removed a second vial. Irene will be the recipient of its contents.

I want to confide in Urania, but I dare not. She would disapprove of my actions. Urania would insist that I communicate with my sister.

I love Josine dearly. There is no one in this world that I trust more. She is more than a sister to me. I worship her. Josine is almost like a deity to me. Too long has she bored the burden of our mother's oath of vengeance. My sister can't be forced to be my protector forever. I too can defend the family honor. I must prove my worthiness to be a Cagliostro.

September 9, 1893: Dr. Cato's establishment, the Sanctuary Club, was founded in the spring of 1890. Located in Hampstead, the rules of the nursing home are very straightforward. Inmates paid an entrance fee of 50 pounds and yearly rent of 10 pounds. The only qualification was that the boarder suffers from a curable malady. After my arrival at the Club, Dr. Cato explained Irene Chupin's case more thoroughly:

"The money for Irene's upkeep has been paid by her uncle, Victor Chupin. For the last three years, Irene has suffered from shock. Her hands were severely damaged. A brilliant French surgeon, Anatole Cerral, reconstructed them. Dr. Cerral's surgery was quite extraordinary. The only signs of physical injury are some scars on her wrists. Unfortunately, Irene suffers from a mental delusion brought about by her ordeal."

"What is the nature of this delusion?"

"Are you familiar with Irene's duties as Madame Fourneau's chief prefect?"

"She imposed punishments on other girls at the school. These disciplinary actions included floggings. Please forgive my bluntness, Dr. Cato, but Irene behaved like a malicious sadist."

"I will not excuse Irene's actions, but you may view her with greater sympathy in light of a salient fact. Irene became an abuser after she herself was abused. Madame Fourneau had Irene whipped shortly after her enrollment at the school. It was only to avoid further beatings that Irene accepted a position as one of Madame Fourneau's assistants. Eventually she rose to the top position."

"Irene told you this?"

"She has never spoken about it. I learned the facts from Irene's uncle. The scars on Irene's back confirmed Victor's story."

The naive Dr. Cato had a garbled version of the truth. I knew the real story from my sister. Irene's scourging had been a consequence of the policies that she herself had persuaded Madame Fourneau to adopt.

"You still haven't explained Irene's delusion, Dr. Cato."

"Irene is consumed by guilt. She's never forgiven herself for her activities as a perfect. She imagines herself to be another girl entirely, Teresa Grévin."

"Wasn't she also one of the victims in the College Girl Murders?"

"Yes, Teresa was slain just before Louis Fourneau's assault on Irene. Prior to her demise, Teresa was being persecuted by Irene."

"Did Irene beat Teresa?"

"No, but Irene was threatening Teresa with a flogging. Irene desired to coerce Teresa into joining the inner circle of prefects. Irene believes that she is really Teresa."

Cato escorted me to Irene's room. Upon viewing my nemesis, I understood why Cato thought that we might be related. Irene has a slender physique and dark hair like my own. However, her eyes are blue while mine are hazel. Our chins were vaguely similar. This bizarre resemblance to my adversary was offset by our totally different hairstyles. My prey wore her hair in a French braid. My own was stacked in a bouffant.

Cato introduced me. "This is Sabine Absalom, Irene."

"The doctor likes to joke, Miss Absalom. My name is Teresa."

"Please call me Sabine. You look tired, Teresa. Have you been sleeping well?"

"I've been having nightmares. Dr. Cato knows about them."

"Please relate your recurring dream to Miss Absalom," requested Cato.

"Sabine, I find myself in a realm of mist. There is a tall man with a beard and burning eyes. He claims to be the ruler of a powerful kingdom. He wants me to become one of his subjects. The bearded man promises me eternal ecstasy. I have only to invite him into my home. I can't do this."

"Why not?"

"Because it's tantamount to suicide. The bearded man wants me to destroy my soul by surrendering to his temptations. He's just like... *her*."

"Who are you talking about?"

"*The Muse,*" whispered Irene.

"Who is the Muse?"

In response to my question, Irene shook her head. "I can't tell anyone about her. Maybe it's her talisman that's causing the bearded man to visit me." She turned towards my host. "Doctor, you need to exorcise the talisman." Opening a dresser drawer, Irene pulled out an object and handed it to Cato.

I recognized the article in Cato's hand. *It was my sister's pentagram brooch!* Josine's suspicions had been correct. Irene had stolen the brooch.

She was a thief like her father. He had stolen often from our family. Lothaire Stepphun even purloined our usage of anagrams. Lothaire Stepphun was an anagram of the master criminal's real name, Théophraste Lupin.

"Doctor, perhaps we should leave Teresa alone," I suggested. "She might be able to rest when this pentagram is removed from her proximity."

Making our farewells to Irene, Cato and I retire to his private office.

"The bearded man from Irene's dreams must be her private personification of Death," surmised Cato.

"Doctor, have you any suspicions concerning the identity of this Muse from Irene's ramblings?"

"The Muse was clearly Madame Fourneau. She had corrupted Irene earlier by making her a prefect."

"But Louis Fourneau asserted that he committed his murders at the urging of the Muse?"

"Louis was constantly told by his mother that he could only be happy with a girl like her. These statements were twisted by young Fourneau into a plan to construct a composite corpse in his mother's image."

I concluded that Cato was been incredibly stupid. Irene was living under the pretense that she was Teresa. The Muse was the girl who had tempted Teresa. In other words, the Muse was Irene herself.

"This pentagram may be the key to curing Irene's personality disorder. Doctor, are you familiar with hypnotism?"

"I've read the recently deceased Jean Marie Charcot's writings on the subject."

"Then you are aware of Charcot's success in treating hysteria."

"Unfortunately, I have no expertise in hypnotism."

"But I do. I learned it from a brilliant Italian member of your profession." I spoke the truth. Hypnotism had been taught me by Antonio Nikola, one of the most influential members of the Black Coats. "If I hypnotize Irene, she will be forced to grapple with her inner demons. Her true self will be restored."

"I'm not sure that Irene will consent to be hypnotized."

"She gave you the pentagram to be exorcised. A shiny contrivance is used to hypnotize the subject. The pentagram can function as such an instrument. We will convince Irene that the hypnotism is part of the ritual to exorcise the pentagram."

"Your arguments make sense, but I need time to consider them. Could you return tomorrow? I would let you know my decision then regarding your suggested treatment."

Concurring with Cato's terms, I made my departure.

Cato is a consummate idiot. He is totally bewitched by the devilish Irene's charms. I have no doubt that he'll agree to my proposal. Under my hypnotic spell, Irene will confess her crimes. I will find an excuse to cause Cato to leave the room. It shall then be child's play to induce the memorized Irene to swallow the Medjora diphtheria. The official medical verdict will be that Irene contracted a fatal disease.

My ancestor, the first Joséphine Balsamo, was a courageous stalker of vampires. My sister bears her name. Irene is little better than the monstrosities slain by my great-grandmother. It's a pity that Irene can't be dispatched in a more poetic matter. If only I could drive a stake into her implacable heart.

My consolation is that Irene's death would be slow and lingering. A burning fever will ravish her. She will grasp for breath. Her throat will swell. Unable to swallow, she will be force to vomit her own saliva. Irene will suffer for days as the disease devours her.

I am not being excessively vindictive. I remember too well my mother's pain as she lied mortally wounded from the stab wounds inflicted by Lothaire Stepphun's accomplice. Even if she was not guilty of the College Girls Murders, Irene must pay for her father's sins.

September 10, 1893: It's almost unbearable to record the events of this day. Tears flood my eyes as I write these words. Yet I must transcribe them

Cato agreed to my recommendation. I convinced Irene to stare at the movements of the pentagram in my hand as part of an exorcism ritual. As Irene fell into a trance, I commanded her to answer Cato's questions. Below is a transcript of their conversation

"What is your real name?"

"I was born Irene Chupin, but I am also known as Irene Tupin."

"Why do you pretend to be Teresa?"

"I am unworthy. I'm responsible for the College Girl Murders."

Cato was taken aback by Irene's answer. I was expecting Irene to finally admit her atrocities. Cato continued his interrogation.

"How are you responsible?"

"With my help, the Muse seduced Louis Fourneau. She instructed him to kill the girls."

"Did you plot the murders with the Muse?"

"No. I didn't know the Muse's real intentions until it was too late. I thought she was merely conducting a romantic dalliance."

"Who is the Muse?"

"A temptress who enticed me into a web of deceit."

"Identify this woman."

"She was my predecessor as Madame Fourneau's chief prefect. Her name is Joséphine Balsamo."

"Tell me the history of your relationship with Joséphine."

"When I first arrived at the College, Joséphine was my tormentor. She kept badgering me about my parentage. She wanted me to acknowledge the identity of my father. She pressured me to confess to a robbery committed by my brother. She insisted that I become her apprentice. I refused. I never wanted to be a prefect."

"Why did you change your mind?"

"Joséphine convinced Madame Fourneau that I was challenging her authority. The headmistress ordered me whipped by Joséphine. After my punishment, Joséphine resumed her demands. I couldn't endure another beating. I agreed to all her conditions. She indoctrinated me into the depraved practices of the prefects."

"Did your persecution cease?"

"Outwardly my relationship with Joséphine changed. I viewed her in a totally different fashion."

"How so?"

"I came to see her as my protector. My former hatred for Joséphine was replaced by reverence. I worshipped her like a goddess. I relished her tender caress. I lived only to secure her favor. She spoke beguiling words in my ear. Joséphine treated me as her confidant. She liked to be called Josine, but I preferred to think of her as Joséphine. Like her namesake, she had the manners of an Empress. Joséphine promised to cherish me as if I was her own sister."

"Was Joséphine telling the truth?"

"I believed so at the time. I now know that I was merely a pawn in a grotesque scheme of vengeance"

"Vengeance against whom?"

"Against Madame Fourneau."

"Why did Joséphine resent Madame Fourneau?"

"Before I came to the school, Madame had insisted that Joséphine become a prefect. When Joséphine refused, Madame personally flogged her. Faced with future flagellations, Joséphine acceded to Madame's ultimatum."

"How did Joséphine manipulate you?"

"Madame was overly protective of her son. She wouldn't allow Louis any contact with her pupils. Joséphine secretly romanced Louis. I distracted Madame Fourneau to prevent her from observing these trysts. I performed this deception even though I detested it."

"Why was this ruse so distasteful?"

"I didn't want to charm Madame. I wanted to spend my time with Joséphine. I was jealous that Joséphine was bestowing her affection on Louis."

"Then why did you participate in Joséphine's scheme?"

"Because she dictated it. I could refuse Joséphine nothing. She inspired me like no other. I told that she was my Muse, and I would always be her loyal handmaiden. When she left the school for Naples, Joséphine rewarded me for my fidelity."

"How were you rewarded?"

"She sponsored me to be her successor as prefect. She also gave me a gift."

"What was this gift?"

"A pentagram brooch. She said that it would protect me from harm."

"When did Joséphine vacate the College?"

"January 1889."

"Did Joséphine ever communicate with you afterwards?"

"She wrote me constantly. I was overjoyed when she revisited the school."

"When was this?"

"September 1889."

"What happened during Joséphine's visit?"

"She asked me to distract Madame Fourneau one more time in order to meet with Louis."

"Did you comply?"

"I initially refused, but Joséphine convinced me by emphasizing the pentagram."

"What did she say?"

"That the pentagram was the symbol of our eternal sisterhood. She swore that I would always be foremost in her heart. She called me her 'little sister.' "

"What transpired after Joséphine's departure?"

"The first girl disappeared. By January, five more girls had vanished. Madame Fourneau believed that they had merely run away. I began to have suspicions when Teresa couldn't be found."

"Tell me about Teresa. What were your feelings toward her?"

"Teresa was innocent and impressionable. She reminded me of what I had been before Joséphine indoctrinated me. I hoped to make her my disciple as Joséphine had earlier done with me."

"After Teresa's disappearance, what did you do?"

"I accused Madame Fourneau of being responsible for the missing girls. She stripped me of my position. I attempted to flee the College. Madame chased me into the attic. There I discovered Louis. *I can't talk about him!*"

"You must," insisted Cato. "Tell me all about Louis."

"He grabbed me by the throat. An axe was in his other hand, He spoke these words: 'Everything I've done was at the bequest of the Muse. Joséphine wants me to punish both you and Mama. You shall wear the mark of a thief, foolish *handmaiden.*' He slammed my head against the wall. Barely conscious, I felt Louis spread my arms outward over a large chest. I opened my eyes in unendurable pain. Beholding my bloody wrists, I collapsed in shock."

Irene paused before resuming.

"I didn't regain consciousness until days later in the hospital. My mangled limbs were wrapped in bandages. It was God's punishment!"

"God's punishment? Why do you say that?"

"I had succumbed to Joséphine's empty promises. I had envisioned myself her handmaiden. In imitation of Joséphine, my hands had abused others. I had to repent."

"What was your repentance?"

"After the bandages were removed, my hands were different. They were no longer strong and firm. They were soft and delicate like Teresa's. I must allow Teresa to live again through me. I could no longer be Irene Chupin. I would become Teresa Grévin."

Absorbed by Irene's revelations, Cato had ignored me. He suddenly realized that I was sobbing. My tears were genuine.

"Miss Absalom," he whispered, "you had witnessed a disturbing story. Is there anything that I can do for you?"

"A glass of wine will restore my nerves," I replied.

Cato left the room. I was alone with the entranced Irene. My late mother had desired this young woman's annihilation. I could easily have removed the bottle of Medjora diphtheria from my purse and order Irene to swallow its contents. Yet I did nothing.

The doctor returned with the glass of wine. After partaking it, I convinced Cato to release Irene from her trance.

"Awaken, Irene Chupin," I ordered. "You will remember everything that you have told us."

Upon regaining her senses, Irene burst into tears. I hugged her as we cried together.

September 14, 1893: I have reflected on the events in the Sanctuary Club for the last four days. I don't condemn Josine for engineering the College Girl Murders. As our glorious ancestor ruthlessly orchestrated the downfall of the tyrannical Marie Antoinette, my sister displayed no remorse in bringing ruination to Madame Fourneau. Count Cagliostro was responsible for scores of deaths on the guillotine. Can I fault my sister for causing the deaths of five innocuous schoolgirls?

My burden is the knowledge that my sister has never trusted me. She consistently lied to me about her actions at the College. I tried to console myself with the argument that she was merely being overprotective. Did she want to spare me the grisly details of carrying out our mother's vendetta? I wanted to believe this, but such an argument won't stand the light of day.

I remember fully the details of my mother's last moments on Earth. Why was Leonard forced to vacate me from my mother's death chamber? What did my mother tell Josine in my absence? Why was Josine so reluctant to shield me from persecution during our early schooldays together?

Why did Josine thoughtlessly surrender her pentagram brooch to Irene? The brooch was the representation of the strong bond between us. Josine always said she loved me. She used similar language with Irene even though she despised her. Josine even called Irene her "little sister," a term of endearment also bestowed continually on me.

The truth has finally dawned on me. My sister feels the same loathing towards me that she exhibited towards Irene. My resemblance to Lothaire Stepphun's daughter was no mere coincidence. Lothaire and my mother were lovers. Arthur Gordon may be Josine's father, but he's not mine. Lothaire was my real father. My mother must have told Josine the truth on her deathbed. How my sister must have always resented me as the child of our mother's slayer. If not for the promise that she made to our mother, Josine would have killed me long ago.

I received today a letter from Dr. Cato. Irene has accepted her true identity. He expects her to be discharged from the Sanctuary Club within a month. Her nightmares have ceased. The bearded man with the burning eyes no longer haunts her dreams.

He now troubles my own slumbers. For a moment, I imagine myself the victim of one of the legendary dream curses of folklore. This is clearly not the case. My own brooding has merely conjured up an imaginary figure prompted by Irene's babblings.

The man with the burning eyes beckons me into his realm of mist. His offer holds great attraction. I have no reason to live. The bedrock of my existence has been the belief of my sister's love. That delusion has been shattered. My sister views me as a millstone around her neck. If I take my own life, Josine will undoubtedly be filled with joy.

I will live one my day before taking an irrevocable step. I must say good-bye to Urania Caber before terminating my life. She at least has always been a stalwart friend. When I return home, I will swallow the bottle of Medjora diphtheria. My passing will be painful, but it will be just punishment. I foolishly believed Josine's hollow declarations of love. She hates me as much as Irene. It is fitting that my fate shall be the doom devised for Irene.

The avatar of Death will seek to seduce me in my sleep tonight. He must be patient. His entreaties will be answered favorably the next evening.

All Predators Great and Small

Excerpt from L'Essence du Dragon *by Charles Maurice Loridan (1866)*

The popular misconception is that vampires are servants of Satan. The Cult of the Undead really owes its allegiance to Slidith, the Dragon Lord from the Pit of Ngoth. Among the secret acolytes of Slidith was the Roman prefect of Judaea, Pontius Pilate. By deliberately sentencing Jesus of Nazareth to crucifixion, Pilate stained his soul with a monstrous sin. After committing this unspeakable crime, Pilate performed a ritual of metamorphosis to become the Great Vampire, Slidith's surrogate on Earth. As a consequence of Pilate's action, vampires became vulnerable to the sign of the cross. Pilate's bloody reign ended when his heart was transfixed by the blade of a Samaritan seer. The mantle of Great Vampire remained unclaimed until Vlad Dracula became the ruler of Wallachia in the fifteenth century.

Slidith will only accept a mortal of pure degeneracy as his supreme satrap. Sometimes the quality of a single bloodthirsty act is enough to win the Dragon Lord's favor. Pilate demonstrated this through a simple judicial murder. Known as Vlad the Impaler, Dracula proved that Slidith can be equally impressed by quantity as well as quality.

Vlad Dracula's brutality sparked his transformation into the Great Vampire. His impaling of thousands in Wallachia encumbered his soul with sins against humanity. The historical accounts of Dracula's death are false. He wasn't killed by the Turks. Dracula was the vassal of King Mathias of Hungary. Repelled by Dracula's barbarity, Mathias imprisoned him for 12 years. Mathias had a change of heart once the Ottoman Empire threatened his borders. The Hungarian monarch released Dracula to lead an army on a crusade against the Islamic invaders. Resentful of his mistreatment by Mathias, the Impaler secretly betrayed the army to the Turks at the battle of Bucharest. The Turks masked Dracula's treachery by unveiling the severed head of a double in Istanbul. Following this crowning deed of duplicity, Dracula committed ritual suicide with poison. The atrocities attached to the Impaler's soul assured his reincarnation as the Undead sovereign.

Dracula's self-indulgence is limitless. He narcissistically pines for a Soul-Mate, a woman forged in his own image.

Claude Gabriel Dupont-Verdier's Journal, October 31, 1892

I invaded the Mexican tomb with Aguilar and his brigands. We read the inscription: "Here lie Count and Countess Frankenhausen–and Frau Hildegarde, their faithful servant who would not abandon them even when they journeyed into the Great Beyond–1885." My quest for the ultimate romance nears its completion.

José Alejandro Balsamo's Diary, November 3, 1892

In 1875, I learned that Count Frankenhausen, the last Great Vampire, was spreading terror throughout Mexico. For 10 years, my agents pursued him. Finally, Frankenhausen was destroyed by one of my vampire hunters at the Haunted Hacienda. I foolishly believed the horror of Frankenhausen had ended.

The crypt of the Frankenhausens has been looted. All three corpses were stolen. The Cult of the Undead must be the responsible. The culprits have to be attempting the Count's resurrection.

The Count's powers validated Grost's theory that "there are as many species of vampire as there are beasts of prey." All victims of Frankenhausen's bite became mindless vampires. Anyone bitten by them was similarly transfigured. These blood-drinking creatures were more akin to the zombies of Haiti than the Nosferatu of Eastern Europe. These lumbering creatures blindly obeyed the Count's commands.

The remains of the Countess and Frau Hildegarde are inconsequential. The Count devoured the blood of Eugenia, a human woman whom he had married. The resulting Undead Countess had the mentality of an idiot. Hildegarde, the Count's daytime protector, didn't even mature into a vampire. After a spear pierced Frankenhausen's heart, she leapt from the second floor of the Haunted Hacienda. The fall didn't kill her. Without a master, the moronic vampires went on a rampage. The injured Hildegarde became a banquet for the Count's former slaves.

Once the vampires returned to their coffins at the onset of dawn, proper steps were taken. I had extracted an acidic liquid from the roots of the black mandrake plant. This substance was fatal to vampires. Hildegarde's Undead resurgence was thwarted by my anti-vampire serum. The same fluid slew Eugenia and the other vampires in their graves. Even the Count's corpse was inoculated. The mandrake vaccine is not infallible. Its prevalence inside the bodies can be defeated with necromancy.

Count Cagliostro, my grandfather, deduced the Frankenhausen family's dominance of the Cult. Vampires of the Frankenhausen bloodline sired human offspring. Upon reaching adulthood, the firstborn of each generation evolved into the reigning Great Vampire. The Curse of the Frankenhausens was exorcised when my mandrake extract cured the Count's daughter. She is now happily married.

My son-in-law has a far-fetched theory. Supposedly, the Frankenhausens acted as figureheads for Vlad the Impaler, a secret Great Vampire hiding in the

Carpathians. Ricardo's speculations are ludicrous. The Turks decapitated the despot in 1476. No headless husk could be afflicted with the Undead pestilence.

I pray for the safety of my daughter Anna and her children. Extra steps will be taken to protect them in our estate. A reanimated Count Frankenhausen would seek vengeance against my descendants. Even though I disowned Anna's sister decades ago, my fears extend to her. There were recent rumors of a Countess Cagliostro in Panama. Was this my Joséphine, or did she have a daughter?

Claude Gabriel Dupont-Verdier's Journal, September 14, 1893

The Great Vampire is in England. The horrible massacre of the *Demeter*'s crew confirmed his presence. He must have guided that derelict ship to land at Whitby. My own *Jarvee* had earlier made a far less dramatic voyage to these shores. The cargo of three Mexican coffins never disturbed Captain Thompson and his sailors. The choice to store the relics here in London rather than Paris was fortuitous.

Count Frankenhausen's remains were cremated in the cellar of my Georgian mansion. My knife slashed the throat of the young prostitute from Mrs. Blake's bordello. Her blood dripped into the ashes as I recited the incantation from Prinn's *Les Mystères du Ver*:

> *In the fane of Yiggurath, the Source of All Malice,*
> > *And his progeny Slidith, Lord of the Blood Chalice,*
> *I summon forth the Great Vampyre*
> > *By his minion's charnel pyre.*

A wave of mist erupted upward from Frankenhausen's ashes. The haze assumed the semblance of a gaunt man. His dark hair and beard were tinged with grey. I was granted an audience with Dracula.

Dr. Caber's Letter to Joséphine Balsamo, September 15, 1893

Dear Joséphine,
A vial of Medjora diphtheria was missing from the storeroom. An investigation established your sister as the culprit. I challenged Sabine about the theft. She ranted incoherently about suicide. Her offense wasn't reported to my uncle and his associates. Please hurry to London. Sabine needs you desperately.
Your friend,
Urania

Claude Gabriel Dupont-Verdier's Journal, *September 15, 1893*

Dracula returned to my cellar after dusk. I handed him the mystical ruby, Akivasha's Tear. He sliced his palm with the scimitar sacred to the Old Ones. The jewel grew brighter as the Great Vampire poured his blood on it. His lips chanted the Aklo hymn to Yiggurath, Father of Serpents.

The two stone coffins no longer contained decaying carcasses. The occupants displayed the fullness of life. Hildegarde Einem climbed out of her coffin. She wore the stern clothes of a housekeeper. Her face exhibited the ravages of age. Her blonde hair was widely streaked with grey.

"Master," she murmured, "you didn't forsake me."

"Look closely, Hildegarde," decreed Dracula. "Who am I?"

"You're Count Franken– No; you're the nobleman whose castle the Count visited before his departure for Mexico."

"I am Dracula, the true Great Vampire. Siegfried Von Frankenhausen merely masqueraded in that role. He and his ancestors belonged to the Stepsons of the Dragon, my inner circle in the Cult of the Undead. Each Stepson owns a ring identical to mine. Every Frankenhausen firstborn inherited my ring until one of José Balsamo's agents intervened."

Dracula showed his ring to Hildegarde. She recognized the thrice-coiled effigy of a winged dragon with three ruby horns. It was Slidith, the Draconic Adder first worshipped in Lemuria and Valusia.

"I don't understand," declared Hildegarde. "Why do you have Stepsons?"

"They act as my eyes and ears. While I rest in my native soil, my Stepsons are awake in diverse parts of the world. They mentally communicate their experiences to me through our rings. The Stepsons transmit glorious visions of carnage and seduction. At the very least, they relieved the oblivion of my dormancy. Vampires normally don't dream."

"Master... I'm thirsty."

"My servant Gabriel has anticipated your hunger. You may dine after I leave. Restrain any designs on Gabriel's blood. He's too valuable as a mortal to me."

Dracula pointed towards the other vampire. "Eugenia, rise from your coffin! I command it!"

A lady in a white nightgown vacated the second casket. Dark curly hair draped her shoulders. There was no intelligence in her eyes. She motioned aimlessly toward my Master. Akivasha's Tear had mutated the Frankenhausen vampire virus into the more common Transylvanian version. Eugenia now had radically different abilities than in Mexico, but her mental faculties were still damaged. Hildegarde's wits were intact because her initial Undead rebirth miscarried.

"Walk with me in the moonlight, Eugenia," ordained Dracula. "The tribe of Cagliostro disrupted my supreme ambition. You shall be the instrument of my revenge." Eugenia exited with him up the stairs.

I opened a locked door with a key. "Your nightly meal," I heralded. The room harbored four female adolescents. Hildegarde immediately attacked them. Within minutes, the captives were all drained of blood. They would never be vampires. In contrast to its Mexican offshoots, the Transylvanian disease only spreads with the victim's additional drinking of the Undead's blood. Jillian Blake has been paid handsomely to deliver these maidens. The girls will not be missed by their procurer. Mrs. Blake falsely believed that her protégés were en route to Madame Delhomme's prosperous brothel in northern France.

Hildegarde advanced toward a wall mirror. "I have no reflection," she lamented.

"There is a special mirror upstairs. Permit me to escort you."

"What does the Great Vampire intend to do with Eugenia?"

"She's the subject of an audacious experiment. Who was destined to succeed Count Frankenhausen as Dracula's Stepson?"

"Frankenhausen's daughter, Brunhilde. She would have been a Stepdaughter."

"More of a Soul-Mate. For centuries, Dracula has schemed to infuse a woman with his own personality. The Soul-Mate requires superior breeding. He ordered Frankenhausen to wed Eugenia Guzman de La Selva because her maternal grandfather was the renowned soldier, Baron Kralitz. Furthermore, Kralitz's mother was a Durward and his wife was a Szandor. The Durwards were the preeminent duelists of England. Eugenia's pedigree extends directly back to Count Szandor and his Bulgarian bride, fierce rebels against King Mathias of Hungary in the 1480's. With her additional Frankenhausen heritage, Brunhilde would have been the perfect Soul-Mate. Unfortunately, she was vaccinated with José Balsamo's purifying acid. Brunhilde is totally immune to vampirism. Denied the daughter, Dracula will settle for the mother."

We finally reached the room where my "mirror" was stored. At our entry, Hildegarde was startled by a painting hanging over the mantelpiece. It was Joseph Bridau's *Hecate Reborn*. "Is this some sort of joke? I posed for that picture in 1840!" She contemplated the portrait with regret. "I was so beautiful."

"Examine your hands! They're young and firm! Blood has restored your youth!"

Hildegarde ripped off her clothes. Seeing her naked skin, she relished in her rejuvenation.

"Those garments were unsuitable, Hildegarde. These are more appropriate."

Hildegarde put on an exact copy of the white Grecian-style gown modeled for Bridau. Although her elegant legs were entirely covered, the dress closely clung to her superbly proportioned physique. A long sleeve sheathed her right arm, but her left shoulder and limb remained bare.

"It's regrettable, Gabriel, that you don't have a copy of the bracelet in the painting."

"But I have a substitute." I slipped the golden Valusian armlet on her left wrist.

"My portrait was commissioned by the Gabriel family while I was their governess in Austria. Gabriel must be your surname."

"It's my middle name. My mother was one of your charges. I've desired you since beholding Bridau's masterpiece as a boy. My adoration drove me to research your subsequent history. You left my mother's family to become young Siegfried Von Frankenhausen's tutor. Accompanying the adult Count to Mexico, you ran afoul of Balsamo'a vampire hunters during a decade-long battle.

"The death of my French father left me a fortune. I nearly exhausted it to bring you back to life. The *Jarvee*, my private vessel, scoured the globe in an occult crusade. In Boneport, Louisiana, I found the sole surviving edition of Loridan's *L'Essence du Dragon*. All other copies had been incinerated with the author in a warehouse fire. Besides Dracula's plans for a Soul-Mate, the book documented the rites capable of resuscitating any vampire. The Great Vampire's blood must envelop the ruby called Akivasha's Tear. It took me years to exhume the gem in an Egyptian tomb. Aided by Mexican outlaws, I violated the Frankenhausen Mausoleum. Locating Dracula in London, I offered him a singular trade. As payment for Eugenia, he would grant me my ideal woman...You."

"A fool's bargain, Gabriel. I only seduce with the lamia's kiss. Dracula forbids me to taste your blood."

"Your bracelet overcomes that restriction, Hildegarde. I wear its mate. Both bear the likeness of Slidith, son of Yiggurath and half-brother of Set. The magic of this Great Old One bonds the intellects of the bracelets' bearers. My mind will penetrate yours. The Master conceded the vampire's inability to dream. I can fill your daytime slumber with carnal delights. Let me be your incubus."

"You tempt me. Gabriel is too angelic a name for a tempter. Our nuptials will be sealed with a baptism. I christen you *Satanas*."

Sabine Balsamo's Diary, September 20, 1893

Dr. Caber related that my sister is coming to London. When she uncovers the truth about the poison, her rage will be monstrous. Death's merciful embrace attracts me. The Grim Reaper haunts my sleep, but his form isn't a hooded skeleton. He's a man with a pointed beard.

The apparition of my delirium beckons me to a spectacular realm. He says it is a glorious world where the dead can savor endless evenings of narcotic bliss. The dark messenger offers me this paradise if I welcome him into my house. So far, I have refused.

Claude Gabriel Dupont-Verdier's Journal, September 21-22, 1893

My days were filled with wanton ecstasy. Lust consumed Hildegarde. Vampires generally arise briskly at dusk. Enthralled by our erotic fusion, my concubine reluctantly left her coffin hours after sunset. I teased Hildegarde by proclaiming her the first vampire to chronically oversleep. Purchases from Mrs. Blake satiated Hildegarde's diet. After moving Eugenia's coffin elsewhere, Dracula ignored us for days. I erred in forgetting his existence.

Soon after nightfall, our sensual refuge in the Dreamlands was interrupted by a husky female voice. "Hildegarde, you lazy slut! Attend me! I command it!"

"I obey only the Great Vampire!" replied my lover.

"Enough of your insolence! Feel my wrath!"

In the world of dreams, my darling disappeared. Waking suddenly in my bed, I rushed downstairs to the cellar. "Satanas....save me!" wailed Hildegarde. She was out of her coffin. Blood splattered her white dress. Holding her stomach, she knelt before a macabre interloper.

I beheld a woman in a black ensemble consisting of a sleeveless tunic, pants and boots. Leather bracelets adorned her wrists and her upper arms. The back of her jet hair was tied in a plaited bun. Two long braids of hair fell to her waist. She wore a dark fur cape. A gold chain clasped the cloak around her neck. A ring with Dracula's dragon crest was on the fifth finger of her left hand. The intruder's long sharp nails were stained with Hildegarde's blood.

"How appallingly domestic!" noted the cloaked brunette. "You've given Gabriel a pet name. Do not seek succor from his quarter. Your Satanas hasn't the courage to defy me."

"Countess Frankenhausen," moaned Hildegarde, "please...no more..."

"Don't address me by that name. Eugenia is dead. My progenitor, Count Szandor, was the first Stepson of the Dragon. I celebrate my lineage as Szandra, Countess Dracula."

"Forgive me, Countess Dracula."

"Effete gods grant forgiveness. I impose penance. My boots are tarnished. Clean them."

"I'll fetch a cloth, Mistress."

"No, Hildegarde. Lick off the dust with your tongue."

My dearest complied with this demand. Szandra put her fingers in her mouth. She sucked the blood off her nails as Hildegrarde debased herself. The Great Vampire had altered Eugenia's appearance through sorcery. Only faint traces of Frankenhausen's wife endured. The Soul-Mate of Dracula is leaner with red eyes instead of blue. Eugenia's brain had been a blank slate. It now housed the cunning of a maniacal warrior. This female surrogate of the Great Vampire gloated over our humiliation.

"My handmaiden has been tardy due to her trysts, Satanas. I suspected a potential pregnancy. The only recourse was to dissect her belly. My suspicions were incorrect. Hildegarde, you may stop. Your odious condition merits a bath. I don't require your services any further tonight."

Countess Dracula vanished as a cloud of mist.

Vampires do not wash in water. Running water is fatal to them. They bathe in blood. I bought more specimens from Mrs. Blake to supply the cleansing fluid. Hildegarde's sanguinary immersion healed her injuries. She put on a duplicate of the torn Grecian raiment in silence. A rift developed between us. Not only had I witnessed her degradation, but I had done nothing to circumvent it.

The next day, Hildegarde's performance was …uninspired. She dismissed me from the Dreamlands long before dusk. I cursed Szandra for ruining my lecherous utopia.

Immediately upon dusk, Hildegarde emerged from her coffin. She stood patiently for hours awaiting the coming of Szandra. Finally, a swirl of smoke transmuted into Countess Dracula.

"You have learned from your mistakes, Hildegarde."

"Yes, Mistress."

"Your improvement deserves a reward. Like my consort, I mandate three Sisters of the Night to be my acolytes." Countess Dracula fondled Hildegarde's yellow locks. "As the most senior of my Sisterhood, you shall conscript another devotee of my choosing."

"Who shall be the next Sister, Mistress?"

"My consort has the ability to sense souls in torment. Do you understand this peculiar skill?"

"The Master can feel the thoughts of a person troubled by visions of death and madness. Is the candidate an asylum inmate?"

"No, merely a contemplator of suicide. Her induction into the Sisterhood shall punish the inventor of the most formidable weapon ever employed against our Cult."

"José Balsamo! Have you chosen Señora Anna Peisser, Don José's daughter?"

"No, our quarry is Anna's niece."

"I would have preferred a daughter. Anna infiltrated the Frankenhausen household posing as a servant 18 years ago. I hunger to repay that strumpet."

"My consort researched the Balsamo family. Anna and her husband Ricardo have five children. The youngest is an eight-year old girl. She's the fourth Joséphine descended from Count Cagliostro. Unlike her predecessors, this Joséphine has black hair."

"We could journey to Mexico and make Anna's daughter the third Sister."

"An excellent idea, Hildegarde. Her niece has a reprieve tonight because a proper invitation is lacking. Would you care to scrounge the streets for a midnight repast?"

"We can partake indoors. Thanks to Mrs. Blake, our food larder is well-stocked."

Joséphine Balsamo's Letter to José Alejandro Balsamo, October 6, 1893

Dear Grandfather,

We have never met. I am the child of your prodigal daughter. Her name was the same as your mother's. It is mine as well.

I discovered your whereabouts three years ago during a visit to Panama. You may distrust the validity of this letter. Permit me to prove its veracity with information available only to our family. Joseph Balsamo, Count Cagliostro, had two wives. The tragic passing of the first, Lorenza, was publicized by the novelist Dumas. She needn't concern us. Shortly after the Affair of the Queen's Necklace in 1785, our forebear wedded Sharita, an Indian priestess. Cagliostro investigated the terrifying depredations of Kurt Von Frankenhausen throughout Germany. This alleged Great Vampire retaliated by converting Sharita into a deranged lamia. The Bavarian Inquisition apprehended Sharita and burned her at the stake.

A grief-stricken Cagliostro had an assignation with Joséphine de Beauharnais in Fontainebleau during 1787. Their daughter was born a year later. She was the first of our line to be dubbed Joséphine Balsamo. After her natural mother became Napoleon's Empress, my namesake posed as the goddaughter of the illustrious beauty. In the wake of Waterloo, the original Joséphine Balsamo was wooed by the enigmatic Henri de Belcamp. Her lover revealed his real identity as Prince Serge Dolgorouki of Russia. Belcamp was merely his alias in Paris. Dolgorouki transported Joséphine to the court of Czar Alexander II. There she adopted the title of Countess Cagliostro. Deserted by Dolgorouki in 1816, she bore his son–you, my grandfather. Born Joseph Alexander Balsamo, you utilize the Spanish variant of your name in Mexico.

The Cult of the Undead still terrorized our family. In 1818, your mother received an urgent plea from her older half-sister, Sara Balsamo. Sharita's daughter was pursued in Moldavia by Gorcha the Vourdalak and his bloodthirsty brethren. My namesake gallantly rescued her sibling by slaughtering Gorcha's band of vampires. Great-grandmother trained you to continue the war against the Undead. Your labors are devoted to combating this abomination. News of vampire outbreaks in Mexico prompted your resettlement there in the 1860's.

You married Felina de Valgeneuse in 1844. My mother's birth in 1845 was followed by that of her sister Anna two years later. In 1867, a serious schism developed between you and my mother. She rebelled against your decision to move the family from Europe to Mexico. The clandestine cabal known as the Black Coats recruited her. She envisioned them as no different from the Masonic societies that your grandfather used to spread liberty, equality and fraternity. You argued that the Black Coats only promote treason, revenge and extortion. All your objections were accurate. Unfortunately, I am also entangled in the intrigues of the Black Coats. It's too late for me to escape my hateful servitude. By writing you, I risk my life. It's an offense punishable by death to disclose our organization's activities to outsiders. This rule is so stringent that no member is permitted to keep a diary.

My mother's affair with a munitions dealer led to my birth in 1868. My sister Sabine was born two years later. While I resemble our mother and great-grandmother, Sabine is slim with black hair.

My father wrongly assumed Sabine to be his child. My mother confessed Sabine's true parentage to me and Leonard, our loyal retainer. Sabine was never intended to learn her real origins.

Your daughter Joséphine perished in 1880. She was lured into a fatal ambush by an ex-suitor. As my mother lay dying from her wounds, she asked me to take two oaths. The first was to protect Sabine always. The second was to destroy the family of the contemptible betrayer. Leonard buried your daughter in a purple robe befitting an Empress. Her ring bearing the golden ram insignia was bequeathed to me. Despite my current ownership, I always imagine my mother wearing this ring.

There was another legacy. You had two sliver brooches fashioned as five-pointed stars. They were presents for your daughters. My mother wanted Anna also to join the Black Coats, but my aunt sided with you. Anna's rejection infuriated my mother. She enticed a burglar to steal Anna's pentagram. My mother later regretted this sisterly feud. She cautioned me and Sabine never to repeat it. Our mother divided the brooches between us.

After the funeral, Leonard persuaded my father to provide for our upbringing. Sabine and I were sent to a wonderful Parisian school staffed by nuns. My fiery nature made me a disciplinary problem. Reports of constant infractions compelled my father to separate me from Sabine. Exiled to a strict boarding school in Provence, I took my pentagram with me. Upon graduation, I gave it as a gift to a fellow student.

I then was initiated into the Black Coats. They served as the means to fulfill my mother's dying wishes. An alliance with the Back Coats allowed me to ruthlessly avenge her. It also permitted me to provide for my sister. Sabine's enrolled at St. Swithin's Medical School in London. To avoid the onus of the Balsamo name, she was registered under the anagram of Absalom. The Black Coats agreed to pay for Sabine's education in exchange for her induction into their medical research center. The director of this group is named Urania. Although her family is a notorious criminal dynasty, she surprisingly has a trustworthy nature. Many denigrate her as scientifically brilliant but impractical. I deem her to be a real rarity: a true friend. Urania acted as a mentor to my sister. During a visit to the laboratory of the Black Coats, Sabine stole some poison. Urania immediately wrote me after covering up my sister's crime.

I own a London abode where my sister resides under the Absalom alias. Arriving there from France on September 22, I interrogated her.

"Urania is convinced you're suicidal. Why are you depressed?"

"There's no use pretending anymore, Josine. You hate me."

"How could I? We're sisters."

"No, we're only half-sisters. My father was the man who betrayed Mama."

Stunned by her words, I sought to console my sister. "You're still my flesh and blood. Mama never wanted you to know. Did Leonard say something?"

"I won't tell you."

"Then don't. The only important thing is that I love you." My voice choked with emotion. "I don't care how you learned Mama's secret. We shall always be sisters."

Sabine hugged me and wept. She still shielded her informant after our reconciliation. It must be Leonard. He has known about Sabine's true lineage since the moment of her birth. Because of Leonard's past fidelity, I haven't acted on my suspicions.

The next morning, my sister was much better. I expected to stay with her. An early morning edict from my superior in the Black Coats interfered. She dispatched me with a proposal for an architect in Bristol. Any flunky could have performed the task, but this heartless tyrant regularly saddles me with unnecessary duties. I departed by train before noon. My return was scheduled the next afternoon.

In my absence, Sabine faced pure horror.

Sabine Balsamo's Diary, September 23, 1893

My endless turmoil is over. All doubts about Josine's affection for me have been eliminated. Why did Madame Koluchy send her to Bristol? I miss my sister's radiant smile.

The day was beautiful and sunny. I decided to stroll down Piccadilly Circus at noon. I met a charming woman by happenstance. She accidentally stepped on my foot. Ashamed of her *faux pas*, she insisted on treating me at the local tea shop.

My acquaintance is Countess Alucard, a fascinating aristocrat with braided raven hair. She recently arrived from Hungary with her husband and maid. The lady seemed very wealthy. She was wearing a stylish black dress and veil. A gold bracelet was on her left wrist.

The Countess was extremely loquacious in her thick Hungarian accent. Labeling tea inferior to coffee, she barely touched her cup. Amused by her ramblings, I invited the Countess to visit my home. She knows me only by my pseudonym of Absalom. The Countess asked if her maid, Fraulein Einem, could come. Of course, I assented. Countess Alucard has the most stilted way of speaking. I remember her awkward question: "Do we have permission to cross your threshold?"

As we were leaving, she noticed her husband in the crowd. He's a bearded man strangely resembling the spectre of my nightmares. I am still

(*Editor's Note*: Sabine's diary terminates abruptly. There are no further entries.)

Claude Gabriel Dupont-Verdier's Journal, September 23, 1893

Hildegarde blocked my entry into her mind for several hours. Finally my paramour opened the door to her thoughts. I created the illusory boudoir where we always rendezvoused. Hildegarde's psychic simulacrum appeared. My astral double embraced her, but she remained cold and unresponsive. Our conversation took curious detours.

"Satanas, does Alucard signify anything?"

"It's the Master's name backwards. Some of his Stepsons use it as a *nom de guerre.*"

"How can Dracula live in the daytime? Sunlight should be fatal to our kind."

"Years ago, the Great Vampire conducted a ritual sacred to Slidith. It was supposed to grant Dracula full immunity in daylight, but the ceremony was only a partial success. He can survive the sun, but all his powers are rendered dormant by it. And he still needs to rest periodically to renew his strength."

"The Master imparted this ability to his Soul-Mate. She braved the daylight today."

"You're in the Dreamlands, Hildegarde. How could you possibly know?"

"Because I told her," announced Countess Dracula. I was startled by Szandra's intrusion. Her astral self wore the same barbaric garb flaunted nightly. One of her wristbands had been superseded by a Valusian bracelet. This accessory must decorate Szandra's arm in the waking world. Her clairvoyant communiqués had beguiled Hildegarde. My lover had degenerated into Sandra's daytime voyeur.

"Did you enjoy my chat with Anna's niece?"

"I did not. She's an insipid creature, Mistress."

"I detect a tone of jealousy. Don't fret; you'll always be my favorite. Sabine will merely be a thrall whose eternal suffering will amuse us."

"Thank you, Mistress. Shouldn't Satanas go elsewhere?"

"Let him stay. Some men wish to watch...such things."

I won't describe what happened next in the Dreamlands. Saturated with disgust, I fled the imaginary region to the actuality of my quarters. I went downstairs and brooded over Hildegarde's coffin. With the setting of the sun, she rose from her resting place. Icy indifference emanated from her.

"I have no time for you, Satanas. My Mistress craves my attentions."

"Don't forsake me. I yearn for your company."

"You can easily satisfy your request. Your bracelet will enable you to observe as I gratify the whims of Countess Dracula. You may even learn *something*."

"Such as?"

"How to make love to a woman." She changed into a bat and fluttered away. Regardless of her taunts, my longing overwhelmed me. Merging with Hildegarde's mind, I perceived the outside as her.

I spied a house from a high distance in the sky. Szandra abided outside the building, I took my natural form. The Countess smiled at me with fondness. "My precious Hildegarde," she intoned.

We glimpsed a light on the second floor of the edifice. Becoming mist, we passed through the cracks of the windowsill. We materialized in a bedroom. Sabine Balsamo was seated at a desk. She was busy writing in a notebook. A diary? I will peruse it later. Finally the chronicler noticed us.

"Countess Alucard! How did you get in? Why are you wearing those clothes?"

Szandra stared into Sabine's eyes. She was plucking memories from this pathetic female. Through our bracelets, my Mistress transferred these remembrances. I projected the silhouette of a blonde in a green dress into the sight of our initiate. In her imagination, I became this other woman.

"Josine!" exclaimed Sabine. "Please tell me what is happening!"

"Countess Alucard is a gifted medium," I explained. "She can contact our mother."

"Mama…"

"Please sit down, my sister. Close your eyes and think of Mama." Sabine foolishly complied. "Remember," I resumed, "when we last saw her alive."

"Mama was on her bed. Her shoulder was mutilated from the stab wounds. She died screaming vengeance against her enemies. I can't continue, Josine."

"Open your eyes, my sister!" I dissolved the illusion and bared my fangs. "Sabine Balsamo, die like your mother!"

My scrawny prey leaped from the chair in panic. "Nosferatu!" yelled Sabine. Grabbing a star-like object from her desk, she waved it in front of me.

"A pentagram is no match for a vampire," I boasted. My right hand snatched the talisman from her and tossed it behind me. I ripped open the left side of the puny girl's blouse. My teeth sank into her shoulder. I feasted heartily.

"Don't be too greedy," Szandra whispered into my ear. "Our novice must not truly die."

I reluctantly ceased. Szandra yanked Sabine's head upward by seizing the top of her hair "Now you know, daughter of the Cagliostros, how your mother felt as life slipped away. She cried for their blood of her tormentors. Do you?"

"Blood…" muttered Sabine groggily. "Give me the blood of the woman who did this to me."

"I'm very generous with the spilling of blood" volunteered Szandra. I extended my left arm. The Mistress cut my wrist with her fingernail. She pressed my bleeding flesh over the mouth of our victim.

"Drink, Sabine," purred Szandra.

Joséphine Balsamo's Letter to José Alejandro Balsamo (continued)

My train arrived in London late in the afternoon of September 24. Urania was gracious enough to meet me at the station with a carriage. Hearing of my unnecessary trip, Urania sought to expedite my reunion with Sabine. At my domicile, we made a horrendous discovery.

My sister was lying unconscious on her bedroom floor. Blood flowed profusely from two gashes in her left shoulder. Luckily, Urania always carried her medical bag. After bandaging Sabine's shoulder, Urania arranged an emergency transfusion with me as the donor. If not for Urania'a ministrations, Sabine would have bled to death.

As she slept in her bed, Sabine mumbled, "Josine… Protect me… Vampires…" I knew all about the Undead from the family stories. My sister had clearly been targeted by the cultists. I didn't expound my beliefs to Urania. As a scientific rationalist, she would be unwilling to accept the reality of these supernatural predators. Presuming Sabine the victim of a demented assailant, Urania left to gather some Black Coat bodyguards.

After my friend's exit, I realized that the sun had already set. "Great-grandmother, grant me strength," I prayed. Vampires are vulnerable to crucifixes. None were in the house. I improvised by retrieving two pokers from the downstairs fireplace. As I wandered back through the passageway to Sabine's chambers, I heard feminine giggling. My sister's persecutors had returned. Crossing the pokers, I entered the room. Two women were near my sister's bed. They had torn open the bandages on Sabine's shoulder. One was a brunette in a black leather outfit with a fur cape. Her companion was a blonde attired in the manner of a Greek goddess. The duo slowly retreated before my impromptu cross.

"You call that makeshift atrocity a crucifix," mocked the brunette.

"Our adversary's religiosity is deficient, Mistress," ridiculed the blonde.

"Of course, Hildegarde. We saw this libertine in Sabine's mind. Joséphine Balsamo, Countess Cagliostro, you're merely counterfeit nobility. I am a true Countess, the Soul-Mate of the Great Vampire."

"You must be the wife of the current Count Frankenhausen."

"The Frankenhausens were merely pawns. The real Great Vampire is Dracula!"

Legends depict vampires cowering in terror at the cross. This pair merely froze as if coerced with a pistol. Are the stories false? Or was my cross diminished by its haphazard structure?

"The cross is only as potent as the purity of its holder," jeered Countess Dracula.

"It's strong enough to hold you here until dawn," I attested.

"The sun will not destroy me," warned the Countess.

"But what about me?" pleaded Hildegarde.

"Do not despair. Our antagonist is flawed. I can read her soul."

The scarlet eyes of the Countess probed deeply into mine. The figure of Hildegarde blurred. She was replaced by a woman in a purple robe. Her face mirrored mine.

I gasped "Mama!"

"Please lower your cross, daughter. I must kiss you."

"You can't be Mama!"

"You always deny those who love you the most," said another speaker. There was a girl next to my mother. She was wearing a pentagram brooch. I dare not write her name. She was slender with dark hair just like Sabine. I was confronted by my former classmate from Provence.

"You were always attracted to me, Josine, but you couldn't admit your true passions."

"That's not true. I only pretended to care for you."

"Remember when the headmistress sent all the students to bed. We didn't fall asleep. You were the prefect with the keys to the residence. We crept out into the night to watch the stars together. I told you my aspirations to be an artist."

Tears filled my eyes as I recalled these excursions.

"Frequently, Josine, we went to an unused portion of the school. There I sketched you in secret. I knew every line of your face…every facet of your body."

"Please stop," I begged.

"You must relinquish the pokers, Josine. I can't come to you unless they're surrendered. Only then will you feel the caress of my lips."

Uncrossing the pokers, I gave one to my mother. She flung it on the ground. I glanced at her hands. She had the ring with the golden ram. That same circlet was on my finger. The contradiction dragged me back to reality. The mirage dissipated. My mother reverted to Hildegarde.

I plunged the remaining poker into Hildegarde's chest. As the writhing vampire fell, my classmate devolved into Countess Dracula. She gripped my throat. My hands tugged on the chain of her cape. The Countess hurled me across the room into a wall. Dazed from the impact, I collapsed.

"Mistress…" wheezed the fallen Hildegarde. "She only scraped the edge of my heart…help me…"

The Countess plucked the poker out of her lackey's torso. Hildegarde rose to her full height.

"You damaged my clasp, Cagliostro," snarled the Countess as the cloak dropped off her back. "Your sister will pay for this sacrilege."

"And so will the younger Joséphine," added Hildegarde.

"All in good time," predicted the Countess. "Both Sabine and Anna's little child shall be yours. First, beat this upstart to a pulp." The Countess handed the poker to Hildegarde. The blonde raised the rod with her right hand. I chanced upon my sister's pentagram on the floor. The brooch is silver, a metal sometimes anathema to vampires. I threw the star at Hildegarde. She blocked the flying object with her left hand. The brooch's pin pierced her palm. She issued a sharp whimper. Tucking the poker under her arm, Hildegarde struggled with her right hand to remove the imbedded pentagram. The star rubbed a gold bracelet on her left wrist. She screamed "My arm is burning!" A blue flame engulfed Hildegarde. It disintegrated her and the poker. The brooch fell to the ground.

"You destroyed my servant! Now I will destroy you!" screeched Countess Dracula advancing towards my prostrate body. Her claw-like fingers slowly inched toward my stomach. "You have maternal instincts, Cagliostro. Maybe you're pregnant. Let's see!"

"Leave my sister alone!" shouted Sabine standing behind our nemesis. The lacerations on my sister's shoulder had vanished. The slaying of Hildegarde had revoked the mark of the vampire

Countess Dracula howled in agony. The tip of a metal stake burst from the front of her tunic.

Sabine had driven the other poker through the lamia's back impaling her merciless heart. The vampire dropped to her knees in front of me. I exulted over the shock and disbelief in her eyes.

"Before you roast in Hell, Dracula, learn this lesson. Never underestimate the Cagliostros."

I laughed triumphantly. Countess Dracula then smiled cryptically. Her face was filled with rapture. Then her eyelids closed as she fell back lifeless. The Countess wore a bracelet akin to Hildegarde's. I picked up the pentagram and dropped it on the gilded ornament. Blue fire blanketed the cadaver. The slain vampire faded from existence. The pentagram was unscathed.

No vampire can infest a home without being invited. My sister divulged how the Countess engineered an invitation during a contrived meeting in the street. The Countess had been with a man professing to be her husband. He must be Count Dracula. Urania arrived later with several men. I gave them Dracula's description: a tall thin man with a dark beard. The Black Coats were slowly mobilizing against the Great Vampire.

Claude Gabriel Dupont-Verdier's Journal, September 25, 1893

I drew Hildegarde's soul into my bracelet when her corporeality was lost. That pentagram must have been consecrated as an Elder Sign, a charm hostile to the symbols of Slidith and the Old Ones. Her right hand had held the star earlier without consequence, but the striking of the Elder Sign against the Valusian artifact on her left wrist ignited a devastating combustion.

Hildegarde's entrapped essence does not receive my thoughts. I can only hear her cries of despair and loneliness. Her mistreatment of me has not dampened my lust. I pleaded with Dracula to reconstitute her flesh with Akivasha's Tear. He would only vow to resurrect Hildegarde along with Szandra. The Great Vampire had witnessed the demise of his Soul-Mate through their enchanted rings.

As a precaution, the Master had linked Szandra's spirit to her cloak. If the mantle was extant, Szandra could live again. To ferret out the cape, Dracula embarked on a bold strategy. He directed me to infiltrate the Black Coats. Hildegarde stole Sabine's diary. It contained valuable data about the criminal organization. The diary cited names of important members–Moriarty, Caber, Koluchy, Dorrington, Saladin and Nikola. This infamous roster included London's purveyor of vice, Jillian Blake.

Excerpt from Confessions of a Black Coat *by Larry Parker (Unpublished Manuscript)*

The biggest dunce in the Black Coats was Urania Caber. In the autumn of 1893, she instructed me to burn a fur cape as a favor for Countess Cagliostro. Of course, I did no such thing. Being grossly underpaid, I sold the item to Jacob Dix the pawnbroker.

Claude Gabriel Dupont-Verdier's Journal, *October 3, 1893*

Contacting the Black Coats under the auspices of Mrs. Blake, I stumbled upon a startling fact. They're searching for Dracula. When I apprised the Master, he instituted countermeasures. Already pursued by Van Helsing, he can't afford to fight the Black Coats. A retreat to Transylvania is warranted.

The Great Vampire is not content with defensive maneuvers. Dracula bids me to orchestrate new aggression. The *Jarvee* will be arriving in Mexico with a message for Aguilar. Once his desperados secure a certain prize, the ship will haul the merchandise across the Atlantic. Captain Thompson was reluctant to lug such freight. I overcame his qualms by promising him ownership of the *Jarvee* for this final service.

Joséphine Balsamo's Letter to José Alejandro Balsamo (concluded)

I'm perplexed by Countess Dracula's dying grin. My sister thinks that our opponent was at peace after her release from the vampire curse. I don't share this opinion. Her smile implied a new conspiracy against our family. The instigator of this offensive must be the Great Vampire. According to our inquiries, Count Dracula fled England by a ship bound for the Black Sea.

Hildegarde mentioned Anna's daughter. Anxiety over her welfare motivates my letter. Dracula's disciples may still seek to turn her into a vampire. Did Anna name her child after my mother? Or was Anna thinking of your mother, the slayer of demons? Two Joséphines have already disgraced the name of your esteemed parent, grandfather. My mother and I were corrupted. The youngest holder of our ancestor's name must be spared an equally cruel destiny.

As a member of the Black Coats, I am little better than a vampire. Like the Undead, the Black Coats prey on humanity. The leaders of my organization are sadistic autocrats. I never informed them about Dracula's true nature. They merely view him as a lunatic stalking my sister. My motives for this subterfuge are simple. I dread that the Black Coats might seek a partnership with the Great Vampire.

My mother during her lifetime kept a picture of Anna. I always admired my aunt's wonderful ebony curls. Is her daughter also a brunette? Does Anna call her daughter Joséphine or the Spanish counterpart, Josefina?

Ever since my experience with Countess Dracula, I've been plagued by a recurring nightmare. I see a child with dark hair abused by fiends. Her persecutors are not vampires but men in black coats. Please cherish and protect Anna's daughter.

Your granddaughter,
Joséphine

José Alejandro Balsamo's Diary, May 6, 1894

Masked bandits raided our hacienda. They kidnapped Josefina. Ricardo and the servants are out searching for her. I implore God to let no harm befall my innocent grandchild.

The Eulogy of Satanas to his Beloved, April 30, 1895

Darling Hildegarde, you cannot read my words. Your disembodied purgatory persists on Walpurgis Night. One prerequisite is absent for your liberation. I require the blood of the Great Vampire, but he is no more. Van Helsing's followers exterminated him in Transylvania.

Your enemies, the heirs of Count Cagliostro, shall not flourish. I plot to avenge you by manipulating the Black Coats. Sabine Balsamo disregarded a cardinal prohibition. She kept a diary with references to the syndicate's hierarchy. Thanks to you, that book is mine. If my criminal peers study her notations, Sabine's life would be in jeopardy. At the proper time, I'll strike at Joséphine's beloved sister.

You always loathed Anna Peisser. Her only daughter is enslaved. Again you're responsible, my sweet, for this development. You proposed Josefina Peisser as a Sister of the Night. Dracula dictated her abduction. Captain Thompson hired Aguilar and his pistoleros to capture the girl. The *Jarvee* smuggled her into Europe. Dracula hoped to personally turn Josefina into a vampire. His destruction caused a modification to this act of retribution. Josefina has been hidden in France. I've sold her to Madame Delhomme's brothel in Chartres. The child will be taught to be a voluptuary rivaling Szandra in depravity. The Balsamo clan rejoices in anagrams like Absalom. I mimic our foes with an anagram of "vampire." Anna's daughter has been renamed *Irma Vep*.

I excuse your flirtation with Szandra. You were attracted to the avatar of the Great Vampire within her. Szandra will no longer be a barrier to our union. I've abandoned my hunt for her cloak. There is no reason to reconstruct her anymore. The essence of the Great Vampire will never separate us. It will dwell inside my breast

Loridan has shown me the way. He described the methods that Vlad the Impaler used to become the Great Vampire. The modern equivalent of Vlad's excesses shall be my pathway to immortality. It may take decades, but I will control my own cadre in the Black Coats. My underlings will commit countless crimes of butchery to befoul my soul. The inevitable outcome will be my arrest by the police. When that calamity arrives, poison will extinguish my life. The Old Ones will reconstitute me as the Great Vampire, the successor to Dracula. My own blood will fuel Akivasha's Tear. You shall feel the fleshly pleasures as my Soul-Mate. We shall walk the Earth for all eternity.

Urania's Babysitter

The woman known as Dr. Urania Caber was in an uproar in 1895. Gabrielle Routh, her governess and bodyguard, had left suddenly to take care of her ailing mother. This was an important night in the history of the Moriarty crime syndicate. A conference was being held in the Northumberland Hotel in London. Former associates of her father, the late Professor James Moriarty, were gathering to reorganize his illegal empire. Urania couldn't afford to miss this meeting. Her position as the chief of the scientific division was being challenged by a ruthless botanist. Yet how could Urania go without a babysitter for her young sons?

The brown-haired mother went over a list of candidates in her mind. Her close friend Joséphine Balsamo was excluded because she was in New Orleans. Joséphine's sister, Sabine, would probably be available, but her near suicide two years ago rendered her unsuitable.

There was Urania's detested half-sister, Trickie Moriarty, an obnoxious girl of 19 years. Through her medical research, Urania had discovered the relationship between nicotine addiction and cancer. She cleverly introduced her half-sister to cigarettes in the hope that eventually Trickie would die an agonizing death. It would be uncharitable to impose on a girl being slowly poisoning. Urania had her ethical standards.

Urania never forgave her father for not remaining a bachelor after her mother's death. Why did he need to secretly marry for as second time? Urania's anger at her father had prompted her to use her mother's maiden name. Urania never adopted Clay or one of the other aliases of her children's father. She refused to do so because that gigolo had abandoned her for other women.

Her only option regarding the babysitter was to request her uncle's help. Born Noel Moriarty, he lived under the false identity of Julius Pavia in the Blackheath district.

With the arrest of Colonel Moran last year, Noel had emerged as the leader of the Moriarty crime network. Despite their family relationship, Urania could not be sure of her uncle's support at the upcoming conference. Noel's wife, Catarina, was not on friendly terms with Urania. Catarina could poison Noel's mind against his niece.

There was a knock on the door of her house. Urania silently hoped this was a babysitter from her uncle. She was surprised to see a slender, dark-haired man

"Antonio Nikola. Don't tell me you're the babysitter?"

"Of course not! Your uncle requested my assistance. Please let my charges come in. I brought Dominick and another boy."

Urania was aghast. She recognized her uncle's nine-year old son, Dominick Damien Moriarty. He had black hair, dark blue eyes and a round face. The other boy was about the same age.

"This young man is Henry Peters, Jr. His father's an Australian business associate."

"Antonio, my uncle was supposed to find a sitter. Instead, he has burdened me with two more children."

"Do not fret, Urania. I already promised Dominick's mother to provide a sitter for her from among my staff. I made a similar commitment to Henry Sr. It just seemed logical that the sitter care for all these boys together. She will be joining us shortly."

Urania called her children to greet their guests.

"Jimmy! Claud! Please come here."

A young slender boy of 12 years with brown hair came prancing down the stairs. He was carrying a massive volume.

"Is my presence really necessary, mother? I was studying grandfather's book on asteroids."

"Cousin Dominick's here with a friend."

Another brown-haired child of six years soon materialized on the stairs. He was clutching a stuffed figure nearly his own size. The manikin resembled an eighteenth century nobleman.

" 'Clod' plays with dolls," jeered Dominick.

"My son's name is Claud Darrell Caber," corrected Urania.

"Please forgive my brother's inanimate companion," explained Jimmy. "Last year, Joséphine Balsamo told Claud a bedtime story about her illustrious ancestor, the Count who secretly launched the French revolution. Claud and I prepared an effigy to be burned on Guy Fawkes Night. I amused Claud by making our Guy look like Count Cagliostro. Claud grew so attached to the Guy that he refused to have it cremated."

"I want to be a Count," said Claud. "I want to make revolutions. I want to blow up Parliament. I'll be Count Guy."

"That's a stupid alias," proclaimed Dominick.

"What's an alias?" asked Claud.

"It's a fake name," interjected Henry. "I have an idea for one of my own. My full name's Henry Lakington Peters, Jr. I could call myself Henry Lakington."

"That's very unoriginal," volunteered Jimmy. "Just replace Peters Jr. with Peterson. Are you related to Karl Peters, the German explorer of East Africa?"

"Never heard of him," responded Henry.

"Karl Peters...Karl Peterson," mumbled Claud.

"Your aliases are foolish," decreed Dominick.

"Could you make a better one?" challenged Henry.

"We should use anagrams like the French crooks," asserted Dominick. "My middle name is Damien. It could easily be Medina."

"Only a sissy uses anagrams," argued Henry.

"I'm not a sissy!" snapped Dominick.

"Now, boys, play nicely with each other!" ordered Antonio.

"I have no desire to play with Dominick," observed Jimmy. "He once tried to hypnotize me into behaving like a dog. Luckily my mind is resistant to mesmerism."

Urania was ready to berate Jimmy for bringing up an old dispute. Her scolding was prevented by a knock at the door.

Antonio answered it. "Here's the babysitter, Milday Nevermore," he said.

A slender Caucasian woman entered the house. She wore a dark kimono covered by a slim coat. She had short brown hair and a black patch covering her right eye. Around her neck was a chain that ended in an amulet shaped like a cat's head. She was holding the hand of a young blonde girl. The child's other hand held a toy rifle.

"Permit to introduce Lily Bugoff," declared Milady. "I also promised her parents to mind her."

"Thank you for letting into your home, Madame Caber," stated Lily.

"A charming young lady," noted Urania. "How old are you, Lily?"

"Seven."

"Why do you have a rifle?" interrupted Claud.

"I'm a huntress. Papa hunts peasants in Russia."

Urania concluded that Lily's English was flawed. She must have meant "pheasants."

"Tell me a story about the peasants," insisted Claud.

Urania was concerned about the impressionable Claud. After the bad experience with Joséphine's fables about Cagliostro, Urania didn't want his head filled with tales of violence and gore. She had always intended her children to excel in the medical and scientific wing of the Moriarty gang. Jimmy was clearly on such a path, but she feared that Claud was too impulsive. She didn't want him to become an assassin when he chose a career. Fortunately, tales about the hunting of birds should do no harm.

Confident that Claud had found a harmless playmate, Urania left with Antonio for the Northumberland Hotel.

The Lady in the Black Gloves

1. 1885-1889: The Initiation of a Prefect

In November 1885, a lecture on French literature was being delivered by Madame Fourneau, the headmistress of the College for Young Women, an exclusive boarding school in Provence. She was a middle-aged widow with brown hair, dressed in a stern black skirt and a white blouse, with a dark brown tie. She always repeated her comments twice while her students, approximately 30 girls, recorded her words in their notebooks.

"Alexandre Dumas was... Alexandre Dumas was... an extremely meticulous writer... an extremely meticulous writer... His historically accurate novel... His historically accurate novel... *Joseph Balsamo... Joseph Balsamo...* revealed the true role of the title character... revealed the true role of the title character... in fomenting our great revolution of 1789... in fomenting our great revolution of 1789."

A 15-year old girl raised her hand. She was slender, with dark hair, and wore a dark orange dress. The headmistress acknowledged her.

"You have something that you wish to say, Mademoiselle Tupin?"

"I disagree, Madame. Monsieur Dumas severely distorted Joseph Balsamo's activities. He was merely a charlatan known as Count Cagliostro. Dumas later compounded his fabrications by exaggerating Balsamo's role in the Affair of the Queen's Necklace. Dumas's assertions about Balsamo's secret passages in the Rue St. Claude are wild speculations, typical of an author who claimed that Louis XIV was replaced with his twin brother."

"So you disagree with my assessment of Dumas, Mademoiselle Tupin?"

"I do, Madame."

"Are you calling me a liar?"

"No, Madame, I am not."

"Then, why are you arguing with me?"

"At my previous school, we were allowed to question our teachers."

"We follow other methods here. But I feel there is an ulterior motive behind your statements."

"I do not understand what you mean, Madame."

"By denying Cagliostro's achievements, you are, in effect, criticizing a fellow student, one whom I have entrusted with a large amount of responsibility."

"No, Madame, I am not saying that at all."

"Yes, you are, Mademoiselle Tupin. I must insist that you apologize for your behavior."

"I will not. I have done nothing wrong."

"Then, you must be punished."

Madame Fourneau approached the desk occupied by a 17-year old student. She had blonde hair, a delicate chin, deep-set eyes and high cheek-bones. She wore a black skirt and a brown blouse, with a black tie.

"Mademoiselle Balsamo, take Mademoiselle Tupin to the isolation room."

The blonde girl rose. The headmistress gave her a key. Pulling Tupin by the arm, Balsamo dragged her out of the classroom. The brunette was taken up a flight of stairs to a Spartan room with a bed and two chairs.

As the blonde was leaving the room, she addressed the younger girl:

"My dear Irene, you brought this upon yourself."

"What do you mean, Joséphine?"

"You should have agreed to my offer. As I told you before, I really run this school."

Two hours later, Joséphine returned with Madame Fourneau and two other girls. The headmistress harangued the detainee.

"Mademoiselle Tupin, are you now willing to apologize for the slanderous remarks that you made earlier?"

"No, Madame."

"If you do not recant, you will have to be punished appropriately."

"If that is your wish, so be it, Madame."

"It is not my wish. It is *your* wish, Mademoiselle." Madame Fourneau handed a whip to Joséphine. "Mademoiselle Balsamo will administer the punishment."

A week later, Irene stood before Joséphine and two other girls who helped her in her prefect duties at the school. The trio was sipping tea.

"Irene," intoned Joséphine, "the last time you were here, I asked you to join our sisterhood. You foolishly refused. I extend that offer again. Do you accept?"

"Yes, Joséphine."

"Very wise. But we need to clarify certain matters. You did not wish to discuss them before. Are you willing to do so now?"

"Yes, Joséphine."

"Your mother's maiden name is Victoire Chupin, but there is no mention of your father's name in your records. Who was he?"

"I don't know."

"Your parents were unmarried. Doesn't that make your mother little more than a common harlot?"

Irene nodded.

"You really have to speak up, Irene. What did you just acknowledge that your mother is?"

"A harlot."

"And you are little more than a common thief. Are you not?"

"That is a lie. I have never stolen anything."

"The interview that Madame had with the lady who brought you here would suggest otherwise. That lady has a son, four years younger than you. Your mother was his nurse, wasn't she?

"Yes, His name is Arsène, although his mother calls him Raoul."

"Arsène's mother claims that a valuable brooch was stolen from one of her friends, the Countess de Dreux-Soubise. This brooch was later discovered in your room. Do you admit your crime?"

"No, Arsène stole the brooch. He hid it in my room."

"Irene, don't make an 11-year old boy a scapegoat for your own inept actions. If you tell any more lies, I will see to it that you are punished again."

Irene did not reply

"To protect your mother's reputation, you were registered at the school under the alias of Tupin," resumed Joséphine. "Admit it. You stole that brooch."

"I stole the brooch."

"You are lucky that thieves are no longer branded on the shoulders as they were in days of Jeanne de La Motte. In Arabia, they remove the hands of the offenders. Fortunately for you, punishments of such a cruel nature are no longer used in this enlightened age. The College received a letter asking about your well-being. It came from a fencing instructor named Théophraste Lupin. Who is he?"

"He is Arsène's father."

"Is he *just* Arsène's father? The surname Tupin is very similar to Lupin."

"That's just a coincidence."

"Is it? It seems strange that Arsène's mother left her husband and abandoned his surname. She now uses her maiden name of d'Andresy. I can only conclude that Théophraste and his wife argued over some important matter. Perhaps it was your very existence?"

"I don't know. I told you earlier. I don't know who my father is."

"My dear Irene, isn't it logical to assume that Théophraste Lupin is also your father?"

"Perhaps."

"Good. Now that we have come to an understanding, I have an assignment for you. I have seen your work in art class. You really are quite talented with those firm hands. I want you to sketch my portrait."

In January 1889, Madame Fourneau had startling news for Joséphine Balsamo. Now approaching her twenty-first birthday, Joséphine was scheduled to graduate in the spring. But a new development caused her to leave the College for Young Women sooner than anticipated. Fourneau had received a letter from the wife of Noel Moriarty, the British railway expert, currently residing in Italy. Because she had a three-year-old boy, Mrs. Moriarty wished to engage a governess fluent in both Italian and English. Joséphine spoke both languages.

"You will be pleasantly surprised," said Madame Fourneau, "to learn that Mrs. Moriarty is the former Mademoiselle Catarina Koluchy, your predecessor as my prefect. I have reviewed the terms of her offer and they are very generous. There is only one issue that remains to be settled."

"What issue would that be, Madame?"

"That of your successor."

"There is no question, Madame. Only one candidate exists. She has proven her reliability, although her first few months were difficult."

"As yours were too," chuckled Madame Fourneau.

"I have not forgotten." Joséphine remembered all too vividly her own flogging. "Do you concur with my recommendation, Madame?"

"I do. In fact, she is already waiting outside." Opening the door, Madame Fourneau said: "Irene, will you please join us?"

After the meeting, Joséphine made her farewells to Irene.

"You have been a loyal friend, dear Irene," she professed. "I have a little gift for you."

Joséphine handed the girl a small box. When Irene opened it, she saw a silver brooch in the shape of a five-pointed star.

"A pentagram," indicated Joséphine, "a sort of good luck charm. You may need it in your new role. Madame Fourneau always compared our school to a ship. She was the captain, and I was her first mate."

"In the British Navy, you would have been called Number One."

"Well, Irene, you are the new Number One."

Although the Italian residence of the Moriarty family was in the northern town of Pavia, they were vacationing in the Bay of Naples. Joséphine Balsamo traveled there to assume her new responsibilities. The Moriartys were guests at the Villa Corbucci. The new governess was greeted by Dr. Nikola, the physician to the Corbucci family. He conducted Joséphine to Catarina Moriarty, a regal woman with dusky hair, rosy lips and extremely dark blue eyes. After Nikola departed, Catarina had a revelation for her new employee.

"Joséphine," she began, "I've been guilty of a slight deception. Although I was truthful about my marriage and my child, I do not really need your services as a governess. I have a different position in mind for you. I have been managing a philanthropic organization, a Brotherhood, since I left the College. It is a branch of the Black Coats. I would like you to become one of my assistants."

"I know the Black Coats, Catarina. My late mother was one of their members."

"Indeed. However, there is a glitch. Some of my associates fear that you may bear a grudge because of the disciplinary actions I took against you at the College."

"Not in the least. Any unpleasantness between us was entirely Madame Fourneau's fault. You only followed her directives. By the time you left the College, we had become friends."

"And I proved it when I recommended you for the position of chief prefect. I was surprised that Madame so readily agreed. You were only 16 at the time; others were older, had more experience."

"I had ways of endearing myself to Madame Fourneau, Catarina. We both loved the novels of Dumas "

"Madame also enjoyed your sketches of her."

"A family trait, perhaps; this obsession with artwork. Did you know that she is the sister of Gaston Morrell?"

"The deranged artist who strangled all those women in Paris during 1878?"

"The same. Naturally, her three children are unaware of this. Her daughter is studying in Paris. Philippe pursues his education in Geneva, but the other son, Louis, is still at the school, due to ill health."

"So the young brat hasn't gotten over his asthma. He must be about 16 now. Madame Fourneau still keeps him tied to her apron's strings?"

"Very much so. In fact, I have devised a scheme to manipulate him in order to repay Madame Fourneau for her mistreatments."

"I am happy to hear it. Like you, I had some distasteful experiences at the hands of Madame Fourneau during my tutelage. What is your scheme?"

"I have already seduced Louis. He must be turned against his mother. I have only gained his affection. Louis is not yet ready, but he soon will be. Because Madame Fourneau forced me to draw her portrait, I intend to persuade Louis to present her with an artistic effigy assembled from... very unusual materials. Her son will soon be following in his Uncle Gaston's footsteps."

"A wonderful strategy, Joséphine. You enlist the children of your enemies to act as your underlings. Was it difficult to arrange secret meetings with Louis?"

"I had an accomplice. A fellow prefect. She made excuses for my dalliances with Louis."

"Is this girl smart, Joséphine? Should I recruit her for my Brotherhood?"

"Certainly not. She is merely a petty thief with delusions of intellect. She has no idea about the overall scope of my plan."

"Like Jeanne de La Motte, whom your ancestor manipulated into stealing the Queen's Necklace."

"Her fate will be similar to Madame de La Motte's, Catarina. She, too, will be branded as a thief!"

"Madame de La Motte's shoulders were scarred. Do you intend to do the same?"

"No, I will impose an Arabian penalty."

2. 1896: The Rampage of Bluebeard III

In the autumn of 1896, Paris was plagued by a series of unexplained murders. Five women had been found, strangled, their bodies floating on the Seine. The crimes bore a strong resemblance to those of Gaston Morrell, the notorious strangler who had earlier terrorized Paris under the sobriquet of Bluebeard. Gaston had drowned fleeing the authorities, but now he seemed to have awakened from his 18-year old grave. *L'Echo de France* dubbed this imitator Bluebeard II. A rival newspaper, *Le Matin*, countered by arguing that this new maniac was the third incarnation of Bluebeard. The original Bluebeard was unarguably Gilles de Laval, Baron de Rais, the slaughterer of children from the fifteenth century. The public accepted *Le Matin*'s argument. The current strangler became widely feared as Bluebeard III.

The hysteria gripping Paris was compounded by the reception of letters sent to the newspapers and accurately predicting each murder. All contained the same identical phrases: *"History will repeat itself tonight. Bluebeard will strike again."* They bore the signature of a woman: *"Clio Gosart."*

The House of Repose was an insane asylum situated in the Ville-d'Avray community just outside Paris. It consisted of several buildings spread over a large area, enclosed by an extremely steep wall. One large edifice housed the administrative staff.

Its director, Doctor Eric Maubeuge, was a man of indeterminable age with piercing eyes and a walrus mustache. Seated at his desk, he had been reviewing the file of a patient who had committed suicide that evening. His perusal, however, was interrupted by a visitor.

Maubeuge critically eyed the young woman seated opposite him. He judged her age to be in the mid-twenties. Tall and slender with black hair, she wore an orange dress with a brooch in the shape of a pentagram on the right side. A short black scarf was tied around her collar. Black silk gloves adorned her hands. Silver bracelets were on her wrists. She had presented a business card that identified her as Irina Putine of the Chupin Detective Agency.

"Are you Russian, Mademoiselle?"

"Yes. I immigrated to this country three years ago."

"I must commend you on your French. You speak it like a Parisian."

"Thank you, Doctor. You have an unusual name. Are you from Flanders?"

"I'm not from the city of Maubeuge, if that's what you mean. I'm from Switzerland. Five years ago, I came to France to become director of this sanatorium. Sometimes, names can be misleading. This recently deceased young man was such an example. Despite being christened Louis Fourneau, he was generally known in Provence by the Spanish variant of his first name, Luis."

"I'm well aware of the College Girl Murderer's background, Doctor."

"The College Girl Murders was a foolish name given to my patient's crimes by sensationalistic newspapers six years ago. I'm rather surprised you

68

heard of his suicide. We only sent a message to the police within the last two hours."

"I didn't know of Fourneau's death until my arrival. How did he die?"

"He cut his throat with a razor. We have concluded that an orderly dropped it in his cell after shaving him. Needless to say, the orderly's employment has been terminated. If you didn't come because of Fourneau's death, then why are you here?"

"A simple request from a client who wished to rule out the possibility that Fourneau may have escaped to become Bluebeard III."

"A ridiculous assertion," stated Dr. Maubeuge. "Like Gaston Morrell, Bluebeard III strangles his victims. Fourneau, on the other hand, slew them with a knife and mutilated their bodies. I see no parallels. Why would your client espouse such an absurd theory?"

"My client learned of a family connection between the two killers. My client was Fourneau's sixth victim."

"Your client must be lying about her identity then, Mademoiselle. The account of Fourneau's crimes contradicts that claim. The murders were committed in a boarding school for young women between September 1889 and January 1890. Louis Fourneau was the son of the headmistress. Detaching the flesh of his victims, he took grisly trophies to a locked storeroom in the school's attic. He was trying to construct a woman in his mother's image. He was confronted in the attic by a student who became his sixth victim. Immediately after this murder, Madame Fourneau found the girl's mutilated corpse in the attic. Louis then locked his mother in the storeroom with the grotesque caricature fashioned in her likeness. Her screams were heard by a janitor. He ran into the attic and overpowered Louis. The headmistress was discovered dead from heart failure."

"Certain facts are missing from your file, Doctor. First, my client was merely knocked unconscious by Louis Fourneau, rather than slain."

"That makes no sense. Why didn't he kill her outright? It goes against the pattern of his other crimes."

"Perhaps he was acting on special instructions from his Muse?"

"His *Muse*?"

"Louis told the police that he had performed his atrocities at the bequest of a woman whom he described only as his Muse."

"Perhaps the Muse was Mary Shelley? Louis's crimes were obviously based on her famous novel, *Frankenstein*... But before we continue any further, I'd like to know your client's name."

"Is it not in your file already?"

"My file does not mention the names of Fourneau's victims."

"Yes, the victimizers are often remembered better than the victims. In any event, my client wishes to remain anonymous, Doctor. Since she was the sixth victim, let us refer to her as Number Six."

"Very well then. I can't imagine how Number Six survived. Even if she'd been merely unconscious, she'd have died from loss of blood. Fourneau had severed both her hands."

"As I said earlier, certain facts are missing from your file. A surgeon treated the girl's wounds and rushed her to a hospital. Some months later, her health improved, but she had been mentally traumatized by her ordeal. Her guardian dispatched Number Six to a private nursing home in England. She spent three years there before returning to France."

"I see. Do you have any further questions, Mademoiselle?"

"Did Louis Fourneau write anything during his confinement?"

"Only meaningless scribbles," said the voice of a man who just entered the office. "My name is Dr. Biron." As Irina Putine introduced herself, he kissed her gloved hand.

"The good doctor is a fellow colleague from Passy," explained Maubeuge. "He was visiting here when this unfortunate suicide transpired. Dr. Biron asked to examine the writings of the deceased."

Biron handed Irina a sheet of paper. It had the heading: "*Je m'abuse*" (French for "I abuse myself"). Under it were the words "Louis–Louis," repeated for seven rows.

"I would also like to see the body, Dr. Maubeuge," requested Irina.

"I see no harm in granting your petition."

Maubeuge escorted Irina to the morgue. He lifted the sheet that covered the cadaver. The body was that of a thin handsome man with brown hair. His age was about 23.

As Irina left, she was met by Biron. He was accompanied by a lean man with grey hair and a beard. The man wore tinted spectacles. He was dressed in a black Inverness cape and a top hat.

"Mademoiselle Putine, a police inspector has arrived to inquire into this suicide," announced Biron. "Permit me to introduce Inspector d'Andresy."

"D'Andresy?"

"My name seems familiar to you," remarked the Inspector. "Have we met before?"

"No, but I have heard of a Raoul d'Andresy."

"A distant cousin. My name is Maurice."

The Regenerator of Fashion was a prestigious dressmaking shop in the Rue de Grammont. Its original owner, Van Klopen, had sold his establishment in 1892 to a London clothing firm, the House of Crafts. The new owner, Mrs. Moriarty, was commonly addressed by her employees as Madame Koluchy.

Both she and her husband, Noel Moriarty, were leaders of the European crime cartel, the Black Coats. Each occupied a seat on the ruling High Council. Koluchy's organization, the Brotherhood of the Seven Kings, was an autonomous branch of the Black Coats.

Koluchy was presently having tea in her office with three of her subordinates. Koluchy was dressed in an elegant black gown. Seated at her right was Joséphine Balsamo in a bright green dress. The other two attendees were attired less flamboyantly. They both wore black skirts and brown blouses with black ties. They were Mary Holder, a pale woman with dark hair and eyes, and Helen Lipsius, a damsel with a piquant smiling face and charming hazel eyes.

"Joséphine, my husband is impressed by your usage of the Morrell motif in this current operation," said Madame Koluchy. "He is quite an admirer of Gaston Morrell's artistry. Noel even has one of his paintings."

"I knew that your husband owns works by Jan Gosart and Jacques Saillard, Madame, but I was unaware that he also possessed a Morrell."

"Noel purchased it from the Duc of Carineaux's collection. The portrait is of Morrell's fourth victim."

"Please tell Mr. Moriarty that I am very pleased with his protégé, Malbodius. His arrangement for the transportation of the corpses to the Seine has been very efficient. Where did your husband find such a talented individual?"

"Malbodius was recruited by my late brother-in-law before his tragic death in 1891. Poor James met him in Switzerland."

Mary Holder refilled her own cup of tea. She noticed that Joséphine's cup was nearly empty.

"More tea, Mademoiselle Balsamo?"

"The correct title is Countess," said Joséphine coldly. "You are guilty of a breach of etiquette, Mademoiselle Holder. I could have you sent to the Alteration Room."

"I apologize, Countess," beseeched Mary. "I meant no disrespect."

Being the daughter of a genuine Italian Count, Koluchy knew that Joséphine's claims were a sham. Nevertheless, Koluchy permitted Joséphine's affectations since the blonde was her most valuable assistant.

"Do not fret, Mademoiselle Holder," interjected Koluchy. "Mistakes are allowed, provided they are not repeated. Countess Cagliostro committed a much more serious mistake two years ago, and suffered no other punishment than being temporarily banished to New Orleans. She tried to recruit Arsène Lupin as her pupil, but he outsmarted her and is now a major threat to us."

"Lupin will soon be eliminated, Madame," said Joséphine.

"Joséphine, I have a fondness for you that dates from our days together as students, but I warn you. Our society will not tolerate a second failure in this matter."

"My spy is keeping me well informed of our adversary's thefts. Arsène Lupin will soon *pay the law*."

"You will be held to that assurance. Let us discuss other matters. The dresses worn by our two colleagues may have a certain nostalgic flair. They are

71

from the new clothing line based on those uniforms that the late Madame Fourneau gave her prefects as gifts."

"Madame intends to propose a new name for the Brotherhood to the High Council," said Helen Lipsius.

"What name?" asked Joséphine.

"The Black Skirts."

Chief Inspector Lefevre of the Sûreté had investigated the original Bluebeard killings of 1878. Now in his late fifties, he was entrusted largely with supervisory duties. The new Bluebeard inquiry had been delegated to Inspector d'Andresy. In his private office, Lefevre showed d'Andresy a recent article in *Le Matin*:

"...Born in Martinique in 1850, d'Andresy had become an official in the constabulary on the island. During 1895, he had achieved considerable fame for breaking up a smuggling ring active in the Caribbean and the Gulf of Mexico. Working closely with American authorities, d'Andresy had tracked the leader of the crime network to New Orleans. Regretfully, the detective was afflicted with pneumonia while fruitlessly pursuing the master criminal in the Louisiana bayous. After his recovery, d'Andresy was transferred to Paris in the same year..."

"The writer of the article has full confidence in your ability to arrest Bluebeard III," commented Lefevre. "Unfortunately, I can only reach the same conclusion by hearing a report of your progress."

The Inspector coughed slightly. Lefevre attributed that cough to a consequence of the investigator's earlier pneumonia. D'Andresy proceeded to summarize his inquiries.

"Since Morrell strangled the women whose portraits he painted, our supposition has naturally been that Bluebeard III must also be an artist. All of his victims posed for either painters or sculptors. My suspicions first focused on a sculptor, Boris Yvain, because three of the victims were amongst his models. But he has no connection to the other two. Furthermore, he has an unbreakable alibi for the night of one of the murders. I now have a new suspect, Jacques Saillard."

"The painter whose work is said to be even more erotic than that of Monet and Renoir?"

"Yes, the same. His so-called art is obscene."

"That is your opinion, Maurice."

"I detest such filth, Chief Inspector."

"Please return to the facts."

"All the victims had posed for him. There's also an intriguing point about Saillard. He has never appeared in public. His physical appearance remains a mystery. I have a suspicion that he may be related to Gaston Morrell."

"Why do you believe that?"

"Madness runs in that family. Morrell's nephew was the recently deceased College Girl Murderer. His brother, Philippe Fourneau, vanished from a Swiss boarding school in 1891. I viewed the corpse of Louis Fourneau in order to get some idea of Philippe's probable appearance. My theory is that Philippe is both Bluebeard III and Saillard."

"Have you been able to trace any of Saillard's other models?"

"Three years ago, Saillard made his debut with a portrait of Isadora Salazar, the celebrated Brazilian beauty. The painting was rather conservative compared to the later trash produced by Saillard's brush. The subject wasn't stark naked. Isadora moved to Germany after marrying the sugar magnate, Otto Klein."

"Do we have any other leads on Saillard in Paris?"

"So far, no. I hope to locate him by interrogating Fritz Kramm, the art dealer who exhibits his paintings."

Lefevre accompanied his lieutenant to Kramm's art gallery. Together they questioned the obese proprietor.

"I've never met Saillard," said Kramm. "The deliveries of the paintings, as well as any financial dealings, have all been handled through an intermediary."

"Who is he?" asked d'Andresy.

"Saillard's proxy is a *she*, Inspector. In fact, she posed for his painting, *The Lady in the Black Gloves*."

"Is that painting here?" asked Lefevre.

"No, it's in London," replied Kramm. "It was sold last year to Julius Pavia, a wealthy British collector."

"What's the model's name?"

"Irina Putine."

The Chupin Detective Agency was a large three-storied building. The firm had been founded in 1868 by Victor Chupin. When Inspector d'Andresy arrived, he immediately asked to see Chupin, but was informed by a secretary that her employer was working on a case in Spain. She directed him to Chupin's chief assistant, Irina Putine.

As the policeman entered Irina's office, she rose from her desk to greet him.

"Inspector, this is a surprise, please have a chair. When I met you the other day, I didn't compliment you on the extraordinary job that you did in the Caribbean."

"Thank you, Mademoiselle. My only regret is that I didn't apprehend the ringleader of the smuggling syndicate in Louisiana. I hope that you'll assist me in finding an equally elusive quarry."

"Whom do you seek?"

"A painter named Jacques Saillard. He's sought for questioning in the Bluebeard murders."

"I'm not surprised. My own investigation has revealed that Bluebeard III is killing Saillard's models. You must have uncovered my role in the exhibition of his work. I'd like to help you, but I'm bound by the rules of confidentiality to protect Saillard's identity. You've placed me in an awkward position "

"No, Mademoiselle, you've placed yourself in this awkward position. Must you continue this pretense that Saillard is merely a client?"

"I don't understand the meaning of your question, Inspector."

"I had initially assumed that Saillard was a man. But now, the thought occurs to me that a clever woman with artistic ability could easily produce such tasteless paintings under a male pseudonym. This would be particularly desirable if the artist in question is pursuing a bohemian lifestyle. You weren't content with just painting other women. You had to immortalize on canvas your own sensuality. I surmise from the title of your portrait that you only wore two small articles of clothing?"

"You have clearly not viewed *The Lady in the Black Gloves*, Inspector. I posed in attire similar to what I'm now wearing. I even wore this brooch. My portrait is no more controversial than the painting of Isadora Klein."

"Dr. Maubeuge told me the details of his earlier conversation with you. Like you, I am aware of the connection between Gaston Morrell and the College Girl Murderer."

"We appear to have both researched Morrell's family thoroughly."

"You have a habit of pretending to represent a client while really acting for yourself. Besides posing as Saillard's confidant, you hide your true relationship to Louis Fourneau's final victim."

"Your statement is ludicrous, Inspector."

"Let us talk about the woman whom you identified as Number Six to Dr. Maubeuge. Have you heard of the *Werewolves*?"

"They were a criminal gang that emerged in Paris during the late 1860s. In 1893, their leader, Lothaire Stepphun, was arrested in New York for murder. Soon after his incarceration, he was fatally shot while trying to escape. What relevance does this have to Number Six?"

"A minor member of the Werewolf gang was a female courier between Stepphun and his fence. She was little better than a prostitute. Her name was Victoire Chupin. She came from the same criminal family that spawned the founder of your agency; in fact, she's his sister."

"It is true that my employer had a checkered past, but he's made amends for it decades ago. Mind you, the same was true of the founder of the Sûreté."

"Victoire was arrested in 1868 for transporting stolen goods and sentenced to a year in prison. After her release, she gave birth to a daughter named Irene. I put it to you that this is Louis Fourneau's sixth victim."

"I do not dispute the fact, Inspector."

"In 1872, Victoire became the personal maid to Henriette d'Andresy, a banker's daughter. The following year, Mademoiselle d'Andresy was disowned by her father because she chose to marry Théophraste Lupin, whom was viewed as an unscrupulous gold digger."

"Did Théophraste truly loved Henriette, Inspector? Or did he marry her in hopes of winning her father's fortune"

"I don't know, Mademoiselle. But what I do know is that, prior to his marriage, Théophraste had long been Victoire's lover. In fact, Irene was their daughter. Théophraste and Henriette moved into a new residence. Despite the awkwardness, Victoire and her daughter were allowed to live with the Lupins. In 1874, Henriette gave birth to Théophraste's legitimate child. Victoire then became the young boy's nurse, Arsène Lupin, who now calls himself Raoul d'Andresy."

"You identified him as your cousin at the asylum, Inspector. Why does Arsène use a false name?"

"Do not play games with me, Mademoiselle. You are well aware of the reason the Lupin marriage soon dissolved after Henriette realized that Irene was Théophraste's bastard child. Henriette fled, reassumed her maiden name and changed her son's first name. For a while, Henriette supported herself by being a servant in the household of old friend, the Countess de Dreux-Soubise. Eventually, Henriette's finances improved. She lived a comfortable existence with her son. Henriette even forgave Victoire for her betrayal."

"I don't understand how Henriette could be so merciful, Inspector."

"She realized that Victoire was merely a stupid woman who had been entirely fooled by Théophraste. Rehired as Arsène's nurse, Victoire with her daughter resided in Henriette's home. In 1885, however, Irene followed in her mother's criminal footsteps. She foolishly stole a diamond brooch. When the robbery was discovered, Henriette insisted that the malefactor be disciplined. The thief was exiled under the alias of Irene Tupin to Madame Fourneau's boarding school."

"Maybe Irene wasn't guilty of the theft of the brooch, Inspector."

"Please enlighten me, Mademoiselle."

"Five years prior, the Dreux-Soubise family had been robbed of a valuable relic."

"The Queen's Necklace, Mademoiselle. I'm very familiar with the unsolved case."

"Was Irene in the household at that time, Inspector? No, she wasn't. What a pity! We can't blame her for that earlier theft. On the other hand, Arsène was. But please, continue with your narrative. I'm curious to see where it'll lead us."

"When Henriette died in 1886, Victoire could have retrieved Irene from the boarding school, but instead she busied herself with raising Arsène. Besides, Irene's letters indicated that she was very happy at Madame Fourneau's College."

"The mail was rigidly censored there, Inspector, by chief prefect. Do you know who she was at the time?"

"No, I do not, Mademoiselle. I fail to see the significance."

"Her name was Joséphine Balsamo. Have you ever heard of a historical figure called Joseph Balsamo, Count Cagliostro?"

"Yes, I've read of him in novels by Dumas. He was involved with the same Queen's Necklace that later came into possession of the Dreux-Soubise family."

"Have you any clues as to the identity of Clio Gosart, the author of the letters predicting the Bluebeard murders?"

"If I did, I would not share them with you, Mademoiselle. I will merely remark that Clio is the Muse of History and Jan Gosart was a Renaissance painter."

"That artist was also known as Jan Mabuse or Jan Malbodius because of his Flemish origins. And Clio Gosart is an anagram of Cagliostro, Inspector. The role of Clio in mythology also suggests that Joséphine Balsamo was the Muse, whom Louis Fourneau cited as the inspiration behind his crimes."

"That anagram proves nothing, Mademoiselle. Cagliostro is the name of a famous seer. The writer of the Clio Gosart letters could merely be familiar with the legends surrounding the clairvoyant Count."

"Have you ever heard of an alleged descendant called Countess Cagliostro?"

"Yes, I remember such a name figuring in a few unrelated cases, but I can't see its connection with these recent deaths."

"There was a confidence trickster calling herself Countess Cagliostro active in Paris during 1870. Twenty year later, a woman appeared in Panama under that name. While too young to be the earlier Countess, she was the right age to be the Joséphine Balsamo from the College. This 1890 Countess romanced Caratal, an important investigator of the Canal scandal. Following his disappearance under highly unusual circumstances, there was speculation that the Countess betrayed his movements to the conspirators behind the swindle. Previously, in April 1889, a woman only identified as Countess de Fenix allegedly ruined General Boulanger's political career by convincing him to flee France after his indictment for treason. The original Count Cagliostro once hid under the alias of de Fenix."

"These are cases of high finance and politics, Mademoiselle. You seem obsessed with Countess Cagliostro. Your fascination might even tempt you to implicate her in the 1880 theft of the Queen's Necklace. Enough of these wild speculations! Bluebeard III is simply a murderous lunatic."

"Joséphine Balsamo could be playing a complicated game for higher stakes. You must have learned that my portrait was purchased by Julius Pavia?"

"Yes."

"Months after Boulanger's disgrace, Joséphine visited her former school. The College Girl Murders commenced following her departure. At that time,

September 1889, Joséphine was supposedly working in the household of Noel Moriarty, the brother of the notorious Professor James Moriarty. The Professor was noted for his art collection. His brother may share the same hobby. Noel and his wife disappeared after the Professor's death in 1891. The reclusive Julius Pavia of London emerged as an art collector shortly thereafter. Noel had owned a home in Pavia, Italy. An illustrious sleuth once compared Noel's brother to an Emperor of France. Julius was the name of a Roman Emperor. Julius Pavia could be Noel Moriarty."

"Mademoiselle, you are playing games with your detours through history. You have been seeking to divert me from my primary inquiry. I have made two accusations, and you have yet to refute them. You are Jacques Saillard! You are Number Six!"

"Regarding the first charge, I met the real Jacques Saillard two years ago in Berlin. Otto Klein engaged the Chupin Detective Agency to prevent his wedding reception from being disrupted by burglars. The bride introduced me to Saillard, and I posed for him. Isadora Klein later hired the Agency to assist in the selling of his work. As I said, I'm not at liberty to reveal Saillard's identity, but Madame Klein is. She arrived in Paris yesterday and is a guest of the Royal Palace Hotel. If I explain the circumstances in a letter that you can present to her, she will likely disclose his whereabouts."

"There still remains the matter of Number Six, alias Irene Tupin. Irina is the Russian form of Irene. You talked about anagrams earlier. Your current surname is an anagram of Tupin."

"You're wrong, Inspector, 'Tupin' has five letters. 'Putine' has six."

"Only because Russian names are transliterated from the Cyrillic alphabet. In Russia, your surname would be spelt with five letters. In other languages employing a Latin alphabet, your surname would be converted into 'P-u-t-i-n' without an 'e.' The extra letter is essential in French to mimic the Russian pronunciation."

"Are you not forgetting a blatant fact, Inspector? Irene's hands were horribly severed. I have a pair of hands, as you can plainly see."

"Yet, you always wear gloves, Mademoiselle. I have heard rumors of great advances in the creation of artificial limbs. Someone may even be able to paint with such appendages. Remove your gloves."

"You're dangerously close to becoming offensive, Inspector, but I will comply."

Irina doffed her gloves. She displayed a set of perfectly formed human hands.

"You may wish to touch them to make sure that they are real."

She rose from behind her desk and then presented her hands to the Inspector. He felt them. They were not synthetic.

"Now that I have acceded to your ridiculous demand, Inspector, please let me write the letter."

At the Royal Palace Hotel, d'Andresy requested an interview with Madame Klein. It was granted by the raven-haired socialite.

"I hope that you were not too upset by Irina's refusal to disclose Jacques Saillard's identity, Inspector," said Madame Klein after having read the letter. "She was bound by promises of secrecy."

"I overstepped, Madame. I falsely accused Mademoiselle Putine of being Saillard."

"That is ironic. Irina told me that she had been an artist in her youth. But she's abandoned such pursuits to join the Chupin Detective Agency."

"We must discuss Saillard, not Mademoiselle Putine."

"I understand the gravity of the situation, Inspector. I will answer all your questions, but you must promise not to make my answers public if they clear Saillard of all suspicion."

"Your terms are acceptable. Who is Jacques Saillard?"

"I am. I use a pseudonym to overcome the prejudices of male art critics. My first painting was a self-portrait. My early work was not as innovative as my recent labors. I sense that you do not approve of my artistic endeavors, Inspector."

"I would not want a sister of mine involved with such paintings."

As Isadora Klein was in Berlin during all of the killings except the last, d'Andresy returned to police headquarters. He reviewed the files on the College Girl Murders. They contained information on Anatole Cerral, a surgeon who advocated outlandish medical procedures. He had treated the injured Irene in Avignon. Once he had finished studying the data, d'Andresy met again with Lefevre.

"Are you familiar with a Dr. Anatole Cerral?" inquired d'Andresy.

"I remember him well. He was hounded out of Paris by the medical authorities. Cerral advocated the application of skin grafts. He proposed that human flesh could be grafted on to patients."

"Did Cerral advocate doing this with severed limbs?"

"I believe he did. Why do you ask?"

"I'm formulating a theory, Chief Inspector. It would be premature to discuss it."

Inspector d'Andresy retired to his home in the Rue St. Claude. He removed the fake wig and beard as well as the glasses that hid his true appearance, that of a much younger man. He then perused a series of papers in which the name of Raoul d'Andresy appeared very frequently.

Among these papers was the birth certificate of Arsène Lupin.

The same night, Irina Putine was conferring with a middle-aged woman inside her office at the Chupin Detective Agency. The lady was her mother, Victoire. There existed a strong degree of resentment in Irina towards her mother. As a result, they rarely saw each other. But now, the circumstances demanded it.

"I have asked you here because I need information about Papa," said Irina. "He was more than just a fencing instructor."

Victoire did not respond.

"He was Lothaire Stepphun," asserted Irina.

"How did you discover that?"

"Your earlier association with the Werewolves. Lothaire Stepphun is an anagram of Théophraste Lupin. Papa loved anagrams. He taught me their usage during my childhood. I believe the daughter of one of Papa's enemies has been using anagrams, too, for her own purposes."

"Who are you talking about?"

"Before I disclose her identity, we need to have an open discussion of a certain event in 1880, the theft of the reconstituted Queen's Necklace. Uncle Victor briefed me about that affair, I know Arsène stole the necklace and gave it to Papa."

"I don't want to talk about this."

"Neither do I, but it's relevant to my current line of investigation. A police official inadvertently suggested today a possible link to my brother's earlier crime. I have only one question. Did anyone try to steal the necklace from Papa?"

"Yes, there was this blonde woman who posed as a purchaser for the gems. I never knew her name, but she belonged to the Black Coats. They attacked your father. One of his paramours stabbed the blonde. I later heard the she died of her wounds."

Irina's mother wasn't being totally candid. She had known the blonde by the name of Gloria Scot. Due to a humiliation inflicted on her by Gloria, Victoire had sworn never to mention that name again. Unknown to Victoire, Gloria Scot was an anagram of Cagliostro.

Victoire's revelation enabled Irina to grasp Joséphine's scheme. The dead woman must have been Joséphine's mother, the 1870 Countess Cagliostro, who likely coveted the Queen's Necklace because of its connection to her ancestor, Count Cagliostro. The current Joséphine had been orchestrating a complex scheme of vengeance against the Lupin family in order to avenge her mother's death. Irina's own debasement at the College was merely part of this vendetta.

"Mama, did Papa commit that murder in 1893 that led to his death in New York?"

"No, your father was a thief and a swindler, but he wasn't a murderer. Evidence was fabricated against him by one of his enemies."

"Probably by the Black Coats. Their doctrine of *pay the law* always causes scapegoats to be falsely charged with crimes. The daughter of the woman who was stabbed in 1880 is behind it all, Mama. Her name is Joséphine Balsamo."

"Joséphine Balsamo! Arsène never mentioned any connection between her and the Queen's Necklace."

"Arsène! What does he have to do with her?"

"Oh! I shouldn't have said anything. I'm sorry, but I can't tell you. Arsène swore me to secrecy."

"Oh really, Mama, we shouldn't keep secrets from each other. We're one happy family," said Irina sarcastically. "I keep my distance from Arsène, but I have followed the news about him. He lives in Normandy with his wife, Clarisse. What's the problem? Were he and Joséphine lovers?"

"Stop it! I agreed to conceal from him that you're back in France. He still thinks you're in England. In exchange, you're not to bother me about him. Why can't you make peace with him? Do you realize that you haven't seen him for 11 years?"

"We must discuss it, Mama. I will not have you place his interests over mine, your own blood. Now, tell me. I want to know what happened between Arsène and Joséphine."

But Victoire remained silent.

As Victoire left the Chupin Detective Agency, she was besieged by doubts. She had to justify her overriding loyalty to Arsène. Victoire remembered an incident from when Irene and Arsène were children. She was taking the youngsters to buy candy. Distracted by the rambunctious Arsène, Victoire accidentally bumped into a pedestrian. The man had called Victoire 'a dumb slut.' Arsène had responded by kicking the man in the shins. She recalled Arsène's words: "No one insults my precious Victoire! No one!" Arsène had always been faithful to her. Victoire would remain faithful to him.

The next day, a letter bearing the Clio Gosart signature was received at *L'Echo de France*. The police were immediately notified that Bluebeard III was about to strike again.

Maurice d'Andresy informed Chief Inspector Lefevre that only two of Jacques Saillard's models were in Paris: Isadora Klein and Irina Putine. Although the real Saillard had been cleared, the two policemen still agreed that the killer was targeting his models.

The pair formulated a strategy to protect the two ladies. Lefevre would take a squad of policemen to shield Madame Klein. Meanwhile, d'Andresy would bring Irina to that same location.

When d'Andresy arrived at the Chupin Detective Agency, Irina was attired in a comparable fashion as the day before, except that her dress was dark red. He requested that she accompany him to a safe house guarded by the Sûreté. His request was quickly rebuffed.

"I'll be safer here surrounded by my own operatives," argued Irina. "I'm convinced that you and your colleagues have been grossly incompetent so far."

"You're acting like a fool, Mademoiselle. Is there anything that I could do to persuade you to change your mind?"

"Being a member of the d'Andresy family, you must know about their affairs. There's a connection between Raoul d'Andresy and Joséphine Balsamo. If you can tell me what it is, I'll accompany you."

"Agreed, but I will only divulge it en route to the safe house."

"I will accept that condition, but I'll add one of my own. We'll use the cab maintained by the Chupin Detective Agency. If I find that you're supplying me with either false or incomplete information, I'll order the cab to return us here."

The Inspector assented to Irina's request. Irina carried a large handbag with her into the carriage. Entering the cab, the Inspector gave the driver an address in the Rue St. Claude.

"I await your information," stated Irina.

"Raoul d'Andresy first met Joséphine Balsamo two years ago."

"Please call your cousin by his real name: Arsène Lupin."

"If we're dropping aliases, then we should do the same with yours. I'm aware of Dr. Cerral's controversial experimentation with hand transplants. Your bracelets cover surgical scars."

"Then there is no need to engage in further subterfuge. I am indeed Irene."

"Joséphine seduced your half-brother in order to turn him into her lieutenant in crime."

Irina silently deduced that Joséphine had devised an elaborate strategy of revenge against the children of Théophraste Lupin. Joséphine had recruited Théophraste's offspring as expendable pawns to be liquidated at her leisure.

"Are they still partners, Inspector?"

"No, Arsène turned against her."

"Tell me the truth now. If you don't, I'll turn this cab around. How do you know all this?"

"I am Arsène Lupin, sister," he admitted with a sigh. "I went to Louisiana to help my cousin, the real Maurice d'Andresy, pursue the leader of the smugglers. Maurice caught pneumonia and died. I assumed his identity."

"Intriguing. Has my little brother been misbehaving?"

"I have formed an organization somewhat similar to the old Werewolves."

"Let us return to Joséphine. Did your affair with her occur after your marriage to Clarisse?"

"It happened before. That was a very impertinent question, sister!"

"Consider it just retribution, brother. You asked me several rude queries yesterday."

"My truculence was motivated by a sense of shame. My own inquiries unearthed all the nasty details of your conduct at Madame Fourneau's boarding school."

"Do you realize, brother, that I am being judged morally unfit by a man who just confessed to be the leader of a criminal fraternity? The question is not whether we are brother and sister of the flesh, but rather brother and sister of the spirit. Both our souls have been tainted by Joséphine Balsamo."

The cab arrived at its destination, Rue St. Claude. Irina ordered it to return to the Detective Agency. As they entered the house, the cabdriver noticed that Irina waved goodbye to him with three fingers.

Across the street, there was another cab. A man and a woman sat inside.

"The mousetrap has been sprung, Herr Malbodius," commented the female.

"The Lupin siblings will be destroyed by Bluebeard III, Fraulein Lipsius," predicted her male escort.

Inside the house, Irina and the fake Inspector entered a large living room.

"The Chief Inspector and Madame Klein hasn't arrived yet, sister."

"I have a difficult decision to make, brother." Irina quickly took a pistol out of her purse. She pointed it menacingly at her companion.

"Sister, what are you doing?"

"I am debating whether to kill you now or turn you over to the authorities, brother. You told me a pack of lies and half-truths in the cab."

"I told you the truth!"

"Joséphine Balsamo is still your lover! You're still in partnership with her!"

"That's not true! I love Clarisse!"

"You weren't in Louisiana assisting the real Inspector d'Andresy to chase the chief smuggler, brother! You were the ringleader! Your only truthful assertion was about the assumption of the genuine Inspector's identity when he perished from pneumonia."

"Sister, you're letting your resentment against me warp your judgment! Can't you see Joséphine's scheme? She started the Bluebeard murders to reawaken your rancor towards me! Her aim is for you to murder me!"

"Brother, have you ever read *Le Vicomte de Bragelonne*?"

"Have you lost your mind, sister? Do you want to turn our conversation into a literary discussion?"

"Answer the question!" demanded Irina.

"Of course, I have. It's a famous book by Alexandre Dumas."

"Doesn't it concern Louis XIV and his twin brother, the Man in the Iron Mask?"

"Yes, but I don't understand why you're bringing that up now!"

"The man incarcerated in the Ville-d'Avray asylum wrote 'Louis' twice for seven rows. In other words, he wrote 'Louis' 14 times! The same inmate also wrote the words '*Je m'abuse*,' reminiscent of an alias of Jan Gosart. The artist was called Mabuse because he came from Maubeuge, a city in Flanders. Maubeuge is the name of the asylum director."

"Surely Maubeuge would have deduced the contents of this alleged message. Why show it to you?"

"Maubeuge didn't show it to me, brother; the visiting Biron did. In Dumas' novel, conspirators replace Louis XIV with his twin. Madame Fourneau had twin sons. She even named them after the siblings in *Le Vicomte de Bragelonne*. Maubeuge works for Joséphine Balsamo, alias Clio Gosart. The doctor replaced Louis Fourneau with his brother. Maubeuge must have abducted Philippe in Switzerland and transported him to the asylum. The prisoner wrote that cryptic message, hoping that it would be deciphered by someone. Poor Philippe didn't commit suicide, Maubeuge murdered him because an accomplice in the French police was about to reveal the family connection between the College Girl Murderer and Gaston Morrell!"

"Maubeuge may be a killer, Irina, but I had nothing to do with the death of that inmate!"

"Au contraire, you had everything to do with it, brother. I have been calling you 'brother' not because we're brother and sister in the flesh, but because we're brother and sister in the spirit. Both our souls were corrupted at your mother's boarding school. You're not Arsène Lupin! You're Louis Fourneau! Bluebeard III!"

The man posing as Maurice d'Andresy took off his wig, false beard and tinted spectacles. The face of a handsome man with brown hair was exposed. He looked exactly like the cadaver at the Ville-d'Avray asylum.

"It's been a long time, Louis," announced Irina. "You went to New Orleans after your liberation from the asylum. How long have you been free? For five years, I imagine. Your brother disappeared from Switzerland in 1891, the same year that your associate arrived from there to manage the asylum."

"Your deductions about Malbodius are correct."

"Malbodius? Like Mabuse, a pseudonym derived from Jan Gosart of Maubeuge. Eric Maubeuge is a man of many names, Louis, just as you are. Your impersonation of the Inspector was quite masterful. You used the Inspector's pneumonia to mask your own asthma. You must have diverted the police into guarding Isadora."

"Lefevre is at her hotel."

"Very clever. But your ploy to pose as Arsène was inconsistent with your behavior yesterday. The true Arsène would never refer to his beloved Victoire as a 'prostitute,' or a 'stupid woman,' even in the middle of a masquerade. Since we were children, Arsène has been devoted to my mother."

Louis Fourneau let the pieces of his disguise drop to the floor.

"The usurpation of my brother's identity was intended to lure me into this house, but it hints at a more complex motivation for your strangulations," continued Irina. "The traditional method of the Black Coats is to *pay the law* by framing an innocent. The name Arsène Lupin has yet to be attached to any significant crimes. Joséphine's plot is to blame my brother for the Bluebeard murders. If my dead body was found floating in the Seine, the police would follow the trail here. There must be evidence in these premises that Inspector d'Andresy is Arsène Lupin in disguise. The authorities would find ample justification to embrace my brother as a convenient scapegoat. The intense panic engulfing Paris will ensure Arsène's conviction. Do you take pride, Louis, in butchering five innocent women as part of such an elaborate charade?"

"It's your own fault, Irene. Joséphine thought you dead until a few months ago."

"She must have seen my portrait at the home of Julius Pavia, alias Noel Moriarty. Besides my resemblance to her former classmate, Joséphine would have recognized the pentagram brooch. After some inquiries in the artistic circles of Paris, she uncovered my new identity at the Chupin Detective Agency. Joséphine was originally under the misapprehension that I was Saillard, but the real facts still fit her false scenario regarding Arsène. With your talk of 'tasteless paintings' in my office, Louis, you behaved like a puritanical censor. No doubt you gave Lefevre and others the similar impression that 'Maurice d'Andresy' is a fanatical hater of sexually provocative art. Such a man would be enraged to learn a sister was peddling Saillard's portraits. Following my death, Lefevre would have concluded that Arsène had been insanely stringing him along in a false identity. You and Joséphine want to depict Arsène as a man driven to murder by my connection to scandalous paintings."

"Exactly, my sister of the spirit. Your own flamboyant behavior sparked the massacre of Saillard's models. You have only yourself to blame for those deaths."

Irina rubbed her pentagram with her left hand before responding.

"You argue like your mother, Louis. You always blame the victims for the abuse that you unleash upon them."

"You seem to be very fond of your pentagram these days. You never wore it at the College. Why flaunt it now?"

"Joséphine gave me this brooch to ensure my blind subservience. I wear it to remind myself never to behave like such a fool again."

"In that case, my dear Irene, you have failed in your purpose!" shouted a new voice. "I also gave that brooch to mock your early ignorance of your father's secret life. My gift is the sign of the werewolf, but you have transformed it into a badge of imbecility."

Joséphine Balsamo, attired in her customary green dress and holding a gun in her right hand, stood behind Irina, the barrel of her weapon pressed against the back of the detective's head.

Taking Irina's gun and handbag from her hands, Fourneau deposited the articles on a nearby table.

"I've been an idiot!" confessed Irina. "This house is in the Rue St. Claude, where the original Cagliostro lived. It must have been part of a string of buildings that he owned and equipped with secret passages."

"I still remember when you refused to accept their existence. You have been very predictable. I used the Clio Gosart alias as bait to draw you into my web, my little fly."

"This is a rare occurrence for you, Joséphine. You usually don't take a direct role in your murders. The Black Coats have trained you well, as you tried to train Arsène. I understand he's started his own competing gang. Your colleagues must not be too happy with that fact."

"You should be more concerned with your brother's carelessness," retorted Joséphine. "A spy inside Arsène's gang has assured us that he has no alibi for the murders. Your brother has been committing robberies in the evenings. The intense scrutiny following the discovery of your corpse will cripple Arsène's syndicate. The only way for Arsène to avoid the guillotine would be to confess to his thefts. Your brother is destined for either a long prison term or the executioner's blade!"

"Enough of this talk!" yelled Fourneau. "I have been waiting a long time to become reacquainted with Irene. This time, my sixth victim must die!"

"Louis has always been frustrated by one fact," said Joséphine. "When I designated you as the final victim in the College Girl Murders, I had specifically instructed him to avoid killing you during the mutilation."

"Why did you order that?" asked Irina. "Did you want me to bleed to death?"

"If you really must know, Irene, dear, I was hoping that the loss of your precious artistic hands would drive you insane."

"My sanity remains intact!"

"Are you sure, Irene? There are times when you act most irrationally."

"Joséphine, stop bickering!" exclaimed Fourneau. "Let me get on with my work!"

"If you must, Louis, do what you do best!" said Joséphine as she backed away from Irina.

Fourneau removed his tie. "I really want to slit your throat, Irene, but such a procedure would upset the standards established by my uncle..."

Fourneau threw the tie around Irina's neck and started to pull. As the girl gasped for breath, Joséphine lowered her gun.

Irina grabbed her pentagram brooch and pulled it from her dress. She stuck the uppermost point of the star into the middle of Fourneau's throat and pulled the brooch across his neck. The murderer released his hold on the tie and fell to the ground with a severed jugular.

Joséphine raised her gun. Irina swung forward. She slashed her enemy's hand with the point of her brooch. Shouting in pain, Joséphine dropped the gun. Irina grabbed her by the throat and pushed her against the wall. Irina now held the uppermost point of the pentagram against Joséphine's neck.

"You seem to be at a loss for words, Joséphine, dear. Do you admire how the points of your gift have been sharpened like razors? I could cut your throat, but I wish to work within the law. I will be happy to see you dispatched by the guillotine, but first there's something I must do. Because of you, I was branded as a thief. The least I can do now is to return the favor."

Irina pulled Joséphine by the nape of her neck and slammed her against the wall. The blonde slumped to the floor, a stream of blood running from a gash in her forehead. Removing her scarf, Irina bound Joséphine's feet. She used Fourneau's neck-tie to secure her hands. She then retrieved her handbag, took out its contents and performed a certain act upon her unconscious foe.

Irina then searched the house. Locating the birth certificate and other papers that implicated her brother in the murders, she burned them in a fireplace. Irina had no love for Arsène. Her destruction of evidence was motivated by self-interest. An investigation of Arsène would reveal too many secrets from her own past.

Irene removed the pistols from the floor and deposited them in her handbag. Leaving the house, she walked three blocks before finding the cab from the Chupin Detective Agency. She had silently signaled the driver with her hand to wait that distance from the building. She told the man to take a message to Lefevre at the Royal Palace Hotel, to inform him that Bluebeard III now laid dead at Inspector d'Andresy's residence.

After dispatching the driver, Irina returned to the house. To her consternation, she discovered that Joséphine was missing. Only the corpse of Louis Fourneau remained. Irina greeted Lefevre when the police arrived at the Rue St. Claude. The Bertillon measurements confirmed the identity of the false Inspector d'Andresy. Irina never mentioned the name of Arsène Lupin. At her suggestion, Lefevre had the Clio Gosart letters compared with certain correspondence that the Avignon authorities had salvaged from the aftermath of the College Girl Murders. The handwriting of a former prefect at Madame Fourneau's College matched Clio Gosart's. A warrant was issued for Joséphine Balsamo's arrest, but she was never apprehended for her role in the Bluebeard crimes.

Dr. Maubeuge, alias Malbodius, never reappeared at the Ville-d'Avray asylum. He left France to seek refuge in another country.

In the Regenerator of Fashion, there was an area called the Alteration Room. There, tailoring mistakes were corrected and clothes were altered to fit patrons. The room contained various knitting devices, ironing implements and branding tools.

There, Joséphine Balsamo now stood before Madame Koluchy, Helen Lipsius and Mary Holder. Joséphine's forehead and right hand were bandaged. At Madame Koluchy's insistence, Joséphine wore the same dress from the Rue St. Claude.

"This is a formal hearing," said Madame Koluchy. "There will be no Christian names or self-bestowed titles of nobility employed here. Is that understood, Mademoiselle Balsamo?"

"Yes, Madame," answered Joséphine.

"Malbodius was assigned to transport Putine's corpse to the Seine. Instead, he saw Putine leave the house unharmed. He and Mademoiselle Lipsius found you tied up like a calf. Do you acknowledge this?"

"Yes, Madame."

"You also appear to have been branded. There are marks on the shoulders of your favorite dress, drawn with ink. What are those marks, Mademoiselle?"

"They are both the letter 'V,' Madame."

"What, in your opinion, is the significance of that letter?"

"It stands for '*voleuse*,' Madame," Joséphine replied, using the French word for a female thief.

"Your two friends here lack the benefit of a strong education in French history. You have expertise in this area. Explain to them the historical significance of those marks."

"Jeanne de La Motte was punished by being branded with these marks."

"They are the marks of a thief, are they not?"

"Yes, Madame."

"Do you confess that you have stolen from the Black Coats, Mademoiselle?"

"I have stolen nothing, Madame."

"You have stolen the Black Coats' dominant position in France by accidentally creating a major competitor in Arsène Lupin. You have stolen the opportunity to rectify that mistake by allowing yourself to be outwitted by Irina Putine. You are a thief, Mademoiselle Balsamo."

"I am a thief, Madame."

"Those marks are an appropriate punishment."

"These marks are an appropriate punishment, Madame."

"Remove your dress, Mademoiselle Balsamo, and give it to Mademoiselle Lipsius. An alteration clearly needs to be performed."

Joséphine complied with Madame Koluchy's commands and handed her dress to Helen.

"Mademoiselle Lipsius, please examine the dress in order to duplicate those marks on a softer and more delicate surface," commanded Madame Koluchy. "Mademoiselle Holder, please assist me in ensuring that the surface in question remains stationary during the duplication."

Joséphine saw the three other women rise from their seats and advance towards her.

"This can't be your wish, Madame!" pleaded Joséphine.

"No, it is *your* wish, Mademoiselle Balsamo."

Some minutes later, the Alteration Room was filled with the screams of Joséphine Balsamo.

Corridors of Deceit

To the population of London in November 1896, the House of Crafts was merely the headquarters of a reputable fashion company. In reality, the building was the center of the nefarious criminal society known as the Black Coats. Its basement served both as a dungeon and a torture chamber. Presently, a young woman wearing a brown blouse with a black tie and a black skirt was unceremoniously dragged inside a cell.

"Your new abode, Dodger," coolly announced her flamboyant jailer.

She was a woman with short brown hair, brushed from the forehead in a wide stock, giving the impression of a bird-like crest. Her tall, lean body was attired entirely in black. A patch covered her right eye. Her open coat was styled like an Inverness cape. Her outfit also comprised a shirt with a cravat plus pants and boots. A ring of keys dangled from her belt. An amulet in the shape of a cat's head was chained around her neck. Her right hand clutched the back of the captive's chestnut hair.

"Please don't hurt me, Milady," whimpered Dodger.

"I don't intend to. As a talented thief, you're a valuable asset for us. A period of incarceration should cure your stubborn streak, however. You disobeyed my order to steal Baron Gruner's diary."

"I couldn't let you blackmail the man I love!"

"You little fool! You were merely expected to flirt with Gruner. He cares nothing for you."

"That's not true."

"Enough of this nonsense! I let you have the 'Dodger' sobriquet. Your insolence merits a demotion. Remember the nickname of 'B. F.' from our schooldays? It suits you so well!"

Releasing Dodger, Milady secured the door and left the basement. The cell's door had a small window covered with bars. Light from a small lamp poured through it. Dodger removed a folded page from her sleeve and held it to the light. Though she knew the inscription by heart, reading it consoled her:

"Dearest Berenice, pray for my soul, I will pray for yours...Irene."

Dodger knew it was dangerous to hide this paper. Milady would punish her if it was found, but seeing the words reminded Dodger to perform a ritual every day. She did it now.

"Our Father, who art in Heaven...."

The White Lodge, a late-Georgian mansion in the Blackheath district of London, belonged to Noel Moriarty, a leading member of the High Council of the Black Coats. His wife, known to London's high society as Madame Koluchy, never appeared in public with her husband. In fact, most people believed her to be a widow. This majestic woman with black hair and dark blue eyes was presently dining at the White Lodge with her father, Count Corbucci, a heavily built man with a large white mustache. Both father and daughter wore gold rings shaped like snakes. The Count was a patriarch of the Camorra, the Italian secret society which had long ago spawned the *Veste Nere*, a.k.a. the Black Coats. His daughter headed another criminal enterprise known as the Brotherhood of the Seven Kings.

"The Espionage Hotel proposed by Malbodius will need a competent architect, Catarina."

"I would recommend the designer of our headquarters, Father. This artisan also worked for Marguerite Chavain and Madame Sara."

"You've reorganized the Brotherhood in preparation for the upcoming meeting of the High Council?"

"Yes, I have a new chief of staff, Milady Nevermore."

"Wasn't she Antonio's principal assassin? I'm surprised that my foster son let her go."

Corbucci was discussing the Black Coats' head of Asian operations. On a trip to Havana, decades ago, the Count had adopted a homeless waif named Antonio. Before her marriage to Noel, Catarina had been engaged to Antonio. Their betrothal had been broken for reasons known only to the Corbucci family.

"Milady was my operative before she was Antonio's, Father. Six years ago, I sent her to Japan to be trained by the Iga ninja clan. Antonio made the arrangements. She was always slated to be in my employ."

"Why happened?"

"Just as her training was concluding, the Koga clan attacked the Iga village. Nearly all the Iga ninjas were massacred by a 'Steel-Skin Kung Fu' expert imported by their Koga rivals. Milady survived, but she suffered extreme injuries. Antonio informed me that she would face a prolonged recovery, so I temporarily lost interest in her and Antonio used her in the meantime."

"So he stole one of your own. How charmingly bureaucratic."

"When news of Milady's activities reached me, I forced Antonio to relinquish her back to me."

"What happened to your prior chief of staff?"

"Joséphine will now report to Milady."

"Considering Joséphine's previous failures, I don't understand why you let her live. Your affection for this former classmate of yours is affecting your judgment, my girl."

"Not true, Father. I have despised her since our very first encounter."

"And yet, you picked her to be your assistant during your tenure as prefect at that school."

"The headmistress required the performance of certain distasteful duties. Rather than bear the burden myself, I chose a pretentious girl to assume those responsibilities. Since Joséphine proved her... expertise, I inducted her into the Brotherhood. But I still relish in tormenting her."

An attractive blonde woman in a green dress entered the House of Crafts. She was ending a short leave of absence that had been granted her to give her time to recover from some injuries she had recently received in Paris. The blonde woman found Milady Nevermore in her private office rubbing her hands together in a smug manner.

"So you are Joséphine Balsamo," said Milady to the newcomer. "The situation is somewhat awkward. I understand this used to be your office, but I needed to move in immediately. Your possessions have been temporarily stored downstairs."

"I understand, Milady," said Joséphine. "Your taste is exquisite. Your necklace is quite lovely."

"A gift from a male admirer." Milady stroked her cat amulet affectionately.

"I notice a Poe collection on your bookshelf. May I look at it?"

Milady handed *Tamerlane and Other Poems* to Joséphine. The blonde woman perused the dedication inside: *To Kaitlin: A great rarity for a great daughter. Love, Father.*

Returning the book, Joséphine pondered the inscription. Milady was an enigma to Joséphine. This dedication was the only clue to her new supervisor's identity.

"I was told that Madame Koluchy has approved my posting to New Orleans," she said. "When do I leave?"

"Your reassignment has been cancelled, I'm afraid. I've reviewed the Bluebeard III affair. It was filled with blunders. You wanted Arsène Lupin to *pay the law* for a murder, but instead of simply committing one, you planned six."

"I had sound motives. I wanted to create a public outcry."

"That is a poor excuse," interjected Milady, wagging a finger.

"Don't treat me like a schoolgirl!"

"I wouldn't mention schoolgirls here, if I were you. Your pawn killed many schoolgirls."

"I used Louis Fourneau because the crimes required his artistry to be credible."

"You little fool!" screeched Milady. "That monster should never have been born. You should have let him rot in his asylum. And you should know that Madame Koluchy agrees with me."

"Does she now?"

"Many of our female colleagues have attended the Fourneau boarding school. Professor Chavain of the High Council has even formed an Alumnae Association."

"I know. I'm a member–unlike you."

"Your membership has been revoked. Professor Chavain was shocked to learn of your involvement with the murderous maniac responsible for the school's closure. Wild rumors circulated after the press publicized your alliance with Louis Fourneau. It was even said that you and Madame Koluchy had plotted the school's destruction together. But she quashed these stories by addressing the Alumnae."

"What did she say?"

"The truth. That you used Louis without her knowledge."

Joséphine knew that Koluchy was lying. Certain details of the recent Bluebeard murders had been withheld from Milady and the Black Coats.

"I want to talk to the Alumnae. I need to explain my conduct."

"Such a meeting has, in fact, been already scheduled. I've taken the liberty to prepare your speech."

Milady handed Joséphine a sheet of paper. The blonde woman's features grew darker as she read it.

"But this is a confession! This is a lie."

"This speech will appease Professor Chavain. The High Council plans to debate Madame Koluchy's proposal to rename the Brotherhood as the Black Skirts. Such a change would consolidate the increased role of women in our society, but for this measure to pass, the Council's only other female member must support it. Be thankful that Professor Chavain, as a botanist, didn't insist that *a branch be cut*."

In Black Coat parlance, the *cutting of a branch* meant the imposition of the death penalty.

"We need to discuss your attire at the Alumnae meeting," resumed Milady. "Our Black Skirt campaign would suffer if you wore your uniform."

"What uniform?"

"Under the Brotherhood's new dress code, uniforms are worn by all female members."

"Ah, yes. I saw them in Paris. Brown blouses, black skirts and ties. They're even sold commercially. But executives are exempt from the dress code."

"Yes, but this exemption applies to me–not you."

"I'm no longer an executive?"

"You're now a mere employee, entrusted with this building's security."

"I've been demoted to *a security guard*! Me–Countess Cagliostro!"

Joséphine defiantly raised her hand. It bore a ring with the image of a golden ram.

"Don't flaunt your little trinket at me. I might be tempted to expropriate it. Another uppity aristocrat was once forced to surrender all her prized possessions to me. As far as I know, your title is unverified. I've instructed the other employees to only call you Mademoiselle Balsamo."

"Yet, everyone calls you Milady."

"Have you researched my lineage?"

"No, I haven't."

"Then you spoke without thinking. In my youth, I suffered from the same fault. But I shall cure you of that habit."

Joséphine delivered her humiliating speech that evening. In another act of humiliation devised by Milady, she had been forced to appear naked before the Alumnae. After the speech, Milady instructed Joséphine to wait in a dressing room for her new uniform. Joséphine stared at her shoulders in a mirror. A "V" had been branded into each shoulder. Even though this disfigurement had been done on Madame Koluchy's orders, Joséphine held Irina Putine of the Chupin Detective Agency responsible. Remembering her triumphant adversary from their days together at the boarding school, the blonde woman began to mutter to herself:

"The Furnace letters... Milady de Winter... Kaitlin de Winter."

There was a knock on the door.

"May I come in, Countess?"

"Yes," responded a stunned Joséphine.

A brunette carrying a box entered.

"Your uniform, Countess."

"Thank you, Maude. You've always understood proper etiquette."

"I haven't forgotten your generous wedding gift, Countess. Besides, my former mistress, Lady Beltham, instilled in me a proper appreciation for titles."

"Maude" had been born Hendrika Pienaar in Pretoria. Her alias was derived from the British aristocrat whom she had once served as a maid. Maude also liked to mimic Lady Beltham's courtly accent.

"Do you still have access to the personnel files, Maude?" Joséphine asked. "I'd like to see Milady's."

"It's too risky, Countess. Anyone caught reading her file would be worse off than B. F."

"B. F.?"

"You might remember her as 'Dodger.' She's a burglar transferred here from Paris. She's in the dungeon now. Milady treats her like dirt. Apparently, they have some prior history together."

"B. F... Those initials are familiar. Can you get me her file instead?"

"That should be easy. I'll get it from Purity."

A week later, two middle-aged ladies from Bristol crossed the English Channel. One had brown hair while the other was a blonde wearing tinted spectacles. Arriving at the Chupin Detective Agency in Paris, they requested to see the firm's owner. A secretary informed them that Monsieur Chupin was in Spain. The visitors were instead directed to the office of Irina Putine, his chief assistant.

Irina was 26, tall and slender, with a glossy mane of black hair. A brooch shaped like a pentagram was pinned on the right side of her orange dress. A black tie was tied around her collar. It matched the black silk gloves on her hands. Silver bracelets graced her wrists.

"My name is Rosette Trevor," said the brown-haired lady. "I live in Bristol with my husband and daughter. This is my neighbor, Eva Relli."

"I teach architecture at a local university," said Eva. "I moved with my son to England from Naples after my husband's death."

"Eva was kind enough to accompany me on this trip," added Rosette.

"Madame Trevor, your maiden name is Morrell," replied Irina. "Your two siblings are deceased. Your brother was a painter. Your sister, Natalie, ran a boarding school in Provence. Two of her three children are dead."

"Why, that's amazing," said Eva. "It's just like Dr. Watson's accounts. Imagine Mademoiselle Putine deducing all that from your appearance, Rosette."

"It's very easy for Mademoiselle Putine to make those statements, Eva. She knows all about my family. A month ago, she killed my nephew, Louis Fourneau."

"I was acting in self-defense," said Irina.

"I don't doubt it. Louis was a fiend."

"Your sister, too, was also somewhat controversial."

"I won't defend Natalie's reputation. The floggings at her school were abhorrent. I'm here about her daughter, Berenice. She and your employer's late niece, Irene Chupin, were close friends."

"Irene's very much alive, Madame Trevor. She told me about Berenice."

"But the newspapers reported Irene's death from shock after my nephew..."

"You were about to say—after your nephew chopped off her hands. The accounts of her death were inaccurate. Irene's relatives wished to protect her from publicity. They never issued a denial."

"May I meet her?" inquired Madame Trevor.

"That's impossible, I'm afraid. Irene now lives in complete seclusion. But I have something else to show you..."

Irina went to a large safe in her office. She entered the combination and opened the door. Among shelves of papers, she removed a bundle of letters tied together and handed them to Madame Trevor.

"These are some of Berenice's letters to Irene."

Madame Trevor untied the letters and skimmed through them.

"I recognize my niece's handwriting. How did you get them?"

"During Irene's recuperation, they came into Monsieur Chupin's possession."

"He couldn't know Berenice wrote those letters. She used an assumed name."

" 'Blythe Furnace,' yes. But the French translation of Furnace is Fourneau. Your niece's alias shares the same initials as her real name. Monsieur Chupin astutely uncovered her true identity."

"Your employer never contacted my niece."

"Monsieur Chupin only found the letters after your niece's disappearance. Perhaps you could confirm Berenice's friendship with Irene, if only to verify our own information?"

"My niece was lonely and friendless during her childhood. My sister Natalie doted on her sons, but woefully neglected Berenice. The three children resided in a segregated area at the school. Natalie forbade Berenice to socialize with her students, whom were regarded as the dregs of society. She was, in fact, planning to send Berenice to a proper boarding school in Paris. Berenice, who was then 13, feared that Parisian girls would see her as a graceless provincial."

"A concise summary, Madame Trevor, but there is one missing fact: Berenice did befriend a student at your sister's school."

"What year was that?" queried Eva.

"It was in August 1885," answered Irina. "But please continue, Madame Trevor."

"Berenice stole a set of keys from her mother. She wandered around the school at night."

"Just like a burglar," observed Eva.

"My niece was a bit of a tomboy, since her only playmates until then had been her brothers. As you noted, Mademoiselle Putine, a new student's arrival changed all that. Her name was Irene. She had been locked in a storeroom while Natalie conferred privately with the girl's guardian."

" 'Guardian' isn't quite the proper term to describe Henriette d'Andresy," noted Irina. "Her son, a cunning thief, had been nursed by Victoire Chupin, Irene's mother. When the girl was falsely accused of one of his thefts, Henriette enrolled Irene at your sister's school."

"Yes, my niece told me all that. Berenice unlocked the storeroom where Irene had been confined. That's how the friendship between the two girls began. Irene had a book with her, a novel by Charles Dickens–I don't remember the title."

"*Oliver Twist,*" said Irina.

"My sister reviled Dickens as a defamer of the French Revolution. Berenice warned Irene that her mother would burn the book if she found it, so Irene gave it to Berenice, and even inscribed it. Over the next few weeks, the girls continued to meet clandestinely. When Natalie eventually enrolled Berenice at the Institution Bachelard in Paris, the girls hoped to correspond, but complications arose in the matter of Irene's surname."

"How was that a problem?" wondered Eva.

95

"Perhaps I should explain," volunteered Irina. "Natalie Fourneau's pupils were unwanted children. She protected the reputation of the people responsible for her students' confinement by changing the surnames of many girls. Chupin became Tupin."

"So Irene wouldn't be able to receive mail!" said Eva.

"Irene was a special case," said Irina. "Henriette d'Andresy had warned Madame Fourneau that Irene's uncle was Victor Chupin, the private detective. Monsieur Chupin had been deceived about the reasons for his niece's presence at the school, but insisted on writing to her nevertheless. Of course, his letters were addressed to Irene Chupin."

"How did Berenice manage to circumvent this peculiar arrangement?"

"My sister kept meticulous records and Berenice was able to break into Irene's file. Then, using the identity of 'Blythe Furnace,' she pretended to be an old friend who had gotten Irene's address from Monsieur Chupin. This subterfuge was necessary because the mail was also being censored."

"Natalie was reading the mail?" asked Eva.

"My sister delegated that task to her prefect," said Madame Trevor.

"Joséphine Balsamo, your nephew's accomplice in the Bluebeard murders," added Irina.

"My niece's stratagem worked and the correspondence went on for over four years," continued Madame Trevor. "During this time, she was badly harassed by a fellow student, Kaitlin de Winter, the daughter of an English Baron assigned to the Paris Embassy. Berenice characterized Kaitlin as 'an uppity aristocrat.' She gave Berenice vicious nicknames. My niece's initials are meaningless in French, but Kaitlin said they stood for 'Bloody Fool.' In a letter, Irene advised Berenice to fight fire with fire."

"Meaning?" asked Eva.

"Kaitlin professed to be related to the de Winter family from Monsieur Dumas's Musketeers novels," continued Madame Trevor. "She insisted on being addressed as 'Milady.' Irene pointed out that the proper title of a Baron's daughter is 'Right Honorable,' so Berenice started calling Kaitlin's 'Right Dishonorable.' Kaitlin was also a devotee of Edgar Allen Poe. She liked the nickname of 'Raven' because of the poem, so Irene suggested that Berenice call her 'Craven.'"

"Irene knew how to handle a bully for a simple reason," concluded Eva. "Because she was a bully herself. She was, in fact, your sister's last prefect."

"But Irene was coerced by Joséphine into becoming a prefect," said Irina. "So Berenice was advised on how to fight a bully by a person who had already submitted to another bully's domination."

"Whatever Irene's motives, my niece was very grateful," said Madame Trevor. "She viewed Irene as her best friend. Berenice was later devastated to learn of her mother's death, her brother's incarceration and Irene's alleged demise. I then traveled to Paris in order to take her back to Bristol. Before we could return to England, a horrible event transpired. Berenice returned from Sunday Mass to discover her room vandalized. Irene's letters had been torn to shreds. The pages of Irene's gift, the Dickens book, were ripped out. My niece saw this as a horrible desecration. All the remembrances of her best friend had been destroyed. Neither I nor the Countess could console her."

"What Countess?" said Irina.

"Countess Corbucci, one of my sister's former students. She came to the Institution Bachelard to offer her condolences."

"Was this Countess a blonde?"

"No, a brunette. Soon after the vandalism, Berenice disappeared. Her room showed signs of a struggle. All her clothes and possessions were missing. The same night, Kaitlin also vanished with her belongings. The police couldn't trace either girl. I believe Kaitlin was responsible for both the vandalism and my niece's disappearance."

"Why reopen this case?"

"I received this letter. I didn't want to go to the French police because of their general ineptitude. Eva recommended your Agency because of Berenice's connection to Irene."

Rosette handed a letter to Irina. The sleuth scrutinized it.

"The person who wrote this is a terrible writer," commented Eva. "Several English words are misused. Do you get the gist?"

"Yes, Madame Relli. The writer identifies himself only as 'Parker.' He wants 50,000 francs for information about Berenice's whereabouts. Parker desires a meeting at a warehouse along the Seine this Sunday night. The signal will be the playing of a musical instrument."

"I don't have that kind of money," pleaded Madame Trevor.

"It doesn't matter. The Chupin Detective Agency will gladly pay for this information in light of your niece's friendship with Irene. We will also be waiving our customary fee. I will contact you to report on the meeting's results."

"You're very generous," said Madame Trevor. "Thank you."

"Rosette has been very honest, Mademoiselle Putine," said Eva. "Don't you think that you should be equally forthcoming?"

"Eva!" reprimanded Madame Trevor. "You must apologize. Mademoiselle Putine has been extremely kind."

"But not altogether candid with us. She's Irene!"

"What has prompted this absurd conclusion?" asked Irina.

"The similarity of names: Irene Tupin–Irina Putine," said Eva.

"Despite the fact that Madame Trevor mentioned the horrible mutilation that befell Irene."

"You're wearing gloves."

"My hands are normal," said Irina. "You may examine them."

Irina removed her gloves. Eva gently touched Irina's hands, but then pushed back the silver bracelets.

"There are scars on your wrists! You have much explaining to do, Mademoiselle."

"My scars resulted from a suicide attempt."

"Why did you attempt suicide?" asked Madame Trevor.

"Are you familiar with the Nihilists?" said Irina.

"They're anarchists who murder Russian aristocrats."

"Yes. Years ago, I was in Paris with my Russian mother. The Nihilists murdered her and took me prisoner. Their vicious abuse prompted me to slit my wrists. Monsieur Chupin rescued me and became my legal guardian. I spent years at an English boarding school. Upon my return to France, Monsieur Chupin changed my name to avoid further Nihilist persecution. My alias is derived from his niece's name."

"Nihilists operate in Russia," challenged Eva. "This is France."

"Madame Relli, did you ever hear of Countess Yalta?"

"No, I haven't."

"I remember the case," said Madame Trevor. "The Countess was poisoned by the Nihilists in Paris 16 years ago. A hospital in Avignon was named after her."

"That is correct. Countess Yalta was my mother," said Irina.

"I don't recall any reference to a daughter in the newspapers."

"My parents were unmarried," replied Irina, lowering her head in shame.

"I'm sorry for forcing that admission. Eva, you must apologize to this gracious lady," said Madame Trevor.

After the two women had left, Irina, who was really Irene, mentally rehashed the lies she had just told. She had, in fact, gone to an English nursing home, not a boarding school, after her discharge from the Countess Yalta Memorial Hospital. One of the hospital's surgeons, Anatole Cerral, had surreptitiously given her a new pair of hands.

On Sunday night, Irina went with a satchel of money to the banks of the Seine. She was armed with an umbrella that concealed a sword. The docks were deserted, except for a person playing a harmonica. The musician was a blonde woman whose physique resembled Irina's.

"Ain't you a swell, dearie," complimented the blonde, speaking English with a Cockney accent. "What's pinned to your chest? A pentagon?"

"Are you Parker?"

"Purity Parker. You must work for Mrs. Trevor. Nice umbrella. What's on the handle? Looks like a horny horse."

"It's a unicorn's head."

"That ain't no unicorn, luv. I'm wearing a unicorn. A Black Skirts unicorn. Ain't it pretty?"

Irina experienced an odd feeling looking at Parker's uniform. Madame Fourneau had given her prefects similar dresses as gifts.

"What are the Black Skirts?"

"It's the new name for Madame Koluchy's Brotherhood. Why not call us the Sisterhood, eh? Maybe Koluchy don't want us confused with them Catholic Huns. I'm a personable jerk. I handle files on them that work for the Black Coats."

"You're a personnel clerk."

"Just what I said," concurred Parker pointing to a brown manila folder lying on a crate. "That's B. F.'s personable file. You can take a gander if you hand over the money."

"How did the Brotherhood hire you?" asked Irina.

"My brother Larry got me this job. He's Colonel Moran's chum."

"Your brother is Parker the Garrotter?"

"My brother ain't no rotter! He's a strangler."

"My apologies. Why betray the Black Coats now?"

"The bigwigs made the Personable Deportment part of Koluchy's gang. The new boss wants to fire me. Bit of a fancy pants. Calls herself Milady Nevermore."

"Is her real name Kaitlin de Winter?"

"That's right. Kitty Winter. Kitty treats B. F. like trash."

"What's happening to B. F.?"

"Her Nibs locked her in the cellar. Very impotent persons are interested in her, too. Balls-Ammo took a peek at this file."

"Tell me more about Balsamo."

"I hear she's going to America."

"Take the money. Hand me the folder."

The two women made the exchange. Irina opened the file and read it under a lamppost. The contents confirmed all her suspicions. Purity opened the satchel, examined the bills and then closed it.

Absorbed in the file, Irina didn't notice a man moving in the shadows. His head was encased in a white, hood-like mask that formed an implacable face with high cheekbones and thin lips. The mask had slits from which the ears protruded. The figure wore a black coat buttoned over a bare muscular chest. Black pants and gloves completed his costume. His right hand gripped a large sickle.

"Traitor!" yelled the man in black. "*Cut the branch!*"

The bizarre intruder leaped out of the darkness. His sickle made a wide sweep towards Purity. The blow was extremely swift. Irina never saw it make contact. All she saw was the Cockney's blood-soaked hand over her face. Stumbling backward with the satchel, Purity fell into the Seine.

"Murderer!" shouted Irina. Dropping the folder, she unsheathed the sword from her umbrella. Irina and the stranger thrust and parried back and forth. The duo locked blades near the dock's edge.

"Who are you?" demanded Irina.

"I am the Pallid Mask! Be grateful that I have no instructions to kill you!"

Pushing Irina away, the attacker jumped into the river. As the Pallid Mask vanished underneath the waters of the Seine, Irina recalled a play suppressed by the French government. The Pallid Mask had been another title for the Phantom of Truth in *Le Roi en Jaune*. The murderer had modeled his costume on the enigmatic character from the controversial drama.

Victor Chupin was back in Paris. His long Spanish trip had ended in failure. Roger Vollin, the leading French authority on the Spanish Inquisition, owned a torture blade created by the infamous Sebastian Medina in the sixteenth century. The blade had been stolen in Paris, and the thief's trail had led to Barcelona. Retained by Vollin, Chupin had futilely searched for the stolen artifact.

Inside his office, Chupin, a short man of 47 years, now read Irina's report on the Berenice Fourneau investigation. Irina was seated in front of his desk.

"I told Madame Trevor that no one arrived for the rendezvous," she said. "She's now convinced that the letter was a hoax. We're fighting the Black Coats. I didn't wish to put her in harm's way."

"Irina, you must drop this inquiry. Berenice's a thief whose family has persecuted you."

"It would be hypocritical for us to abandon her. We both have our own dubious pasts and questionable relatives."

"I just don't understand your sense of obligation to her."

"When we were at school, she confided all her secrets to me. I was like a priest hearing a confession. She even told me her greatest fear."

"We have no hints to Berenice's whereabouts."

"The Black Skirt uniform is the key. It is sold by the House of Crafts, a London fashion firm operated by Madame Koluchy. Joséphine Balsamo left the Fourneau school to work for Mrs. Moriarty, a former prefect. Years ago, I read the school's files on all my predecessors. Mrs. Moriarty was registered at the school under the surname of Koluchy, but her real maiden name was Corbucci. Koluchy has to be Countess Corbucci."

"She must be related to Count Corbucci, the Camorra leader, Irina. Rumors exist surrounding a daughter named Catarina. He hid her during a civil war inside the Camorra. Her sanctuary must have been the school."

"Quite right, Victor. Berenice's file confirmed that Koluchy recruited Kaitlin de Winter at the Institution Bachelard. The two then abducted Berenice and coerced her into thievery. Berenice maintained her love of Charles Dickens, for her nickname is 'Dodger.' Kaitlin's is 'Milady Nevermore,' an alias derived from Dumas' *The Three Musketeers* and Poe's 'The Raven.' Berenice is now her prisoner at the House of Crafts in London. She's in danger. I want us to go to London at once to deliver her."

"I'm afraid we can't," said Chupin. "We won't be ready for at least another week. 50,000 francs of our funds are lost at the bottom of the Seine. I must arrange a loan to avoid bankruptcy. If only the police had found the money when they recovered Purity's body."

"Waiting isn't an option. I'll go to London by myself."

"Someone needs to watch your back. Take another operative with you."

"You know very well we can't spare anyone at the moment."

"We've had this conversation before, Irina. Why are you constantly running alone into danger? Are you punishing yourself for having been Madame Fourneau's prefect? You need to forget about that cursed school."

"I'll always have *these* to remind me," said Irina, extending her hands. "You know why I wear these gloves. It's because I can't stand to see the flesh beneath. Dr. Cerral gave me the hands of a girl whom I persecuted. I'm still haunted by her memories."

"You didn't kill her. In fact, you avenged her death."

"That act alone doesn't wipe the slate clean. I fear that I'll be damned for all eternity. If I rescue Berenice, then maybe God will forgive me."

"Very well," said Chupin. "Go to England alone then. But you must recruit a regular assistant."

"You want me to hire someone in London?"

"Yes. From one of our English competitors. I've tried to make inroads into the British market for years. The Agency needs someone familiar with London. Here's a list of candidates."

"Anna Beringer of Tyler's," said Irina. "I've heard of her. May I hire someone not on this list?"

"Only if it's someone with top credentials."

At the House of Crafts, Madame Koluchy had asked Milady to come to her office.

"Do you know Purity Parker, Milady?"

"A scatterbrain currently on vacation in Paris. We should remove her in the upcoming purge."

"That's no longer necessary. Her recent performance review indicated a potential for betrayal. As a precaution, I had her kept under surveillance. She was caught passing information to Irina Putine of the Chupin Detective Agency and was–terminated."

"Do we know what information she leaked?"

"One file was missing. Fortunately, we keep duplicates. Here it is."

"My old schoolmate's! Why is Putine interested in her?"

"They met at a boarding school. This is Putine's file."

Milady took the second file and read it. Besides Irina's role in solving the Bluebeard murders, she had known nothing about the sleuth's past until studying this dossier.

Later, she went to the Archives to find more information about Irina. She returned to her office with a file on the Countess Yalta Memorial Hospital in

Avignon. As she put the file on her desk, she felt something brushing against her boot.

"Apollyon!" cried Milady with delight. She reached down to pick up a black cat. Petting it affectionately, she saw in the doorway a thin figure with dark hair and eyes. He wore a ring similar to Count Corbucci's. He had come to London to attend the gathering of the High Council.

"Our mutual friend missed you, but not as much as I," declared Dr. Antonio Nikola.

Putting the cat aside, Milady embraced Nikola in a passionate kiss. Some minutes later, he studied the hospital's file while stoking the cat.

"I understand your interest. Dr. Cerral could theoretically engineer a limb transplant, but an optic replacement is beyond even his skills."

"I was hoping..." murmured Milady, rubbing her eye-patch.

Nikola touched her cheek affectionately. "Don't worry about your outer beauty, my love. Nothing will ever mar your inner radiance."

"Excuse me," said Madame Koluchy entering the room. "I need to talk to *my* chief of staff."

Inside Tyler's Investigations in London, Irina met with Anna Beringer, a detective nearly her own age. Irina had enlisted Anna to help rescue Berenice. If she performed well, Irina planned to offer her a permanent job.

"I've been hearing rumors about these Black Skirts," volunteered Anna. "I've seen women wearing the uniform at a local thieves' den, *The Old Fellow*. My informant there, Porky Shinwell, says the women work at the House of Crafts. They even have identification cards."

"One of us needs to sneak inside that building by posing as a Black Skirt. Once we determine the layout, we can rescue Berenice by breaking in during the night."

"Your plan won't work. I'm too well known by the local criminals, and Joséphine Balsamo knows you."

"She's probably in America by now. Is it unusual for the Black Skirts to wear gloves?" asked Irina.

"In this autumn weather, it's quite common. Black is the preferred color," Anna replied.

"Do any of the Black Skirts resemble me?"

"Yes, two: Mary Holder and Maude North."

"I must replace someone unimportant. What's their backgrounds?"

"Mary's the cast-off lover of Sir George Burnwell. Some small talent as a thief. A minor underling, at best. Maude, on the other hand, is a versatile impersonator. She instigates complex swindles with her husband. Our decision seems obvious."

"Clearly Mary. Maude is irreplaceable."

That night at *The Old Fellow*, Porky Shinwell invited Mary Holder to share a glass of champagne with him in a backroom. When Mary entered the room, she was easily overpowered with chloroform by Anna and Irina. An identification card was found inside her purse. Irina quickly removed Mary's uniform and immediately left the tavern.

The next morning, the Black Skirts reported for work at the House of Crafts. Scores of employees stood in a long line at the door. A gloved woman wore a scarf over the lower portion of her face. Irina Putine, now attired as a Black Skirt, prayed the scarf would sufficiently disguise her as Mary Holder. She presented Mary's card to the Black Skirt on duty at the front door. Irina's face was still largely covered by the scarf, but she glanced at the guard. Her eyes widened upon recognizing Joséphine Balsamo.

Once inside, Irina wandered around the main floor for a few minutes. She was about to open a door leading to the basement when a hand tapped her shoulder.

"Excuse me, you're in a restricted area," said a harsh voice. "We haven't been properly introduced. I am Milady Nevermore." She pulled off Irina's scarf exposing her full face. "Show me your identification card!"

Hoping that Milady had never met Mary, Irina complied. Watching the one-eyed woman, Irina felt she was in the presence of a relentless enemy. Milady returned the card.

"Your name is Mary Holder. What are you doing here?"

Before Irina could spin a yarn, Joséphine Balsamo surfaced abruptly.

"Mary's eyes are black. Yours are blue. You're–Irina Putine!"

Irina punched Joséphine's jaw. The blonde woman fell down. The detective hit Milady in the left eye, causing her to stagger a few steps back. Irina twirled around to run, but her neck was quickly grasped from behind by Milady. The detective grabbed the wrists of her attacker, but she couldn't break the Black Skirt's hold.

"Balsamo, are you alright?" asked Milady, as Irina struggled futilely.

"Yes, Milady," answered Joséphine rising from the ground.

"Our captive here is squirming. I could render her senseless by pinching a nerve, but a severe punch to the stomach should suffice. Will you oblige?"

"With pleasure," joyfully proclaimed Joséphine as she delivered a sharp blow to Irina's stomach.

When Milady released her hands, the detective toppled forward. Milady bent down and patted the slumbering Irina's head in mock affection.

Elsewhere in the House of Crafts, three members of the High Council, Dr. Nikola, Madame Koluchy and Count Corbucci, were being harangued by one of their agents. The lecturer was Dr. Malbodius, a man of indeterminable age with a goatee. Malbodius was outlining his proposal for the Espionage Hotel.

"The hotel will be equipped with secret listening posts. Two-way mirrors will permit the listeners to spy upon the guests. The architect will be here soon."

Milady interrupted the meeting.

"I have captured an intruder–Irina Putine."

Koluchy, dressed in a black gown, extended her hand.

"Will there be daylight?" interrogated the matriarch of the Black Skirts.

"It will be daylight from midnight to noon if it's the will of the Mother," answered Milady, ritually.

She then stooped down to kiss Koluchy's ring. An order of execution had been issued against Irina. As Milady left, she passed the architect who had just arrived to join the conference. Eva Relli and Milady exchanged greetings.

Irina regained consciousness in the basement of the House of Crafts. She was lying on a raised slab in the back of a dimly lit dungeon. Her arms and legs were bound to the slab by shackles on her wrists and ankles. Six feet over her neck was an axe-like blade. Approximately 15 inches in width, it was attached to a metal pole leading upward to a series of clockwork-like gears in the ceiling.

"The Medina blade!" uttered Irina.

"You recognize my new toy," said Milady. "I crossed swords with your employer when I stole it. My false clues sent him on a wild goose chase to Barcelona. Medina's creation inspired a famous story by Poe. This blade was an early prototype. A later, larger blade could slice through a person's midriff, but this particular model is most effective at decapitation. I have attached it to a mechanism constructed in the best traditions of Poe."

Milady pointed to a series of levers on the ground.

"The lever near your right foot starts and stops the pendulum. The middle lever restores the blade to its starting position. The far lever opens and closes the shackles."

The farthest level was pointing towards Milady. She gazed at her reflection in a wall mirror.

"I'm very sensitive about my remaining eye. Your death would be more merciful if you hadn't struck me there."

"I merely struck a craven bully, the Right Dishonorable Nevermore."

"You seem familiar with certain exchanges between two schoolgirls. Our files documented your friendship with my other prisoner. No doubt you corresponded with her during her stay at the Institution Bachelard."

Milady pulled the innermost level toward her. Swinging back and forth, the blade descended with each movement. The one-eyed woman went to a small table and picked up a ball of black yarn with two long needles.

"If you don't mind, Mademoiselle Putine, I'll knit to pass away the time."

"Do I get a last request?" asked Irina.

"I will grant it within reason."

"May I see my friend before I die?"

"Your reunion will be diverting. You probably haven't seen her in over a decade."

Putting the needles and yarn back on the table, Milady marched towards another cell. Opening the door with the keys from her belt, she hauled Dodger out.

"A friend desires your company," mocked Milady. "You're hiding something!"

Milady yanked a page out of Dodger's right sleeve. Throwing her back into the cell, Milady locked the door. She returned to the slab.

"Regrettably, Dodger–B. F.–has broken the rules of her confinement. Her visiting privileges have been revoked. I'm courteous enough to read this paper aloud. Maybe you'll find it entertaining. *Dearest Berenice, pray for my soul, I will... pray...*"

Milady couldn't finish. A tear formed in her eye. She placed the paper gently on the table.

The pendulum was now five feet above Irina. Suddenly the truth consumed the detective.

"*The prisoner is not Berenice–she's Kaitlin! You're Berenice!* You abducted Kaitlin and forced her to join the Black Coats! You gave her the B. F nickname that she created for you! You called her Dodger! You took her title of Milady! You stole Kaitlin's belongings!"

"Am I supposed to be impressed? You already knew this. Parker gave you Kaitlin's file."

"We've both been fed false information. I never met Kaitlin before in my life."

"You met her at an English boarding school before she moved to Paris."

"I was never at an English boarding school."

"Yes you were. Victor Chupin sent you there to escape the Nihilists."

"What Nihilists?"

"The Nihilists who murdered your mother."

"My mother?"

"Countess Yalta."

"Countess Yalta is not my mother! My mother's Victoire Chupin! *I'm Irene!*"

Irina felt trapped in a nightmare of her own making. Her own lies were now being used against her. Eva Relli must belong to the Black Coats. She had manipulated Rosette Trevor into contacting Irina to find Berenice, and had reported the cover story the detective had told them.

The pendulum plunged to four feet above Irina. Milady was outraged by Irina's claims.

"You lie! Irene's dead!"

"Compare the names Irina Putine and Irene Tupin."

"Victor Chupin gave you the alias of Irina Putine as a homage to his late niece."

"I know all the contents of your letters to Irene. I can prove it, too. Ask me any question."

"A pointless exercise. My letters must have come into Victor Chupin's possession. He showed them to you after seeing my real name in Kaitlin's file."

"But the letters were signed Blythe Furnace."

"The truth could easily be deduced. The same initials. The surname. Your claims are ludicrous. You have a pair of hands."

"My hands are the result of an experiment by a surgeon named Cerral."

"Most ingenious. I learned of Dr. Cerral while researching your Russian mother. You must have kept abreast of what transpired at the hospital named after her. Our files are very explicit. Cerral has yet to put his proposals on limb transplants into practice. You're simply using his theories as a ploy."

"Check the scars on my wrists!"

"The result of a suicide attempt during your imprisonment by the Nihilists."

The blade was swinging two feet above Irina.

"Koluchy hated your mother. She secretly loathes you too. She only wants to manipulate you into killing your best friend!"

"Parker must have told you about the false rumor that Madame Koluchy ordered the destruction of my mother's school."

"She did! She worked in concert with Joséphine. They were both abused by your mother–just as I was! I couldn't tell you that in my letters."

The blade now dangled only a foot above Irina's neck.

"Stop lying about my mother!" screamed Milady.

"At school–in the storeroom–there, you told me things that were not in your letters. Your greatest fear..."

"You're stalling for time!"

The blade was beginning its final descent.

"Be very careful now," hissed Milady. "The blade's even with your chin."

The blade rotated to the right.

"Berenice, your greatest fear was becoming..."

Irina stopped talking as the blade passed over her Adam's apple and swooshed to the left.

"...someone like your mother."

Irina closed her eyes in anticipation of her own death, but it did not come. She opened her eyes. Milady had pressed the switch to stop the blade. Its edge was an inch from slicing the left side of her neck. The shackles sprang open. Moving slowly to her right, Irina rose from the slab.

"Irene," sobbed Milady.

"Yes–Berenice."

"I'm not the girl from the storeroom anymore... I was full of despair when I thought you died. I wanted to strike out at the world. Koluchy offered me power. You wouldn't understand..."

"I understand all too well. Your mother and Joséphine made me the same offer."

Milady opened Kaitlin's cell door with her keys.

"Kaitlin de Winter, I grant you your freedom. You know the exits from this building, Please take Irene to safety."

"Kaitlin, why did you keep that dedication page torn from *Oliver Twist*?" asked Irina, helping the other woman to get back to her feet.

"At the Institution Bachelard, Berenice claimed to have proof that I had vandalized her quarters. I went to see her with the page, hoping to trade it in exchange for her silence. But I was overpowered by her and Koluchy. During my years of servitude, my only comfort was prayer. Reading your inscription reminded me to pray."

"You'll soon all be saying your prayers!" said a woman's voice.

The wall mirror had swung open, revealing a secret passage behind it.

Madame Koluchy emerged with a pistol. Following her were Dr. Malbodius and Count Corbucci, both holding pistols, Joséphine Balsamo, Eva Relli, the Pallid Mask, armed with his sickle, and a woman with black hair. She pointed to her uniform.

"My Black Skirt unicorn lured you here," announced the woman in an unmistakable Cockney accent.

"Purity Parker!" said Irina.

"No, I'm Maude North," said the Black Skirt, switching to a cultured voice. "The Pallid Mask is Mr. North. The real Purity accepted my offer to take a joint vacation to Paris. I used a blonde wig to impersonate her. My husband's blade never touched my face. A vial of pig's blood was concealed in my hand. I streaked my face with it before falling into the Seine and swimming to safety with your 50,000 francs. After that, we killed the real Purity, disfigured her and threw her body into the river."

While the others covered the three women with their guns, Joséphine strolled over to the pendulum. By manipulating the switches, she retracted the deadly blade back to its original height.

"The concept of an Espionage Hotel came from this prototype," explained Eva, pointing at the mirror. "It's enabled us to see everything."

"Milady, lie down on the slab," said Koluchy. "Maude and Eva, restrain the others."

After Milady had complied, Joséphine closed the shackles. Maude held Irina's arms from behind. Eva did the same to Kaitlin.

Joséphine pulled out one of the needles from the ball of thread on the table.

"You shouldn't have mocked my title, Berenice. And you not even being a true 'Milady.' But I remembered a letter to Irene in which the writer described a classmate with a valuable collection as an 'uppity aristocrat.' When you cited your theft of the possessions of an 'uppity aristocrat,' I suspected you were Blythe Furnace. Your prisoner's real personnel file later identified you as Berenice Fourneau."

"Joséphine came to me after she deduced your identity," said Koluchy. "She warned me that you might betray us if you ever found out that Irina Putine was your best friend, Irene Chupin. For years, Eva Relli had been spying on your aunt. We arranged this affair to test your loyalty. Joséphine's title of nobility is hereby restored as reward for her cleverness. Her executive rank is also restored. You're the branch that needs cutting, Nevermore."

"I'll appeal to the High Council," said Berenice. "Dr. Nikola won't permit this."

"He can speak for himself!" said Count Corbucci. "Antonio, please join us."

Nikola entered from the wall panel.

"Excellency, do I have your permission to speak freely to the condemned?"

Corbucci nodded his head in approval. Nikola treaded slowly towards the woman he had known as Milady. His hand brushed the ball of thread with the remaining needle. He stoked the hair of his shackled lover gently.

"Berenice, I owe everything I am to the Black Coats. They rescued me from starvation in Cuba. I cannot defy them. Not even for you."

Nikola bent down and kissed her on the lips. As he walked away, he spied Irina being held by Maude. Nikola moved in front of the detective. He seized her wrists.

"I curse the day when my precious Milady befriended you."

Nikola spat in Irina's face and then released her hands. He turned to Corbucci.

"I do not need to witness this execution, Excellency. I ask permission to return to my hotel."

Although a ruthless man, Corbucci possessed genuine affection for Nikola. He sensed the younger man's need for solace.

"Your request is granted, Antonio. Furthermore, I shall accompany you."

Corbucci and Nikola left the dungeon.

"I know why you're doing this, Koluchy!" said Berenice. "My mother isn't the only reason. There's Antonio! You couldn't stand the thought of another woman in your ex-fiancé's arms!"

"Countess Cagliostro, perform your duty. *Cut the branch!*" ordered Koluchy.

Standing over Berenice's right side, Joséphine raised the needle like a sacrificial knife.

"You will die by the pendulum, but you will only hear the blade. I'm removing your other eye."

While the Black Coats focused their attention on Joséphine, another needle dropped from Irina's right sleeve into her hand.

She stabbed Maude's left hand. Crying in pain, the woman let go of her grip on the detective. Irina broke completely free and sprang toward the slab. She pushed the outermost lever forward. Berenice's shackles snapped open. Irina then tackled Joséphine.

Berenice whirled off the slab. Malbodius and Koluchy both fired their pistols, but the shots missed. A swift leg kick from the one-eyed woman hit Koluchy in the stomach. She collapsed, overcome by pain. Berenice then delivered a brutal punch to the face of Malbodius . He, too, fell unconscious.

Meanwhile, Eva Relli was struggling to restrain Kaitlin. Busting loose, the former schoolgirl had turned around and delivered a devastating series of blows to the blonde woman's body.

The Pallid Mask swung his sickle at Berenice's head, but it passed harmlessly over her as she dropped to the ground. Swinging around, her extended right leg hit the man's feet. He smashed into the ground. Maude's uninjured hand snatched Malbodius's gun from the ground, but Berenice was faster and grabbed her arm. The Pallid Mask got up and sprang forward, lunging with his sickle. Berenice threw Maude in his direction. The blade pierced her stomach.

"Juan..." gasped Maude as she died.

Dropping his sickle, the speechless Pallid Mask let his wife's body slump to the floor. He gripped Berenice's throat with both hands. The one-eyed woman delivered two karate chops to her antagonist's arms. The Mask released his clasp. Plucking the man's right arm, Milady flipped him off his feet. As the chalk-faced assailant was lifting himself up, she kicked him in the jaw. The Pallid Mask crumbled in a senseless heap.

Berenice saw Kaitlin standing above a vanquished Eva. Irina and Joséphine, however, were still struggling on the ground. The needles were in each combatant's right hand. Each woman was holding the other's wrist with her free hand.

Berenice seized the back of Joséphine's neck and pulled her away from Irina. The blonde woman dropped her needle. Berenice then shoved Joséphine into Kaitlin's former cell and locked the door. With Irina and Kaitlin's help, she deposited the other Black Coats in neighboring cells.

"You'll regret sparing my life!" screamed Joséphine from her cell. "I know how you escaped. Nikola hid the other needle up his sleeve before kissing you. He then slipped it to Irina and maneuvered Corbucci to safety. Koluchy will figure out everything. Someone will die for this. *Cut the branch*! This time, that *branch* will be your lover!"

"I doubt it. Koluchy will shield her former fiancé. She still loves him. You exploited her jealousy to ruin me. Now Koluchy will destroy you. You're a more convenient *branch*! This is your third failure! Farewell–Countess!"

"What happened to Kaitlin and Berenice after your escape?" asked Victor Chupin.

Irina was briefing her uncle at the Chupin Detective Agency.

"Kaitlin insisted on being taken to the home of Baron Gruner. He should protect her from any further persecution. Before leaving London, Berenice burglarized Maude's apartment. Here are the 50,000 francs that Maude stole from us. Earlier in the dungeon, Berenice detached the Medina blade from the torture device. We delivered it to the Vollin estate. This is Roger's check for its retrieval. Berenice's staying as a guest of the Vollins for the present."

"Roger has an impressionable 14-year old son. I hope Berenice doesn't give young Richard any bad ideas. We need to discuss one final matter, your new assistant."

"This employment contract merely needs your signature. My choice wasn't on the list."

"This contract is for Blythe Furnace!"

"Berenice is reviving her old alias."

"But I said it had to be someone with top credentials."

"Besides the skills of an Iga ninja, Blythe possesses a rich knowledge of the London underworld. And she solved a mystery that even stumped you: The Case of the Purloined Pendulum."

"This isn't funny, Irina! The woman's a homicidal lunatic. She nearly beheaded you."

"A clear misunderstanding–atoned for by her subsequent actions."

"Not in my eyes! Let her seeks atonement in a nunnery or an asylum."

"If you persist, I might resign and open a competing agency with her."

Victor Chupin sighed. He couldn't bear the thought of a separation from his niece. Reluctantly signing the contract, he silently prayed that this document wasn't her death warrant.

Cut the Branch

Inside her prison cell, the blonde awaited her execution. For the last month, she had languished in the underground dungeon of the Black Coats. One of the proverbs of the European crime cartel was "Cut the Branch." The saying meant that any underling who outlived their usefulness must be eradicated. In December 1896, this dictum was about to be applied to Joséphine Balsamo, the woman feared as Countess Cagliostro.

The London headquarters of the Black Coats was located in the House of Crafts, a building ostensibly the home of a fashion company. The decision to terminate Joséphine's life had been made by the ruling High Council weeks earlier. The delay is carrying out Joséphine's sentence was due to the construction of an appropriate execution chamber outside her cell.

Joséphine was about to be dispatched on an unusual scaffold. The structure harbored neither a gallows nor a guillotine. A rectangular airtight enclosure of unbreakable glass had been erected. A small circular opening had been cut in the bottom of the glass. A hose connected to small metal tank was connected to the round aperture. The container housed a poison gas developed by Dr. Antonio Nikola, a prominent member of the High Council.

Countess Cagliostro had been condemned by Nikola and his former fiancée, Catarina. Born into the Corbucci family, a powerful Neapolitan clan in the Black Coats, the dark-haired Catarina had been slated to marry Antonio since her early teens. A series of events prevented their wedlock. In 1879, a civil war erupted in the Black Coats between the forces of Catarina's father, Count Salvatore Corbucci, and Professor James Moriarty. When Catarina's mother was assassinated by Moriarty's allies in the following year, Count Corbucci sought to protect his daughter from harm. Under the alias of Mademoiselle Koluchy, Catarina was secretly placed in Madame Fourneau's College for Young Women, a boarding school in Provence. If Corbucci had known the true nature of the school, he never would have permitted his offspring to attend there. Catarina was sexually abused at the school. She had been forced to indulge in practices that called her own femininity into question. When she graduated at the age of 21 in 1884, Catarina rushed home to her beloved Antonio. She wished to be married immediately, but her father delayed the nuptials in order to plan an elaborate ceremony. Concerned about her own womanhood, Catarina begged Antonio to consummate their love before their formal wedding. Antonio declined because such an action would have offended Count Corbucci. Catarina then made a fateful decision. She conducted a brief romantic liaison with another man, Norman Head. This Englishman meant nothing to her. Her heart had always belonged to Antonio. When Antonio learned of this affair, he broke the engagement. One year later, Corbucci arranged a diplomatic marriage for his wayward daughter. In order to cement a peace treaty with his rival in the Black Coats, Corbucci had negotiated the wedding of Catarina to Noel Moriarty, the Professor's younger brother.

At the Fourneau College, Catarina had met Joséphine. Although Catarina secretly despised her younger classmate, the brunette soon recognized the younger blonde's talents for deceit. Under the alias of Madame Koluchy, Catarina emerged as the leading female agent of the Black Coats. In 1889, Joséphine left the college to become Catarina's chief of staff. With Catarina's permission, Joséphine put the final touches to a complex scheme of revenge that resulted in Madame Fourneau's death in 1890. With Joséphine as her surrogate, Catarina had avenged her debasement by the corrupt headmistress.

A humiliating defeat by Irina Putine, an operative of the Chupin Detective Agency, resulted in Joséphine's demotion. Joséphine had found herself under the brutal supervision of Milady Nevermore, Catarina's new chief of staff. Nevertheless, Joséphine persuaded Catarina to have her launch a new conspiracy. Catarina resented Nevermore because she had become Antonio's lover. Playing on Catarina's jealousy, Joséphine inaugurated a plot to cause the deaths of both Putine and Nevermore. Joséphine's stratagem backfired. Maneuvered into a compromising situation by Joséphine, Nevermore disrupted the Black Coats by defecting to the Chupin Detective Agency. Blamed for Nevermore's desertion, Joséphine was marked for death by her murderous colleagues.

The cell door was opened briefly for Joséphine Balsamo to receive a visitor. A brown-haired woman of 34 years entered. She was Urania Caber, the chief of a scientific division of the Black Coats. Although she was the daughter of the late Professor Moriarty, Urania was isolated from the overall operations of the Black Coats. Judged to be too merciful by her malevolent peers, she was solely responsible for technical research.

Urania was in tears. She harbored genuine affection for Joséphine.

"My uncle refused my pleas for leniency," insisted Urania. "There's nothing more I can do."

"I resigned myself to my fate long ago. Has my sister discovered the truth?"

"As you instructed, I told Sabine that you returned to New Orleans. She has no idea of the doom hanging over you."

"After my demise, you must tell Sabine the truth. Watch over her, my friend. She may be tempted to do something foolish."

"I promise to shield Sabine from all harm."

"16 years ago, I made the same pledge to my dying mother. She gave me this just before I swore an oath of fidelity to Sabine's welfare." Joséphine indicated a ring on the fourth finger of her right hand. The circlet bore the emblem of a golden ram, the Cagliostro family crest.

"Do you want it given to Sabine?"

112

"If my sister received this ring, she would feel obligated to fulfill an oath of vengeance imposed on me by our mother. Sabine is incapable of pursuing a vendetta. Let the ring be buried with me. It is the only remnant of my noble heritage."

Joséphine pointed to her attire. She was clothed in a brown blouse with a black tie and skirt. It was the uniform of the Black Skirts, the criminal organization led by Catarina. An alliance of secret societies constituted the Black Coats. In addition to the Black Skirts, the confederation included such sinister associations as the Gentleman of the Night and the Camorra. Normally Joséphine wore an elegant green dress. Due to her demotion, she had been forced to wear the garments of a minor functionary.

"I will make sure that your last wishes are respected," vowed Urania. "I won't be present in the audience tonight. I can't be part of Catarina's ceremony."

Joséphine knew that Catarina was turning her execution into a private spectacle for the top echelon of the Black Coats.

"I understand, Urania. You've always been a loyal friend."

Hugging Joséphine, Urania kissed her gently on the cheek. Noel Moriarty's niece departed.

One hour later, Joséphine Balsamo's cell was invaded by a red-haired woman attired as a Black Skirt. She was Orianne Coyatier. Years ago, Joséphine and Orianne had been fellow students at the Fourneau College for Young Women. Madame Fourneau had tyrannically presided over her school with an elite guard of student prefects. After Joséphine had been made chief prefect, she had recruited Orianne and another girl, Rochelle Moreau, as her assistants. Both Orianne and Rochelle were the same age as Joséphine. They should have graduated together in the spring of 1889, but Joséphine was offered employment by Catarina in January. Orianne and Rochelle had been formidable lieutenants. Orianne was strong and athletic while Rochelle was witty and clever. When Joséphine left the school, Rochelle had expected to finish out the term as the chief prefect. Instead Rochelle was stunned when Joséphine recommended a younger prefect to be her successor. Passionately devoted to Rochelle, Orianne shared her classmate's chagrin. When the two girls graduated, Catarina recruited both of them into her organization. The pair had long harbored resentment of Joséphine.

Grabbing Joséphine roughly by the arm, Orianne pulled the captive outside the cell. Joséphine found herself confronted by Rochelle. With the disgrace of Milady Nevermore, the position of Catarina's chief of staff had been bestowed on Rochelle. An attractive woman with brown hair, Rochelle always dressed in black.

"You once joked that my raiment was suitable for funerals, Balsamo," commented Rochelle. "I'm now attending yours."

Rochelle was standing with an entourage of high-ranking Black Coats. Catarina was wearing a purple gown that exposed her shoulders. This was an act of contempt directed at Joséphine. As the consequence of an earlier failure to outwit Irina Putine, Joséphine had been brutally punished by Catarina. Both the blonde's shoulders had been branded with the letter "V." The symbol stood for "*voleuse*," the feminine form of "*voleur*," the French word for thief.

Alongside Catarina were her father, Count Corbucci, and Antonio Nikola. Corbucci, a stout man with a large mustache, stared whimsically at Joséphine. The younger Nikola looked away from her.

"As much as I appreciate your labors, Antonio," declared Corbucci, "I would have preferred a simple lynching. I witnessed many a hanging during my travels in America, my boy. I even saw Ramirez, the notorious bandit, strung up on two different occasions. Incredibly, he survived both times."

"I'm surprised you never depicted Ramirez's multiple executions in one of your novels, Excellency," observed Antonio.

"Unfortunately, a rival chronicler of the American West, Bob Robertson, wrote an epic about Ramirez before I had a chance."

Also present was Professor Chavain, a botanist whose scientific research team competed with Urania's. Four years older than Catarina, Chavain was the first graduate of the Fourneau College to join the Black Coats. She had recommended the College to the Corbucci family. Unlike Catarina, Chavain relished the depraved practices of the school. A handsome woman with black hair, she was reputed to be the most vicious member of the High Council.

Rochelle opened the door to the glass chamber. Orianne shoved Joséphine inside. The door was slammed shut. Catarina turned the knob of the tank connected to the glass cabinet. Gas flooded the compartment. Pounding on the glass, Joséphine gasped for breath. As the fumes overcame her, Joséphine beheld the smiling faces of Catarina, Rochelle, Orianne and Professor Chavain. The blonde sank lifeless to the ground.

At the House of Crafts, Catarina conferred with Rochelle.

"There is only the disposal of the corpse to be settled," noted Catarina.

"I've received a written communiqué for your husband, Madame. He wants Balsamo's body delivered to Sara's shop in the Strand."

"Noel never mentioned this to me! Who delivered these instructions?"

"Your niece, Madame."

"The meddling Urania! She always had a soft spot for Balsamo. Did my husband dictate anything else of importance?"

"Merely that Balsamo's signet ring was not to be removed from her hand."

"So that blonde strumpet desired burial with her family heirloom. No doubt this last request was conveyed to Urania. We shall frustrate Balsamo even in death. Who's conveying the cadaver to the Strand?"

"Coleen Pegler, Madame."

"An excellent choice. Order her to remove Balsamo's ring."

"What should Coleen do with it?"

"Let her wear it. Tell her it's a gift from me. I am dining with my husband and father at the White Lodge. Contact me if there are any complications."

Joséphine Balsamo's remains were locked in an oblong wooden box. The trunk was placed on a carriage by three men. Joséphine's unofficial pallbearers were all American outlaws. Joséphine had once run a smuggling ring in New Orleans. There she had recruited numerous American criminals who had returned with her to Europe.

One was Frank Moran. With a penchant for gunplay and gambling, Frank professed to be related to Colonel Sebastian Moran, the former Black Coat leader now residing in an asylum for the criminally insane. If anyone challenged the validity of Frank's dubious declaration, their objections were overridden by a bullet. A long coat hid a belt with a holstered six-shooter.

Patrick Dickson wore an eye patch. In a Texas bar fight during 1882, a Chinese brawler had gouged Dickson's right eye. An expert marksman, Dickson relied on stealth. He kept a small derringer up his sleeve.

Completing the trio was Hamish Webb, a blond man with hardened features. Sporting an elegant suit, he looked more like a lawyer than a hired killer. He always carried a book. His current reading material was Stangerson's *Dissociation of Matter Through Electricity*. The pages had actually been hollowed out to conceal a pistol. Protruding from the edge of the book was a string ending in a metal loop. Pulling on the cord would cause the concealed gun to discharge. The volume was stuffed into a large pocket of Webb's coat.

Supervising the three brigands was an American woman in a Black Skirt uniform. Around 40 years old, she was very attractive with auburn hair and dark eyes. A black beret crowned her head. Brown gloves covered her hands. The right glove was altered to hide an injury incurred during a gun battle in a train yard. Her last two fingers were missing. The slender woman had been wounded by a Pinkerton agent in 1879. The gloves had originally been designed with holes to expose all the fingers, but the openings over her dismembered digits had been sewed shut.

This unscrupulous female used the alias of Coleen Pegler. Pursuant to Rochelle's commands, Coleen proudly displayed Joséphine's ring on the fourth finger of her left hand. Extremely attractive, Coleen dominated male colleagues by bestowing her sexual favors on them. Rochelle had often referred to Coleen's underlings as a "male harem."

Coleen's seductive charms had proved invaluable to her superiors in a difficult transition. In 1884, the High Council had bestowed on Catarina total dominion of the Brotherhood of Seven Kings. As its name implied, the criminal association was traditionally male-dominated. Recently Catarina had reorganized the Brotherhood into the more feminist Black Skirts. The male employees in the former Brotherhood resisted this radical transformation. Coleen's ability to charm the opposite sex had greatly assisted in calming the reluctant traditionalists under Catarina's authority.

Coleen and her subordinates mounted the wagon. Driven by Moran, the vehicle eventually reached an unpretentious shop in the Strand. The establishment was wedged in between a hosier and a printer. The windows of the shop were stacked with perfume bottles. A small brass plate on a mahogany door bore these words: "Madame Sara, *Parfumeuse*."

Coleen rang the doorbell. It was opened by a stout Mexican with curly hair and a mustache. He was clothed in the red uniform of a doorman. The sleeves of his coat were rolled up. A snake was branded on his left arm.

"I am Gordo Reloj. Are you making the delivery from the House of Crafts?"

After Coleen acknowledged Reloj's assumption, the Mexican escorted the American quartet into the shop. The men carried the oblong box.

Two raven-haired women awaited Reloj inside. The taller of the duo had a bouffant hair style. Her outfit included a white shirt, an embroidered vest and a brown skirt.

"This is my wife," indicated Reloj.

"Pilar the Casino Bandit!" shouted Dickson. "You were supposed to have perished with the rest of the Aguilar gang! A bounty hunter collected the reward on you!"

"My death was a falsehood," said Senora Reloj. "The lying *gringo* who collected the bounty on my *amigos* lied. He merely knocked me unconscious. Despite my absence among the corpses of the Aguilar gang, the foolish authorities paid the bounty on my head."

"I never knew you were married," mentioned Dickson.

"Gordo and I are newlyweds. We married shortly after I fled Mexico,"

"Enough of this small talk!" interrupted the other brunette. "There's business to transact."

The speaker was 5 feet and 4 inches tall. She was dressed in a gold tunic that ended at her thighs. Black pants and boots encased her legs. A dark gendarme-style cape with a gold lining draped her shoulders. Her hair was cut in an unusual manner. The ends were severed at chin length. The left side of her hair was draped around her ear while the right side hung down close to her face. A small black fur cap adorned her head. She wore a black belt. Stuffed inside the belt was a black glove. The right side of her belt was covered by her cape.

"I'm sorry, Comandante," pleaded Senora Reloj. "I didn't expect to see an old friend."

"I am not heartless, Pilar," stated the Comandante. "You know what kind of person I am."

"The Comandante is a just woman," responded Senora Reloj.

"You can reminisce with your old *compañero* once the merchandise has been delivered to the laboratory."

Led by the Comandante, the Americans carried the trunk into the basement. Coleen and the Relojs followed. Underneath the store was a much larger underground sanctuary Navigating a series of corridors, they finally reached a room filled with medical instruments. A large table was in the center of the room. The Comandante directed the Americans to deposit the oblong box on the floor.

"Gordo, I will need you to stay here and assist me," ordered the Comandante. "Pilar, you can take our guests to the pantry and talk about old times."

After Senora Reloj had left with the Americans, the Comandante opened the trunk. Together with Gordo, she lifted Joséphine's body and placed it on the table. The Mexican was dismissed by the brunette. He left to find his wife and the Americans. The Comandante knocked on a nearby door.

"Your patient awaits, Doctor."

Holding a syringe in his hand, Antonio Nikola entered the room.

The prostrate Joséphine Balsamo opened her eyes. She recognized Nikola.

"Why am I not dead?"

"The gas put you in a cataleptic trance. I merely had to inject the antidote."

"Why did you save me? You have as much reason to hate me as the others."

"You bear responsibility for separating me from Milady Nevermore, but you were also made a scapegoat for my own role in facilitating her escape. Unlike my associates, I am not infatuated by the doctrine of *pay the law*. I won't let another be punished for my own actions."

"The High Council will murder you once they learn the truth."

"The Council is effectively dominated by Noel Moriarty and Count Corbucci. Both have agreed to this subterfuge. Your execution was a ruse to satisfy Catarina's vindictiveness."

"You won't be able to keep my survival secret from her."

"We have no intention of keeping her in the dark. Noel will take a perverse delight in informing Catarina of your exoneration."

"I don't understand. Why would Noel and the Count defy Catarina?"

"They seek to garner favor with your godmother."

"Sarah Warrender? The All-Father expelled her from the High Council in 1878. Not even Noel's older brother trusted her. With the loss of Sarah's patronage, my mother had no choice but to shift her allegiance to Professor Moriarty."

"Your godmother fled to her refuge in Brazil. In her alternate identity of Madame Sara, she patiently erected a formidable syndicate extending throughout South and Central America. She even has agents in Mexico and the southwestern United States. Over the last few years, I have engaged in several joint enterprises with her. Inevitably I negotiated her return to the ranks of the Black Coats. She has resumed her place on the High Council."

"The All-Father would never have sanctioned her reinstatement!"

"You underestimate Noel's powers of persuasion."

Joséphine digested Nikola's revelations. Who really was the supreme power in the High Council? In theory, the All-Father was the unchallenged overlord of the Black Coats. However, Joséphine had heard rumors that the All-Father had been forced to relinquish his power to Professor James Moriarty, Lord of the Night. Moriarty's title was derived from his leadership of the Gentleman of the Night, the London subsidiary of the Black Coats. With the Professor's death in 1891, Colonel Moran was invested as the Lord of the Night. After the Colonel's incarceration in 1894, Noel Moriarty succeeded him in that role. Nikola's statements implied that the Lord of the Night was the true master of the Black Coats. Was the All-Father merely a figurehead?

"Your godmother insisted that you be pardoned," continued Nikola. "You are currently in her recently opened perfumery. Before I introduce you to her subaltern, we must come to an understanding."

"Concerning what?"

"I wish for peace to exist between us, Countess. Let us forget the turmoil of the Nevermore affair. We have too much in common to be enemies."

"You're referring to our joint Italian ancestry?"

"More than that, Countess. You remember when we first met?"

"At the Villa Corbucci. You interviewed me when I arrived as a governess."

"You later learned that I was secretly evaluating your fitness to join the Black Coats. If not for my recommendation, your duties would have been merely supervising Dominick Moriarty's education."

"What prompted you to sponsor my inclusion in the Black Coats?"

"I sensed a kindred spirit. We both witnessed the demise of our mothers at an early age. Your soul also cried out for vengeance. The Black Coats gave each of us the means to quaff our thirst for justice."

"You shall have your wish, Antonio. There shall be no war between us."

"Thank you, Countess. Before summoning your godmother's emissary, let me help you to your feet. You should receive her fitting your proper station"

With Antonio's assistance, Joséphine rose from the table. Briefly leaving the room, Antonio returned with the Comandante.

"Countess Cagliostro," said Antonio, "permit me to introduce Marga Sandorf."

The Comandante knelt in front of the Countess. The brunette bowed her head in subservience.

"My heart belongs to the Cagliostro clan. My soul belongs to the Cagliostro clan. I am your slave. Command me, Excellency."

Extending her right hand, Joséphine asked *"Will there be daylight?"*

"It will be daylight from midnight to noon if it's the will of the Mother," answered Marga. She kissed Joséphine's hand.

Feeling the touch of Marga's lips, Countess Cagliostro realized that her ring was missing.

In the pantry of Madame Sara's shop, Coleen and her three henchman were seated around a table with the Relojs. They were all sharing a bottle of whiskey. Suddenly the celebrants were interrupted by the intrusion of Marga, Antonio and Joséphine.

"Balsamo!" shouted Coleen. "But you're dead"

"Her Excellency is very much alive," asserted Marga.

"My proper title is Countess Cagliostro," insisted Joséphine. "You always addressed me correctly as my servant in New Orleans, Coleen."

Joséphine spied the signet ring on Coleen's left hand. "You have my property. Surrender it immediately "

"I will not. Madame Koluchy granted me this reward for my loyal service."

"The reigning Madame here is named Sara!" proclaimed Marga. "Her decree is that the Countess be granted anything she wishes."

"I don't give a damn for your Madame Sara! She can go to Hell!"

Before replying, Marga removed the glove from her belt and put it on her right hand. She pulled back her cape to expose a holster on the right side. Her gun was lodged with the butt facing outwards. It could only be drawn with her left hand. The firearm was made of solid gold.

"Your name shouldn't be Pegler. You have a penchant for filth. Your name should be Piglet."

The three gunslingers rose from the table. Hamish Webb was holding his massive volume. His finger was touching the loop that could activate the pistol. Dickson positioned his right arm behind his back. His derringer lowered into his hand.

Frank Moran pushed back his coat to display his own revolver.

"I believe you owe Miss Pegler an apology."

"You're Frank Moran," retorted Marga. "You claim to be Sebastian Moran's cousin. You're a liar."

Moran reached for his revolver. Marga was much quicker. Grabbing her gun with her left hand, she fanned the hammer with her gloved right. The first bullet entered Webb's forehead. The second penetrated Dickson's his left eye. The third found its home in Moran's heart. Marga's fourth bullet shot the beret off Coleen's head.

Coleen raised her hands in the air.

"Don't kill me! I have no gun!"

"Kill you! What kind of person do you think I am? Enlighten this Piglet, Pilar."

"The Comandante is a just woman!" contended Pilar.

"Pilar, remove the ring from this Piglet's hand and give it to the Countess."

Senora Reloj complied with Marga's command.

"I have a boon, Excellency," remarked Marga. "Let me deal with this Piglet in my own fashion."

"Your request is granted," said Joséphine.

Marga raised her gun menacingly at Coleen.

"But you're a just woman!" yelled Coleen with her arms still extended upwards.

"I am indeed."

Marga fired twice. The first bullet blasted the fifth finger of Coleen's left hand. The second disintegrated the adjacent finger.

Coleen Pegler dropped to the floor in agony.

Marga holstered her golden gun.

"You now have matching hands, Piglet."

Catarina was livid. After treating Coleen's wounds, Antonio had returned the injured woman to the House of Crafts. Rochelle Moreau immediately summoned Catarina at the White Lodge, Noel Moriarty's mansion in the Blackheath district of London. Upon learning the news of the violent shootout at Madame Sara's, Catarina swiftly returned to the White Lodge to confront her husband.

Noel Moriarty was a tall man of 56 years. His shoulders were bent as if from years of study. His delicate face had a long and pointed chin. His silver hair was brushed low on the forehead. Tinted spectacles covered his pale gray eyes.

"Ah, Kate, it's a pity that you didn't return earlier. You just missed Antonio. He left with your father."

"Both of them were afraid to face me! You all conspired to reprieve Balsamo!"

"A necessary concession to bring Madame Sara back into the fold. Have you forgotten your enthusiastic support for her reinstatement? You relished the idea of a third woman on the Council."

"My operatives have been slaughtered by Madame Sara's gunslinger! I demand satisfaction!"

"Did Rochelle Moreau relay my directive about Balsamo's ring?"

"Yes, she did."

"You didn't countermand me? Did you, Kate?"

"Of course not!" lied Catarina.

"According to Antonio, Pegler stole Balsamo's ring. That pilferer is solely responsible for the unfortunate incident at Madame Sara's. You should consider having Pegler executed. At the very least, you should have her flogged."

"I will consider your recommendations, Noel, but reprimanding Pegler doesn't settle the issue of Balsamo."

"Do not fret, my dear Kate. I have already factored in your disdain for Balsamo. Your desire to see her chastised will be fulfilled."

"How?"

"A further disciplinary matter relative to Balsamo has come to my attention. I have delegated Madame Sara to deal with the matter promptly. Balsamo soon will undergo an ordeal far worse than asphyxiation."

"I don't understand."

"Balsamo will be forced to kill the one person she truly loves."

Noel Moriarty proceeded to explain in detail. When her husband finished, Catarina laughed gleefully. She couldn't imagine a more fitting revenge.

Madame Sara's perfumery also functioned as a beauty salon. In preparation for her meeting with her godmother, Joséphine was bathed and glamorized. Pilar Reloj was a skilled manicurist. Her husband revealed himself to be a talented hairdresser.

Wrapped in a towel, Joséphine Balsamo sat in a chair. As Pilar worked on the blonde's nails, Gordo curled her hair.

"Pilar, I'm curious about the Comandante," disclosed Joséphine. "Tell me about her."

"Her father was Aristide Orlowsky Sandorf, the younger brother of an Hungarian count. Her mother, Ivonne Von Schulenberg, belonged to a celebrated family of Austrian marksmen."

"Marga's uncle was Baron Von Schulenberg," added Gordo. "He was quiet a shootist. 24 duels. 23 widows."

"Aristide was an officer in the Imperial Austrian navy," resumed Pilar. "There he became a protégé of the Navy's Commander-in-Chief."

"You mean Maximilian, the Emperor's brother?" questioned Joséphine.

"Yes," affirmed Pilar. "In 1864, Maximilian became Emperor of Mexico with the support of French bayonets. Resigning his commission, Aristide traveled with his wife to serve Maximilian in Mexico. When Maximilian was executed by Juarez three years later, Aristide was left stranded in Mexico."

"Why didn't he return to Europe, Pilar?"

"The disgrace of his brother prevented such a contingency. Count Sandorf was arrested for treason during Aristide's sojourn in Mexico. Enraged at the Mexican authorities for killing his patron, Aristide terrorized the Mexican coast as a pirate. In 1868, his beloved Ivonne died giving birth to Marga."

"Did Marga's father train her to shoot proficiently?"

"He neglected her shamefully. Aristide blamed Marga for her mother's death. When she was 16, she ran away from home. Migrating to Texas, she met Manny Bennet."

"Is he related to Solly Bennet, the Mexican-American outlaw?"

"His brother, Excellency. Manny taught her how to handle a gun."

"Were they lovers?"

"Yes, Excellency. She loved him passionately, but Manny could not fully return her ardor His soul still longed for a woman who had married his best friend, Corben Caine. Sensing Manny's reluctance, Marga left him. Later, the Caine family quarreled with a rancher, Wilmot Rogers, over cattle. Corben and his wife were killed in the resulting feud. Manny retaliated by slaying Rogers and his sons. The rancher also had a daughter. She fatally shot Manny. When Marga learned of Manny's death, she avenged him by planting a bullet in the stomach of the Rogers girl. Marga was wanted for murder. A price was placed on her head. Jefferson Gonzales hoped to collect it."

"I've heard of him. Count Corbucci wrote a novel based on Gonzales. He was a bounty hunter notorious for carrying a golden pistol."

"That gun is now the Comandante's. Gonzales tried to dry-gulch her. She was faster. Marga lifted the pistol from his bullet-riddled corpse."

"Gonzales wasn't the only bounty killer sent to Boot Hill by the Comandante," contributed Gordo. "There was also the Lanky Gunman. He was quite a character. His weapon was a rifle with a scope. When he trained his rifle on Marga, she dispatched a bullet straight through the scope into his eye. Another bounty killer was nicknamed the Yankee Whistler because he always whistled the same song. Marga shot him in the mouth."

"Marga has a sense of irony," concluded Joséphine. "She proved that in her treatment of Pegler."

"The Comandante should have killed Pegler," contended Gordo. "A friend of mine had a saying: 'When you wound a man, you better kill him.' That adage applies to women as well. I learned that lesson the hard way. I left a man for dead after shooting bullets into his hands and legs. Miraculously he recovered. My enemy tracked me down. After wounding me in the same way, he turned me over to the tender mercies of a town raided by my gang. Luckily, the local priest convinced the populace not to lynch me without a trial. Madame Sara's agents broke me out of jail. From that day forward-, I became her loyal follower."

"Why did my godmother rescue you?" queried Joséphine.

Gordo pointed to the snake branded into his left arm.

"Madame heard that I bear the mark of the sidewinder. She's a snake worshipper."

"Excellency, may I ask you a question?" said Pilar.

"You have graciously answered my own inquiries. Please do."

"Do you know someone named Dupont-Verdier?"

"Calls himself Satanas. He's part of Jillian Blake's prostitution ring. Why do you ask?"

"Madame Sara interrogated me about him. Aguilar had some dealings with him in Mexico. Unfortunately, I could tell our mistress nothing. All of their business ventures happened before I joined Aguilar's desperadoes."

Upon completion of her beautification, Joséphine Balsamo put on appropriate apparel for her presentation to Madame Sara. Aware of Joséphine's fashion tastes, Marga Sandorf permitted the blonde to choose from a wardrobe of stylish green dresses.

In the confusion surrounding the gunfight in the pantry, Joséphine had pocketed the derringer of the deceased Dickson. Suspicious of her new associates, Joséphine hid the gun up her sleeve.

Marga showed Joséphine into Madame Sara's study. Awaiting them inside was a short woman with blue eyes and dazzling golden hair. Her gown was made of white satin, A medallion bearing a serpent with seven heads hung around her neck.

The woman ran up and embraced Joséphine. "Godchild, I haven't seen you since you were a little girl."

Joséphine was taken aback. "You can't be Sarah Warrender! You're too young!"

The woman called Madame Sara moved away from Joséphine. "But I am Sarah Warrender. The Cagliostro blood flows too in my veins. I drank our ancestor's elixir of youth when I was 25."

"Do you take me for a fool! I know this scam all too well. It was taught to me by my mother. Like her, I exploit a resemblance to my namesake, the original Joséphine Balsamo, born in 1788. You must be Sarah Warrender's daughter. You're no more immortal then I am!"

"Once when you were nine years old, godchild, you crept in my dressing room. You gasped upon glimpsing the birthmark between my left thigh. It is a red crescent. Shall I show it to you?"

"I was shocked because my gypsy governess told me that only a witch bore such a mark. I don't doubt that you have a similar crescent. It could easily be a tattoo!"

"I anticipated your skepticism. Marga, please summon our other guest."

Marga left the room. She returned with a distinguished gray-haired man with a beard. Joséphine immediately recognized the visitor as Leonard, her mother's former lieutenant.

"Josine, I have never lied to you. This woman is the Sarah Warrender from your childhood."

Leonard was one of the few people whom Joséphine trusted explicitly. She was overwhelmed by Leonard's confirmation of Madame Sara's identity.

"You may leave us, Leonard." The bearded man left the three women.

"Please sit down, my godchild," instructed Madame Sara.

Joséphine seated herself in front of a desk. Sara sat down behind the desk. Marga Sandorf stood behind Sara's chair.

Sara smiled benignly.

"You have grown into a beautiful woman. You look just like my sister."

"My mother was your sister?"

"No, your great-grandmother was my sister. Surely you know the story of how she saved me from the Moldavian vampires."

Joséphine knew the story by heart. Her gypsy governess had enraptured her with tales of her great-grandmother. The first Joséphine Balsamo had an older half-sister. She had been named Sara.

"If you are the original Sara Balsamo, then your mother was an Indian woman named Sharita. Your features display no evidence of Indian ancestry."

"My mother was only half-Indian. She was the daughter of a French colonel, Etienne Cressy Raimond D'Arcourt, and a Thuggee high priestess. My grandmother was also named Sharita."

"While I accept your claim to be Sarah Warrender, I need further proof that you are the original Sara Balsamo. What was your father's true ancestry?"

"Most historical accounts portray him as a mountebank. In reality, he was the dethroned heir to the Duchy of Strackenz. He assumed the alias of Cagliostro because it was the ancient Roman name for Strackenz. In order to hide his identity from the usurper who stole his kingdom, my father dyed his naturally blond hair black."

Joséphine pointed to Sara's medallion. "Is that a Hydra?"

"No, the symbol has nothing to do with Greece. It represents a Naga. Thuggee, the religion of my mother's forebears, is allied with Naga worship."

"Thuggee was suppressed by the British in the 1830's."

"The British Raj pretends that the cult was suppressed, but it still flourishes. I briefly gained control of Thuggee decades ago. Under my English alias of Warrender, I married Achmet Genghis Khan, the chief acolyte of Kali. My husband was slain by the British during the Sepoy Revolt. I escaped by romancing a British officer. He smuggled me out of India."

"Gruesome Clayton! He mentioned you in his memoirs! You were the Countess Cagliostro of 1857!"

"Yes. I was forced to hide my identity as Achmet's widow by posing as Countess Cagliostro. Technically the title is rightfully mine since your great-grandmother was my junior. I permitted my younger sister to use the title out of gratitude for her intervention in Moldavia. It was inherited by both you and your mother. Clayton took me to Mexico where he had been posted as a military adviser. He abandoned me for another woman."

"Clayton suspected that you were pregnant with his child."

"Enough talk of Clayton! I hate him! Don't remind me any further of that rake!"

"Perhaps we should speak of other matters. We need to discuss my sister."

"There is a very urgent matter pertaining to Sabine. Acting for Jillian Blake, Satanas recently purchased Carfax Abbey. He found something there. The previous owner seems to have stolen an object from your sister three years ago. Satanas turned the article over to Jillian, who placed it in the hands of Noel Moriarty. He subsequently gave it to me."

Joséphine vividly recalled the horrific events of 1893. Her sister had been attacked by vampires. Carfax Abbey must have belonged to the Great Vampire, Dracula. Unknown to Joséphine, Satanas was misleading everyone about his relationship to the previous occupant of Carfax Abbey. Dracula had actually given Satanas one of Sabine's possessions.

Sara reached into a drawer and pulled out a small black book. She presented it to Joséphine.

"This is my sister's writing!"

"I suggest you review it carefully, godchild."

For the next 15 minutes, Joséphine read her sister's diary. Joséphine finally learned the details of Sabine's discovery that they had different fathers. As Joséphine read the pages, tears flooded her eyes. When Joséphine closed the book and placed it on the desk, Sara finally broke her silence.

"Your sister is guilty of a most heinous offense. The Black Coats forbid any member to keep a diary. She lists the most prominent leaders of our society. Her indiscretion merits death."

"Surely you can intervene with Noel Moriarty! Just as you did for me!"

"You are overlooking a most salient truth. Her betrayal extends beyond the Black Coats. She has played Judas to her own family."

"What are you talking about?"

"Sabine had it within her power to remove one of our family's enemies. Irene Chupin became the woman called Irina Putine. If Sabine had murdered her three years ago, you would have been spared two ignominious defeats at Irina's hands."

"That's irrelevant. Sabine's still my sister. Still your kinswoman. She's a Cagliostro."

"She's a weakling unworthy of our family. Your sister is also an untrustworthy fool. She must be exterminated."

"No! Not Sabine!"

"And you must be the one who kills her!"

"Never! I swore an oath to my dying mother to protect Sabine!"

"As the elder of the Cagliostro family, I remove the burden of that oath from you!"

"She's still my sister! I don't need an oath to justify protecting her!"

"How can you defend Sabine? Her treachery reduced you to tears!"

"I cried from reading my sister's heartbreak. I never wanted her to discover the truth about her father."

"Think carefully, my godchild. There is more at stake than Sabine's life. If you slay her, you would prove your worthiness to me. You'll be rewarded. I'll let you run my entire network in the Western Hemisphere. You'll have tremendous power."

"I still refuse!"

"You idiot! Sabine bears the polluted blood of the Lupins! How can you have any loyalty to this worthless half-breed?"

"No one insults my sister!"

Joséphine slapped Sara backhanded across the face. Her ring cut into Sara's lip. Touching her bleeding visage, Sara stared at Joséphine with intense hatred.

"Marga...*Cut the Branch!*"

Joséphine reached for the concealed derringer. She aimed it at the brunette, but Marga had already drawn her gun. The golden pistol fired first. The bullet seared into the blonde's head. Joséphine fired harmlessly into the air before falling from her chair. As Joséphine's form sprawled motionless on the floor, her blood stained the carpet.

Days later, a woman awoke in a bedroom. There was a bandage circling her head.

Suddenly the woman noticed that she was not alone. Madame Sara was seated near the bed.

"Why do I still live?" asked the bedridden Joséphine Balsamo

Sara lowered her head in shame.

"Forgive me, godchild. My conduct was unworthy of a Cagliostro. Fortunately Marga's aim faltered. Her bullet only creased your skull."

"You no longer desire my death?"

"Godchild, you displayed great courage in defying me. Seeing you on the ground wounded, I was reminded of my own sister. She never lost faith in me. Your great-grandmother was as loyal to me as you are to Sabine. I realized the great sin that I was asking you to commit. I swear in my father's name to safeguard Sabine. No harm will come to her. Please forgive me for my earlier actions."

"I forgive you, godmother."

"You will be rewarded for your devotion to your sister. My offer to administer my business holdings in the Americas still stands."

"I accept. If you have no objections, New Orleans will be the center of our operations."

"Agreed."

"Of course, I will need a capable chief of staff to assist me."

"You formed an alliance with Ballmeyer during your previous stay in New Orleans. He's still in the United States. You could easily recruit him."

"I have a different candidate in mind than Ballmeyer."

An hour later, Marga entered Joséphine's bedchamber.

"Excellency, Madame said that you wished to see me."

"Thank you, Marga Sandorf. I own you my life as well as that of my precious sister."

"You can't be serious. I almost blew out your brains."

"Your shot wasn't happenstance. You deliberated creased my skull. You defied Madame Sara's order to extinguish my life."

"Excellency, you're mistaken."

"Your code of honor prevents you from admitting the truth. I will respect your reticence, but I have deduced something else. You did more than just show mercy. Madame Sara was consumed by rancor. Her heart would not have opened up to me and my sister easily. Someone convinced her to show compassion as I lied unconscious. That person is truly a just woman. I need such a woman to be my chief of staff. Will you honor me by accepting the position?"

"Excellency, it is you who honor me."

As a gesture of her acceptance, Marga kissed Joséphine ring.

After Marga left, Joséphine contemplated her future. She could never trust Madame Sara fully. Her kinswoman was too mercurial. Joséphine must shift the loyalty of Sara's followers to herself. Marga had already fallen under Joséphine's influence. The Comandante was only the beginning.

Joséphine plotted vengeance. Irina Putine would pay for the indignities inflicted on Joséphine. So would Catarina Koluchy and Milady Nevermore. Joséphine conceived the perfect act of retribution. Both Koluchy and Nevermore loved Antonio Nikola. During their conversation, Joséphine sensed that Antonio was attracted to her. Joséphine would avenge herself on both women by romancing him.

As she fell asleep, Countess Cagliostro smiled. All her enemies would suffer in the days ahead.

Unseen Stratagems

In early January 1897, a conclave was held between the two most dangerous men in London. The setting was the White Lodge, a mansion in the Blackheath district. The doors of the domicile closed behind Dr. Malbodius. A massive butler escorted the visitor into the private study of Noel Moriarty, the Lord of the Night. Moriarty was the physician's superior in the Black Coats, the European crime cartel.

The Lord of the Night was a tall, lean man with tinted spectacles. The walls of his private sanctum were covered with paintings. The works of Raeburn, Mabuse, Greuze, Coswell, Bridau and Hallward graced the study. Prominently displayed was a more recent work by Jacques Saillard, *The Lady in the Black Gloves*. It featured an attractive woman in her twenties. She had dark hair arranged in a French braid. On the right side of her orange dress was a brooch in the shape of a pentagram. A black tie was draped around her neck .Black gloves and silver bracelets covered her hands and wrists. Her blue eyes gave the impression of infinite despair.

Malbodius, a clean-shaven man of indeterminable age, scrutinized Saillard's painting. "How appropriate, Herr Moriarty! This portrait of Irina Putine will no doubt inspire our discussion."

"Putine has emerged as a serious threat, Doctor. By arranging the defection of Milady Nevermore, Putine alerted the Chupin Detective Agency to our future projects. Several operations have been scrapped by the High Council."

"Including my Espionage Hotel."

"You chatted with Putine during the Bluebeard murders. What is your appraisal of her?"

"She is a woman haunted by betrayal, guilt and temptation. Her relatives conspired to make her *pay the law*. Putine was consigned to a school as hellish as any penitentiary. She has never forgiven herself for her actions as Madame Fourneau's prefect."

"I'm well aware of the unique educational methods of the Fourneau College. My wife was always reluctant to discuss the school. My late brother and I had to plant our own spy there to learn that institution's true nature. Putine's sense of guilt is understandable. Your reference to temptation eludes me."

"At the College, Putine engaged in controversial sexual practices. Jacques Saillard indulges in similar hedonistic endeavors. The nude portraits done by Saillard are assumed to be evidence of the artist's romantic conquests. Yet Saillard uncharacteristically painted Putine clothed."

"You believe that Putine turned down Saillard's lustful advances?"

"Precisely, Herr Moriarty. Despite Putine's rebuff, Saillard still remained on friendly terms with the female detective. The portrait proves that."

"As well as the fact, Doctor, that Putine delivers Saillard's art to Fritz Kramm's gallery."

"Putine is both repelled and attracted by Saillard."

"This ambivalence on Putine's part raises an interesting point, Doctor. If not for this needless vendetta of Joséphine Balsamo, Putine would probably have been recruited into the Black Coats like the other Fourneau College students. Would it be possible to form an alliance with her?"

"Out of the question. Putine suffers from a Messianic urge to redeem others. Her partnership with Nevermore is the latest manifestation. Although we could never achieve an entente with Putine, we could impose a détente?"

"A lessening of tensions?"

"I have a plan, Herr Moriarty. It's a variation on the 'invisible weapon' stratagem employed by the Black Coats in 1838 against the d'Arx family. The services of two female members of the Black Coats are essential to my undertaking."

"Who are these women?"

"One is Marga Sandorf. I have already gained Madame Sara's permission to use her services. The other lady is well known to you. She is Putine's former classmate. In fact, I have taken the liberty to invite her to our parley."

The butler disturbed the meeting.

"Forgive my intrusion, Mr. Moriarty, but your sister is here."

That same evening inside her London perfumery, Madame Sara showed an Indian box to her goddaughter, Joséphine Balsamo. The box's lid had a carving of a seven-headed snake. Opening the box, Sara revealed four golden rings. They were molded to resemble snakes with women's heads.

"They're like the rings worn by the Corbucci family," observed Joséphine.

"The rings of Salvatore Corbucci and his brood have the heads of reptiles," explained Sara. "Those rings are merely ornaments of high office. The Black Coats are an outgrowth of the snake cults of Acheron and Valusia. This box contains wedding rings carved in the shape of the Naga Princesses, the servitors of the Snake Mother. Our ancestor, Count Cagliostro, was an acolyte of the Serpent Gods: Adana, Sithra and Ixcatl."

"Why are you showing me these rings, godmother?"

"Godchild, the time may soon come for the Cagliostro clan to cement an alliance by marriage."

Sara's words surprised Joséphine. She had been contemplating a romance with one of their colleagues in the Black Coats, Dr. Antonio Nikola. Had her godmother guessed her intentions?

A new group of tenants occupied an office building in Paris. They called themselves the Neptune Society. Ostensibly they were a philanthropic organization dedicated to oceanic research.

One of the Society's officers was Dorcas Spode. She was a thin, aristocratic Englishwoman in an austere khaki dress. A black bonnet covered her blond hair. Her handsome face was obscured by rather large glasses. She was extremely nearsighted.

In her private office, Dorcas sat listening to another female member of the Neptune Society. She was a slender woman in a blue dress. Her black hair was styled into a bouffant.

"You wish to see me, Dorkie?" asked the brunette. "Does this involve the new firearm regulations?"

"Partially, Sabine."

Dorcas reached into her desk drawer and pulled out a derringer. She handed it to Sabine. "Since our relocation from London, our superiors have instructed me to requisition weapons to all female employees. There have been recent incidents of women being assaulted. Do you know how to handle a gun?"

"I've never used one before, Dorkie."

"I'll be more than happy to give you some lessons once they fix up the firing range in the basement. "

"You implied that there was another matter to discuss."

"Yes, Sabine. What do you know about Milady Nevermore?"

"She recruited you to handle security matters for the Society."

"I've just heard a very disturbing story about Nevermore. Please sit down, Sabine. This concerns your sister."

Elsewhere in Paris, a new painting by Jacques Saillard was unveiled at Fritz Kramm's art gallery. A large crowd had gathered to view the controversial artist's labor. Saillard was a reclusive celebrity whose true guise was unknown to the general public. One of the few people to have seen Saillard was the woman who delivered the painting to Kramm. Her name was Irina Putine. Her appearance was identical to Saillard's artistic rendering with two notable differences. She carried an umbrella whose silver handle culminated in the sculptured head of a unicorn. A Cordobes hat adorned her head. Her uncle, Victor Chupin, had given it to her as a gift after recently returning from Spain.

Irina stared cryptically at the canvas. As with the overwhelming majority of Saillard's output, the portrait featured the erotic image of a nude female. Suddenly Irina's private thoughts were interrupted by a male voice.

"Not Saillard's best work."

The speaker was a boy not yet 14.

"Aren't you a little young to be here?" replied Irina.

"My mother takes a progressive view of sexual education."

Irina then felt a tug on her skirt. She looked down to see a younger boy. He couldn't have been any younger than seven.

"Why do you have a unicorn?" asked the child.

"It's from a bedtime story that my father told me. A nobleman owned the last unicorn on earth. The saddest day of his life was when he discovered it slaughtered by a wolf."

"I know you!" declared the urchin. "You're a lady. You have gloves."

"Yes, I'm a lady. And I'm wearing gloves."

"Please forgive my younger brother Claud," said the other boy. "Sometimes his immaturity garbled his thoughts. He meant to identify you as *The Lady in the Black Gloves*. Your artistic incarnation is well known to both of us. Our great-uncle owns your portrait."

"You're related to Noel Moriarty?"

"Yes, my late grandfather was his older brother."

"Your grandfather was Professor Moriarty?"

"Yes. In fact, I bear his name, James."

"Jimmy!" yelled a disheveled woman with brown hair. "I can't find Claud."

"He's right here, Mother. No doubt you recognize my beguiling conversationalist."

"Irina Putine!" announced the mother of the two boys. "You look just like your painting!"

"You must be Trickie Moriarty," noted Irina.

"Trickie! She's my obnoxious half-sister. I'm Urania Caber. Surely you've heard of me."

"I'm sorry, but your name is unknown to me."

"How could you not have heard about me? I'm in charge of scientific research for my uncle. Aren't you familiar with the Neptune Society?"

"Is that the same as the Nightingale Hierarchy?"

"Don't confuse my operation with Professor Chavain's. I'm surprised you don't know my name. After all, my aunt attended the Fourneau College with you."

"Your aunt Catarina actually graduated long before I was a student there."

"I'm not talking about Catarina. She's only my aunt by marriage. I'm talking about my aunt by blood. It's hard to imagine her as my aunt. I'm roughly a decade older. She's so helpful. I wouldn't be here if she and Dorkie hadn't volunteered to take over my duties. You're very familiar with my aunt's congeniality. Remember how she aided you with the lottery."

"Auntie's here!" screamed Claud pointing to another woman who just entered the studio.

The arrival had a flamboyant appearance. Her short brown hair, brushed backwards from the forehead, gave the impression of a bird-like crest. She was attired entirely in black. A large patch covered her right eye. Her unbuttoned coat was an Inverness cape. Her ensemble included a shirt with a cravat plus pants and boots. A chain bearing an amulet in the shape of a cat's head encircled her neck. Formerly known as Milady Nevermore, she now answered to the name of Blythe Furnace.

"*She's your aunt!*" uttered a puzzled Irina.

"Oh no," responded Urania. "Claud just calls her 'Auntie' out of affection. Milady Nevermore used to be his babysitter,"

Blythe joined the other two women.

"Urania! What are you doing in Paris!"

"The Neptune Society has recently relocated here. I'm surprised, Milady. You haven't told your friend anything about me!"

"Irina, could you please excuse me and Urania? We need to briefly talk in private." Blythe led Urania away.

Left with the two children, Irina decided to pump the older boy for information.

"Jimmy, how long has your mother known Milady?"

"They've been great pals for almost two years. Mother's very fond of Milady. They share the same views on sex and violence."

"Please elaborate."

"While our mother has no problem with my brother and I studying adult biological relationships, she feels that romantic stories of bloodshed could warp us. Therefore she instructed our babysitter to only tell us uplifting tales lacking in violence."

"Milady told you fairy tales?"

"Actually Milady has a vast reservoir of legends preserved by the Iga ninjas."

"But all those stories must be about Japanese assassins!"

"You obviously are unfamiliar with the heroes described by Milady. Hattori Hanzo III was concerned about cleaning up the Japan capital. He opened a bathhouse there. The adventures of Zatoichi prove that the blind can overcome any obstacle. He helped peasants erase their gambling debts. Daigoro was a three-year old left motherless. His father made a living by performing odd jobs. This caring parent built a special baby cart in order not to be separated from his offspring. The saga of Dr. Baian reveals the true nature of the medical profession."

Irina concluded that she had done Blythe an injustice. Neither an hygienist, a blind man, a young child being raised by a widowed father, nor a physician could be a brutally efficient killer.

Blythe returned with Urania. The latter pressed a card into Irina's right hand.

"This is my address in Paris. Please come tomorrow for lunch. Your old school chum will be there."

Urania quickly left with her children.

Irina and Blythe vacated the art gallery together. They both lived in separate apartments at a boarding house in the Rue de Choiseul. The two women shared a cab together. Inside the carriage, Irina confronted Blythe.

"You deliberately withheld the fact that Professor Moriarty has another daughter."

"Irina, please understand. Urania is my friend. She even entrusted her children to me. When you debriefed me about the Black Coats, I felt obligated to protect her. You can't expect me to backstab all my old compatriots.".

"I respected your feelings. I never pressured you to divulge information about Antonio Nikola's enterprises due to your former relationship with him. All other members of the Black Coats are potential enemies of the Chupin Detective Agency."

"Not Urania. She's extremely impractical. You saw that for yourself. Her uncle keeps her ignorant of all illegal enterprises. She's confined to the research department."

"What's about her aunt?"

"You know all about Catarina."

"There's another aunt. Urania mentioned that she attended the Fourneau College with me."

"Irina, I honestly don't know this other aunt. Did Urania say anything else about her?"

"Urania mentioned her aunt helping me with the lottery."

Blythe grasped the reference immediately. As the chief prefect at the Fourneau College, Irina had secretly organized a lottery. The winner was permitted a romantic liaison with a handsome laborer who delivered firewood. The lottery had inadvertently saved Irina's life. One of the lottery's winners had persuaded the workman to post a letter which led to a doctor arriving at the school. The medical visitor prevented Irina from dying from a murderous attack.

"Did any student help you organize the lottery?"

"The idea came from one of my subordinate prefects, Rochelle Moreau. Of course! The name Moreau is very similar to Moriarty."

"Her personnel dossier gives a totally different story about her family. She lived with her father, a prominent surgeon, in England. Dr. Moreau fled Europe after a scandal concerning experimentation on a dog. She was left in the care of her uncle, a lawyer in Avignon. He enrolled Rochelle at the College."

"Blythe, you and I both know that the Black Coats sometimes alter their records."

"It's possible. There was a rumor that Professor Moriarty's father, the infamous Dr. Noel, had a French mistress, Madame Zephyrine. She could be Rochelle's mother."

"Why did you examine Rochelle's file?"

"When I was Catarina's chief of staff, Rochelle was one of my lieutenants. Catarina had suggested that Urania share power with a more practical manager in the Neptune Society. Rochelle was being considered for that position."

"What is this Neptune Society?"

"It was the original scientific branch of the Black Coats. Urania is its leader. Professor Moriarty derived the name from the Roman god who lives hidden in the sea."

"How does it tie in with the Nightingale Hierarchy?"

"Marguerite Chavain and others on the High Council were skeptical of Urania's competence. In order to placate these critics, Noel Moriarty made a decision at the Northumberland Hotel Conference of 1895. Chavain was permitted to create her own scientific unit. Unlike the Neptune Society, the Hierarchy takes a direct role in the regular operations of the Black Coats."

"What about the other members of the Neptune Society? Urania cited someone called Dorkie."

"Dorcas Spode. Urania's security expert. Beside her, Urania's only other noteworthy employee is a female physician whom I've never met. She's the younger sister of Joséphine Balsamo, "

"My archenemy's sister! I don't understand why you protected this woman. You hate Joséphine as much as I."

"Out of loyalty to Urania, I couldn't expose any of her subordinates. Besides, Joséphine's sister has a reputation of ineptitude as bad as Urania's."

"What name does this sister use?"

"Her alias is an anagram of Balsamo. Absalom. Dr. Sabine Absalom."

Irina was shocked. Four years ago, Irina had been suffering from hysteria at a London nursing home. A young female medical student had been instrumental in curing Irina's dementia. Her name was Sabine Absalom.

After their arrival at the Rue de Choiseul, the two women went to their respective apartments. They were going to freshen up before having dinner with their landlady, Madame Vabre. Blythe answered a knock on her door. She opened it expecting to see Irina. Instead, Blythe was confronted by a woman whom she did not recognize. The stranger wore a long blue coat.

."My name is Sabine Balsamo. My sister Joséphine is dead because of you."

Reaching into her pocket with her right hand, Sabine pulled out her derringer. Blythe delivered a swift kick to Sabine's wrist. The gun flew out of her hand. Blythe delivered a karate chop to Sabine's neck. The intruder fell unconscious into Blythe's arms.

Sabine opened her eyes. She was lying on a couch in the living room of Blythe's apartment. The one-eyed woman was no longer there. Standing over

Sabine was Irina Putine. At Irina's request, Blythe had gone to Madame Vabre's dining room. Irina intended to interview Sabine alone.

"Irene..." murmured Sabine.

"I'm called Irina now, Sabine, or perhaps I should address you formally as Dr. Balsamo. You restored my sanity in the Sanctuary Club. Rather ironic considering the feud between our families."

"Do you know why that feud started?" questioned Sabine.

"My brother stole a valuable necklace. My father was trying to market the gems. Your mother posed as a buyer for the illegal merchandise. She attempted to murder my father. One of his paramours stabbed her."

"That's not true. The necklace was supposed to be a gift for my mother. Our father lured her into a trap."

"*Our father!*" exclaimed Irina.

"Sabine Balsamo is your half-sister!" stated Blythe Furnace.

"As well as Joséphine's half-sister," explained Irina. "Sabine shares the same mother with Joséphine, but the same father with me and Arsène. I have no reason to doubt Sabine's word."

"But Sabine's assertions about your father contradicts statements by your mother!"

"My mother has lied to me in the past. No doubt she will do so in the future."

"Outside of your uncle, you have quite an untrustworthy group of relatives. Your sister is as deceitful as your brother."

"Sabine doesn't fall into the same category as Arsène. She was extremely honest with me. Unaware of our joint parentage, Sabine originally intended to kill me in the Sanctuary Club. Instead she was prompted to cure me. Sabine's been a more caring sibling than my treacherous brother. Oddly enough, she has somehow managed to be true to both me and Joséphine."

"Is Joséphine really dead?"

"Sabine was told by a reliable source that her sister was executed by the Black Coats. Your prediction that Joséphine's associates would 'cut the branch' proved accurate."

Blythe held Sabine's derringer in her hand. "Sabine holds me responsible for Joséphine's demise."

"I convinced my sister to refrain from any further murderous attempts."

"Sabine lacks the competence to be a successful murderess. This gun wasn't even loaded."

Sabine Balsamo's mind was in turmoil. Before taking a cab back to her apartment, she had conversed with Irina for hours. News of Joséphine's death had thrown her into a deep depression. During her time with Irina, Sabine had felt a strong kinship. Could the void in her life left by Joséphine's death be filled by Irina?

Sabine was about to unlock her apartment's door when she was confronted by two women in the hallway. Both were dressed identically. Their outfits consisted of brown blouses with dark neckties and skirts. Sabine recognized their clothes as the uniforms of the Black Skirts, a subsidiary of the Black Coats. Joséphine had belonged to the Black Skirts. Due to the cold January weather, the pair wore black shawls. The taller of the duo was a stunning woman with curly flame-colored hair and dazzlingly white teeth. Her companion was a brunette.

"Dr. Absalom, I am Mademoiselle Coyatier," acknowledged the redhead. "This is Mademoiselle Holder. There's been a breach of security at the Neptune Society. Please accompany us."

The two Black Skirts escorted Sabine into an a waiting cab.

"This isn't the Neptune Society!" protested Sabine as she alighted from the carriage.

She and her two companions had arrived at a building bearing this sign: "The Regenerator of Fashion."

"The head of security has felt it necessary to meet at different location," professed Coyatier.

The three women entered the doors of the establishment. Inside the fashion business was an area called the Alteration Room. Supposedly only clothes were modified there. The room housed numerous knitting tools and branding instruments. Ushered into the Alteration Room, Sabine found herself in the presence of an alluring woman with brown hair and eyes. She was dressed in an elegant black gown. A dark jeweled stud graced her collar. Seated on a chair, the woman sipped a glass of sherry.

"You were expecting Dorcas Spode. My name is Rochelle Moreau. Did your sister ever mention me?"

"No," answered Sabine.

The lamp in the Alteration Room shined on Rochelle's stud. The light was reflected into Sabine's eyes making her uncomfortable.

"I'm not surprised," continued Rochelle. "I was Joséphine's assistant prefect at the Fourneau College. Serving her loyally for four years, I was the most senior of her lieutenants. When Joséphine graduated unexpectedly in early 1889, she repaid my fidelity by recommending a less experienced girl to succeed her. Your sister was always a traitor to those who trusted her."

"Don't insult my sister!"

"While I failed to replace your sister as Madame Fourneau's primary prefect, I assumed her prior role as Madame Koluchy's chief of staff. I intend to serve my mistress more faithfully than your ignoble sibling."

"I demand to see Dorcas Spode or Urania Caber! Catarina Moriarty has no authority over me!"

Coyatier seized Sabine roughly by the right arm. "Our mistress is known as Madame Koluchy! If you don't show proper respect, I'll snap your arm like a twig!"

"Orianne, please release Sabine's arm," said Rochelle.

"As your wish, Rochelle," replied Coyatier.

"You are guilty of treason, Sabine," pronounced Rochelle.

"I don't know what you are talking about!"

"You deny visiting the residence of Irina Putine and Blythe Furnace, two operatives of the Chupin Detective Agency?"

"My movements are not the concern of the Black Skirts! I belong to the Neptune Society!"

"However, the activities of Furnace are my concern. She's a former member of the Black Skirts. I have ample justification to apprehend you. In addition to treason, you are guilty of insubordination. Unlike you, Orianne Coyatier is loyal and respectful. I intend to reward her. Orianne, you shall have the pleasure of reprimanding this turncoat."

"Absalom, you're a thief," hissed Coyatier. "You've stolen from the Black Coats!"

"I've stolen nothing."

"You stole information. You gave that information to Putine and Furnace. Madame Koluchy once found your precious sister guilty of thievery. Do you remember how she was punished?"

"No!" yelled Sabine.

Coyatier smiled gleefully as she turned towards Holder. "Mary, prepare the branding iron. Absalom will be marked as a thief!" Coyatier violently ripped the right shoulder of Sabine's dress exposing her flesh. Sabine screamed.

"What barbarity is this!" shouted a masculine voice with a German accent. Dr. Malbodius had suddenly invaded the Alteration Room.

"This isn't your concern!" argued Rochelle.

"As the newly appointed Satrap of Paris, all Black Coat activities here fall under me. Who is this lady?"

"She's known as Sabine Absalom," disclosed Rochelle.

"I've heard of her. She works for the Neptune Society. You have no jurisdiction over her."

"She consorted with a disgraced former member of the Black Skirts."

"Since Dr. Absalom belongs to a different branch of our confederation, this matter should have been brought to my attention. Mademoiselle Moreau, leave this room with your associates. I wish to interrogate Dr. Absalom in private."

As Rochelle and the two Black Skirts departed, a whimpering Sabine slumped to the ground. Dr. Malbodius gently helped her rise from the ground. "Dr. Absalom, please seat on this chair. Let me get you something to drink."

Rochelle had left a bottle of sherry next to a group of glasses. Filling a glass, Malbodius gave it to Sabine.

"Thank you, Monsieur."

"We haven't been properly introduced. I am Dr. Eric Heinz Malbodius. I must apologize for those arrogant Black Skirts. A lady of your accomplishments needs to be treated with respect."

"You're familiar with my work?"

"Your paper on vocal modification was quite illuminating. I've been told that you are quite skilled in mimicry. I've also enjoyed your monograph on hypnotism."

"You're very kind, Dr. Malbodius."

"An advantage of this room is its ample supply of dresses. There must be one in your size. Let me leave while you change into something suitable. Once you are ready, we shall call upon your superior. She surely will be able to rectify this disgraceful incident."

"You'll take me to Dr. Caber?"

"No. We'll consult Urania's recently appointed co-manager. She's very adept at bureaucratic maneuvering."

The next afternoon, Irina and Blythe visited Urania at her new Parisian home.

"Is your aunt here?" asked Irina.

"Here she is," indicated Urania pointing to a dark-haired woman in her twenties.

"Suzanne Noel!" remarked Irina.

"I'll let you two old school comrades reminisce," said Urania. "Blythe, Claud has become unmanageable again. Could you soothe him with one of those sweet Japanese fables?"

"A Daigoro story should do the trick," declared Blythe. After showing Blythe to Claud's room, Urania retired to the kitchen in order to make sandwiches for her guests.

Suzanne had been registered in the Fourneau Colleague in January 1889. Until the school closed down a year later, she had been the most popular girl at the school. Her vivacious personality had captivated the other students. Judging Suzanne to be of average intelligence, Irina had never considered recruiting her as a prefect.

"I'm now Professor Noel," imparted Suzanne. "I've a doctorate in Mathematics."

"But you barely passed Algebra at the Fourneau College!"

"My mediocre test grades were a ruse, Irina. If I had displayed my real academic potential, I would have come to the attention of Madame Fourneau. She always recruited the best and the brightest of her pupils as prefects. I had no desire to participate in the debauchery sponsored by our headmistress. A prefect's role would have complicated my mission."

"Your mission?"

"Marguerite Chavain and Catarina, my sister-in-law, were regularly recruiting Fourneau College graduates into the Black Coats. All these women were proving to be capable agents, but they were reluctant to discuss their alma mater with outsiders. Not even Catarina would unveil the mysteries of the school to her husband. He and my other brother, Urania's father, decided to place their own informant inside the College."

"So, the Moriarty brothers put their own sister inside the Fourneau College. You must have been frustrated by your inability to communicate frankly with your siblings."

"Actually, I wrote them detailed reports."

"That's impossible! I personally censored all your mail."

"You created a loophole."

"The lottery!"

"By expropriating Rochelle's lottery idea, you maintained your control over the other students. Every three weeks, a young man delivered firewood to the school. I remember him well. His name was Henri. He was so handsome and muscular. All the girls drew lots. Whoever won was allowed to have a rendezvous with Henri. The arrangement ran smoothly for you until Henri proved rebellious."

"He was rather fond of one girl. You."

"Henri refused to continue his participation in the lottery unless he saw me on a more regular basis. You came up with a novel solution. The other girls would have rebelled if you just rewarded me with Henri. Since you and the other prefects weren't fond of boys, none of you ever took advantage of winning the lottery. You and your lieutenants relinquished the prize to some deserving student. That individual always became me. No one complained because I was so popular. The other girls even gave me the nickname of Lucky. I prefer to be called that rather than Suzanne."

"I always thought Henri was acting on his own volition. You actually put the idea in his head."

"It's all comes down to beating the odds. The number of students at the Fourneau College never exceeded more than 30 girls, and the number of prefects was generally three or four. The others had a 1 out of 30 chance of winning. My chances were 5 out of 30. I'm a master of probabilities. My doctoral thesis was on Probability Theory."

"You had Henri smuggled out letters to the Moriarty brothers behind my back!"

"Don't look so cross, Irina. Have you forgotten? I had Henri post a letter to someone other than my brothers. If not for the letter to Teresa's mother, Dr. Cerral never would have come to the school. You would have bled to death if not for my connivance."

"Why did you send that letter? It had nothing to do with your mission."

"I'm not as ruthless as my brothers. In some ways, I'm like my niece. I couldn't stand by and watch you persecute Teresa. It was sickening."

Upon hearing Suzanne's words, Irina became overcome by emotion. All the guilt that she had suppressed regarding Teresa flooded her mind. Irina was visibly upset.

"Forgive me, Irina. Considering the history of my own family, I have no right to be judgmental. Ultimately we both failed Teresa. I need your help to save the life of another being unfairly victimized."

"Who are you talking about?"

"Sabine Absalom. Your sister."

"How did you learn that she's my sister?"

"Sabine told me last night. She becomes a pawn in my sister-in-law's machinations."

"What does Catarina Koluchy have to do with Sabine?"

"Catarina has a rivalry with Professor Chavain on the High Council. Ever since Chavain formed the Nightingale Hierarchy, Catarina has felt outmaneuvered. My sister-in-law hopes to acquire her own scientific division."

"The Neptune Society."

"Exactly. Catarina argues that Urania is an incompetent manager. My sister-in-law lobbies Noel to allow the Neptune Society to be fully absorbed into her own Black Skirts. She hopes to prove Urania's unfitness to lead by manufacturing a scandal. Sabine is the key."

"Catarina discovered Sabine's relationship to me."

"She put Sabine under surveillance. Her agents followed her to your apartment. They apprehended Sabine. Your sister found herself at the mercy of Rochelle Moreau and Orianne Coyatier. Remember them?"

Irina recalled a harrowing event from her past. When she was 15, Rochelle and Orianne had been Joséphine Balsamo's assistants at the Fourneau College. As Coyatier held Irina down, Joséphine had whipped her. During the ordeal, Rochelle had counted the number of times the lash struck.

"What happened to my sister?"

"Fortunately, nothing. Another member of the Black Coats summoned me. We prevented Sabine from being harmed."

"Why were you sent for?"

"One of Catarina's earlier ploys against the Neptune Society was to saddle Urania with a co-manager beholden to the Black Skirts."

"Rochelle Moreau."

"Urania countered by sponsoring me as a substitute. I now run the Society alongside her. Let us evaluate this situation objectively. With Joséphine's recent death, Sabine longs to see you, her other sister. You may harbor dreams of having Sabine defect to the Chupin Detective Agency. Don't be deceived by your success with Blythe. Your friend has the skills of an Iga ninja. If your sister fled from the ranks of the Black Coats, she would easily be hunted down and killed."

141

"What do you propose, Lucky?"

"I can persuade my brother to permit supervised meetings between you and my sister for the correct price."

"Name it."

"There are two conditions. First, you only meet Sabine in my presence and Urania's."

"You outnumber me 2 to 1. Can I bring Blythe? I'm sure that Urania would like to socialize with her."

"Agreed."

"What you're second condition?"

"The Neptune Society has openly relocated to Paris. The Chupin Detective Agency must make no effort to investigate our activities."

"You wish me to turn a blind eye to your crimes?"

"What crimes? The Society only engages in research."

"You still make weapons for the Black Coats."

"We are no more responsible for the crimes done with those weapons than the manufacturers of Winchester rifles are for the slaughter of American Indians. Both the Black Skirts and the Nightingale Hierarchy have offices in Paris. They will jointly veto any participation by the Neptune Society in illegal operations."

"I detect an ulterior motive. If I frustrate the endeavors of Koluchy and Chavain, I enhance the status of the Neptune Society at the expense of your rivals."

"You have gauged the situation accurately. What is your answer?"

"I accept your second condition."

In the evening, Eric Malbodius was taking Sabine to dinner at the Restaurant Imperial. It was Sabine's birthday.

"I've rented a private banquet room for the evening, Sabine. I have a birthday surprise for you. We will be joined by two special guests."

"Do I know them, Eric?"

"One is your godmother."

"Sarah Warrender? She must be in her fifties now."

"Your godmother now calls herself Madame Sara. She has a remarkable talent for preserving a youthful appearance. The other lady will be a surprise."

An usher showed the two doctors into the banquet room. There were two glamorous blondes seated at the table. Sabine immediately recognized the taller of the pair.

"*Josine! You're alive!*"

Joséphine embraced her sister.

"Eric, let us leave the two sisters," said Madame Sara. "They have much to discuss. Joséphine, I've asked your chief of staff to stand guard outside. She will see that you are not disturbed."

After their companions departed, Joséphine related to Sabine how her execution had been staged to placate Catarina Koluchy. Sabine followed with an account of her own ordeal at the Regenerator of Fashion.

"Rochelle and Orianne dared to maltreat you," emphasized Joséphine. "They shall pay for this outrage."

Opening the door, Joséphine summoned the individual outside. A petite woman joined the sisters. She was dressed in a gold tunic. Black pants and boots enveloped her legs and feet. A black gendarme-style cape with a gold lining draped her shoulders. Her short raven hair was covered by a black fur cap.

"This is Marga Sandorf, a loyal servant of the Cagliostro clan," proclaimed Joséphine. "She will avenge our family honor."

Before reporting to work at the Regenerator of Fashion every morning, the redhead performed a regular ritual. She had been raised in an orphanage at Sartene, Corsica. No one knew her true antecedents. She had been left at the foundling home in a basket. A note had been pinned to her blanket identifying her as Orianne Coyatier.

As she grew older, she received frequent visits from an old man, the Cavalier Arom. He claimed to be a friend of her grandfather. Arom told her exciting stories about her grandfather. Her forebear was known as the Marchef because he had been a quartermaster in the French army. The Marchef had saved Arom's life on numerous occasions. The Marchef had slain many men who had aroused Arom's wrath. Orianne's favorite story concerned how the Marchef had walled up a man alive in an apartment at the Rue de Jerusalem. When she was 16, Arom took Orianne out of the foundling home and placed her in the Fourneau College.

After her graduation, Orianne along with Rochelle Moreau was inducted in the Black Coats by Catarina Koluchy. Hearing the history of the murderous association, Orianne realized that her elderly patron must be the All-Father, the reputedly immortal ruler of the Black Coats. Many in the Black Coats dismissed the All-Father as a charlatan. Furthermore, he was even labeled a mere figurehead for the Lord of the Night. In her heart, Orianne knew differently. Noel Moriarty was merely the minion of the reclusive Cavalier Arom.

In Paris during 1891, Orianne searched for the house in the Rue de Jerusalem where the Marchef had sealed his victim. Unfortunately, the original building had been burned down by the Communards in 1871. Orianne's frustration at not being able to visit the site of her grandfather's celebrated crime was visibly expressed to her fellow Black Coats including Joséphine Balsamo

One morning in 1897, Orianne awoke to find an intruder in her bedroom. It was Marga Sandorf. Her left hand held a golden pistol.

"Get out of your bed, granddaughter of the Marchef!"

"Who are you?" asked Orianne rising to her feet. "How did you get into my room?"

"I am the emissary of the Cagliostro clan. I picked the lock on your front door."

"If you weren't holding that gun, I would throttle you with my bare hands!"

"What kind of person do you think I am? I'm a just woman!" Marga placed the gun down on top of a cabinet. "Kill me if you can!"

Orianne leapt at Marga, The redhead's hands gripped the brunette's throat.

Sometime later, Joséphine Balsamo arrived at the Regenerator of Fashion. She asked to see Rochelle Moreau. Joséphine was directed to the Alteration Room. There she found Rochelle drinking a glass of sherry.

"Remember your last visit here, Balsamo?"

"My proper title is Countess."

"Your claim to the nobility has always been dubious. Perhaps a compromise is in order. I will call you simply Joséphine."

"As you wish. I'm here concerning your treatment of my sister."

"Poor sweet Sabine. What a pitiful creature! Her voice is so high-pitched. She seems in a permanent state of hysteria. No one takes her seriously. Sabine shall always be a millstone around your neck."

"Worry about your own Achilles heel, Rochelle."

"Who are you talking about?"

"Orianne Coyatier. She's more than a sister to you."

"Orianne is quite capable of protecting herself."

"You overestimate her talents. Your fondness for Orianne clouds your judgment. Haven't you notice that she hasn't reported for work yet."

"What have you done to Orianne?"

"Marga Sandorf has paid her a morning visit. Consider it ample payment for the assault on Sabine. Orianne is resting in her apartment. She'll be fine provided her supply of oxygen remains. I suggest you hurry."

A distraught Rochelle left the Alteration Room. Taking a cab with Mary Holder, Rochelle rushed to Orianne's apartment. The door was unlocked. Inside, Rochelle and Mary saw a group of tools lying on the floor. A wall paneling had recently been replaced. Nailed to the panel was a note: "Orianne Coyatier, born 1868."

Grabbing crowbars from the floor, Rochelle and Mary tore open the wall panel. They found a bound Orianne inside. She was unconscious. There were bruises on her neck. Rochelle immediately dispatched Mary to get a doctor.

Once his examination of Orianne concluded, the physician conferred with Rochelle.

"Your friend is out of danger, Rochelle. She should be fully recovered after a week's rest."

"When Madame Koluchy ordered me to cooperate with you, Dr. Malbodius, I was told that you would restrain Joséphine from any acts of retaliations."

"Joséphine will be content to let the matters rest. There will be no further reprisals by you."

"I refuse! Joséphine won't have the last laugh!"

"You have no choice, Rochelle. Madame Koluchy will insist on a medical report to justify Orianne's absence. I can tell her one of two stories. Either Orianne has influenza or she has suffered a severe beating at the hands of Marga Sandorf. When Coleen Pegler endured such a defeat, Madame had her flogged. Orianne doesn't have the strength to survive a similar chastisement. Are we in accord?"

"Yes, Doctor," conceded Rochelle.

Departing Orianne's apartment, Malbodius went to a perfumery. This shop was a Parisian version of the business that Sara presided over in London.

"How is your plan proceeding, Doctor?" inquired Madame Sara.

"Joséphine reacted exactly as anticipated. She and her sister are easy to predict. Marga Sandorf now occupies the perfect position on the chessboard that we've constructed."

The following week, five ladies gathered for lunch at the Restaurant Imperial. They were Irina Putine, Blythe Furnace, Sabine Absalom, Urania Caber and Lucky Noel. It was a pleasant meal without incident. Sabine wore a pentagram brooch that was identical to Irina's. During their previous talk at Blythe's apartment, Irina had learned the full history of the two brooches. They had originally been made by Sabine's maternal grandfather. He gave them as presents to his two daughters, Joséphine and Anna. The two sisters quarreled with each other. Joséphine was being courted by a daring young thief, Théophraste Lupin. He stole Anna's brooch and gave it to Joséphine as token of his love. Later Joséphine gave birth to a daughter with the same name. This caused a momentary separation between the two lovers because the child was fathered by another man. Both Joséphine and Théophraste reconciled leading to the birth of another daughter, Sabine. Another of Théophraste's love affairs resulted in Irina's birth. Joséphine was supposedly fatally betrayed by Théophraste.

Joséphine's older daughter and namesake swore revenge on Théophraste's family. By a strange quirk of fate, Sabine's half-sisters both found themselves students at the Fourneau College. There the current Joséphine Balsamo entangled Irina in a complex scheme of murder. Joséphine had given Irina the brooch as a gift. The haughty blonde had once stated her motives for the gift. Joséphine allegedly been mocking Irina's then ignorance of the feud between the Balsamo and Lupin families. Had Joséphine spoken the truth? Confronted by the truth of Sabine's ancestry, Irina wondered if Joséphine's gift had been prompted by a different rationale.

As they were separating after the meal, Sabine pressed a note into Irina's hand. Once the members of the Black Coats had departed, Irina examined the paper:

I wear this brooch today because of the bond that connects us for all eternity. You will always be my sister. I will never betray you.
Sabine

In the successive weeks, the women met regularly at the Restaurant Imperial. Irina noticed a distinct improvement in Sabine. She exuded radiance. Sabine seemed to have achieved a state of inner peace. She also now always wore blue gloves and never removed them. Was this another sign of her bonding with Irina? Since Irina never doffed her own black gloves, she concluded that Sabine was imitating her.

The quintet discussed many things–music, fashions, books, the theater, and even Urania's children. Ironically, they deliberately shied away from the major topic of the Paris newspapers. A spectacular crime wave had descended on the city. During the months that followed, Paris was plagued by a brazen series of robberies. Jewelry stores and warehouses were being constantly plundered. At the scene of each crime, the letter M was found scrawled on a wall. The newspapers recorded rumors of an inscrutable mastermind. Only known as M, this individual was the organizer of every illicit deed in Paris.

An impatient press clamored for action. Chief Inspector Jacques Lefevre convinced the police commissioner to take bold action. As a reward for its earlier role in ending the atrocities of Bluebeard III, the Chupin Detective Agency was hired to assist the authorities. Irina Putine knew instinctively that the Black Coats were responsible for the M crimes. She immediately arranged for daily surveillance of both the Regenerator of Fashion and the Nightingale Hierarchy.

Outwardly the Nightingale Hierarchy was a philanthropic association promoting the protection of avian sanctuaries. The Paris headquarters of these alleged international ornithologists seemed harmless. The sign of the society was a bird with the motto "What good deed have you done today?" Despite long hours of spying on the Nightingale Hierarchy, Irina's agents reported no signs of suspicious activity.

A constant watch on the Regenerator of Fashion was proving equally fruitless until a minor incident. In May 1897, a visibly angry woman in a Black Skirt uniform with a dark beret was seen leaving the dressmaking business. Acting on a hunch, a Chupin detective followed her. She stopped briefly before a poster advertising the newspaper *Le Matin*. Playing on the coincidence that its own name began with the same initial of the enigmatic criminal discussed in its recent issues, the poster for *Le Matin* displayed a huge M. The Black Skirt stopped momentarily and spat on the poster. This minor act of irreverence could be a potential lead. The incident was mentioned in a report to Irina Putine. She showed it to Blythe Furnace. As Milady Nevermore, Blythe had been familiar with many of the Black Skirts. The description fit Coleen Pegler. Tracing Coleen to a disreputable tenement, Blythe sent her a message. She requested Coleen to meet her in an alley near the Rue des Martyrs.

That night, Coleen kept the appointment. She followed Blythe deep into the alley in order to speak unobserved with her.

"You were always square with me, Milady. The Black Skirts became Hell for me after you left."

"I believe you have reason to hate M, Coleen."

"I want to see M dead! M treats me like dirt!"

"Who is M?"

"M is someone you probably never met. M is Doc Malbodius."

"I'm acquainted with Malbodius. How do you know the doctor?"

"Doc personally requested me to be the liaison with the Black Skirts. The London office relays information about financial transactions to the Regenerator of Fashion. I then take it to Malbodius. I thought that I was getting a plush assignment, but Doc just abuses me. Doc and that Hungarian won't even call me by my real name. They call me Piglet."

"Who's this Hungarian?"

"Marga Sandorf."

"Marga! Has the Order of the Serpent Heart joined the Black Coats?"

"Madame Sara sits on the High Council. That Marga hates me. She turned Malbodius against me. You recall how I was wounded by a Pinkerton. Marga made my left hand matched my right."

Coleen raised her left hand. The last two fingers were missing.

"Why did Marga maim you?"

"Because I was wearing Joséphine Balsamo's ring. After you fled London, Balsamo was condemned to death. She was—"

"I know all about her execution. We haven't much time. Tell me what Malbodius and Marga are planning."

"You're right, Milady, Doc was looking at me very strange today. Marga is training Doc. Marga is—"

"A just woman, Piglet!" shouted a shadowy figure near the entrance of the alley.

A gun was fired. Clutching her stomach, Coleen fell to the ground. Blythe pressed against the side of the alley as five bullets whirled by her. Before Blythe reached the start of the alley, she heard a door slam. A carriage rode into the night.

Blythe Furnace came from an artistic family. She was sketching a figure on a pad while delivering a report to Irina Putine at the Chupin Detective Agency.

"I've seen Malbodius twice," commented Irina, "His physical appearance was radically different on each occasion. When we first met, he used the alias of Eric Maubeuge."

"Malbodius occupies a unique position in the Black Coats," added Blythe. "He reports personally to Noel Moriarty. The Lord of the Night frequently lends out Malbodius to others on the High Council. His current employer must be Madame Sara."

"I've never heard of her?"

"I didn't tell you about her earlier because her organization was separate from the Black Coats. When I was working for Antonio Nikola, I had some dealings with Sara. She built up a syndicate in South and Central America based on the cult of Quetzalcoatl. Her followers are called the Order of the Serpent Heart. Antonio long hoped to bring them into the Black Coats. He must have recently succeeded."

"You mentioned a Marga Sandorf."

"Sara's personal assassin. She kills with a golden pistol. I recognized her voice in the alley. In the Americas, they call her *La Hija del Diablo.* Here's what she look like." Blythe presented her sketch to Irina. "Marga's never been known to miss a target."

"This 'Devil's Daughter' missed you five times."

"Those shots were deliberate misses. Marga and I have a history."

Blythe lowered her right arm. An object swiftly fell into her hand. Rapidly rising her arm, Irina saw a small silver plated gun with four barrels.

"I've never seen you use a gun before, Blythe."

"After my education by the Iga ninjas, Antonio sent me to New Orleans to study with a semi-retired gunslinger. My tutor lives under the name of Jake Silver today, but he was the notorious Ace Sartana in the 1870's. Normally, I don't use a gun. Reliance on weapons can dull an individual's fighting skills."

"You're still remarkably swift."

"Marga shared your opinion. Antonio once entrusted me with retrieving a relic from the Brazilian jungle. The Order of the Serpent Heart assisted me. Marga was my companion during my foray into the Amazon. We fought off a horde of native warriors with our pistols. Impressed with my abilities, Marga challenged me to a duel. I won."

"Shouldn't Marga be dead?"

"It was a mock duel. Neither of our lives was ever in danger. To be brutally honest, I think Marga let me win."

"At least she isn't your equal in hand to hand combat."

"Don't be so sure. Marga is an expert of copeira, a Brazilian fighting style vaguely similar to *la savate.* I've never combated a practitioner of that technique."

"How friendly were you and Marga?"

"I know what you're thinking, Irina. You're wondering if I have divided loyalties. Marga may have once been my friend, but you're my best friend."

"You proved that in the House of Crafts. I'm not concerned about your fidelity but your resolve. You might hesitate in fighting Marga because of your earlier camaraderie."

"I have no illusions about Marga. She's a curious mixture of chivalry and cruelty. Her chivalrous side was indicated by those deliberate misses in the alley. Her cruel side was present by her removal of Coleen Pegler. Marga normally dispatches an opponent by a bullet to the heart or to the head. Those wounds generally cause a quick death. If Marga has contempt for an opponent, she delivers a bullet in the stomach. Marga believes that a wound there causes intense pain. The victim agonizes briefly before expiring."

"Marga's animosity towards Coleen resulted from the theft of Joséphine Balsamo's ring. What link exists between Marga and Joséphine?"

"There's probably a connection between Joséphine and Marga's employer. Madame Sara is obsessed with religions that worship snakes. She even poses as the high priestess of the Naga cult of Asia. There's a legend that Joséphine's ancestor, Count Cagliostro, sold his soul to the Serpent Gods in exchange for an immortality elixir. Sara may have concluded a similar pact."

"What are you talking about?"

"When Antonio introduced me to Sara a few years ago, she looked no older than 25. Antonio knew Sara in the 1870's. She had the same youthful appearance."

"Balderdash, Blythe. The Sara of the 1870's must be mother of her current namesake. Joséphine employed the same illusion of immortality by exploiting her resemblance to her own mother."

"Perhaps you're right. I never liked Sara. She encourages Marga's ruthlessness. Marga's sadism may prove to be her undoing."

"In what way?"

"Before she died, Coleen had time to scrawl a single word on the pavement in her own blood: TRANSAS.

The word had immediate significance for Irina. Transas Shipping was a delivery and hauling company that did business all over Paris. Their black horse-drawn vans were a well-known sight along the boulevards. The company was extremely efficient with very cheap rates. Even the Chupin Detective Agency utilized Transas Shipping to deliver packages.

Irina was acquainted with Martin Stedor, the manager of Transas Shipping. He was a jovial man with a receding hairline. The Chupin Detective Agency now monitored Transas Shipping in addition to the offices associated with the Black Coats Irina and Blythe tracked the movements to Stedor. Watching the main office, the ladies noticed that Stedor did not go home one night. At midnight, Stedor finally left the office accompanied by two other men. The trio rode away in a Transas van driven by a fourth man.

The Transas vehicle arrived in the jewelry district of Paris. Stedor and his two companions alighted from their van. After a half hour, three men returned to their conveyance. The van transported its passengers to a warehouse.

Throughout, its nightly travels, the van had been followed by a carriage belonging to the Chupin Detective Agency. Inside had been Blythe and Irina. Skilled in Japanese ninja techniques, Blythe expertly blended into the darkness of the night. She had trained Irina in these ninja methods as well. Irina was dressed in her normal attire with the addition of a long black cape that covered her orange dress. Irina carried her umbrella. It housed a concealed sword. The two sleuths clandestinely penetrated the warehouse.

Hidden behind a group of stacked crates, Irina and Blythe gazed on a bizarre meeting. Stedor and his two confederates stood before a curtain. On the other side of the curtain, a bright lamp cast a dark slender silhouette on the screen.

"Did the burglary go as planned, Stedor?" questioned a female voice from behind the curtain

Blythe immediately recognized the speaker. "That's Marga Sandorf," she whispered to Irina.

"Yes, Chief," replied Stedor. "Your intelligence from London was correct. In order to cover his debts, Lord Faber had secretly sold the Ripening Rubies to a jeweler in the Rue de la Paix. We liberated it from his safe."

Stedor held up a belt of stunning Burmese rubies.

Irina and Blythe burst forth from their hiding place. Stedor pulled a knife. Irina smashed the handle of his umbrella on his wrist. Dropping the knife, Stedor was rendered senseless by a punch to the jaw by Irina. Blythe slammed the heads of the two men together. They fell senseless to the ground.

Irina pulled out her sword. A bullet fired from the behind the curtain hit the sword's handle. Irina dropped her blade. Blythe suddenly grabbed her. As a bullet whizzed by Blythe, the two women fell to the ground. Blythe rolled on the floor underneath the curtain.

Irina heard a blow. A pistol slid from underneath the curtain towards her. Blythe must have knocked the gun out of Marga's hand and kicked the weapon away.

Two shadowy figures engaged in a brutal duel of martial arts behind the curtain. Grabbing the gun, Irina aimed it at the curtain. It was her intention to kill Marga Sandorf. Irina doubted Blythe's ability to defeat Madame Sara's assassin. However, Irina couldn't tell the combatants apart. Both were approximately the same height. Both were wearing coats, pants and boots. Neither wore their hair on their shoulders. All Irina could see was a jumble of blows and counterblows delivered by arms, elbows and legs.

The vicious contest ended when one of the pugilists delivered three leg kicks in succession to her adversary's stomach. The recipient of the blows collapsed. Having retrieved her sword, Irina cut open the curtain. She beheld a triumphant Blythe standing over her conquered nemesis. The motionless woman was not Marga Sandorf. The vanquished fighter was Irina's sister, Sabine.

The driver of the Chupin Detective Agency carriage had been sent to the Prefecture of Police. He returned with Chief Inspector Lefevre and a squad of gendarmes. Inside Blythe awaited him with four bound captives. They were Stedor, his two fellow burglars, and the driver of the Transas Shipping van. Blythe had apprehended him after her victory over Sabine.

Blythe handed the Ripening Rubies to Lefevre.

"M's gang was Transas Shipping," announced Blythe.

"M is Martin Stedor?" asked Lefevre.

"No, M is a woman. She hid behind the curtain. M escaped. Irina Putine is still pursuing her."

Blythe had lied. The unconscious Sabine had been removed from the warehouse by Irina. Inside the bedroom of her apartment in the Rue de Choiseul, the sleuth had secreted her sister.

For hours, Irina watched over her slumbering sister. Lying on Irina's bed, Sabine's right wrist was handcuffed to a bedpost. Her left arm lied by her side. On the fourth finger of her left hand was a gold ring fashioned like a serpent with a woman's head. Sabine was garbed in a long blue coat with wide sleeves. A three-pronged spear was emblazoned on the right side of the garment. The coat reminded Irina of a mandarin's robe.

Sabine's gun lied on top of a bureau. It was a C96 Mauser Pistol.

The bedchamber was illuminated by a single lamp. The curtains were drawn.

Sabine suddenly murmured in the bed.

"It was not I. It was Eric. He made me lie."

She opened her eyes. She looked around. Her eyes caught a clock on the bureau. It was nearly half past three.

"Irina! What am I doing here? Why am I chained?"

"Don't you remember what happened?"

"Eric Malbodius and I were conducting an experiment in hypnotism. He used me as his subject."

"Malbodius! How can you trust that man?"

"He helped me when I was being tormented by Rochelle and Orianne. Eric prevented them from torturing me."

"How long have these hypnotic experiments been going on?"

"For four months."

"Do you know Marga Sandorf?"

"She's Eric's assistant."

Sabine gazed at her hand. "Why am I wearing this ring?" She looked down on her chest. "Why am I in this coat? What does this pitchfork design mean?"

Taking a key, Irina unlocked the handcuff. She assisted Sabine to her feet.

"Eric betrayed you. He hypnotized you to commit crimes. You can't trust the Black Coats anymore. You need to come with me to the police. You must tell them everything about Eric."

Sabine seized the Mauser pistol. She held it covering Irina.

"I can't do that. You don't understand. I have to leave. Don't try to stop me."

"I understand everything, Sabine. You lied about the hypnotism to make me drop my guard. It's time to discuss your husband."

"You know Eric and I are married!"

"The ring on your finger is proof. Madame Sara is the high priestess of a religion that reveres snakes. She officiated over your wedding. You hid your wedding ring from me by wearing gloves doing our regular luncheons. How could you have participated in such a ritual?"

"It was a beautiful ceremony. You don't understand the true nature of the Naga faith."

"You tried to mislead me, Sabine, with your comment about a pitchfork on your coat. That's no pitchfork. It's a trident, a symbol associated with gods of the sea. The trident represents your allegiance to the Neptune Society. Lucky Noel is ambitious and clever. The Neptune Society had lost most of its influence just before she became its co-manager. Only by committing a successful series of crimes could the Neptune Society maintained its autonomy in the Black Coats. Lucky's brother assigned Eric to help her. The Black Coats knew that the Chupin Detective Agency would pose a threat to them. They took advantage of our family relationship to neutralize the Agency. Can't you see? With Eric's coaching, Lucky manipulated Urania into meeting me at the gallery. Lucky even tricked you into visiting Blythe. Who gave you that empty derringer? Dorkie or another of Lucky's subordinates? The Black Coats had being pulling your strings like a puppet. Eric doesn't love you! You're only a pawn to him!"

"That's not true!"

"Because you're my sister, you were chosen to direct the Neptune Society's operation. Eric persuaded Madame Sara to allow Marga to instruct you. Marga gave you lessons in marksmanship and copeira. You became the mysterious M, the ruler of the Parisian underworld. You issued orders concealed behind a curtain. Since your own voice is far from commanding, you imitated Marga's. What happened to you, Sabine? How could you emulate that sadist?"

"Marga Sandorf is a just woman! She nearly killed Orianne for her attack on me!"

"Your husband is as treacherous as he is cunning. He must have orchestrated the assault on you by Orianne and Rochelle. He needed you to revere Marga. He ordered her to punish Orianne."

"You're wrong. It was Joséphine's idea!"

"*Joséphine's alive!*"

"I didn't lie to you about her execution. After our meeting, I discovered that her death was an elaborate illusion. I couldn't tell you. You're both my sisters. I'm trying to be loyal to you both."

"Pointing that gun is hardly proof of your sisterly regard. By contrast, you're very protective of Joséphine. Marga told you about Coleen Pegler's theft of your sister's ring. In order to reprimand Coleen further, you had her placed under your authority. You respected Marga as the defender of your family's honor. You strove to behave like her. You even copied her wanton disregard for human life."

"Pegler merited death!"

"When Blythe met with Coleen, there was a misunderstanding. Blythe thought that Coleen's references to Doc Malbodius meant your husband. Coleen was referring to you, Dr. Sabine Malbodius. You realized that Coleen might turn informer. You followed her and killed her. Your mimicry of Marga's voice misled Blythe. She thought that Marga deliberately missed her. Actually you tried to hit Blythe, but your shooting is inferior to Marga's. You genuinely missed. You want to kill Blythe."

"I hate her! She caused Joséphine's disgrace!"

"Just as you really hate me for my victories over Joséphine."

Sabine looked genuinely hurt. "That not true, sister!"

"Don't lie to me! You shot at me in the warehouse!"

"I wasn't trying to kill you! I shot the sword out of your hand!"

"You fired a second shot!"

"That was at Blythe!"

"You're aiming a gun at me now."

"I can't let you turn me over to the police. I assume Blythe surrendered my henchmen to them."

"Correct."

"It's been about two hours since the fight in the warehouse. Blythe will be too busy to get back here to prevent my escape. Don't try to stop me. I won't kill you, but I could stop your pursuit by putting a bullet in your leg. Don't make me do that, sister! I don't want to hurt you!"

Sabine opened the bedroom door. Blythe Furnace was standing outside. She had been listening to the entire conversation. Pointing her Mauser at Blythe, Sabine pulled the trigger several times in succession.

"Poor Sabine!" mocked Blythe "You still don't know when a gun is empty. Irina removed the bullets during your beauty rest." Blythe's silver pistol slid swiftly into her hand. "Mine is fully loaded." Blythe raised her gun. "I could have drawn and fired my pistol behind the curtain, Sabine. I didn't because you're Irina's sister."

"You couldn't have gotten back from the police so quickly!" said Sabine.

"What is it the Black Coats say, Sabine?" interjected Irina. "Will there be daylight?" Irina pulled back the curtains. Sunlight flooded the room. "It's not 3:30 in the morning. It's 3:30 in the afternoon."

"The police raided Transas Shipping this morning," disclosed Blythe. "All the employees are being held for questioning. Your criminal apparatus is smashed. As for you, Dr. Malbodius, there's the murder of Coleen Pegler. You have a date with the guillotine."

Sabine looked pleadingly at her sister. "If you knew everything, why participate in this farce?"

Opening her bureau's drawer, Irina pulled out Sabine's luncheon note. "Because I wanted to believe this! I wanted my suspicions to be wrong! I wanted you to give me a different explanation! You could have been duped! You could have been coerced! I wanted to embrace your story about hypnotism! You promised never to betray me! You lied!"

"No! I didn't betray you! Don't you understand? I did it all for you! Eric, Lucky, Sara-they all made me a promise. If I did what they wanted, they would keep you and Joséphine apart. The Black Coats would send Joséphine far from Europe. The two of you are locked in a horrible vendetta. You're both my sisters! I can't allow one to kill the other! I love you both!"

Irina stared into Sabine's haunted eyes. In her strange twisted way, Sabine was telling the truth. She did genuinely care for Irina.

"Sabine, you were a true sister to me at the Sanctuary Club. I owed you a debt. That debt is now paid. I'm letting you go. Blythe, lower your gun."

"You can't be serious, Irina! Your sister killed Coleen! She'll kill again!"

"She's still my sister, Blythe."

Blythe obeyed Irina's order. Irina gazed sternly at her sister.

"Sabine, you've chosen a dark road to travel. If you have any decency left in you, abandon this path. If you don't, I'll have no choice but to bring you to justice." Irina turned her back on Sabine

The woman known as Dr. Malbodius left Irina's apartment.

Irina tore Sabine's note again and again. She wept uncontrollably.

Whatever anger Blythe felt from Irina's leniency swiftly dissipated. Blythe hugged Irina as she sobbed. Blythe was Irina's best friend, and Irina truly needed a friend that afternoon.

Eric Malbodius was quite content. Despite the police raid on Transas Shipping, only a small amount of the stolen merchandise had been recovered by the authorities. The Neptune Society had transported the bulk of the booty to England. With Sabine at liberty, no one could tie the Neptune Society to Transas Shipping. The entire operation had ended very well. The Moriarty family felt indebted to him for restoring the prestige of the Neptune Society. An important alliance with Madame Sara and the Cagliostro clan had been consummated. He even bagged a pretty wife as a bonus. Sabine had her deficiencies, but they could be corrected. Eric would methodically continue the renovation of her personality.

Most of his colleagues committed crimes because they believed the end justifies the means. For Eric, the means justifies the end. He delighted in causing the suffering of others. Eric had successfully maneuvered every player in this profitable affair into acting according to his desires. His ultimate destiny was a certainty. Someday he would be the supreme master of the Black Coats. When that day came, the world would be engulfed in chaos.

Consequences of a Funeral

"Raffles must die!" swore Dr. Nikola. "The murder of Count Corbucci must be avenged!"

This death sentence was pronounced during October 1897. Nikola was presiding over a meeting in the Villa Corbucci. This residence of the Corbucci family was located in Baiae, a resort area in the Bay of Naples. The relatives of Salvatore Corbucci had gathered for his funeral. In the previous September, the body of the Count had been discovered in London. He had been poisoned. After a sensational inquest, the corpse had been released by the British authorities to the Count's family. To the Italian public, Corbucci was merely an eccentric nobleman who wrote novels about the American West. He was actually one of the most dangerous criminals in Europe.

Antonio Nikola had felt genuine affection for Count Corbucci. In 1868, Corbucci had encountered the young Antonio, then a 12 year-old orphan, in the streets of Havana. Developing a fondness for the boy, Corbucci transported him from Cuba to Europe. Antonio became Corbucci's foster son. Besides adopting Antonio, Corbucci inducted him into the Camorra, the Neapolitan criminal organization. Antonio soon learned how the Camorra was part of a much larger confederation, the Black Coats. The other individuals in the room were all members of the Black Coats.

Noel Moriarty, the Count's son-in-law, was the leader of the Gentlemen of the Night, the London branch of the Black Coats. He was a thin man in his fifties. Colored spectacles covered his pale gray eyes.

Catarina, Noel's wife, was a glamorous brunette of 34 years. She could be properly addressed as Countess Corbucci or Mrs. Moriarty. However, Catarina rarely used those names. In European society, she assumed the alias of Madame Koluchy. With her father's support, Catarina had taken over another Neapolitan secret society, the Brotherhood of the Seven Kings, in 1884. In the autumn of 1896, Catarina had reorganized the Brotherhood into the Black Skirts. Taking advantages of the legitimate grievances of suffragettes and feminists, Catarina had sought to recruit female followers by pretending to be an advocate of women's rights. Unlike Susan B. Anthony and Emmeline Pankhurst, Catarina cared nothing about righting the oppression of women in a male-dominated society. In contrast to the heroic pioneers of feminine equality, Catarina was only interested in furthering her own ambitions.

Five years younger than her sister, Carolina Corbucci was an attractive woman with raven hair and dark blue eyes. Like Catarina, Carolina was dressed in a black dress suitable for mourning. Count Corbucci's late wife had been an American from Texas, Kate Washburn. When Kate had been killed by her husband's rivals in the Camorra in 1880, the Count had taken measures to ensure their daughters' safety. Catarina had been registered under a false surname in a boarding school in southern France. Carolina had been dispatched to Texas to live with her American relatives. Only recently had Carolina returned to Europe. During her sojourn in America, Carolina had corresponded regularly with her sister. In fact, it was one of Carolina's letters that inspired Catarina to create the Black Skirts. Carolina described how a protest march by American women had prevented a murderess, "the Queen of the Outlaws," from being hanged. Carolina's description of this incident prompted Catarina to attempt to hijack the suffragette movement for her own selfish goals.

The only other individual listening to Nikola's assertions was not a member of the Corbucci clan. He was a freelance assassin often employed by the Black Coats. Called the Pallid Mask, he was a man of many aliases. Although he had previously been known as Juan North, his current cover identity was Dirk Gurn. Despite his somewhat autonomous relationship to the Black Coats, Gurn's late wife had been one of Catarina's Black Skirts.

Gurn was extremely ambitious. He did not wish to continue as a mere lackey of the Black Coats. He harbored dreams of running his own criminal network. Gurn had recently been in New York where he was in the process of defrauding a wealthy French businessman, Etienne Rambert. In order to conclude this elaborate swindle successfully, Gurn was required to briefly return to Europe. He soon found himself summoned to the Villa Corbucci.

"How did this feud between the Count and Raffles result?" asked Gurn.

"Raffles quarreled over a woman with Stefano, the Count's trustworthy retainer, in November 1895," replied Nikola.

"That must have been some months after Raffles was publicly exposed as a burglar. The public mistakenly believes that Raffles drowned in the Mediterranean."

"Exactly, Gurn," confirmed Catarina. "Not only did Raffles survive, but he made his home in this very neighborhood."

"I've heard of Stefano's demise," acknowledged Gurn. "Raffles must have slain him."

"Papa was always so loyal to his subordinates," noted Carolina. "He was bound by honor to avenge Stefano. It took Papa two years, but he eventually tracked down Raffles in London. Before Papa could exact justice, that filthy brigand poisoned him."

"Raffles must be living under a false identity in England," concluded Moriarty. "Unfortunately, my late father-in-law did not confide to us how he had found Raffles. It will be up to you, Gurn, to force this swine out in the open."

"That could take years, Sir," said Gurn.

"The Black Coats can afford to be patient," stated Moriarty. He scribbled a figure on a notepad and showed it to Gurn. "This will be your compensation, Gurn, once you dispose of Raffles. Is it satisfactory?"

"More than satisfactory."

The funeral of Salvatore Corbucci was attended by the highest echelons of the Black Coats. All of these underworld luminaries visited the Villa Corbucci to pay their respects to the family. Among the mourners was the Cagliostro clan. They were led by Madame Sara, the petite matriarch. Included in the Cagliostro delegation were Sara's two goddaughters, Joséphine Balsamo and her sister Sabine. A recent newlywed, Sabine was accompanied by her husband, Dr. Eric Malbodius. Joséphine had initially been scheduled to depart for New Orleans, but the trip had been delayed. Joséphine had proven invaluable in the construction of Madame Sara's European enterprises.

Joséphine, an alluring blonde, embraced Antonio.

"Antonio, you have my condolences."

Catarina was annoyed by Joséphine's actions. While Nikola had established amicable relations with the Cagliostro clan, Catarina had nothing but contempt for them. Once Catarina's subordinate in the Black Coats, Joséphine harbored a grudge concerning her mistreatment by her former superior. Joséphine intended to irritate Catarina by romancing Antonio. 13 years earlier, Antonio and Catarina had been betrothed. The engagement had collapsed due to Catarina's infidelity, and the Count had forced his wayward daughter to consummate an alliance with the Gentlemen of the Night by marrying Noel Moriarty. Due to his failure to wed Catarina, Antonio had gained the reputation of being a woman-hater. Joséphine knew these rumors of misogyny to be false. Antonio had conducted a passionate love affair with a former colleague in the Black Coats, Milady Nevermore. For totally different reasons, Catarina and Joséphine had conspired to successfully disrupt Antonio's romance. Joséphine was well aware of Catarina's true feelings. The older daughter of Count Corbucci felt trapped in a loveless marriage. She still harbored strong desires for Antonio.

Focused on Joséphine's machinations, Catarina didn't notice that her sister was consorting with another member of the Cagliostro party. Carolina approached a slight woman wearing a gold tunic, black pants and boots. A black cape with a gold lining covered her shoulders. She was Marga Sandorf, the personal assassin of the Cagliostro family. Normally, a black fur cap covered Marga's short dark hair. In deference to the late Count Corbucci's memory, Marga had removed her cap and stuffed it under the black belt across her waist.

"Excuse me," said Carolina, "are you *La Hija del Diablo?*"

"I've been called that title," admitted Marga.

"I heard of your exploits in Texas. I'm Carolina Corbucci."

"I've never met your father, Signorina Corbucci, but I read all his novels. They were published in America under the pseudonym of Stanley Corbett. For a European, your father had a great understanding of the American West."

"He traveled extensively in America during the 1860's and 1870's. It was during that period that he met the gunslingers whom were fictionalized in his novels."

"Of course, Ignacz Djanko was the most prominent. I regret that I never knew him. Unfortunately, I had a brief acquaintance with a less reputable adventurer immortalized by your father in *The Gilded Pistolero*."

"You mean Jeff Gonzales."

"Yes. You must be aware that I killed him."

"I bear no resentment about your disposal of Gonzales. He was my least favorite of the gunfighters celebrated by my father. He was a thorough egotist. In the exploit recorded by my father, I always blamed him for the death of the saloon hostess."

"I appreciate your frankness, Signorina."

"Please call me Carolina. May I call you Marga?"

"Of course, Carolina."

"Could I see the golden pistol that you took from Gonzales?"

Marga pulled back the right side of her cape. A holstered firearm on her belt was exposed.

"You wear your gun with the butt facing outward," noticed Carolina.

"Being left-handed, I draw my gun crossways. It's been claimed that Djanko wore his guns in a similar fashion. Your father's version of his exploits, *The Undertaker's Big Gun,* states otherwise."

"There were many Djanko impersonators. Djanko established a reputation just before the Civil War. Since most Americans couldn't pronounce his Croatian surname properly, it often became corrupted. Many other gunfighters took the name Djanko or a close variation in order to steal the original's fame. You remember Djanko's red-haired lover?"

"Her name was Maricruz Juana."

"After Djanko deserted her in Texas, Maricruz Juana became the paramour of John Forest, a bounty hunter. He gave her the nickname of Mijanou. In return, she bestowed on Forest the alias of Djanko because of his similarities to her earlier lover. It was Forest, a false Djanko, who wore his guns like you."

"You're as knowledgeable on the American West as your late lamented father."

"Marga, would you do me the honor of having a drink with me?"

"I never drink alcohol, Carolina. It dulls my senses."

"An opinion shared by Angel-Face Brown and Death-Sentence Cash. Like those Western gentlemen, I assume you only partake of milk."

"Quite correct."

"Then let us retreat to the kitchen, Marga, for two glasses of milk."

Marga followed Carolina into the kitchen. Carolina found a pitcher of milk and two glasses.

"I have my own glass, Carolina." Marga reached into a pocket in her pants. She pulled out a foldable metal cup. "My mother was a member of the Von Schulenberg family. This is one of the famous Von Schulenberg drinking goblets. Extending the cup to its full height, Marga poured the milk into it and Carolina's glass.

"To the memory of your late father," toasted Marga. "His immortality was guaranteed by his novels."

The two women clicked their glasses. After Carolina tasted her milk, she had a request.

"Could I examine your pistol?"

Marga handed her gun to Carolina.

"Thank you, Marga. Although Jeff Gonzales was unworthy, it means much to me to touch an object that Papa wrote about."

Carolina twirled the gun. Facing the wall, Carolina put the gun to her side and drew it forward against an imaginary opponent.

"You're very swift on the draw," remarked Marga. "You truly know the mechanics of how to handle a gun. It's regrettable that we can't fight a mock duel."

"A mock duel?"

Marga elaborated in detail.

"And you have all the necessary tools for this mock duel in Paris?" questioned Carolina.

Marga nodded her head.

"Catarina and I will be in Paris in two weeks. Let us arrange a rendezvous in the Bois de Boulogne."

Later that evening, Carolina revealed to her sister the arrangement with Marga Sandorf.

"A mock duel!" exclaimed Catarina. "Are you insane?"

"Antonio is arranging the details," explained Carolina. "He assures me that this is a harmless exercise. He once arranged a similar contest between Marga and one of his subordinates."

"Antonio is deluded by feminine wiles! The Cagliostros have arranged this demonstration to humiliate you. Marga Sandorf is a treacherous upstart! She's not to be trusted!"

Despite Catarina's protests, the mock duel went ahead as planned. On an early morning, the various parties met in the Bois de Boulogne. Each contestant was represented by two seconds. Joséphine and Sabine acted for Marga while Antonio and Catarina performed the same function for Carolina.

Marga was sporting her usual attire, but Carolina was dressed flamboyantly for the occasion. Her ensemble was a "cowgirl" outfit largely modeled on the clothing worn by Louise King, the notorious train bandit of the 1880's. Carolina's slender shape was clad in tight-fitting black shirt and pants. The hair of the tall brunette was tugged inside a black hat. A bright yellow bandana encircled her neck. An empty holster hung from a belt around her waist.

Marga's holster was similarly empty. In order not to give either party any particular advantage, it was agreed that the duelists would use a pair of identical dueling pistols. The firearms were carried in a box by Sabine. Carolina was given the choice of which pistol to use. After detecting no visible difference between the pair, Carolina arbitrarily selected one. Once the weapons were designated, Joséphine loaded Marga's with a single bullet. Catarina did likewise with Carolina's.

With their guns holstered, Marga and Carolina advanced away from their seconds to the center of an open field.

"Before we begin," said Marga, "there is the matter of the Von Schulenberg Ritual."

"Ritual? What ritual?"

"My mother's family has long prized the art of dueling. When a Von Schulenberg challenges a worthy opponent, that individual is asked to perform a rite of mutual respect. We exchange weapons."

"Catarina warned me about this!" shouted an angry Carolina. "You and that Joséphine Balsamo are planning some sort of trick! You're rigging the duel! Your gun is sabotaged!"

"But you examined the pistols!" protested Marga.

"Don't try to fool me!" Carolina spat on the ground. She motioned to Antonio. "Let the contest begin!"

Antonio was somewhat repulsed by Carolina's violent outburst. He quickly regained his composure.

"The duelists will walk 20 paces from one another!" As Antonio counted from 1 to 20, the two women turned and stepped away from each other. When he reached 20, Antonio gave new directions. "Stop! Turn and face each other! When I count to three, you will draw and fire. One...Two... THREE!"

Carolina drew her gun, but she never fired it. Marga's bullet slammed into her neck. Dropping her gun, Carolina fell backwards. A gruesome red stain formed across the prone Carolina's yellow bandana.

At the Paris residence of the Corbucci family, Catarina expressed her outrage.

"Carolina could have been killed."

"She only has a bruised neck," diagnosed Antonio. "Carolina never would have been injured if you hadn't painted the false seeds of distrust in your sister's brain. Marga Sandorf had only intended a friendly contest until Carolina's behavior offended her."

"You're sure none of that blood on Carolina's neck was real?"

"I examined her carefully. The breakaway bullets only contain red paint."

A couple of days later, Catarina conferred privately with Gurn.

"My sister was assaulted by that Hungarian hussy. I want you to temporarily suspend your search for Raffles. You must exterminate Marga Sandorf. Do it in a manner that can't be traced to me."

"I believe in poetic justice, Madame. Your sister was defeated in a duel. Shouldn't Marga be killed in a duel?"

"I would be quite pleased if such an event occurred."

"Tell me more about these fake bullets, Madame."

"They were developed by a former Confederate gunsmith, Leeman Bailey, living in Mexico. He made them for a bounty hunter called Gunsight Eyes. Years later, Bailey sold some of the same bullets to Jeff Gonzales. When Marga killed Gonzales, she found a supply of these bullets among the bounty killer's belongings. She's been using them in mock duels."

"Has anyone ever been known to defeat Marga in a mock duel?"

"A former member of the Black Coats did once, Gurn. You have ample reason to remember her. I'm referring to our mutual enemy, Milady Nevermore alias Blythe Furnace."

A surge of hatred flashed through Gurn. Furnace had been responsible for his beloved wife's death a year ago.

"Furnace would be the perfect cat's paw! We will manipulate her into removing Marga! We win either way! If Furnace fails, she dies instead of Marga!"

A few days later, Gurn paid a visit on Joséphine Balsamo. When they stayed in Paris, the Cagliostro clan utilized a large perfumery belonging to Madame Sara. Gurn located Joséphine there.

"It's been over a year since I last saw you, Juan," observed Joséphine.

"I'm now called Dirk Gurn. I have a favor to ask you, Countess."

"Name it. I haven't forgotten the services that you and your late wife performed on my behalf."

"I've been granted the commission to avenge Count Corbucci. In order to complete my assignment, I emulated you. When I was in America, I talked to Ballmeyer. Remember the series of robberies that you committed with him there?"

"Ballmeyer and I amused ourselves by stealing the weapons of famous murderers confiscated by the police." Joséphine and her accomplice had enacted these robberies in the United States during 1895.

"I have performed a similar act in London. Do you recognize my cane?"

"It used to belong to poor sweet Sebastian! Scotland Yard seized it when he was arrested for Ronald Adair's murder."

"I liberated Colonel Moran's cane from the Yard's Black Museum. As you're aware, it's really an air-gun developed by Julius Von Herder."

"You intend to kill Raffles from afar."

"Yes, Countess. Unfortunately, my talents as a sniper are a trifle rusty. I need tutelage by an expert shootist. You have such a person in your employ."

"Her name is Marga Sandorf. She's superb with both a pistol and a rifle. I'll arrange for her to instruct you, Dirk."

In the basement of Madame Sara's perfumery was a target range. It was here that Marga coached Gurn. The pair soon developed a cordial friendship. Gurn used the opportunity to gain information from Marga.

"You taught Countess Cagliostro's sister as well, Marga."

"Yes, she's quite proficient with a pistol, Dirk."

"I've never met her. Does Sabine ever practice here?"

"She'll be here tomorrow. I'll introduce you."

The next day, Gurn met Sabine Malbodius. She looked nothing like her blonde sister. In fact, Gurn was stuck by an unusual resemblance of Joséphine's dark-haired sibling to Irina Putine of the Chupin Detective Agency. Having an errand to perform for Joséphine, Marga left Sabine and Gurn alone at the firing range.

"You use a most unusual gun," said Gurn, "a C96 Mauser Pistol."

"It was a gift from my sister. She discovered the existence of a distant American relative notorious for using this type of weapon."

"The Mauser fires 10 bullets. Doesn't it?"

"Yes. It took me a while to adapt to that fact after being trained with a six-shooter by Marga. When I fist employed the Mauser in an assassination, I had two targets. One of my quarries escaped due to my carelessness. I mistakenly assumed my ammunition exhausted after firing six bullets."

"I heard about that incident. You were trying to kill Blythe Furnace in an alley. She deserves to die. My late wife, Maude, was a staunch supporter of your sister in the Black Skirts. She thought the treatment of the Countess by Furnace was a disgrace."

Sabine paused before responding. "Josine never told me the full details of that ordeal. Could you tell me?"

"I'm not sure if I should."

"Please, Dirk. I need to know!"

"Furnace did more than demote your sister to the position of a security guard. She forced the Countess to strip naked in a room full of women."

On the evening of the next day, Madame Sara was confronted by Joséphine Balsamo.

"I never wanted Sabine to become deeply entangled in the schemes of the Black Coats. You manipulated her into marrying Eric Malbodius, godmother."

"There was no viable alternative, godchild," insisted Sara. "A marriage to Malbodius undid the damage caused by the revelations of Sabine's diary. The nuptials prevented Sabine's execution by the Black Coats."

"For that reason, I reluctantly consented to my sister's wedding. However, you and Malbodius are continuing to put Sabine in danger."

"What are you talking about?"

"Blythe Furnace! You and Eric forced Sabine into conflict with Furnace in the past! My sister is no match for Furnace! She defeated Sabine when they fought in the warehouse!"

"Neither Eric nor I have any intention of engaging Sabine in a vendetta against Furnace."

"Gurn told Sabine the full details of my mistreatment by Furnace when she was Milady Nevermore. Sabine is planning to attack Furnace in order to avenge my honor."

"Ah, I understand. You give me and Eric too much credit. We aren't using Gurn to plant ideas in Sabine's head."

"I apologize, godmother. We must do something to restrain Sabine!"

"I will alert Eric. He will placate her. However, the issue of your earlier harassment by Furnace should be addressed. Luckily, the Cagliostro clan has an enforcer to punish our enemies."

"Darling, you can't engage in another battle with Furnace," implored Eric Malbodius. "She nearly killed you the last time."

"She merely knocked me unconscious!" argued Sabine.

"Such blows can be fatal. I love you too much to risk your life. You can never defeat Furnace in physical combat. She has a genetic advantage. Her maternal grandmother was a member of the Vadarasse family of female wrestlers. Don't fret, darling. Furnace shall pay for the indignities inflicted on your sister. I've talked to your godmother. Marga Sandorf shall eradicate Furnace."

In the Rue de Choiseul, Madame Vabre owned a boarding house. One of her tenants was a woman with an unforgettable appearance. She possessed short brown hair. Her right eye was covered by a large black patch Her dark garments consisted of a shirt with a cravat, pants, boots, and a coat in the style of an Inverness cape. An amulet in the form of a cat's head hung from a chain around her neck. Born Berenice Fourneau, she had adopted the alias of Milady Nevermore during her service with the Black Coats. Having defected to the Chupin Detective Agency, this formidable damsel assumed the name of Blythe Furnace.

One afternoon, Blythe was returning to her apartment after concluding her work at the Agency. As she approached the door to her apartment, Blythe sensed that something was wrong. Skilled in the art of stealth by the Iga ninjas, she had unusually sensitive hearing. Barely audible sound of breathing could be detected from her apartment. Some intruder was inside. Pushing the door open, Blythe was confronted by an unexpected sight A dark lean man with a pale complexion sat on a chair. He stroked a cat in his lap.

"Antonio!" announced Blythe.

Putting the cat aside, Dr. Nikola leaped from the chair. He and Blythe embraced.

Betweens her passionate kisses, Blythe asked a question.

"How is our Legacy?"

"She's safe in Japan."

Some hours later, Blythe stroked Antonio's hair as they laid together in her bed.

"I can't leave the Agency, my love. It's impossible for me to return to the Black Coats."

"True, Berenice. But you could seek sanctuary in the Iga village. Our daughter needs a mother."

"Someone needs me more than Legacy."

"Who?"

"Irina, my best friend. She's been extremely vulnerable since learning the truth about Sabine. If I desert Irina now, the Black Coats will destroy her."

"You always has a strong sense of loyalty. I have a message to convey from another old friend, your fellow gunslinger from Brazil."

"Marga? What does she want?"

"Merely to see you. She's rented a suite at the Royal Palace Hotel."

"Marga's now allied with Joséphine Balsamo."

"Marga has given me her word that this isn't a trap."

"I learned long ago to respect Marga's word."

The next evening at the Royal Palace Hotel, Marga poured Blythe a glass of milk as they sat across a table.

"I have always appreciated our shared affection for milk, *compañera*," said Marga.

"Considering my necklace, it would be unusual for me to dislike milk."

"Dr. Nikola gave it to you as a gift. Where did he find this necklace?"

"Antonio has been very vague about its origins. Supposedly he found both it and his cat in some place called Ulthar."

"It seems to be made of a metal that I can't recognize."

"It's supposedly orichalcum."

"The metal of Atlantis discussed by Plato! How fascinating!"

"You didn't summon me here to discuss my jewelry."

"Unfortunately, there is an official meeting that must be arranged. We fought side by side in the Brazilian jungle. I have never met a gunfighter with better reflexes. I even challenged you to a mock duel."

"Which you let me win."

"Your lover was watching. I could not humble you in his eyes. Recently I met a woman who was almost as talented as you. She and I had a similar mock duel in front of her relatives."

"Did you let her triumph as well?"

"I would have, but she insulted me just before we contested."

"I get the impression that this conversation is headed beyond mock duels."

"I only worked for Madame Sara when we first met. I'm now chief of staff to her goddaughter."

"Joséphine Balsamo, I presume."

"Exactly, *compañera*. When you were her superior as Milady Nevermore, you stripped her bare like an animal."

"You're in no position to judge me. You style yourself 'a just woman,' but your justice can be very rough. For example, your treatment of Coleen Pegler."

"Touché, *compañera*. Despite the accuracy of your observation, Countess Cagliostro is still my patron. It's my solemn duty to defend her honor. Believe me, I take no pleasure in this action."

Marga removed a glove from her belt. She threw it on the table.

"I, Marga Sandorf, challenge you, Berenice Fourneau, to a duel to the death. Your death will be quick, but my mistress has instructed me to slay you in a contemptible manner. I apologize in advance."

"A duel with Marga Sandorf! You can't be serious!"

The speaker was a slender woman with dark hair tied in a French braid. Clothed in an orange dress, she wore black gloves and sliver bracelets. A pentagram brooch adorned the right side o her dress. Known as Irina Putine, she was Blythe Furnace's closest friend. Irina resided in a separate apartment at Madame Vabre's.

"I know this is difficult for you to understand, Irina, but Marga proceeds according to defined rules of etiquette. As with all duels, the principals have seconds. Antonio Nikola has agreed to be one of my seconds. I want you to be the other."

"And who will be Marga's second? Joséphine Balsamo?"

"Yes. I know what you're contemplating, Irina. Joséphine is still wanted for her role in the Bluebeard murders. You want to tip off the police and ambush her. I can't let you do that. This is an affair of honor."

"There's nothing honorable about Joséphine. Have you forgotten how she promised to tear out your left eye?"

"Sabine will probably act as Marga's other second. Irina. You wouldn't want the police interrogating her."

Irina was silent. Sharing a common mother, Sabine and Joséphine were half-sisters. Sabine's father had also been Irina's. Sabine was Irina's half-sister as well. Finally, Irina responded.

"I disagreed with your decision, but I will always be your friend. Just as you have stood by me in difficult times, I'll stand by you. I'll be your second."

"There's another matter, Maître Durnais."

"My uncle's lawyer? What does he have to do with this?"

"Durnais is my lawyer as well, Irina. In the event of my death, Durnais has instructions to give you an envelope. It concerns the location of my Legacy. If anything happens to me, I want you to protect my Legacy."

"What is this legacy?"

"Legacy is a person. I never told you about her before, Irina, Legacy's in Japan. She's my daughter."

"Is Antonio the father?" asked a surprised Irina.

"No, he always calls Legacy 'our daughter,' but he's not the father. You remember how I lost my eye.".

"You were training with the Iga ninjas. The rival Koga clan raided the Iga village. You were attacked by an assassin that they imported from China."

"After he defeated me in combat, he raped me. When I discovered my pregnancy, I wanted Antonio to perform an abortion. He refused. Antonio convinced me that I carried an innocent who shouldn't be made to suffer for her father's crime."

The next morning, Gurn reported at the perfumery's firing range for his daily session with Marga. Instead, Gurn was greeted by Sabine Malbodius.

"Marga isn't here. She's refraining from gunplay for an entire day. It's part of a family ritual."

"I've heard of the traditions of the Von Schulenberg family. They generally rest the day before a duel. Is Marga going to fight a duel?"

"Yes."

"Let me guess. It's with Blythe Furnace."

"You're very astute."

"You must be one of her seconds. You have the means to guarantee Marga's victory."

Although Madame Koluchy, Gurn's secret employer, desired Marga's destruction, he harbored no animosity against the Hungarian sharpshooter. Blythe Furnace was another matter. Gurn held her responsible for his beloved wife's death.

"Explain," demanded Sabine.

"There are fake bullets developed by Leeman Bailey."

"Marga's supply is almost exhausted. There's only one of those phony bullets left."

"One is sufficient. You can arrange for this bullet to be in Furnace's gun."

"But I load Marga's gun."

"Marga and Blythe were once friends. The Von Schulenbergs have a tradition of exchanging weapons with enemies considered to be worthy opponents. The two combatants will trade firearms. By placing the bullet in Marga's gun, you will really be loading Blythe's."

"I will consider your proposal, Dirk."

In the evening, Gurn was summoned by Marga to the Royal Palace Hotel. He wondered if Sabine told her about his suggestion. Marga's code of chivalry would cause her to be outraged. Suspicious of Marga's request for an audience, Gurn arrived with Colonel Moran's disguised air-gun.

He was received by Marga in a golden nightgown.

"Like the matadors, I make love the night before a kill. It's a Von Schulenburg family tradition."

She dragged him into her bedroom.

Four hours later, Gurn left. He couldn't recall a more exhilarating evening in his life.

The duel was scheduled in the early morning at the Bois de Boulogne. The duelists with their respective seconds arrived in separate carriages. Some distant away secretly resided a third carriage in a wooded area. It had carried Gurn and Madame Koluchy to the scene. With binoculars, they spied on the combatants.

"How predictable!" concluded Catarina. "Marga chose the same spot where she disgraced my sister."

"My plan is foolproof," assured Gurn holding Moran's cane. "Madame, one of your enemies will surely die today."

As usual, Marga wore a holster, Today it was empty. Blythe was attired in her customary apparel with the addition of an empty holster strapped to her belt. Wearing a Cordobes hat and carrying an umbrella, Irina scrutinized Marga's seconds. Joséphine was displaying another fashionable green dress. Sabine was sporting the same blue coat that Irina had first seen in a Parisian warehouse

Joséphine glared at the former Bernice Fourneau with intense animosity. Their mutual hatred had been spawned in the Provencal boarding school run by Berenice's mother. The two females had resented each other since the summer of 1884. Joséphine had then been 16, and Berenice merely 12. Berenice and her family were visiting their cousins, the Cascabels, in Normandy. Madame Fourneau's aunt, the former Cornelia Vadarasse, was married to César Cascabel, the acclaimed circus acrobat. Since Berenice and her two brothers were quite a handful for a widow, Madame Fourneau had her favorite student, Joséphine, accompany them to Normandy. Joséphine was assigned the difficulty task of supervising the rebellious Berenice. One year later, Berenice had been sent away to Paris. More than a decade passed before the two antagonists re-encountered each other. By that time, Berenice had become the totally unrecognizable Milady Nevermore.

The Von Schulenburg pistols were presented in their case by Joséphine. Sabine loaded Marga's. Irina did likewise with Blythe's. Both female warriors placed their weapons in their holsters. They walked together to the center of the fields. Marga turned toward Blythe.

"We were once comrades, *compañera*. Will you honor that former camaraderie by participating in the Von Schulenberg Ritual."

"Let us exchange weapons," agreed Blythe.

As the two women traded pistols, Gurn wondered if Sabine had acted on his advice.

While Antonio Nikola counted to 20, the two adversaries walked that number of paces. Marga and Blythe faced one another. Blythe left hand rested on her cat's head amulet. Her right hand hung next to her holstered gun. Antonio gave the final instructions.

"When I count to three, you will draw and fire. One...Two...THREE!"

Marga pulled out her gun and fired.

Blythe's left hand raised the amulet of her necklace in front of her left eye. Marga's bullet crashed into the orichalcum metal. The bullet shattered from the impact.

At the Royal Palace Hotel, Marga had mentioned Joséphine's orders to inflict an ignominious death on Blythe. Later Irina had remembered Joséphine's vow to remove Blythe's sole remaining eye. Reasoning her left eye to be Marga's target, Blythe had blocked the shot.

Under the rules of dueling, Blythe was entitled to have a free shot at Marga. Aiming her pistol towards Marga, Blythe looked at Joséphine Balsamo.

"Countess Cagliostro, regardless of your misdeeds, I once treated you in a reprehensible manner. No human being should ever be wronged as I wronged you." Blythe raised her arm up toward the sky. "Consider this act an apology." Blythe fired harmlessly into the air.

"You failed, Gurn!" scolded Catarina. "You guaranteed that one of them will die!"

Gurn coolly attached a scope to the air-gun. He raised the weapon. Through the scope, he could see both Marga and Blythe.

"I only have one shot. Who shall die? Sandorf or Furnace?"

Even though Catarina despised Marga, her hatred was more intense for Blythe.

"Furnace!"

"I was hoping for that choice, Madame."

Gurn could see Blythe's large eye patch through the scope. Adjusting his aim, he fired. The bullet slammed into Blythe's patch. She fell forward to the ground. A shocked Irina ran toward her. Turning over Blythe, Irina screamed upon seeing the blood-drenched face of her best friend.

The carriage carrying Gurn and Koluchy quickly departed. Inside, Koluchy giggled with delight.

"Marga Sandorf will be very angry," forecasted Gurn. "She will guess my interference. It will be necessary for me to hide in the Western Hemisphere for a year or so. At the proper time, I will return to eliminate Raffles."

"It was the Pallid Mask who fired the air-gun," concluded Marga gripping her drinking cup. "Sabine warned me about his possible interference. Therefore, I diverted him the evening before the duel. He never noticed that I replaced his real bullet inside his air-gun with my remaining counterfeit projectile. As it turned out, it was a wise precaution. Even though the pellet was harmless, its impact did stun you. The false blood unnerved your seconds."

"They regained their composure after realizing I was unhurt," acknowledged Blythe holding a glass of milk in Marga's hotel suite. "Your decision saved my life."

"Considering you planned to spare my life, *compañera*, it was a prophetic action. We can never fully be friends again. Despite your gallant gesture, Countess Cagliostro will continue to loathe you and Irina Putine."

"Then let us be the best of enemies," proposed Blythe.

Clicking her cup against Blythe's, Marga made a toast: "Enemies Forever!"

Kingdom of the Blind

"A woman stands in a field of blood. Her face is vague, but she wears dark goggles. She generates an aura of death and destruction. Her hands hold a spear with a blade on both ends. The blood-splattered corpse of a mortal enemy rests at her feet."

The speaker was a statuesque woman wearing a silver turban and a scarlet tunic. She was a self-styled seer named Sylvia Pence. Seated at a table in a room lit only by candlelight, she held the hand of another woman.

Sylvia's blue eyes opened widely. "This battle should have been one of the greatest triumphs of the woman in the goggles ... but it shall be her destruction! An intruder has arrived to snatch the laurels of her victory."

"Describe this intruder," ordered the veiled woman.

"The invader is a woman. She wears a black patch over one of her eyes."

"Her right eye?"

"No, her left. She carries a small sword sheathed in a wooden staff. Drawing her blade, the one-eyed woman challenges the other to a duel to the death. The two combatants fight fiercely. The woman with the spear is no match for her one-eyed antagonist. The woman in the goggles is beheaded. The one-eyed woman holds her adversary's head in triumph. I can see no further into the future."

"Is there any way to change the grisly destiny of the woman in the goggles?"

"I have merely described the course of events based on their current trajectory, Mademoiselle Corbucci. If you warn the woman in the goggles, she can take precautions to ensure a different outcome."

"Thank you, Madame Pence."

The soothsayer's client rose from the table. Leaving a large amount of money, she left the seer's house.

Carolina Corbucci was nearing her thirtieth birthday in the early spring of 1898. Her family had long been prominent in European crime. Carolina's late father, Count Salvatore Corbucci, had led the Camorra in Naples. Her sister, Catarina, was married to Noel Moriarty, the leader of the Gentlemen of the Night, the dominant criminal gang in London. Both the Camorra and the Gentlemen of the Night were branches of the Black Coats, the international crime syndicate. With her husband's support, Catarina had transformed another Neapolitan secret society, the Brotherhood of the Seven Kings, into the Black Skirts, the female auxiliary of the Black Coats.

Some months ago, Catarina had purchased an abandoned theatre in Paris. Christening it the Agnes de la Fere Athletic Club, she converted the structure into an indoor circular amphitheatre. Her intention was to entertain her loyal followers with gladiatorial spectacles. Over a hundred members of the Black Skirts sat in the circular stands.

Residing on a throne in the front row seat was Carolina. She had spent several years in Texas. It amused her to dress up as a female gunslinger. Her black "cowgirl" ensemble consisted of a hat, shirt, pants and boots. A revolver was holstered in a belt around her waist. A yellow bandana was tied around her neck. Next to Carolina was an Eurasian girl wearing a kimono. She was six years old.

Seated near Carolina were Rochelle Moreau and Orianne Coyatier. Rochelle, an attractive woman with brown hair, was dressed in a black dress that seemed appropriate for mourning. She functioned as Catarina's chief of staff. Orianne, another member of the Black Skirts, was Rochelle's frequent collaborator. An athletic woman with red hair, Orianne wore a brown blouse with a black tie and skirt. This was the formal uniform of a member of the Black Skirts. Seated to the other side of Carolina were two women who were garbed in somewhat different uniforms. Their skirts were black, but their blouses were silver.

Another woman in a black skirt stood in the center of the arena's pit. She wore a red vest over a white blouse and bowtie. The waistcoat was tightly buttoned. Her right hand griped a cane whose handle was carved to resemble a snake's head. Her left hand carried a samurai sword. Her light brown hair was bound by a chignon at the nape of her neck.

"Ladies of the Black Skirts, I am your mistress of ceremonies, Ecstasy Parker. It's my honor to present our beloved Queen, the Blind Spinner."

Carolina led the audience in thunderous applause.

From a side doorway, Catarina Moriarty entered the amphitheater. The ruler of the Black Coats was five years older than her sister. Like Carolina, Catarina was a statuesque brunette. She was dressed in a purple leotard which covered her arms and legs. Her black boots stood on the deep layer of sand that covered the floor of the arena. Her dark hair was covered by a fur hat with a large white brim. The top of the hat had been dyed purple. Her eyes were covered by black goggles. Her hands held a staff with a long scimitar at each end.

"Fourteen years ago in Naples," proclaimed Ecstasy, "when we were still the Brotherhood of the Seven Kings, our gracious Queen recruited a man into our order. Deserting our society, that man fled to England. When our sovereign later moved to London, this apostate devoted his life to frustrating her designs. In December of last year, he led a squad of policemen in an assault on our liege's headquarters. A fire resulted during the raid. The treacherous dog believed that our Queen had burnt to a crisp, but she escaped. We all shall see how treason is punished. Our society has captured the traitor responsible for her flight from London."

Ecstasy drove the samurai sword into the sand. "Bring forth Norman Head."

Three men entered the pit. Two were burly men dressed in brown robes with a black sash tied around their waists. These were male members of the secret society led by Catarina Moriarty. While the former Brotherhood was reorganized to have women in the primary positions of power, men continued to do most of the menial tasks. These monk-like underlings were called the Black Sashes.

The muscular pair held a struggling captive whose arms were tied behind his back. A blindfold covered his eyes.

"Release the prisoner," ordered Catarina. The Black Sashes untied the captive's hands. As Ecstasy and the Black Sashes exited the pit, the captive removed the blindfold

"Are you surprised to see me?" asked Catarina.

"I thought the world was rid of you and your accursed Brotherhood, Madame Koluchy," replied Norman Head.

"The Brotherhood has evolved into the Black Skirts, Norman, and I have abandoned the alias of Madame Koluchy. I am now the Blind Spinner. Do you recognize the weapon in front of you?"

Norman pulled the samurai sword out of the ground. "I spent a few years in Japan before you reappeared in London. This is a fine blade. It's the work of Koutatsu of Shimosa Province."

"You know how to use such a weapon?"

"I was trained by a Japanese swordsman."

"Then I challenge you to a duel to the death."

"Even though you're a woman, I accept. You must be punished for your crimes."

Raising his sword, Norman rushed at her. Catarina easily dodged his blow before striking. A blade on her staff sliced through Norman's right shoulder. Still holding the Koutatsu blade, his amputated arm fell into the ground. The lifeless fingers maintained their grip on the weapon.

"YES!" screamed Ecstasy watching from the entrance to the pit. Her eyes gaped in. She was breathing heavily.

"Does she always act like this?" whispered one of the Black Sashes.

"You're new here," replied the other. "Every time blood is drawn, it's like she's overcome by lust."

Catarina severed Norman's other arm. Another slash of her staff cut off both his legs at the knees. The remnants of Norman's torso fell backward into the sand.

"KILL HIM!" screamed Ecstasy. The Black Skirts in the stand echoed Ecstasy's cries. "Kill him! Kill him!"

Catarina's staff sliced into Norman's neck. She grabbed the severed head by the hair and raised it triumphantly. The crowd exploded in applause.

Watching from the passageway, Ecstasy prepared to regain her composure to formally declare Catarina the victor. Another Black Sash arrived. The features of the newcomer were obscured by the raised hood of the monk-like robe. The Black Sash carried a wooden cane.

"What are you doing here?" asked Ecstasy. "Only two men are permitted to work with me."

The Black Sash responded by swiftly unsheathing a sword from the cane. Within a few seconds, the two Sashes were fatally stabbed. With another blow, the killer cut off the head of Ecstasy's cane. The attacker grabbed Ecstasy and pressed the blade against the announcer's throat.

"If you want to live, Black Skirt, you'll do as I say."

Shortly thereafter, Ecstasy entered the arena. She was followed by the other woman. The tip of her sword plodded Ecstasy to move forward. The interloper was no longer disguised as a Black Sash. Having removed her robe, she was revealed to be a Japanese woman wearing an eye-patch over her left eye. Dressed in black, she wore a sleeveless waistcoat over a honeycomb body stocking. The raised collar of her waistcoat extended outward like the wings of a bat.

"There will be a unscheduled bout," announced Ecstasy. "Queen Catarina has been challenged by Sumeru Yuki, a ninja of the Iga clan."

The one-eyed Yuki lowered her blade from Ecstasy's back. "Leave, you Black Skirt slut," ordered the ninja. The mistress of ceremonies quickly ran to the safety of the exit. With her left hand, Yuki picked the sword futilely used by deceased Norman Head.

"A Koutatsu blade. My own sword was made by his student, Senzo." Yuki gripped both swords defiantly. "Queen of the Black Skirts, you have lost your advantage of dual blades. You have abducted a child who was under my protection. Return her to me and I'll withdraw my challenge. What is your answer?"

Catarina laughed. "This is my answer."

Yuki screamed as a samurai sword pierced her back. The blade rammed through her body. The tip of the sword burst through the front of Yuki's tunic. Grabbing Yuki's shoulder, the assassin withdrew the sword from the ninja's body. Dropping her swords, Yuki collapsed. Lying on the ground, she beheld the image of her attacker in her right eye. The blade stained with Yuki's blood was held by a woman wearing a ninja-style outfit consisting of a dark tunic and pants. Emblazoned on the chest of the garment was a white circle with the face of a horned demon in the middle.

"Hannya ..." murmured the dying ninja. She looked in the direction of the Eurasian child. "Your mother will succeed where I have failed!" Shouted in Japanese, those were the last words of Sumeru Yuki of the Iga clan.

Ecstasy returned to the arena. "Ladies of the Black Skirts, we must not let this vandal spoil our victory celebration. She has been aptly punished for her arrogance. Let us applaud Her Majesty's execution of a despicable traitor. I declare the loser to be Norman Head."

Rising from their seats, the Black Skirts delivered a standing ovation to their leader. Catarina advanced towards Ecstasy. The announcer knelt in obeisance.

"Enjoying the taste of blood, Ecstasy?"

"Yes, my liege." Ecstasy lowered her head to the ground. She licked a pool of blood with her tongue.

In the stands, Carolina raised her pistol in the air. She fired six shots in celebration of her sister's victory.

Marga Sandorf belonged to the Order of the Serpent Heart, another branch of the Black Coat crime syndicate. Her height was 5 feet and 4 inches. Her gold tunic ended at her thighs. A black cape with a gold lining draped her shoulders. Black was also the color of her pants and boots. A black fur cap covered her raven lock. Her hair was cut short. The left side of her hair was draped behind her ear while the right side hung loosely against her face. Born in 1868, Marga was thirty years old

Her ancestors had been European soldiers. In 1864, her Hungarian father along with his Austrian brother-in-law, Baron Von Schulenberg, and the Baron's cousin, Colonel Skimmel, had joined an elite corps of European mercenaries supporting Maximilian's ill-fated attempt to reign as Emperor of Mexico. Colonel Skimmel perished in the fighting against Benito Juarez's followers in 1867. Skimmel had been survived by a wife and a one-year old daughter, Heidi. Settling in Texas, Baron Von Schulenberg provided sanctuary for Mrs. Skimmel and her child. In 1869, the Baron married the Colonel's widow. Their daughter, Sigi, was born in 1873. Following Maximilian's defeat, Marga's father, Aristide Sandorf, had remained in Mexico. Aristide and the Baron regularly corresponded and would even occasionally visit each other. Since their ages were only separated by two years, Heidi and Marga often played together as children.

During her career as an assassin in the Black Coats, Marga became friendly with Dr. Eric Malbodius, Noel Moriarty's trusted lieutenant. When Marga mentioned her two cousins living in Texas, Malbodius recruited them into the Black Coats. Nearly every subsidiary of the Black Coats had an office in the French capital, Noel appointed Malbodius the Satrap of Paris in order to coordinate the activities of all the various divisions of the criminal confederation in the city. Heidi and Sigi assumed the role of the Satrap's liaisons to the Black Skirts. The two half-sisters frequently visited Marga at Madame Sara's Perfumery, which served as a front for the Order of the Serpent Heart. Late last year, Dr. Malbodius had temporarily relinquished his duties in order to undertake an important mission in South America. His duties as Satrap had been assumed by his wife, the woman known as Frau Doctor.

Marga's cousins shared her penchant for militaristic apparel. Heidi Skimmel was dressed like a naval officer. Although her father had served in the infantry, her stepfather, the Baron, had served in the Austrian navy. Heidi wore a bright silver blouse and a black skirt. Her silver cap was decorated with black band with a metallic skull and crossbones in the center. Black gloves extended just below her elbows. A pouch was strapped to her belt. Marga's mother and Heidi's maternal grandfather had been Von Schulenbergs. The two distant cousins resembled each other.

Sigi Von Schulenberg was very different from her half-sister. While Heidi was the same height as Marga, Sigi was four inches taller. Heidi's hair was dark like Marga's, but Sigi's was red. Although she also wore a black skirt, Sigi's blouse was a lighter shade of silver and had two chest pockets. Gaudy epaulettes adorned her shoulders. A sliver knife rested in a sheath strapped to her belt. With the death of her father, she assumed the title of Baroness Von Schulenberg.

Also present was Senora Pilar Reloj, a former bandit from Mexico. She was dressed modestly in a white blouse and brown skirt. Her only display of ostentation was an embroidered vest. Subordinate to Marga in the Order of the Serpent Heart, Pilar always referred to her superior as the Comandante.

"I love your new uniforms," observed Marga. "What prompted Frau Doctor to have you wear them."

"Because of this," answered Sigi. She pulled out her knife and held it in the air.

"The silver blade of the Von Schulenbergs!" exclaimed Marga. "The talisman of the Holy Vehm!"

"Excuse me, Comandante, what is this Holy Vehm?" inquired Pilar.

"They were a secret society that administered justice in the Holy Roman Empire for centuries. A Von Schulenburg was one of the founding members."

"The Holy Vehm championed our cultural integrity," volunteered Heidi. "Their secret tribunals condemned violators of our Teutonic traditions to death."

"They sound like the Ku Klux Klan in the United States," said Pilar.

"More or less," replied Heidi.

"Did they execute their enemies with daggers?" asked Pilar.

"Not normally," replied the Baroness. "They generally used knives like this as a warning. However, my ancestor, Fritz Von Schulenberg, enjoyed to carve the letter 'A' in the stomachs of dissenters. The letter stood for *abschaum*, the German word for scum."

"I emulate our illustrious forebear by shooting my enemies in the belly," stated Marga.

"I prefer the Holy Vehm's more traditional means of execution," said Heidi. "It was hanging. When we lived in Texas, I always liked to see a good lynching."

"I'm confused," admitted Pilar. "What does the Holy Vehm have to do with Frau Doctor?"

"The Holy Vehm was abolished in 1811," explained Heidi."The High Council has accepted a proposal drafted by Frau Doctor. The Black Coats intend to revive the Holy Vehm. Sigi and I will be going to Germany to participate in this new enterprise. These are our uniforms for the resurrected Vehm. We will miss you, Marga."

"I assume Frau Doctor's husband will head this new branch of the Black Coats," said Marga.

"That is yet to be determined," declared the Baroness. "His South American assignment prevent him from assuming leadership of the Holy Vehm. There is speculation that the Vehm project may be entrusted to the Pallid Mask."

"He is a logical alternative," noted Pilar. "The Pallid Mask is familiar with Germany. He once impersonated the Archduke of Heisse-Weimar."

"Whoever our superior is, the German assignment will be a vast improvement on our current duties," predicted the Baroness. "Catarina Moriarty has delusions of grandeur, and her sister struts around in that ludicrous gunslinger outfit."

"Actually, I find Catarina and Carolina rather sweet," interjected Heidi. "It's that Hannya that I can't stand."

"Someone needs to put that Corsican upstart in her place," indicated Sigi.

Heidi giggled. "You forget that Marga already did that."

Marga was perplexed. "I know no Black Skirt named Hannya."

"Hannya is a *nom de guerre*," disclosed Heidi. "Her real name is Orianne Coyatier."

"The alleged granddaughter of the legendary Marchef? " said Marga. "She was insolent enough to assault a member of the Balsamo family. Her victim was Sabine Balsamo, the future Frau Doctor. As the vassal of the Balsamo clan, I was ordered to discipline Orianne."

"I remember now," said the Baroness. "You nearly suffocated her."

"Rochelle Moreau tried to keep Catarina unaware of Orianne's humiliation," added Heidi. "When Catarina learned of Orianne's defeat, she was furious."

"Was Orianne demoted?" asked Marga.

"No," said Heidi. "Somehow Orianne convinced Catarina to send her to Japan to be trained by Koga ninjas. Upon her return to Europe, that arrogant redhead instructed Catarina in the same fighting techniques. Orianne assumed the alias of Hannya, a demon from Japanese mythology. Tread carefully, Marga, Orianne may seek revenge."

Marga pulled back her cape revealing a holstered gun. "Even if Orianne has improved as a pugilist, she's no match for my golden pistol."

"Enough talk of that infernal Corsican!" interrupted the Baroness reaching into one of her shirt pockets. She took out a foldable metal cup and extended it. "Since the same blood flows in our veins, we all possess a Von Schulenberg drinking goblet. We must perform the family toast."

Marga pulled a similar collapsible cup out of her belt. Opening her pouch, Heidi pulled out an identical cup as well as a metal flask. Heidi poured the flask's contents into her cup and her half-sister's.

"I would offer you some of our wine, Marga, but you always drink milk."

"You're correct, Heidi. Pilar, please fetch the pitcher."

"Yes, Comandante." Pilar filled Marga's cup with milk.

"This may be our last family toast," said Heidi. "Sigi and I will be leaving for Germany in a few days."

"You're forgetting another Von Schulenberg tradition," asserted Marga. "When members of our family go on a vital mission, their kin always drink a toast with them immediately before their departure. It's my duty to take you to the train station."

"Then we shall perform another toast at the station," concluded Sigi Von Schulenburg raising her glass "As the reigning Baroness, it's my role to perform the toast. Let us remember the family motto. Purity of blood brings victory."

"Purity of blood brings victory," repeated Heidi and Marga. The women clinked their glasses together and drank.

After the Baroness and Heidi had departed, Pilar made an observation.

"You were visibly moved during the toast, Comandante."

"Yes, my younger cousin, the Baroness, has finally accepted me. While Heidi and I have always been close, I had previously detected a veiled hostility from her half-sister."

"Why should the Baroness resent you?"

"Possibly she viewed my blood as impure."

"But you're a Von Schulenberg!"

"On my mother's side. My father was a Magyar of Hungary."

"Didn't all the hostility between the Austrians and the Hungarians end with the creation of the Dual Monarchy decades ago?"

"For some people, Pilar, prejudice never dies."

"This torso was found in an alley not far from the Chupin Detective Agency," pronounced Chief Inspector Jacques Lefevre removing a sheet over human remains at the morgue. "As you can seem the head and limbs have been severed. On the chest is tattooed a purple diadem. Dr. Bertillon believes the tattoo was made after death."

"I recognize the symbol," admitted Blythe Furnace. The speaker was a slender woman whose short chestnut hair was cut short. It was combed backward to give the impression of a bird-like crest. A large eye patch covered her right eye. With the exception of white gloves, she was dressed entirely in black. Besides pants and boots, she was wearing a black coat with an Inverness cape. The coat was worn over a shirt and an ascot tie. A chained necklace with an amulet bearing the image of a cat's head completed her ensemble.

Blythe was an operative of the Chupin Detective Agency. Together with her associate, Irina Putine, Blythe was conferring in the morgue with Lefevre. Irina wore a orange dress with a black tie. In contrast to Blythe's white gloves, Irina's were black. A Cordobes hat covered her black hair. A pentagram broach adorned the right side of her dress. Her right hand held an umbrella with a unicorn's head on the handle.

"The tattoo is the Purple Crown of the Blind Spinner. It is based on a occult legend. The Blind Spinner was Vathelos, a warrior queen of Atlantis. She established seven Atlantean colonies across the globe. Vathelos appointed satraps to rule these outposts. With her death, the satraps became independent kings. The Neapolitan secret society, the Brotherhood of the Seven Kings, derives its name from this ancient legend."

"Why was Vathelos called the Blind Spinner?" asked Lefevre.

"Born sightless, Vathelos spun elaborate plots to trick her opponents into fighting battles on her terms," responded Blythe. "A veritable Amazon, she was formidable in combat. Like Commodus, the Roman Emperor, she even personally participated in gladiatorial duels in an arena."

"The legend is ridiculous," argued Lefevre. "I've heard of blind swordsmen reliant on their sense of hearing, but a blind gladiator would be unable to hear due to the bloodthirsty roars of the crowd."

"Vathelos supposedly had a magical talisman to overcome her blindness." Blythe paused. "This mythological discussion is a diversion. We need to verify the identity of the victim."

"You are correct, my friend," said Irina. "I fear that the dead man is Norman Head, the man responsible for foiling the Brotherhood of the Seven Kings in England. My friend, Anna Beringer, telegraphed me from London that Monsieur Head had disappeared."

"Can you think of any reason why the killers would leave the body so close to your Agency?" queried Lefevre.

"I've always suspected that the Brotherhood was behind the Bluebeard III murders," answered Irina. "When I solved that case, I earned the Brotherhood's enmity. That mutilated corpse was intended as a warning."

Inside the Agnes de la Fere Athletic Club, a storage room had been converted into a target range. Here Carolina Corbucci practiced her marksmanship on life-size dummies. The human replicas hung from ropes tied around their necks.

Carolina was reloading her pistol when she was joined by Ecstasy Parker.

"I want to discuss the next competition, your Ladyship," informed Ecstasy. Although the mistress of ceremonies had spoken impeccable French in the arena, she addressed Carolina in English. When Ecstasy used her native tongue, she had a distinct cockney accent. "I've always dreaded that a gatecrasher might upset the apple cart. Blimey! That Japanese blighter could easily have sent me packing in a coffin."

"You have a new cane."

"It was made by my sweetheart, Lenny Wolfe. He's an engineer in the Gentlemen of the Night. Lenny's here in Paris conducting some business for our

Queen's consort. He gave me this as a present. The cane's identical to my old one except it's has a useful feature. You notice how the bottom is shaped like a barrel. Then there's the head. See the fangs inside the snake's mouth. They're really triggers." Ecstasy pointed her cane in the direction of one of the dummy. Her fingers gripped the upper portion of the mouth of the snake. "When I press the fangs..."

A slender dagger shot out of the cane. Its steel blade pierced the chest of the dummy.

"Very ingenious." noted Carolina. "An air-gun that shoots a dagger."

"The dagger's handle is made of aluminium in order for it to be light. It may prove useful if there is any further unpleasantness. I have a favor to ask your Ladyship. Sometimes members from the other branches of the Black Coats are allowed in the audience. Can Lenny be my guest the next time the Queen executes a traitor?"

"Of course, Ecstasy. Consider it a reward for introducing me to Sylvia Pence."

"Sylvia's a class act. We worked together at the Grayson Music Hall in London. She performed a mindreading act in those days, and I was her assistant. I tried to recruit her into the Black Skirts, but Sylvia prefers to work solo."

"You realize that I deliberately mislead Lefevre," said Irina to Blythe as they rode back to the Chupin Detective Agency in a private coach.

"Of course," confirmed Blythe. "Like myself, Norman Head was a former subordinate of Catarina Moriarty. The warning was directed at me."

"There was no reason to inform the Chief Inspector of your criminal past. I got the impression that you held something back concerning the legend of Queen Vathelos."

"Your instincts are correct, Irina. Vathelos supposedly manufactured a mystical lens which allowed her to see. It was attached to the visor of her helmet during combat."

"And your reason for not telling Lefevre?"

"It's a sensitive matter." Blythe touched her eye patch. "When I lost my right eye, Antonio Nikola had hopes of finding the Helmet of Vathelos to create a monocle to restore my sight. According to legend, the Helmet was buried with Vathelos. Her tomb is somewhere in the Hoggar Mountains. The crown symbol of Vathelos may have been used to mock me by someone in the Black Coats who resents my romantic relationship with Antonio."

"Catarina and Antonio were once betrothed."

"In fact, it was her affair with Norman Head that caused Antonio to break the engagement. Scotland Yard never recovered Catarina's body after the fire. I fear that she still lives."

Blythe recalled the details of Catarina's supposed death. Norman Head and the police had cornered the female mastermind in her laboratory. Superintendent

Ford of Scotland Yard had leaped at Catarina. She touched a switch to release a monstrous flame that fatally burnt Ford. Blinded by the flame that seared into their eyeballs, Head and his allies fled the house. After the fire was extinguished, Ford's remains was found but not Catarina's. It was assumed that she had been completely incinerated.

The next day, the Chupin Detective Agency received a second message from Chief Inspector Lefevre. Another corpse had been found in an alleyway close to the Agency. Since Irina Putine was in the midst of discussing another case with other members of the investigative bureau, Blythe Furnace arrived at the site cordoned off from the public by the authorities. She was greeted by Lefevre.

"The body resides in that barrel over there," informed the Chief Inspector.

"That's not a barrel. It's a Japanese coffin. Caskets are circular in Japan."

"This note was attached to the lid of the coffin." Lefevre handed the paper to Blythe.

It contained a single sentence: 'She failed to protect her friend's Legacy.' The message was signed with the purple crown symbol plus the face of a horned demon.

"Mademoiselle Furnace, are you alright?"

"No, I need to see the body ..."

Lefevre escorted Blythe to the coffin. Blythe gasped upon viewing the corpse inside.

"Yuki ..."

"If you need time to compose yourself..." began Lefevre.

"The victim's name is Sumeru Yuki. I met her in Japan, Inspector. Please permit me to return to the Agency. I promise to come to your office today to give you the full story."

"I haven't forgotten your valuable assistance in solving the 'M' crimes. You have my permission, but can you at least tell me the significance of this satanic face next to the crown of Vathelos."

"It's Hannya, a female demon from Japanese mythology. She's known for devouring children."

"Legacy is Blythe's daughter," explained Irina. "she was born six years ago in Japan."

Irina was addressing her uncle, Victor Chupin, the director of the Chupin Detective Agency.

"Is Dr. Nikola the father?" asked Victor.

"No. When Blythe was studying with the Iga ninjas, their secret village was attacked by the rival Koga clan. The Koga ninjas were assisted by a Chinese assassin, the White Priest. This brute delights in wounding women by plucking out their eyes. He then rapes and kills them. He captured both Blythe and Yuki. After maiming them, the White Priest violated Blythe. He was about to kill her when Nikola fortuitously arrived. After driving off the White Priest, Antonio attended to Blythe's and Yuki's wounds. Legacy was born nine months later. Blythe had difficulty accepting Legacy as her child. She left her in Yuki's care before leaving Japan with Nikola. Blythe hasn't seen Legacy since she was an infant."

"The Black Skirts must have Legacy. What strategy do you propose to rescue her?"

"Blythe and I intend to take the police fully into our confidence."

"But Blythe will have to reveal her criminal background to the authorities. That will compromise you as well. Lefevre is totally ignorant of your true origins."

"I'm prepared to make that sacrifice."

Arriving at police headquarters, Irina and Blythe conferred with Lefevre in his private office.

"We have a confession to make, Inspector," declared Irina. Both of us have withheld our real identities from you."

"Yes, I know. You are really Irene Chupin and Berenice Fourneau."

Both female detectives were stunned.

"Permit me to explain, Mademoiselle Putine," continued Lefevre. "You unmasked Bluebeard III as the former perpetrator of the College Girl Murders in Avignon. Under your real name, you had been hospitalized at the Countess Yalta Memorial Hospital during those earlier crimes. My wife saw you there during your recovery. When the press lionized you for ending the Bluebeard III killings, my wife recognized your photograph in the newspapers."

"Why was your wife at the Countess Yalta Memorial Hospital in 1890?" asked Irina.

"She was visiting her brother. He works there."

"That doesn't explain how you know my real name." said Blythe.

"Soon after the Bluebeard III case, Mademoiselle Putine reported the murder of an Englishwoman named Purity Parker. She informed us that Parker was murdered because she possessed information concerning the whereabouts of Berenice Fourneau, a woman who had vanished in the aftermath of the College Girl Murders. Shortly thereafter, you appeared in Paris as Mademoiselle Putine's assistant. You bear the same initials as Berenice Fourneau. Furthermore, Furnace is the English translation of Fourneau."

"Have you inform your Sûreté colleagues of your deductions?" asked Blythe.

"They remain in ignorance. My wife persuaded me to respect your secrets."

The two operatives of the Chupin Detective Agency proceeded to share all their information regarding Yuki's death.

The next morning, a personal advertisement appeared in the morning edition of *L'Epoque*:

Compañera, we need to drink together at the usual place. I will be there after the stroke of six. Come when convenient.

That evening, Marga Sandorf arrived at the Royal Palace Hotel. There was a room there that she jointly rented with another woman. Neither of them regularly lodged there, but they maintained it as a secret meeting place. When Marga opened the door, she was greeted by Blythe Furnace.

"I need your help, old friend," stated Blythe.

"We were allies once, *compañera*," noted Marga, "but now we are on opposite sides."

"All I ask of you is information."

"I won't reveal any secrets of the Black Coats. I'm no traitor."

"Quite true, but you are a just woman. You do not war on children."

"Children?"

"Legacy has been abducted by Catarina Moriarty."

"But Legacy was in Japan under the protection of your friend, Sumeru Yuki."

"Yuki is dead."

"The newspapers reported the discovery of a murdered Japanese woman? Was that Yuki?"

"Yes."

"How could Catarina have found out about your daughter? You kept Legacy's existence a closely guarded secret. The only two people who knew of her existence in the Black Coats were Antonio and myself."

"It was Catarina who originally dispatched me to Japan to be trained by the Iga ninjas. She must have sent someone to Japan to investigate my past."

"I've always been confused by these ninja clans, *compañera*. What is the relationship between the Iga and the Koga ninjas?"

"The clans are deadly rivals, It was the Kogas who attacked the Iga village when I was violated. Why are you asking me about them?"

"Recently Catarina sent one of her Black Skirts to Japan to be tutored by the Koga clan."

"Everything begins to make sense. The Koga clan is constantly spying on their Iga rivals. The Kogas knew the circumstances of my rape. They must have learned that a Eurasian child was being reared by Yuki. It wouldn't be difficult for them to conclude that the child was mine."

"The Kogas must have imparted that information to Catarina's operative. You must know this Black Skirt. Her name is Orianne Coyatier."

"She was one of my subordinates when I was Catarina's chief of staff."

"Orianne has risen to a high position in the Black Skirts. She's now Catarina's personal combat instructor. I may have been indirectly responsible for that she-devil's recent good fortunes. Her decision to study in Japan seems to have originated from a sound thrashing that I gave her."

"You called Orianne a 'she-devil.' Any particular reason for using that term?"

"She's adopted an alias from Japanese demonology. Orianne calls herself Hannya."

"A note bearing the likeness of the legendary demon was pinned to Yuki's body."

"Then you have ample reason to seek out Orianne. You have tested the boundaries of my loyalty to the Black Coats. There is no more that I can tell you, *compañera*."

"The Black Skirts used to have their Paris headquarters at the fashion shop, the Regenerator of Fashion. They have since moved their base elsewhere. Do you know where?"

"I don't. Even if I knew, I would be honor bound to keep it secret. It's a pity that I can't help you further in your quest for retribution. I have no love for either Catarina or Orianne."

"Your information about Hannya was still helpful. All that remains is for us to drink our toast." Blythe advanced towards a pitcher of milk residing near a glass on a table. Removing the collapsible drinking cup from her belt, Marga extended it. After pouring milk into Marga's cup, Blythe filled her own glass.

"Enemies forever!" said Blythe.

Marga echoed Furnace's toast. After clicking their glasses together, the two women drank as they stood next to an open window.

From a different hotel across the street, Heidi Skimmel and Sigi Von Schulenberg had been watching the conversation between Marga and Blythe through binoculars.

"You have seen the evidence for yourself, Heidi. Our half-breed cousin is a traitor."

"We can't be sure, Sigi. We couldn't hear what was said."

"Don't be a fool, sister. They acted like old friends."

"But Marga tried to kill Furnace in a duel!"

"Madame Moriarty told us the details of that duel. Blythe blocked Marga's shot and then fired in the air. The duel must have been cleverly staged between them. You know what we must do!"

"Marga is our cousin!"

"That only makes her treason more reprehensible," argued Sigi.

The next day, Sigi conferred with Catarina Moriarty at the Agnes de la Fere Athletic Club. Wearing a purple robe, the Black Skirt leader still wore her black goggles.

"As you predicted, Catarina, Furnace contacted Marga. How did you know they would meet at the Royal Palace Hotel?"

"The Pallid Mask had told me that Marga challenged Furnace there to fight their duel last year. Marga and Furnace have an unusual bond. They saved each other's lives in the Brazilian jungle before Furnace's defection to the Chupin Detective Agency. A clerk at the Hotel was bribed to tell us if either of them rented a joint room there. I was pleasantly surprised that they maintained a joint apartment there."

"Why not inform Marga's superiors of this apartment. Surely the Order of the Serpent Heart would punish her for disloyalty."

"Both Madame Sara and Josephine Balsamo value Marga too highly, Baroness. Your cousin would easily bamboozle them with some talk that she and Furnace are honorable adversaries like Saladin and Richard the Lionhearted."

"I understand, Madame. My half-sister could easily swallow such a story. Heidi is reluctant to *cut the branch*." Sigi was using underworld parlance for executing a fellow member of the Black Coats.

"Don't worry, Sigi. My own sister is cultivating Heidi. Carolina will persuade your sibling to be your accomplice in Marga's removal. Everything should be ready in two days. Don't send the invitation for Marga to meet you here until we're sure that Furnace has swallowed our bait."

"I don't understand Furnace's role in Marga's assassination, Madame."

"I have valid reasons for hating both Furnace and your cousin. As Milady Nevermore, Furnace was my trusted aide until her defection. Marga humiliated my sister. Last year, I tried to manipulate them into fighting each other to the death. That plan failed."

"Yes, I know. I told Heidi a false version of their duel."

"Now, I have decided to eliminate Furnace personally to prove to my subjects that no one betrays me with immunity. An opportunity also presents itself to exterminate Marga. Since she is a fellow member of the Black Coats, your cousin must be eradicated with a certain finesse. A scapegoat must be found to *pay the law*. Blythe Furnace must appear to be Marga's killer."

"This is where Furnace's pistol plays an important role."

"Exactly, Baroness. Her weapon is rather unusual. It was a gift from Ace Sartana, the American bounty hunter. The gun's bullets are a unique caliber. Once Marga is killed, her corpse will be presented to the Balsamo family. They will be told that Furnace accused Marga of revealing Legacy's existence and then shot her in a duel witnessed by her two loving cousins. Madame Sara will want to perform an autopsy. It will confirm that the bullets came from Furnace's pistol. You remember my instructions concerning them?"

"All four bullets will be shot into my mongrel cousin's stomach. I have a small request, Madame."

"What is it?"

Sigi pulled out her knife. "Let me carve the letter 'A' into Marga's belly. It is the more traditional method for killing Magyar scum in the Von Schulenberg family. I'm confident that the bullets would eliminate all evidence of Marga's true demise."

"Your request is aptly poetic, but it must be refused. I can't risk Madame Sara discovering the truth, Baroness."

"Are you confident that Furnace's gun will be delivered into my hands?"

"Leave that to Hannya and Rochelle Moreau."

"That duo is extremely effective, but their assistant worries me. She has proven unreliable in the past."

"This time she will not bungle her assignment. She's too deathly afraid of Hannya to be intimidated by the ladies of the Chupin Detective Agency. Did you pass all that false information to Marga?"

"Yes. Marga falsely believes that both my sister and I have grown to hate Orianne Coyatier since her elevation as Hannya."

"Excellent. Marga doesn't suspect that Hannya is really a respected colleague of both you and Heidi."

"Hannya is indeed very formidable. What drives her?"

"Shame and love. The shame of being trounced by another woman prompted her to become a lethal warrior. Her unrequited love for a man is her other major motivation."

"Whom does she love?"

"The Pallid Mask. Years ago, she and the Mask had an affair. The Pallid Mask had two great loves. He was engaged to La Bouchère, an athletic assassin. A vigilante drowned her before they could be married. Later he wedded a confidence trickster known as Maude, but she was slain by Furnace. It was Maude who stole the Pallid Mask away from Hannya. The Mask was then attracted by Maude's superior skills. Since Maude's demise, Hannya has vastly improved. I consider her my most versatile agent."

"You must intend to exploit Hannya's passionate desire to your advantage, Madame,"

"It was my father, Count Corbucci, who first realized the great potential in the Pallid Mask. Since that time, my family has sought to make him our pawn. Maude was a member of the Black Skirts. During their brief union, I was able to control the Mask through her. After her death, the Pallid Mask has pursued his own destiny."

"Will Hannya will be able to bring him back into the fold?"

"I have sought a replacement to seduce the Pallid Mask. Hannya is the perfect choice. She now combines La Bouchère 's physical prowess with Maude's cunning. Once Furnace is dead, I intend to have her corpse stuffed. Orianne Coyatier is an expert taxidermist. The body will then be delivered to the Pallid Mask by the woman whom I have chosen to be his bride."

"Furnace's carcass could be Hannya's passport to the realization of all her desires."

"Just as Marga's corpse will perform the same function for you, Baroness." Catarina gently stroked the back of Sigi's neck as she leaned forward to whisper into the redhead's ear. "I have spoken to my husband. If I recommend it, you will be made the supreme ruler of the revived Holy Vehm. Within a year, your new position will inevitably lead to a seat on the High Council."

Carolina Corbucci and Heidi Skimmel were in the gunnery range at the Agnes de la Fere Athletic Club. Heidi opened a locked case which kept weapons exclusively used by her half-sister and herself. The case contained two Borchardt C.93 pistols and a Nagant M1895 revolver. The two women took turns firing at the dummies dangling from nooses. Heidi used one of the Borchardt pistols while Carolina was armed with a Colt M1892.

"I enjoyed reading your father's novel, *The Man from Minnesota*, in the original Italian edition," said Heidi. "The English version cut out the closing scene where the hero shot out the lenses of the eyeglasses."

"Your idea to have these effigies hang from the roof was very efficient," noted Carolina.

"When I was a little girl, I was thrilled by the tales of the Holy Vehm slaying outlaws. I used to take dolls and hang them from tree branches. As I grew up in Texas, I never missed a chance to witness a public execution. I've always been captivated by the gallows."

"For a woman who understands the necessity of the scaffold, Heidi, you are unexpectedly squeamish about punishing your disloyal cousin."

"Why do we have to kill her? Can't we just maim her? I have a plan. When she comes to take Sigi and me to the train station, I will ask Marga to lend me her golden gun. I will claim that I need to photograph it in order to make a silver duplicate to match my uniform. While I'm taking pictures, Sigi will ask Marga to participate in a round of target practice. My sister will give Marga this Nagant revolver. It's been sabotaged to explode. Once Marga fires, her left hand will be horribly injured. She'll never handle a gun again."

"A very quaint notion, Heidi. I can't endorse your proposal, but I shall incorporate portions of it into Catarina's plan. You will depart with Marga's pistol. Blythe's gun will be delivered to you outside. Upon your return, you will hand it to Sigi. Your sister will then *cut the branch*."

"Won't you reconsider? Why must you side with Sigi?"

"I understand your feelings. It's not easy being the junior sister."

"I'm Sigi's senior by seven years."

"But you are removed from the line of succession to the Von Schulenberg barony. Your are Sigi's junior in authority while I am Carolina's junior in both age and authority. You must trust Sigi's judgment as I trust Catarina's. Marga has not only betrayed the Black Coats, but she has affronted the Corbucci family. By rightfully executing your cousin, the future of your family will be assured. The Schulenbergs will be as powerful as the Corbuccis and the Moriartys."

Carolina extended her right hand. It bore a ring in the shape of a coiled snake.

"Will there be daylight?" asked Carolina.

"It will be daylight from midnight to noon if it's the will of the Mother," answered Heidi. She kissed Carolina's ring.

The next morning, a slender brunette arrived at the Chupin Detective Agency. Dressed in a Black Skirt uniform, she asked to see Irina Putine. A receptionist escorted her to Irina's private office. Blythe Furnace was also there.

Once the secretary departed, Blythe grabbed the visitor's right arm and twisted it behind her back.

"You have nerve, Black Skirt, coming here," snarled Blythe.

"Don't hurt me," pleaded the Black Skirt. "I'm just a messenger."

"Release her, Blythe," interjected Irina. "I recognize her. She's Mary Holder."

Blythe relinquished her hold on the Black Skirt.

"Mary Holder?" said Blythe. "Ah, I remember now. You're the discarded mistress of Sir George Burnwell. You have some value as a petty thief."

Mary rubbed her arm. "You remember me from when you were Madame Moriarty's chief of staff."

"Actually you were beneath my notice," claimed Blythe. "Irina told me about you. She needed to find an innocuous Black Skirt to impersonate. You're not much of a fighter. Irina easily chloroformed you at the *Old Fellow* in London."

"She had help," noted Mary. "There was that Beringer woman."

"I doubt that Anna's contribution was significant," stated Blythe. "You're just a minor functionary in the Black Skirts --- a disposable pawn easily sacrificed."

"Enough petty bickering, Blythe," said Irina. "You have a message for me, Mary."

"It's actually for both of you," admitted Mary. "Orianne Coyatier requests a meeting. I'll take you to her."

Mary and the two detectives hailed a cab. The Black Skirt told the driver to transport them to the Restaurant Imperial. When the carriage arrived at the destination, the women alighted and entered the dining establishment. They found Orianne Coyatier awaiting them. Dressed in her Black Skirt uniform, the redhead sat at a table. Next to her was a bottle and four glasses. Mary immediately sat to the right side of Orianne.

"Please be seated, ladies," said Orianne. "I took the liberty of ordering the best La Frenaie wine. I chose a public place in order for none of us to be tempted into committing an indiscretion."

As Orianne poured the wine, Irina and Blythe took their places. Irina grabbed the glasses swapped the glasses closest to her and Blythe with those next to Orianne and Mary.

"You think that I'm trying to poison you, Irina," observed Orianne. "Don't you trust me? Have you forgotten how we were students together at the Fourneau College."

"It's because I remember those days that I don't trust you," claimed Irina.

"And you, Milady Nevermore," said Orianne. "It's difficult thinking of you as Blythe Furnace. Your resignation from our association was regrettable, but it did provide an opportunity of advancement for our mutual friend, Rochelle Moreau. She really wished to be here, but her duties as chief of staff give her little time for socializing."

After sipping her wine, Blythe responded. "You can dispense with the hypocritical pleasantries, Hannya."

Orianne angrily grabbed Mary's wrist. "She called me Hannya! You little fool! What have you been telling them about me! Must I punish you again. "

Blythe lied to protect Marga Sandorf. "Your stooge revealed nothing. The image of Hannya was prominently displayed on the note found with Sumeru Yuki. Clearly Catarina now has a lieutenant who uses that name. I merely took a guess. Your reaction has confirmed my suspicion."

Releasing Mary's wrist, Orianne smiled. "Your very bold, Blythe. Your Japanese friend was similarly headstrong. Madame Moriarty sent me to Japan to study under the Koga ninjas. It wasn't difficult to discover your little secret. One day when Yuki was away on an errand, I removed your Legacy from the Iga village. Picking up my trail, Yuki followed me to France. She wanted to erase her failure to protect your daughter. Yuki should have contacted you, but her pride compelled a solo rescue effort. Her foolhardiness prove to be her undoing."

"As your overconfidence will lead to your own Waterloo," concluded Blythe. "So you're a Koga ninja now. Let us test our skills against each other."

"Nothing will give me greater pleasure," professed Orianne, "but that exhilarating experience is reserved for my mistress, Madame Moriarty. Only two people have successfully revolted against her authority. One was an Englishman. He has been punished. That leaves you. My mistress emulates the Blind Spinner of Atlantis by engaging in gladiatorial contests with her adversaries."

"Is Catarina challenging Blythe to a duel?" asked Irina.

"Of course," acknowledged Orianne. "The prize will be Legacy. It's my liege's intention to publicly defeat Blythe in front of the Black Skirts whom she so wantonly betrayed."

"I didn't betray the Black Skirts, Hannya," objected Blythe. "Catarina manipulated me into an untenable position. She couldn't stomach that I had won the affection of Antonio Nikola."

"When you meet her, Madame Moriarty will prove that Dr. Nikola values her favors more than yours," predicted Orianne.

"Do you really expect Blythe to foolishly stroll into Catarina's trap?" questioned Irina.

"If Blythe is suspicious about Madame Moriarty's sincerity, she will be permitted to carry a firearm to the rendezvous. However, she will be required to relinquish it before entering the arena."

"How does Catarina intend to fight this duel?" asked Blythe.

"Madame Moriarty will be armed with a two-bladed spear," revealed Orianne. "You'll be permitted to bring an equivalent weapon into the arena."

"Would a samurai sword be permissible?" said Blythe.

"Yes," conceded Orianne.

"Then I accept your challenge."

"No!" protested Irina.

"Don't interfere, Irina," admonished Blythe.

"Excellent!" said Orianne. "You will return here alone tomorrow at noon, Blythe. Mary will be waiting for you. She'll escort you to the location of the arena. Now Mary and I shall take our leave. If you value your Legacy's safety, you won't try to follow us."

"One final matter, Hannya," interposed Blythe. "Once I'm finished with Catarina, you and I will have a reckoning."

Orianne laughed. "You'll never get that chance."

At Madame Sara's beauty shop, Marga Sandorf received a message from her cousins. They would be leaving by train for Germany tomorrow. In the morning, Marga should pick them up at the Agnes de la Fere Athletic Club. Marga had never heard of this establishment before.

"Two woman grapple in an arena," said Sylvia Pence in her private chambers. "Their figures are obscure. One wears goggles. The other wears a necklace with an amulet in the shape of a cat's head. The combatants taunt each other. The woman in the goggles argues that her adversary is unworthy to wear the necklace. The wearer of the necklace sprouts hatred as she proclaims her enemy to be the obstacle to her union with the man she loves. The woman with the goggles impales the woman with the necklace on a spear.

"Another woman approaches. Her back is towards me, but I recognize her voice. It is my friend, Ecstasy Parker. She proclaims the loser of the match to be Blythe Furnace. She then drops to her knees in front of the victor. The woman in the goggles asks Ecstasy if she enjoys the taste of blood. Esctasy's face touches the blood-soaked sand.

"You are watching this from a throne. Next to you is a shorter woman. She is dressed in a silver tunic and a black skirt. A cap bearing a skull insignia covers her dark hair. She informs you that her cousin is dead.

"Gunshots reverberate in the stands. The source is you, Carolina Corbucci. You are firing a revolver in response to the victory of the woman in the goggles."

Carolina was pleased. She always shot into the air when her sister was triumphant.

"Can this future be changed?" asked Carolina.

"That depends on you. If you don't alter your plans, this destiny is etched in stone."

Carolina saw no need to change the scheme that she had engineered with her sister. The deaths of Blythe Furnace and Marga Sandorf were assured.

"This is the second time that you're foolishly engaging in a duel orchestrated by the Black Coats," said Irina at the Chupin Detective Agency.

"I owe it to my daughter," replied Blythe as she polished a samurai blade.

"You haven't seen your daughter since her infancy. Does she even know what you look like? Even if you rescue this child, she could be an impostor manufactured by Catarina Moriarty. "

"When I left Legacy in the Iga village, I asked Yuki to instruct my child in the secret identification ritual of our ninja clan. Legacy will expect me to prompt her with the sacred words of Tarao Hanzo. If the girl knows the proper response, then she is truly my child."

"I could follow you and Mary to the site of this arena. It would be simple to contact Inspector Lefevre and have the police raid it."

"I won't put my daughter's life at risk, Irina. I selfishly abandoned Legacy after her birth. It's now time to make amends. Promise me that no one in the Chupin Detective Agency will follow me."

"I promise. Considering the odds are overwhelming against your survival, you'll need to exploit the traditional weakness of the Black Coats. Their schemes are often undermined by their internal feuds. Hannya's behavior inadvertently revealed a weak link in Catarina Moriarty's organization yesterday."

"You're talking about Mary Holder."

"There was intense fear in Mary's eyes when she sat next to that bullying redhead. Hannya's threatening words indicate that she regularly beats Mary. You must entice Mary into betraying Hannya."

While Irina conferred with Blythe, Victor Chupin was secretly meeting with Chief Inspector Lefevre.

"Irina anticipates that Blythe will insist that no one in the Agency follow her tomorrow when she meets Mary Holder at the restaurant," divulged Victor.

"You want the police to substitute for the Agency," concluded Lefevre,

"Precisely. Trailing Blythe Furnace will lead you to the killers of Norman Head and Sumeru Yuki."

"I'll give this assignment to my best man, Justin Ganimard."

At 11 o'clock in the morning, Marga Sandorf arrived at the Agnes de la Fere Athletic Club. She was met by Sigi and Heidi.

"There's been a change of plans," explained Sigi. "Frau Doctor wants us to stay in France for another week. Since you're here, we might as well show you around."

"What is this place?"

"It's the new headquarters of the Black Skirts."

An hour later, Justin Ganimard was seated at a table in the Restaurant Imperial. Mary Holder was waiting inside. It had been easy for Ganimard to identify her because she wore her Black Skirt uniform.

Entering the establishment, Blythe Furnace carried a long box containing her samurai sword. She approached Mary. Two other women in elegant clothes went into the lavatory. One of them was carrying a shopping bag.

"We need to talk in private," said Mary. "Follow me."

Mary led Blythe into the lavatory. There didn't seem to be anyone else inside. Mary whistled. Two lavatory stalls opened revealing the women who had previously entered. They had changed their clothes. One woman was dressed like Blythe Furnace. Wearing a wig to duplicate Blythe's unique hairstyle, the woman also wore an eye patch. Her companion was dressed in a Black Skirt uniform.

"You have a distinct habit of always dressing the same clothes," said the false Blythe. "I noticed that when you were known as Milady Nevermore. You still wear the same coat."

"You always were an expert mimic, Helen," replied Blythe. She had recognized her double as Helen Lipsius, one of her former subordinates in the Black Skirts. "Who's your friend?"

"I'm called Cesarine Caoutchouc," answered the other woman. "Perhaps you heard of me?"

"A former associate of Colonel Clay. You look enough like Mary to pass for her from a distance. This really isn't necessary. No one from the Chupin Detective Agency is following me."

"But the police are," revealed Helen. "I spotted Inspector Ganimard outside. You shall leave ten minutes after Cesarine and I depart. Mary, remember Hannya will punish you if you don't arrive on time."

Vacating the lavatory, Helen and Cesarine proceeded to lead Ganimard on a wild goose chase across Paris.

"How often does Hannya punish you, Mary?" said Blythe.

"Spare me your questions," retorted Mary.

"The Black Coats treat you like a slave. I can change all that."

"No one escapes the Black Coats."

"I did. Irina Putine offered me sanctuary at the Chupin Detective Agency. The same can be done for you."

"You won't live long enough. Even if you defeat Madame Moriarty in the arena, Hannya and the others won't let you leave with your daughter. They'll kill you."

"With your help, I'll be able to outwit all of them."

Mary was silent. She appeared lost in thought. Minutes passed. She beckoned Blythe to follow her. Outside, a coach waited for them. They got inside. As the horses drew away from the curb, Mary finally spoke.

"If I help you, there are two things that you must promise me."

"Name them," said Blythe.

"In case I die, but you survive, I want you to take a message to my uncle. He's Alexander Holder, the senior partner of Holder and Stevenson in London. Tell him I'm sorry for betraying him and John."

"I promise. And your other condition?"

"Kill Hannya."

"I had every intention of doing that."

"Don't underestimate her. She's a monster. When Orianne Coyatier went to Japan, she took me with her as a servant. Every evening after her training sessions with the Koga ninjas, she practiced her fighting techniques on me. Even though I helped Rochelle rescue her when she was left for dead by Marga Sandorf, Orianne used me as a punching bag."

"How long did Hannya study with her Koga tutors?"

"About three months."

"I studied years with the Iga ninjas. She's no match for me."

"Hannya will do everything within her power to see you die. Madame Moriarty intends to use her to romance the Pallid Mask. Orianne and the Mask were once lovers."

"Orianne Coyatier romancing a man? I find that hard to imagine. Besides I don't see any reason why the Pallid Mask would find her attractive. She's not exactly his type of woman."

"She resembles his lost love."

"Maude North? Maude was dark and slender. She didn't resemble Orianne at all."

"I'm not talking about Maude. I'm referring to La Bouchère. She was brawny like Hannya."

La Bouchère had perished before Blythe's service with the Black Coats, but she had heard of her. "Hannya will soon be as dead as La Bouchère. So will Catarina Moriarty."

"You can't kill Madame Moriarty. If you defeat her in combat, you'll need to use her as a hostage to secure your daughter's release."

"If I let Catarina live, then Sumeru Yuki's death won't be avenged."

"It wasn't Madame Moriarty who slew Yuki. It was Hannya."

"Hannya!"

"Your friend was preparing to battle Madame Moriarty. While Yuki was distracted, Hannya stabbed her in the back. The same thing could happen to you. Hannya will be standing in the passageway though which the arena can be entered. If Madame Moriarty's life is in jeopardy, Hannya will attack you. You must direct the combat away from Hannya. Once you incapacitate Moriarty, you can them challenge Hannya openly. Her arrogant pride will compel her to fight on your terms."

Blythe removed the lid of her long slender box. She pulled out a sheathed samurai sword. Removing the weapon from the scabbard, Blythe held it up for Mary to see.

"This was one of the last blades made by Muramasa, the great swordsmith. It was used by the legendary Yagyu family to slay demons. Catarina's minion shall regret adopting the name of a she-demon."

"Promise me that your sword will taste Hannya's blood."

"I promise." Sheathing the sword, Blythe put it back in the box.

"This is the underground arena," announced Sigi. "The amphitheater is empty now, but they will be executing a traitor here in about an hour."

"Will I be able to watch it?" asked Marga.

"That wouldn't be wise," advised Heidi. "Carolina Corbucci still holds a grudge about that mock contest you had with her."

"Also that detestable Orianne Coyatier will be there," added Sigi. "She hasn't forgotten your little wrestling match. We have to take you somewhere else."

"We should go to the target range," suggested Heidi. "It'll be deserted because all the Black Skirts will be preparing to gather here."

Leonard Wolfe was a short man with a lean figure and blond hair. In the firing range, Wolfe fired the two bullets of his derringer into one of the dummies. He was left-handed. Ecstasy Parker stood next to him.

"Any reason why this target range is located on the second floor overlooking the entrance?" asked Wolfe.

"Madame Moriarty wants us to be able to defend ourselves in case the police ever raid us. Here we have an ample supply of guns. We can easily pick off the peelers by shooting through the windows." Ecstasy looked at a clock on a stand. "It's getting late, Lenny. We'd better go."

"Let me just reload my derringer. Where do you store the bullets?"

"There isn't time for that now. Lenny. If we dally, you'll get a lousy seat in the arena. You can come back here to reload after the show. It isn't like you're going to need to blast someone soon."

"You're right as always, my love." Lenny gave Ecstasy a passionate kiss.

The carriage deposited Blythe and Mary at the Agnes de la Fere Athletic Club. As they walked into the building, Blythe extended her right arm. A small silver-plated pistol with four barrels slid out of her sleeve into her hand. The entrance hall was deserted.

"All the Black Skirts will be gathered at the arena. I'll take you there."

"One moment," said Blythe. Putting the box on the ground, she unsheathed the samurai sword. With the sword in her left hand and the pistol in her right, Blythe was escorted by Mary to the amphitheatre.

"Can I borrow your pistol, Marga?" requested Heidi.

"Why?" asked her cousin inside the target range.

"I want to photograph it. I'm going to have Julius Von Herder make a silver duplicate when we arrive in Germany."

Pulling back her the right side of her cape revealed a gold-plated pistol in a holster. The gun faced butt first since Marga was left-handed. Withdrawing her gun, Marga handed it to her cousin. "I'll be back shortly," said Heidi before exiting.

Sigi unlocked the box resting on the counter. "While Heidi's gone, we can practice our marksmanship."

"A Nargant revolver!" exclaimed Marga. "I've never handled one of those."

"Unfortunately, it's defective. We need to use the two Borchardts."

Mary guided Blythe down a dark corridor towards one of the two entrances into the arena. When they reached the alcove that opened on to the combat area, they beheld Rochelle Moreau, Ecstasy Parker and Orianne Coyatier. Rochelle and Ecstasy were attired as they had been during the prior competition. Orianne wore a long gray robe. On her chest was a white circle with the face of a Japanese demon in the center.

Blythe pointed her gun in Orianne's direction. "The image of your Japanese namesake makes a convenient bull's eye, Hannya."

"If you harm me, your daughter will perish," warned Orianne.

Rochelle sought to defuse the situation. "There is no need for threats. Mademoiselle Furnace, you came here under the terms of the challenge. Will you please open your coat, I must search you for other weapons."

Blythe complied. She extended her arms but moved sideways to keep her gun pointed at Orianne. "I can fire very quickly," proclaimed Blythe. "If you try anything, Rochelle, Hannya dies."

Rochelle concluded her examination. Other than a roll of money in the right pocket of Blythe's jacket. Rochelle found nothing. She restored the money to Blythe's pocket.

"You will be escorted by Ecstasy into the arena."

"You refused to promote me when you helped Madame Moriarty reorganize the Brotherhood into the Black Coats," said Ecstasy in English. "You call me a bloody satirist."

"The word is sadist," corrected Blythe. "You mangle the English language as badly as your sister Purity did. Your appetite for violence makes you unreliable."

"So what if I like the taste of blood! You should talk! You're a blooming ninja! Your crowd is always sticking swords into each other."

"Ecstasy acts as the referee," explained Rochelle. "It will be her duty to announce you and Madame Moriarty. Ecstasy, please revert to French. You're more eloquent when you speak French."

"Hostilities will commence once I yell 'Let the battle begin,' " added Ecstasy in French. "I won't be present when you and Madame start fighting. I only come back when it's time to declare the loser. That will be you, Blythe. It's too bad you won't be able to hear me. You'll be dead."

Exiting the alcove, Ecstasy walked to the center of the arena. Her serpent-head staff was in her right hand.

"Ladies of the Black Skirts, I am your mistress of ceremonies, Ecstasy Parker. It's my honor to present our beloved Queen, the Blind Spinner."

A long round of applause erupted.

"Madame Moriarty has entered the arena," declared Rochelle. "I must ask you to surrender your gun, Mademoiselle Furnace."

Blythe handed her gun to Rochelle.

"Two years ago, our sovereign elevated a woman to be her chief minister," resumed Ecstasy. "In November 1896, that woman betrayed our ruler. After assaulting our monarch, this traitor cowardly fled. Today, the turncoat has returned to face our Queen in open combat. This renegade lived amongst us as Milady Nevermore. Today she calls herself Blythe Furnace. Let the apostate face our liege."

As Blythe walked towards Catarina Moriarty, The occupants in the stands booed her. She looked at the crowd. Her eye caught Carolina Corbucci in her cowgirl outfit seated on a throne. Blythe had met Carolina in Texas when she was working for Antonio Nikola. Next to Carolina was a young girl. Was she Legacy?

The young child keenly observed the newcomer. This woman wore an eye-patch like her murdered guardian. She carried a samurai sword. During her captivity, the Blind Spinner had shown the girl a photograph of such a woman. Asked if she knew the one-eyed woman in the picture, the girl had replied in the negative. The child only knew that her mother had been a member of the Iga clan. Could this be her mother?

Catarina Moriarty stood in the center of the arena. She gripped her twin-bladed spear. Blythe stood before her.

"Before the duel starts, Her Majesty has some private words for the traitor," shouted Ecstasy. She walked toward the alcove where Orianne was waiting.

"Once you're dead, Blythe, your daughter shall be raised by me," revealed Catarina. She spoke softly in order for her words not to be overheard by the spectators. "She shall eventually assume the role abandoned by you, the premier assassin of the Black Coats."

"Even if you kill me, Catarina, you'll always be haunted by the knowledge that Antonio preferred me to you."

"That isn't true, my dear. Don't you wonder why I'm now called the Blind Spinner? Look into my eyes." Catarina raised her goggles up on her forehead towards the rim of her fur hat. Her dark blue eyes were not as Blythe remembered them. They gave the impression of being turned inward.

"You're blind!" exclaimed Blythe.

Catarina lowered the goggles over her sightless eyes. "A consequence of the fire caused by Norman Head's raid. I had intended to unleash the flame to cover my retreat. However, Superintendant Ford's unexpected attack caused me to start the fire prematurely. I failed to adequately protect my eyes.

"Remember the Helmet of Vathelos? Antonio finally found it in the Hoggar Mountains. Regretting his flirtation with you, he came to me begging my forgiveness. He made these goggles from the visor. Antonio proved his love for me by restoring my sight instead of curing the blindness in your right eye." Catarina paused. "The traitor's audience with me has ended!" she loudly proclaimed.

"Let the battle begin," screamed Ecstasy before running inside the alcove.

In a hallway near the target range, Rochelle Moreau handed Blythe's pistol to Heidi Skimmel. Heidi opened the gun to make sure it was fully loaded. She shoved the pistol into her belt.

When Heidi returned to the target range, Sigi Von Schulenberg and Marga Sandorf had exhausted all the ammunition in the Borchardt pistols.

"Thank you for lending me your pistol," said Heidi returning the weapon to Marga.

"You're welcome," replied Marga. "What's this? Something's wrong. My gun's too light." Marga opened the pistol's cylinder. The bullets were missing.

While Marga had been preoccupied with inspecting her firearm, Heidi handed Blythe's pistol to Sigi.

"Your gun isn't loaded," declared Sigi pointing Blythe's gun at Marga's stomach. "This one is. Die, you filthy Magyar pig!" Sigi pressed the trigger four times.

The gun clicked harmlessly.

Marga threw her golden gun at Heidi. It hit her in the forehead. She fell senseless to the floor. Dropping Blythe's gun, Sigi pulled out the silver dagger on her belt. She lunged at Marga. Dodging the thrust, Marga seized Sigi's right arm and slammed her back into the wall. Marga's right hand grabbed Sigi's throat. The brunette's left hand held the redhead's right wrist. Sigi's hand still held the knife.

"You can't defeat me," snarled Sigi. "Your blood is impure."

"Let's check your blood's purity, Sigi," replied Marga.

Twisting Sigi's wrist inwards, Marga drove the knife into her cousin's stomach. Marga pushed it diagonally upward and then diagonally downward in the opposite direction. Pushing the knife upward towards the middle of the second diagonal, she then pushed it across until the blade met first diagonal.

"The letter 'A' for *abschaum*. You have been marked as scum, Sigi. Only scum would betray their blood kin."

Marga released her cousin's wrist. Sigi's lifeless body slid to the floor.

Examining the silver-plated pistol, Marga recognized it as Blythe Furnace's. With ammo stored in the target room, the Hungarian gunslinger quickly reloaded her golden gun.

She slapped Heidi gently in order to revive her. When Heidi opened her eyes, she felt Marga's gun barrel pressing against her stomach.

"The gun should have fired," moaned Heidi.

"Blythe's gun has a special feature," explained Marga. "If a thin rod is removed from the side, the gun won't shoot."

"Where my sister?"

"In Hell. You'll be joining her there unless you answer my questions."

Catarina Moriarty slashed viciously at Blythe Furnace. The shaft of Catarina's weapon was of metal not wood. The leader of the Black Skirts was able to block Blythe's sword effectively with her two-edged spear.

"You can't break my weapon!" shouted Catarina. "It belonged to Vathelos! It's made of orichalcum!"

One of the blades on Catarina's spear swung towards Blythe's neck. Blythe raised her sword to block the blow. The Muramasa blade snapped. Blythe swirled sideways in order to avoid being decapitated. She threw her broken sword at Catarina. The purple-clad gladiator raised her spear crosswise with both hands. The Muramasa sword was deflected sideways as it bounced to land in the sand. Leaping forward, Blythe's hands grabbed the shaft of Catarina's spear.

Each woman held the two-edged spear sideways, they struggled to wrestle sole control of the weapon. Blythe pushed the shaft forward into Catarina's forehead. Momentarily stunned, Catarina's grip weakened. Blythe pulled the spear out of Catarina's hands. Blythe's right leg delivered a devastating kick to Catarina's midriff. Twirling the spear behind her with her left hand, Blythe's right hand swept downward in a brutal karate chop that struck Catarina's neck. The self-styled Blind Spinner collapsed into the sand.

Blythe quickly looked at the entrance where Orianne Coyatier stood near Ecstasy Parker. The redhead was too distant to launch a surprise attack. With lighting speed, Blythe stuck one edge of the spear into the sand. The weapon stood upright with its other blade pointing to the ceiling. Blythe swiftly pulled off Catarina's hat and removed her unconscious adversary's goggles. Catarina's taunts about Antonio Nikola had wounded Blythe. There was something the one-eyed warrior needed to know. Pulling her eye patch down around her neck. Blythe donned the goggles. She still only had sight in her left eye. Blythe realized the truth.

Antonio would have tested the mystical properties of Vathelos's visor. He would have concluded that it was ineffective to restoring sight to an empty eye socket. Besides being Antonio's ex-fiancée, Catarina was the daughter of Count Corbucci, a man whom Blythe's lover had viewed as a surrogate father. Antonio would have felt morally obligated to cure Catarina's blindness. Catarina had not supplanted Blythe in Antonio's heart. Blythe decided to wear the goggles a little longer in order to completely validate her conclusions.

"Your Queen has fallen!" she proclaimed. "She is at my mercy!" Blythe glared at Orianne. "Let her lackey, Hannya, fight me for her life! Hannya, I challenge you!"

Blythe's utterances were interrupted by a noise behind her. She twisted to the side avoiding a sword thrust that would have fatally stabbed her in the back. Blythe was now separated from the orichalcum spear as she confronted a new attacker.

The assailant was dressed in the dark garments of a ninja with the symbol of Hannya embroidered on the chest. The intruder had attacked from the opposite doorway from which Catarina Moriarty had entered the arena.

"You!" yelled Blythe.

"I am the real Hannya!" admitted Mary Holder. "Prepare to die!"

"Orianne Coyatier isn't Hannya," said Heidi Skimmel. "She was demoted by Catarina as punishment for being defeated by you. Mary Holder had suffered a similar debacle earlier at the hands of Irina Putine. Catarina had forgiven Mary's failure because she saw great potential in her. Having already proven that she had the beauty to attract the Pallid Mask, Mary just needed the proper skills to regain her ex-lover's affection. Catarina hoped to make Mary the replacement for Maude North. Mary even physically resembles Maude.

"Rochelle Moreau and Orianne were originally assigned to be Mary's tutors. When you nearly killed Orianne, Mary saw the opportunity for promotion. Rochelle tried to keep Orianne's disgrace a secret, but Mary informed Catarina Moriarty. As a reward for her act of betrayal, Mary became Orianne's superior in the Black Skirts. Mary was sent to Japan to learn Koga fighting techniques. Orianne accompanied Mary as her servant. During that trip, Mary established her total domination over Orianne, Mary's new ninja skills brutalized Orianne into submission. Adopting the alias of Hannya, Mary abducted Legacy from the Iga village."

"Why did you tell me that Orianne was Hannya?" asked Marga Sandorf.

"Catarina and Mary suspected you of passing information to Blythe Furnace. They constructed an elaborate scheme to deceive Blythe. Orianne pretended to be Hannya. All the other Black Skirts referred to Orianne as Hannya."

"Why all this misdirection?"

"To prevent Catarina's death if Blythe defeated her in the arena. By pretending to be an abused subordinate, Mary hoped to gain Blythe's confidence. Mary would convince Blythe that Catarina's life must be spared in order to secure Legacy's release. Furthermore, if Blythe was diverted into watching Orianne, she would be vulnerable to an attack from behind by Mary. I've answered all your questions. Please release me! I beg you!"

Dressed only in her underwear, Heidi was standing on a stool. Her hands were tied around her back. Loosening the noose that held one of the target dummies, Marga had placed it around her cousin's neck.

"I'm going to leave you there, Heidi. You always relished a good lynching."

"You're going to kill me!"

"What type of woman do you think I am? If Pilar Reloj was here, she would tell you that I'm a just woman. Your chances for survival are excellent. You have only to maintain your balance until your Black Skirt allies discover you. I must now depart."

"Where are you going?"

"To the arena."

A safe distance separated Blythe Furnace and Hannya. The duelists paced around the arena seeking an opportunity to strike. Hannya was pointing her sword straight at Blythe.

"You were easily fooled, Furnace! You are now weaponless!"

"I still live!"

"Not for long!"

As Hannya's sword slashed downward, Blythe quickly stepped backward to avoid the blow. The sword's tip rose upward hooking under the amulet on Blythe's necklace. The necklace flew in the air over Blythe's head. Catching the necklace with her left hand, Hannya placed it around her own neck.

"You have no right to that necklace! It was a gift from my lover!"

"I shall wear it on my wedding day. Your death will unite me with the Pallid Mask!"

Hannya continued to slash at Blythe. Avoiding the blows, the one-eyed woman was forced backwards. Her back was pushed against the arena's wall. There was no more room for retreat.

With both hands, Hannya raised her sword over her head. The blade sliced downward towards Blythe's forehead. Flattening her palms, Blythe caught the blade with her hands. The sword was a fraction of an inch from Blythe's forehead. Twisting the sword out of Hannya's hands, Blythe threw it into the sand. Blythe then leapt at Hannya.

A furor of blows and counterblows erupted between the two opponents. Blythe tried to deliver a kick to Hannya's jaw. Catching Blythe's leg, Hannya threw her into the earth. Blythe fell face forward.

As Blythe pushed upward with both her arms. She had raised herself to her knees when Hannya's left arm twisted around her neck. Caught in a debilitating choke hold, Blythe couldn't breathe.

"I'll strangle the life out of you!" swore Hannya.

"Kill her!" screamed the crowd. "Kill her!"

Blythe's right hand groped in the sand searching for a weapon. She stumbled upon the broken shard of her Muramasa sword. Seizing the shard, she drove it into Hannya's arm. Consumed by pain, Hannya's hold weakened. Breaking free, Blythe's hands reached backward to grab the necklace around Hannya's throat. Blythe twisted the necklace to tighten her hold. With all her might, Blythe threw Hannya over her shoulder. Hannya flew in the air towards the orichalcum spear. Falling downward, Hannya landed on the spear. The upturned blade pierced Hannya's back. The tip of the spear rammed through the image of the demonic face on her chest.

Impaled on the spear, the corpse of the treacherous Mary Holder was suspended above the ground. The cadaver's shadow fell across the unconscious Catarina Moriarty resting below.

"I kept my promise to you, Mary Holder," said Blythe Furnace. "I killed Hannya." Blythe walked towards her vanquished foes. Pulling her necklace off Mary's body, Blythe placed it back around her own neck.

A hush had fallen over the crowd. Ecstasy Furnace re-emerged in the arena. Holding her cane towards Blythe. Gripping the snake-head, she pointed the cane in the direction of Catarina and Hannya.

"I declare the loser to be ---." Ecstasy rapidly shifted to aim the cane at the victor. "Blythe Furnace!"

Pressing on the teeth in her cane's snake head, Ecstasy released the aluminium dagger. It flew straight at Blythe's heart, but Ecstasy's intended victim had the reflexes of an Iga ninja. Blythe's right hand caught the handle of the dagger before its tip could reach its target. The blade was a hair's breadth from her heart. Quickly reversing the projectile, Blythe threw it back at Ecstasy. The knife rammed into Ecstasy's stomach. Blood erupted in her mouth as she dropped to her knees.

"Are you enjoying the taste of blood, Ecstasy?" mocked Blythe.

Ecstasy's only reply was to fall lifelessly at Blythe's feet.

"Nooooooo!" screamed Leonard Wolfe in the stands.

Seated on her throne, Carolina Corbucci had viewed the events in the arena with shock. The prophecy of Sylvia Pence had unfolded in a unexpected fashion. Sylvia had foresaw that Carolina would respond to the victory in the arena by firing her gun. Rising from her seat, Carolina reached for her firearm with every intention of fatally shooting Blythe. Before Carolina could touch her revolver, she found her wrist caught in a grip of steel. Carolina turned to face the woman who had grabbed her hand.

"Marga!" hissed Carolina.

Removing her own clothes, Marga had put on Heidi's uniform before leaving the target range. Blythe's pistol was tucked inside the uniform's belt. The Hungarian gunslinger's golden pistol plodded into Carolina's back.

"I borrowed Heidi's clothes in order to approach you without opposition. She's waiting for you in the target range. My other cousin is dead. If you don't want to find yourself in a similar state, do as I say. I shall release your hand. Grab your pistol and fire all its contents into the air. Then repeat what I whisper into your ear."

After Marga released her hand, Carolina removed the gun from her holster and shot it harmlessly into the air. As Marga whispered, Carolina shouted her words.

"The Black Skirts acknowledge your victory. What do you want?"

Blythe remove the goggles. She restored her eye patch to its proper place. Picking up Hannya's sword from the ground, Blythe raised it in the air with her right hand while holding the goggles in her left.

"Let the child next to you hear my words without interruption and let her reply." Blythe spoke the next words in Japanese. "My body is iron. My soul is air. I destroy evil. Who am I?"

The child answered in the same language. "So long as there is light, there will be shadows that kill to protect their young. You are my shadow. You are my mother."

Catarina Moriarty moaned at Blythe's feet. The one-eyed woman seized Catarina by her hair and pulled her to her feet. She was groggy but conscious. Blythe placed her sword against Catarina's neck.

"Bring me my daughter, Carolina Corbucci," shouted Blythe, "or I'll slit your sister's throat!"

Accompanied by Marga, Carolina escorted Legacy to a stairway.

Blythe placed the goggles over Catarina's eyes.

"Look, Catarina. See your precious Hannya. You intended to wed her to the Pallid Mask, but I have made her bridegroom the Grim Reaper."

Marga, Carolina and Legacy walked through the entrance that Catarina had previously used to come into the arena.

"Mother," said Legacy in Japanese. Reaching out her arms. she implored to be embraced.

"I shall properly welcome you, my daughter," said Blythe in Japanese, "once we have left this den of *yakuza*." Blythe recognized the woman next to Carolina. "Marga, what are you doing here?" asked Blythe. "Why are you wearing that uniform?"

"It's a long story. Let me apologize for being used to pass false information regarding Hannya. I have your pistol tucked into my belt. Catarina plotted to have me murdered with your gun. Fortunately you rendered it inoperative. I returned the favor by persuading Carolina not to shoot you. The gun barrel of my golden pistol is massaging her back."

"Since we have two hostages, I suggest we leave with my daughter."

"If you have no objection, *compañera*, we could share a cab. It can drop you off at the Chupin Detective Agency before proceeding to my own destination."

"A wonderful idea," replied Blythe. She turned her attention towards Catarina. "You will instruct your minions to remain here until your return. Obey my instructions, and I'll spare both your life and your sister's."

Catarina did as she had been ordered. Looking at the stands, Blythe spied Rochelle Moreau and Orianne Coyatier. They had undoubtedly found it expedient to leave the alcove once the situation spiraled out of control. Blythe and Marga should encounter no other Black Skirts during their exit from the Agnes de La Fere Athletic Club.

Once Blythe and her companions entered the alcove, Leonard Wolfe rose from his seat.

"Where are you going?" protested Rochelle. "Didn't you hear our Queen's orders?"

"I'm not one of your Black Sashes. I'm a Gentleman of the Night. Noel Moriarty's my Lord. His consort has no authority over me."

Wolfe ran to the exits. He was determined to avenge Ecstasy. Cursing himself for not reloading his derringer earlier, he ran towards the area of the building where there was an ample supply of guns and ammo.

Blythe and the others navigated through the passages which Mary Holder had originally guided her. Catarina and Carolina walked in front as Marga kept her pistol trained on them. Leading her daughter with one hand, Blythe held the sword in the other.

"Madame Sara and Countess Cagliostro will have you executed, Marga, when they hear of your actions," said Carolina.

"Madame Sara will not appreciate your scheme to assassinate me," argued Marga. "As for the Countess, the marks branded on her flesh during her tenure with the Black Skirts will influence her judgment."

"But will they forgive the destruction of a Black Coat base?" added Catarina. "As soon as Blythe Furnace leaves, she'll go straight to the police. They'll raid the Club."

"Catarina is trying to sow dissension, *compañera,*" observed Marga, "but she does have a point. Madame Sara would find herself in a difficult position on the High Council if scores of Black Skirts are arrested because of my interference. May I suggest a compromise to avoid a conflict between us?"

"Please do," requested Blythe.

"Give the Black Skirts forty-eight hours to abandon their base."

"Make it twenty-four, and you have a deal, Marga."

"Agreed. I assume you have that little metal rod for your pistol on your person."

"It's in my coat pocket. I pulled it out right before handing my gun to Rochelle Moreau. I didn't want her shooting me in the back while I entered the arena."

"Let me give you back your pistol." Gripping the barrel, Marga extended it towards Blythe. Tucking the sword under her arm, Blythe let go of Legacy's hand. Pulling the rod out her pocket, she restored it to the gun. With the gun pointing at Catarina and the sword under her arm, Blythe led her daughter towards freedom.

They reached the hallway where Blythe had left her scabbard inside the long box. Opening the box, she sheathed the blade. Even though the sword was different, it fit the scabbard.

"Marga, could you take my daughter and my new sword outside. Please hail a cab. I'll be joining you shortly."

"Of course, *compañera.*"

As Blythe pointed her gun at Catarina and Carolina, Marga and Legacy departed.

"Catarina Moriarty, not only did you abduct my daughter, but you caused the death of one of my oldest friends. Now you pay the price. Two bullets will be my justice. "

"But you promise to spare our lives!" protested Carolina.

"What kind of woman do you think I am? If Marga Sandorf was here, she would tell you that I'm a just woman."

Blythe's left hand reached out to rip off Catarina's goggles and toss them in the air. The pistol fired upwards twice. The goggles fell to the ground with both lenses completely shattered by Blythe's bullets.

"What happened?" demanded the Blind Spinner.

"She ruined the goggles!" exclaimed Carolina

"Catarina Moriarty, you are condemned to live in darkness," coldly stated Blythe.

The Blind Spinner howled in anguish.

Leonard Wolfe rushed into the target range. He barely glanced at Sigi's blood-spattered body.

"Help me," pleaded Heidi standing on the stool with the noose around her neck. She was positioned close to the nearest window.

Wolfe ignored her. Grabbing a gun from the counter, Wolfe ran to the window and opened it. He saw Blythe Furnace below as she moved towards the cab inside which Marga and Legacy awaited. He pointed the gun downward and fired. The gun exploded. It was the sabotaged Nagant revolver. With a mutilated hand, Wolfe fell against Heidi's stool. Hitting his head against the stool, Wolfe was knocked unconscious. The stool slid sideways out from under Heidi's feet. She swung sideways as the noose tightened.

Inside the cab, Blythe smothered her daughter with kisses as they hugged each other.

"You realize this changes nothing," interrupted Marga. "We remain enemies."

"With enemies like you, Marga, who needs friends?"

"An interesting twist on an old adage. Let me reply with a variation of my own. Your victory over Catarina Moriarty proves that a proverb about men equally applies to the opposite sex. In the kingdom of the blind, the one-eyed woman is queen."

Incident in the Boer War

A little spark can sometimes cause a huge forest fire. There are men who are like sparks. If snuffed out early, these human predators would do relatively little harm. If allowed to burn brightly, they can grow into a conflagration that consumes countless lives. During the Boer War, one such human spark lit a fuse that would unleash countless deaths around the globe. In March 1900, a fatal decision was made in Bloemfontein, South Africa. In his last night of freedom, Arthur J. Raffles wrote a letter:

Dear General Beltham,

Since I robbed an Australian bank in 1882, I have lived a dual existence. By day, I was a respected member of society, admired as a competent cricket player. At night, I became a burglar with countless robberies to my discredit. I was no Robin Hood. The poor never benefited from my thefts. I kept all the money for myself.

Despite my devotion to brigandage, I always remained a loyal subject of the British Empire. In 1895, a Polynesian monarch openly insulted our beloved Queen. The Kaiser sought to reward this island upstart for his effrontery by bestowing upon him a pearl of great value. Hoping to punish the Kaiser for his brazen act, I attempted to steal the pearl on a ship in the Mediterranean. My plan backfired. Inspector Mackenzie of Scotland Yard not only foiled my robbery, but publicly exposed me as a thief. Rather than face a long prison sentence, I jumped off the ship.

The world believed that I drowned. In actuality, I washed up on the island of Elba. Eventually, I took a vessel for the Bay of Naples. There, I fell in love with a woman named Faustina. Alas! Our union was not meant to be. She was also being courted by Stefano, a member of the secret society known as the Camorra. Faced with losing Faustina, Stefano fatally stabbed her. I avenged my beloved's death by shooting her murderer. The death of Stefano made me a marked man. Count Savaltore Corbucci, the primary leader of the Camorra, swore to kill me. For the next two years, his minions dogged my trail.

In the summer of 1897, I caused the death of Count Corbucci. I tricked the bloodthirsty ruffian into drinking poison. I harbor no regrets over my actions.

Yet, the Camorra is part of a larger tapestry of evil. Together with the Red Hand and the Brotherhood of the Seven Kings, the Camorra owes allegiance to the Black Coats. The ruler of this powerful confederacy is Il Padre d'ogni, the All-Father, a recluse hidden in the mountains of Corsica. Corbucci was his protégé. The Count was connected to all the major felons of Europe. His daughter Catarina married Noel Moriarty, brother of the notorious academician slain by

Sherlock Holmes. Corbucci's foster son became feared in the Far East under the name of Dr. Nikola. These associates of Corbucci now control the Black Coats. By killing Corbucci, I earned the eternal hatred of the most powerful criminal syndicate in the world.

From the various fences that purchased the fruit of my burglaries, I learned that the Black Coats had hired an assassin to track me down. This man uses the alias of Juan North. I know precious little about my stalker. There are rumors that he is an aficionado of a notorious play, The King in Yellow. *He supposedly models himself on the Phantom of Truth, a character in the play who hides his features behind a pallid mask.*

Ever since Inspector Mackenzie publicized my illegal endeavors, I had been living a clandestine existence under numerous aliases. North made no progress in tracing me. Not content to wait for the inevitable assault of the Black Coats, I have opted to launch a counteroffensive of my own. Learning that Noel Moriarty resided under the alias of Julius Pavia in the Blackheath district of London, I broke into his mansion. I ignored his expensive art collection to focus on his private papers. I will always regret not appropriating a painting of a beautiful woman by Jacques Saillard.

The papers in my possession dealt with the corrupt financial dealings of the Black Coats in the Panama Canal scandal. I had it within in my power to bring them to their knees. The documents proved the complicity of Noel Moriarty and his associates in the demise of Louis Caratal, an important witness in the Canal scandal.

I secreted the papers in a safe location. It was my intent to let the Black Coats sweat over their inevitable exposure. The war broke out in South Africa. With my trusted friend Harry Manders, I enlisted in the British Army. My intention had been to defend my country loyally. If I survived this conflict, I would have returned to England and sent the incriminating papers to Scotland Yard. Unfortunately, my incognito has been penetrated. An old friend serving in our ranks recognized me. Realizing that I was serving the Empire in my own way, this gallant gentleman held his tongue. Our conversation was overheard by the treacherous Corporal Connal. When I exposed Connal's treasonable contact with the Boers, he retaliated by disclosing my true identity.

General, you have been kind enough to let me fight for one more day before sending me back home to answer for my crimes. I am writing this letter in order to reveal the location of the evidence against the Black Coats. I hid it in a box in the vaults of Cox & Co in Charing Cross. As a joke, I rented the box in Mackenzie's name. Perhaps by destroying the Black Coats, I will finally atone for my sins. Manders knows nothing of the Black Coats. I didn't want to put his life in jeopardy by informing him about that diabolical conspiracy.

A. J. Raffles.

Having finished his letter, Raffles folded it in an envelope. He entrusted the letter to the sergeant.

"Please see that the General receives this in the morning, Sarge."

"I certainly will. I have to confess that I'm long been an admirer of yours. I always knew you were a true patriot ever since you try to spike the Kaiser."

"While the Kaiser's pearl was priceless, I didn't try to steal it to make myself rich. I wanted to avenge the insult that Wilhelm II had levied against our beloved Queen."

"It's a pity that Inspector Mackenzie didn't see it your way. Good night, Raffles."

That evening, Raffles slept in great contentment in his bunk on the soil of South Africa.

The next day, the fighting was intense between the British and the Boers. Harry Manders was wounded by a bullet in the thigh. Raffles carried Manders behind a shallow rock. As Raffles bandaged his comrade's leg, he was approached by the sergeant.

"There's a sniper over there, Raffles. Try to draw his fire while I circle behind him."

Raffles saw the gray felt hat of his antagonist. As he conversed with Manders, Raffles shot a bullet in the hat. The sniper wasn't wearing it. The crafty Boer had stuck the hat on a pole to draw fire. Crouching behind the rock next to Manders, Raffles wondered if he should show his face to bring the Boer marksman out in the open. It was a calculated gamble. The sergeant should be able to get a clean shot at the Boer. Raffles raised his head. The Boer revealed himself and aimed his rifle. Suddenly, the Boer fell forward. The sergeant had shot him in the back.

Then, the sergeant raised his rifle and pulled the trigger.

Sergeant Gurn's bullet went straight into the standing figure of A. J. Raffles.

The official military report claimed the Boer sniper had killed Raffles before being dispatched by Gurn.

Formerly called Juan North, Gurn had search fruitlessly for Raffles for three years. From analyzing the gentleman burglar's conduct in the affair of the Kaiser's pearl, Gurn had concluded that Raffles was often motivated by chauvinism. Gurn predicted that Raffles would eventually volunteer for the Boer War. Waiting patiently for his quarry, he had enlisted himself.

Perusing the letter written by Raffles, Gurn knew that this assassination would indeed prove incredibly profitable. Besides collecting the bounty posted by Corbucci's associates, Gurn had the location of the material that incriminated Noel Moriarty and his co-conspirators in the Panama Canal Scandal.

Gurn was extremely ambitious. He had no desire to be the pawn of the Black Coats. Armed with paper stolen by Raffles, Gurn would force them to allow him to build his own independent criminal empire. In the past, the assassin had mimicked the Phantom of the Pallid Mask from *The King in Yellow*. Garn would now become a personage much more formidable.

Starting with the liquidation of A. J. Raffles, a new series of murders would terrorize the world. The age of Raffles was no more. The new century would usher in the era of *Fantomas*!

The Last Vendetta

In the course of his 83 years, Arthur Gordon had been a fighter for Texas independence, a captain of a slave ship, a gambler, a duelist and a bigamist. He had been married to both Hermine de Chalusse of Paris and Francine Xavier of Austin at the same time. During 1900, he was living a quiet existence in El Paso when a letter arrived.

The author of the letter was Ignacz Djanko, alias the Undertaker. Descended from Croatian immigrants who settled in the American West, Djanko had been one of the most bloodthirsty gunslingers of the West. He had slain easily over 50 men in the course of his brutal career. Gordon first met Djanko along the Pecos River in 1878. At the time, Gordon was selling Lee Bailey's machine guns. Bailey had been a former Confederate gunsmith who had been forced to flee to Mexico when he got into trouble with Federal troops in Texas during Reconstruction. Bailey was a genius who had made a vast improvement on the Gatling gun over a decade before Maxim invented his version of the machine gun. Wishing to reside in obscurity in Mexico, Bailey went into partnership with Gordon to market the machine guns. Gordon had sold one of these weapons to Djanko. The Undertaker had promised Gordon to convince a group of Mexican revolutionaries hiding out in Texas to purchase more. These revolutionaries were stragglers from General Santillana's aborted attempt to overthrow Porfirio Diaz in 1877. Unfortunately, Djanko's impatience and greed had caused the potential Mexican clients to prematurely return to their country and be massacred by Diaz's forces.

Many people mistakenly believed that the Undertaker's machine gun was an 1884 Maxim. This misunderstanding always irked Gordon. This fallacy was largely spread by Stanley Corbett's dime novel, *The Undertaker's Big Gun*. Djanko was feuding with the Red Scarf Gang, a group of ex-Confederates who took over a Texas town once Reconstruction ended. In the dime novel, Djanko had his final showdown with the Red Scarf Gang in a cemetery. Djanko had sought shelter behind a grave that bore the inscription 1889. This was not an error by Corbett. The local gravedigger had gotten intoxicated one day, and transcribed 1889 instead of 1869 on the marker. If Corbett's narrative was read carefully, it would be noticed that Djanko was depicted as a young man in his late thirties who fought for the North during the Civil War. Also Corbett's narrative accurately described Djanko's revolver as an 1873 Peacemaker, a weapon that would have been outdated by 1889.

Sometime in the 1880's, Djanko had shocked his criminal associates by suddenly becoming gripped by religious fervor. Seeking atonement for all the blood on his hands, Djanko had joined a monastic order in Mexico. Two years ago, Djanko had suddenly broken his vows and returned to a life of mayhem. He had written to Gordon seeking replacement parts for his old Bailey machine gun. Unfortunately, Gordon couldn't help him because Gordon had retired from the armament business when he reached his seventieth birthday. He had no idea whether Bailey was even still alive. Gordon had informed Djanko to try other arms dealers. Despite his failure to satisfy Djanko's request, he and the old gunslinger continued to correspond. Gordon perused Djanko's letter.

Dear Arthur,

While buying a new machine gun from a Swedish arms dealer, I received an unusual invitation from his associates. It's for the New Orleans Assassins' Auction, a gathering held for a rather unique clientele. The items being offered for sale include various weapons used to murder our fellow human beings over the centuries. They even have a Bailey machine gun. I am unable to attend because of other business matters. My Swedish supplier suggested passing on the invitation to a friend. I chose you because of an item of fairly recent vintage. The item is marked in the brochure.

Sincerely,
Ignacz

Besides the invitation, enclosed with the letter was a detailed catalogue of merchandise at the auction. An article circled in red immediately caught Arthur's attention:

#37 - C96 Mauser Pistol. Formerly the property of the Mute Shootist of Utah, a man who conducted a violent campaign against bounty hunters by either shooting off their thumbs or killing them outright. In good working order. Capable of firing 10 bullets.

Joséphine Balsamo, also known as Countess Cagliostro, was staging the Assassins' Auction in a large mansion on the outskirts of New Orleans. She was an attractive blonde woman of 32 years. Her personal office had been made virtually sound-proof with steel paneling just in case it was necessary to liquidate any customers who refused to pay. Her partner in this remarkable endeavor was the American known as Aguirre.

His real name was not Aguirre. After a career as a bounty hunter in Utah, this gunslinger decided to leave the state because the governor had ordered an investigation into his activities. Joséphine had christened her partner Aguirre because only the notorious sixteenth century conquistador of the same name had matched him in bloodthirstiness. During his travels in the West, Aguirre had been able to locate many firearms and knives that belonged to the most notorious killers. This huge arsenal would be dispersed at the auction.

For her own part, Joséphine was making contributions to the auction from various different sources. Since the eighteenth century, her family had engaged in extensive dealings with the secret societies of Italy. Joséphine had come into possession of the lethal inventions of the Camorra, the Red Circle, and the Brotherhood of the Seven Kings.

In additions to her assortment of Italian instruments, Joséphine had also profited from her love affair with the French swindler Ballmeyer. Joséphine had seduced the brigand during an earlier sojourn in New Orleans. The romantic couple had amused themselves by plundering the evidence rooms of police departments across the United States. In Baltimore, they had purloined the complete paraphernalia of the mass murderer known as the Butcher. His instruments included a hook, a meat cleaver, a rapier and a single-shot revolver. From the San Francisco authorities, Ballmeyer and Joséphine had stolen the seven idols that had been left beside the victims of Professor Malaki.

These robberies had been committed in 1895. Joséphine had departed for Europe in the following year. The loot from the thefts had remained hidden in America. In 1898, Joséphine unearthed that a French merchant was secretly transferring gold to New Orleans. Remaining in France, Joséphine dispatched her loyal underling, Marga Sandorf, to America. Marga had been instructed to enlist Ballmeyer's assistance. Together with Marga, Ballmeyer murdered the merchant. Cheating his female confederates, Ballmeyer fled America with the gold. Marga found a taunting message for Joséphine from Ballmeyer. Rather than divide the merchant's hoard, Ballmeyer had merely left Joséphine all of the spoils of their 1895 alliance as a token of affection. Ballmeyer had assumed that Joséphine had been saddled with items of questionable value in exchange for a more tangible asset. The trusting Ballmeyer had been totally unaware that Malaki's statues were made of ivory. Joséphine would soon convert Ballmeyer's legacy into substantial money.

The final supplier of Joséphine's stockpile of death devices had been the mysterious Dr. Antonio Nikola, a man who had journeyed substantially in the Far East. In 1898, Nikola had announced his intention to leave Europe and met his final destiny in an Asian monastery. In exchange for assistance rendered in the past, Nikola had bequeathed Joséphine an assortment of Asian weapons collected during his travels.

On this morning in 1900, all the participants in the auction had arrived. Before the bidding began, the potential purchasers were allowed to view the items in a massive ballroom. Numerous armed guards were present to make sure nothing was pilfered. The guests had been allowed to gather together with one notable exception, Arthur Gordon. He was being held in a separate room by two of Aguirre's guards because his invitation was not in order. Arthur was clearly not Ignacz Djanko. While he was examining the prisoner, Aguirre sent a guard to inform Joséphine.

Joséphine was interrupted in her office as she was perusing an Italian novel that concluded with a violent bloodbath.

"As you know, Countess, Peterson delivered an invitation to Djanko with our permission," explained the guard. "Then this fellow Gordon showed up with Djanko's invitation. He claimed that Djanko send him the invitation because the Undertaker purchased his Bailey machine gun from him years ago."

"Could you describe this man Gordon?"

"A tall elderly fellow. Must have been an athlete in his youth, but now he looks like he has one foot in the grave."

When Joséphine was escorted into the prisoner's presence, Arthur stared at her in shock.

"Josine, is that you? My God, you are the splitting image of your mother!"

"And the splitting image of my great-grandmother. This is quite a surprise, Arthur."

"You know this man?" queried Aguirre.

"Yes, Arthur was an old friend of my mother's in the late 1860's. In fact, he helped my mother to become a hostess in Paris shortly before the Franco-Prussian War. Upon my mother's tragic death, Arthur arranged for me and my sister to be properly educated. When I was 12, he paid the cost of my enrollment and my sister's at the Marie Gilbert School in Paris. When I reached the age of 15, Arthur arranged my transfer to the Fourneau College for Young Women near Avignon."

"Josine, I never expected to find you in New Orleans" uttered Gordon. "I heard you were in France."

"A dispute with an ex-partner prompted me to come to America last year. You knew the father of my treacherous ex-associate. He's the son of Théophraste Lupin."

"If the son is anything like the father, then he's the last person in the world that I would ever trust."

Joséphine had ample reason for hating Théophraste Lupin. She believed him responsible for her mother's death. Joséphine devoted her existence to ruining the lives of his descendants. Her first act of vengeance against the Lupin family had actually transpired at the Fourneau College. The mistress of that school had chosen Joséphine to be the senior prefect of all the girls and entrusted her with helping run the school. It had initially been very difficult at the Fourneau College for Joséphine. She had been exiled there after being put on probation at the Marie Gilbert School for the relatively harmless prank of putting a frog in the bed of a classmate. Discipline was incredibly sterner at the Fourneau College where corporal punishment was not unknown. With grim resolve, Joséphine had risen to a position of power.

A younger girl known as Mademoiselle Tupin was later enrolled in the school. Having access to all the school's records, Joséphine uncovered that Tupin was actually the illegitimate daughter of Théophraste Lupin. Tupin was seemingly a variation of Lupin. By the time that Joséphine graduated, she had thoroughly corrupted Tupin and recommended her to the headmistress to be the new chief custodian of all the other students. Joséphine had been far less fruitful in her efforts to dominate Arsène Lupin, the son of Théophraste. In 1894, Arsène had cheated her out of a medieval treasure. However, she had recently enacted a cunning scheme. Her agents in France had abducted Arsène's son. Hiding in America, Joséphine would be safe from Arsène's retaliation.

"Are your uncle and sister here as well?" wondered Gordon.

"Yes, Uncle Leonard is working in the showroom. Sabine is currently roaming around this wonderful city. She's never been in New Orleans before."

"I've heard that you employ a female gunslinger as a bodyguard."

"Marga's not here. She's acting as Sabine's escort."

Turning to Aguirre, Joséphine made a request. "Please release this old family friend. His presence at the Assassins' Auction is most welcome."

When Gordon entered the showroom, he was immediately struck by a large metal Chinese abacus on display at one of the tables. According to the catalogue, it had once been the property of the Bookkeeper, a member of the Ten Killers of the Underworld. Next to the abacus was a large circular metal object that that looked like some sort of hatbox. Blades extended from the side of the object almost making it resemble a buzz saw. Gordon looked up the item in the catalogue:

#235 - Flying Guillotine. This weapon was created on the orders of Emperor Yung-Cheng (1722-35). Execution squads armed with multiple versions of this device roamed the Chinese countryside inaugurating a Reign of Terror similar to that which transpired in the French Revolution. This instrument is not only designed to behead the victim, but to capture his head as a grisly trophy for the executioner. According to Kegan Van Roon's Secrets of the Thirty-Sixth Chamber *(New York: Golden Goblin Press, 1897), Yung-Cheng was slain by rebels who had captured one of these Flying Guillotines. The Manchu Dynasty allegedly obfuscated the assassination by pretending that the Emperor had died a natural death. This particular model offered for sale was used by a blind assassin who reported directly to Yung-Cheng.*

"I see that you are admiring the glorious handiwork commissioned by the enlightened Yung-Cheng," remarked a small Chinese gentleman dressed in Western attire. Accompanying the diminutive Asian, who appeared to be in his fifties, was a fellow Chinese attendee, a tall, thin man in his very late thirties. The older man identified himself as Hong Chen and his younger companion as Huan Tsung Chao. Both presented themselves as the envoys of an enigmatic Dr. Natas. They neglected to mention that Natas was an alias adopted by the powerful governor of the Chinese province of Honan.

"I am appalled by the misleading representation of this artifact in the catalogue," complained Hong Chen. "Did you notice the glaring historical error, Mr. Gordon?"

"I am afraid that I haven't."

"Does not the description imply that the Emperor ordered the creation of this instrument in order to emulate the guillotine introduced into Europe with the French Revolution?"

"Yes, it does."

"When was this Chinese artifact invented?"

"In the early eighteenth century."

"When was the guillotine invented?"

"Well...It must have been manufactured during the early years of the French Revolution. The Bastille fell in 1789. I see your point. The guillotine didn't originate in France until decades after the reign of Yung-Cheng."

"In our country, this device is known by another name that would more properly translate into English as the Flying Executioner," noted the younger of the two Chinese aristocrats. "The term 'Flying Guillotine' was completely a concoction of Kegan Van Roon, a mountebank who pretends to be a serious scholar."

"It is regrettable that such an error occurred in the catalogue considering the ancestry of our hostess," interjected Huan's older colleague.

"I don't understand your comment, Mr. Hong," replied Gordon.

"Her great-great-grandfather, Count Cagliostro traveled extensively in Asia. There he encountered Yung-Cheng's great contribution to the science of capital punishment. Cagliostro became obsessed with our Flying Executioner. Upon his return to Europe, he tried to persuade others to create a similar wondrous means of death. Initially he prevailed upon the Brotherhood of the Seven Kings to investigate the practicality of an equivalent device. Unfortunately, that Italian secret society could only achieve decapitation with a rather crude Iron Circlet. The Brotherhood's creation is another item on display in this showroom. Cagliostro didn't achieve his dream until he persuaded Dr. Joseph Guillotin to promote a French decapitation machine."

"But I also thought that Cagliostro was a mere confidence trickster. You talk about him as he was a personage of incredible influence."

"I can't fault you for your lack of knowledge, Mr. Gordon. You and most of the world have fallen victim to the Masonic campaign to hide the true facts of history."

"What do the Freemasons have to do with all this?"

"Cagliostro was the secret Grandmaster of the Masonic Lodges. In this role, he orchestrated the French Revolution from behind the scenes. The Cagliostro family is famous for hatching convoluted schemes in which others are manipulated. The Count later instructed his Masonic minions to alter all the historical records concerning him when France nearly conquered all of Europe. All the so-called facts about Count Cagliostro are false. These distortions involve his physical appearance as well as his death. Only the great French novelist Dumas was aware of the truth. He portrayed the real Cagliostro in a series of novels."

"Why didn't the Masons murder Dumas if he was revealing their secrets?"

"Not being a Mason, I do not know. Possibly they concluded that most readers would simply surmise that Dumas was spinning wild yarns from his own imagination."

"I would never have envisioned the indirect responsibility of a Chinese Emperor for the fashioning of the French guillotine. I guess that Van Roon's account of Yung-Cheng's death is false."

"You are correct," inserted Huan Tsung Chao. "The story is simply the legend of Shogun Iemitsu's beheading by one of his own Yagyu assassins. The Japanese tale was transposed to a Chinese setting. Our lord, Dr. Natas, was particularly inflamed by Van Roon's lies concerning the Emperor's death. Our noble master swore that if Van Roon ever set foot in China, he would meet with a violent end. Please excuse us; we want to express our grievance about the Flying Executioner to one of the managers."

The Asian pair approached a gray-haired Frenchman at the other side of the vast showroom. Gordon recognized the man as Joséphine's uncle. The Chinese duo was expressing their outrage in a loud manner that caught the attention of many spectators. Gordon suddenly heard an old familiar voice.

"Well, Arthur, it looks like our old friend Leonard has been captured by the Chinese."

"Good Lord! Count Bielowsky. I though you would be dead by now."

"That's a strange comment coming from a man who is 12 years older than me."

The speaker was dressed in the uniform of an officer of the Second Empire. His face sprouted whiskers in the style of Emperor Franz Joseph of Austria-Hungary. His hair was parted in the middle. Both his hair and his whiskers had been dyed dark brown.

"When Napoleon III abdicated, you suddenly disappeared from Paris. Where did you go, Count?"

"I have been serving as an aide-decamp at the court of Antinea, the Sultana of Ahaggar."

"Ahaggar? I never heard of such a kingdom. Where is it located?"

"You're better off not knowing. The Sultana believes in keeping the knowledge of her kingdom's existence confined to her loyal subjects. The Sultana is a woman of unusual pursuits. She has dispatched me here to bid on a group of small statues. Apparently of Sumerian origin, these idols materialized in San Francisco a decade ago. Queen Antinea suspects that they were actually plundered from the tomb of the wizard Surama in her own kingdom. My chances of acquiring the items are debatable. One of our fellow attendees is Oliver Haddo, the purchasing agent of a wealthy consortium of occultists. Haddo has also expressed an interest in bidding on the idols. Perhaps I can placate Her Majesty by buying some Punjabi strangling lassoes as a substitute. But that's enough about my commission. Do you still live in Germany during the summer and in France during the winter?"

"Those days are long gone. Like you, my fortunes were severely depleted by the consequences of the Battle of Sedan in 1870. I tried to borrow money from my son Wilkie, the heir to the Chalusse millions. That spoiled brat refused to have anything to do with me. I was forced to return to Texas where my son John helped me establish a munitions business. Eventually, I made enough money to visit Europe regularly in the 1880's. I've been in Texas for the last decade.

"I wasn't aware that Hermine bore you another son."

"She didn't. Hermine wasn't the only woman that I married. My other wife was an actress, Francine Xavier. She went by the stage name of Xaviera LeFrank. She bore me three sons. All of them were superior to Wilkie."

"Wilkie's behavior towards you is really quite extraordinary. I generally find daughters to be more considerate of their parents than sons. It's too bad that you never had a daughter."

Gordon was tempted to reply that he had two daughters, but he hadn't been married to the mother. Furthermore, her late mother had made him promise never to reveal his parentage to them. Instead, Gordon decided to change the topic of conversation.

"Well, my dear Count, it looks like Leonard has escaped Chinese captivity only to be assaulted by a female blizzard from Hell."

Leonard had been able to placate the Chinese delegates by promising to publicly announce that the catalogue contained errors about Yung-Cheng's execution device. As soon as the Chinese duo had left satisfied, a Japanese lady in a white kimono accosted Leonard. She proclaimed that a large wooden baby cart with concealed muskets was a forgery. The lady argued that the genuine baby cart had been destroyed in the eighteenth century.

"Joséphine's uncle has no luck," continued Gordon.

"I am confident that Leonard will sidestep this lady's thrusts. He's a very slippery eel. You won't believe the story that he told me in a Bourbon Street bar last night. He was an extremely caring brother."

"What are you implying?"

"Leonard just pretended to be the brother of the earlier Countess Cagliostro. This deception permitted the Countess to have another lover who thought that she was his exclusive mistress. Leonard confessed all this in confidence, but he didn't mention the name of the other man. When Joséphine and Sabine were born, the Countess informed her deluded lover that he was the father. In truth, Leonard is their father. It's very funny."

"Yes, it is," Gordon acknowledged with a bitter laugh.

"In fact, Arthur, I heard it stated that Leonard convinced the other man to fund Joséphine's and Sabine's education after they was left destitute. The poor fool sent Joséphine to the Fourneau College, the place where all our old comrades sent their illegitimate daughters. I heard from a Frenchman who visited Ahaggar that this unique learning institution was closed down by the authorities due to a scandal. The principal's son apparently became overly affectionate with several of her students."

"He tried to emulate Casanova, I presume."

"I suspect Bluebeard was more the boy's model. Believe me; you don't want to know the details."

Gordon proceeded to show the Count numerous items from the American West being exhibited. These included the knives of Manuel Sanchez, Doc Holliday's revolver (recently found in Clifton, Arizona), and a banjo with a Winchester rifle concealed inside.

Gordon motioned the Count over to a table displaying several unusual rifles plus a large derringer.

"These weapons, my dear Count, were all the handiwork of my partner, Lee Bailey. I sold them to one of my best clients, the bounty hunter called Gunsight Eyes. Bailey and I even developed special ammunition for Gunsight Eyes. These capsules were seemingly bullets, but were really harmless. They contained a red liquid that looked like blood."

"Why would Gunsight Eyes need those?"

"He needed to join a circus in order to track down a counterfeiter. The capsules with fake blood were used an act in which he functioned as both a marksman and an illusionist. He and other people pretended to kill each other in the act. Here's another of Bailey's great creations. This is one of his famous machine guns. Looking at the serial number inscribed on the weapon, I can verify it's the one utilized by the Rojos brothers to ambush Mexican soldiers at Rio Bravo in 1873."

"Pardon me, sir, but perhaps you can settle a friendly disagreement between me and another gentleman."

The speaker was a tall muscular man with curly black hair. He was dressed in a black suit with a white carnation in his lapel.

"My name is Washburn. I am the sales representative of Washburn-Peterson Armaments."

"I believe that I am familiar with your company," declared Gordon. "You sell arms throughout the Caribbean. Has business been good?"

"Yes. We are even branching out into new territories. My brother John, who runs the company with a Swedish partner, is currently filling a rather large African order for a client aptly known as Killer. Countess Cagliostro was invaluable in negotiating the contract. Please allow me to introduce my friend, Monsieur Satanas of Paris."

Satanas was a thickset man in his thirties. He wore a monocle over his left eye. "My friend, Mr. Washburn, and I were debating about a weapon of similar nature. I am a devotee of Corbucci. One of his best novels was a fictionalized treatment of the real-life outlaw known as the Undertaker. He described such a weapon being employed by the Undertaker in the 1880's. Mr. Washburn insists that the Undertaker's exploit really happened in the 1870's."

Gordon was thoroughly confused.

"Who the dickens is Corbucci?"

"Count Corbucci, the late Camorra leader of Naples and a very close friend of our charming hostess. He was a rather ingenious fellow who once rigged a grandfather clock to fire a pistol. His clock is being offered for auction here. He became infatuated with the stories of the American West during extended visits there in the 1860's and 1870's. The various gunfights of your country reminded him of the blood feuds in his native Italy. Corbucci loved American dime novels so much that he decided to write them himself. His ambition was to be the Ned Buntline of Italy. Having researched several actual events, he wrote a series of books about the West. Being multi-lingual, he first wrote them in Italian and then translated them into English himself. His stories are incredibly popular in Italy. Foolishly, his American publisher, Pickman and Sons, refused to distribute the English version of Corbucci's greatest work, *Il Grande massacro,* because it had a brutally depressing ending."

"I never heard of this Corbucci. I did read a dime novel about the Undertaker by a man named Stanley Corbett."

"Stanley Corbett is Corbucci's pseudonym in America. In Italy, his novels appear under his real name."

Gordon then proceeded to elucidate how a gravedigger's error must have misled Corbucci.

"That explains everything," concluded Satanas. "Corbucci did mention to me that he had visited the graveyard in the ghost town where the Undertaker disposed of the remaining members of the Red Scarf Gang."

"Being such an aficionado of Corbucci, do you intend to bid on the machine gun?" questioned Count Bielowsky.

"If the Undertaker had owned this weapon, then I would have been tempted," answered Satanas. "I'm more interested in finding something for my own business endeavors. I have my eye on a small canon made by Professor Schultze in his factory at Stahlstadt, Oregon."

The group clustered around the machine gun was then joined by a thin young man clad in a white suit with a flamboyant blue scarf. He gave his name as Adam Saxon. He was curious as to where one might purchase a machine more portable and lighter than the weapon being auctioned. Washburn began to enunciate various models sold by his brother's company.

Gordon was intently listening to this litany of machine guns when he was accosted by another newcomer. The fellow was a tall mustached man in his fifties.

"Are you the Arthur Gordon who fought for Texas independence in 1836?"

"Indeed, I am."

"I also fought for Texas. I was an 18-year old lieutenant in the final year of the War Between the States. People know me as Nine Fingers. May I have the pleasure of shaking your hand?"

As he shook the hand of the Civil War veteran, Gordon noticed that his new acquaintance was missing the top joint of one of his fingers.

"I see that you are missing the tip of your trigger finger. You must have difficulty in handling a gun."

"There is still enough of my finger left to pull a trigger."

"You're lucky that you weren't wounded in the thumb. A man can't hold a gun if he's missing a thumb."

Gordon remembered how he had once told the same thing to a young boy that he trained how to shoot.

"Have you ever been to Utah?" inquired Gordon.

"Utah? No, why do you ask?"

"It's just that I knew a lot of Utah bounty hunters with injured hands. You weren't ever a bounty hunter?"

"No, but I was a close personal friend of one of the best bounty hunters. I even served with him in the Confederate army. He was called Gunsight Eyes."

"I was also his friend." Gordon paused for a few seconds. "Wait a second. You aren't the fellow who lost 5,000 dollars to Gunsight Eyes in a poker game and then skipped town without squaring the debt."

"You are confusing me with another man, Sir. The Major and I have always been on the best of terms."

"Major? Gunsight Eyes was a Colonel."

"He was a Colonel when he served in the United States army before Fort Sumter. During his time in the Confederate army, he only rose to the rank of Major."

"I remember now. That's correct, but he preferred to be called Colonel."

"To me, he will always be the Major. Did you know the Major long, Mr. Gordon?"

"Yes, in fact I sold him his derringer and rifles."

"Are you planning to bid on the derringer?"

"Why would I? I sold it. Why buy it back now?"

"I am glad to hear that. I intend to bid on that item. It has a sentimental value for me. Since you are such a close friend of the Major, perhaps you could settle a matter of some mystery to me. In 1879, I suddenly stumbled upon the Major in a circus using a very weird alias."

"Yes, I know all about that. Some Spanish name. Wasn't it Zapata?"

"That's close enough. Why did the Major change his name?"

"Gunsight Eyes had a younger sister. While he was off fighting the Yankees, she and her husband were killed by a Mexican bandit known as the Indian. When the Civil War ended, Gunsight Eyes tried to find the Indian. In 1867, he got a lead that took him to Mexico when the Juaristas were about to finally defeat the forces of Maximilian. A mercenary was fighting alongside the Juaristas against Maximilian's forces. This soldier of fortune had a name like Zapata, but he was also called the Black Indian."

"Black Indian? Was he an African?"

"No, he just had a horrible taste in fashion. He wore the most outlandish black outfit imaginable. Mistakenly concluding that the Black Indian was his sister's murderer, Gunsight Eyes killed him. He was deeply upset after learning the truth. Years later, Gunsight Eyes would be reminded of his tragic error in judgment. In 1876, there was a corrupt Justice of the Peace in Utah. In partnership with an equally dishonest sheriff, he wanted to get rid of a gun runner who settled there. The man was selling guns to Mormon settlers whose land the two corrupt officials were hoping to steal. The devious officials came up with a plan to frame the gun trafficker for a crime that he didn't commit. In order to keep their own hands from getting dirty, the duo opted to trick a famous bounty hunter into killing their enemy. The man that they duped was Gunsight Eyes. At first, Gunsight Eyes didn't suspect a thing. His target had a rather common surname in this country. The name didn't mean anything to Gunsight Eyes until he viewed his quarry. The wanted man greatly resembled an older man with whom Gunsight Eyes was friendly. It turned out the intended victim was actually the son of the old friend. Gunsight Eyes did some investigating and discovered the truth. That's why he took the Spanish alias. Gunsight Eyes had almost killed an innocent man again. By adopting the Black Indian's name, Gunsight Eyes was constantly reminding himself never to make that mistake again."

"I remember reading a recent scandal about bounty hunters in Utah massacring Mormon settlers," recalled Nine Fingers.

"That whole mess was caused by the same Justice of the Peace," maintained Gordon. "He finally mastered the art of orchestrating bounty hunters to further his ambitions. The Mormons responded by hiring a gunslinger to kill the bounty hunters. The conflict in Utah's Snow Hill County in 1898 was nearly as bloody as the 1878 Lincoln County War in New Mexico."

"Well, thank you, for clearing that matter about Gunsight Eyes, Mr. Gordon. Please allow me to take my leave. I have to make some arrangements concerning an upcoming poker game in Doc Malbodius's hotel suite."

When Nine Fingers left, Gordon turned around and suddenly saw Count Bielowsky. The Count had been standing behind Gordon the whole time during the discussion about Gunsight Eyes. The shrewd aristocrat had heard everything.

"You didn't trust that huckster enough to confide in him the whole story, Arthur. Reading between the lines, I can deduce that there's more to the tale. Gunsight Eyes must have left Utah to warn his old friend that his son was marked for death. Am I right?"

"Yes, nothing seems to get by you. Of course, the father rushed to his son's assistance."

"Did the father arrive there in time?"

"No. The sheriff and his partner decided that they had wasted enough time toying with bounty hunters. They personally shot the son and his wife. Both were dead when the father arrived."

"But there was another family member."

"Yes, there was a grandson. The killers didn't waste any bullets on him. They just cut his throat. He would have bled to death if his grandfather hadn't rushed him to a doctor. He lived, but he never spoke again."

"That's...very tragic."

"It's not as tragic as it might have been. As the grandfather told the boy, you don't need vocal cords to learn how to handle a gun."

At the auction, Count Bielowsky purchased the Punjabi lassoes, but Oliver Haddo beat his bid on Malaki's six Sumerian statutes.

Washburn was quite surprised that Gordon spent a substantial amount of money on a Mauser pistol. Such a weapon could be bought for a much cheaper price from Washburn-Peterson Armaments.

Very late into the evening, Joséphine Balsamo invited Gordon as an old family friend to have a drink of rare Amontillado with her and her partners. Both Leonard and Aguirre joined Arthur and Joséphine in her office.

"I must say, Josine, you presided over the auction with the grace of an Empress."

"In a sense, you're responsible for that talent of mine. I learned how to affect a regal bearing by closely observing the headmistress of the Fourneau College. I owned much of my success in my profession to the training given by that skilled lady."

Joséphine was totally sincere in her praise. She had learned the fine art of manipulation from the headmistress of the finishing school. Nevertheless, Joséphine always resented the indignities that were inflicted on her person in the early phases of the tutelage by the matriarch of the Fourneau College. Joséphine succeeded in a diabolical revenge on the headmistress. Joséphine's patron had kept her teen-age son segregated from the female students. Unknown to his mother, Joséphine secretly contacted the boy during her last days at the school. She suggested an idea to him regarding the remaining students. Following Joséphine's departure, the boy acted on her advice and brought ruination to his mother.

"I'm curious. Arthur. Why did you buy this Mauser pistol that's lying on my desk?"

"You probably know that I sold Bailey's weapons to bounty hunters. Many of those men were my close personal friends. That damn Mute Shootist murdered some of my best clients. I intend to break that pistol with a mallet in order to honor their memory."

"Well, Sir," intoned Aguirre in a nice Southern drawl. "There's a piece of information that you might find interesting."

"What's that?"

"I'm the man who gunned down the Mute Shootist. I set an ambush for him with a few of my friends. I shot him in the head, and then I removed that Mauser from his stinking corpse."

"Well. Mr. Aguirre. I think that you and I should shake hands."

Aguirre extended his right hand. Gordon seized the Mauser from Joséphine's desk. His first bullet blasted into Aguirre's right thumb. As Aguirre fell to the ground screaming, the second bullet from the Mauser stuck the thumb on his left hand.

"You murdered my grandson!" yelled Arthur as he sent his third bullet into Aguirre's forehead.

"As for you, Leonard, there is the matter of the unnecessary tuition that I paid to the Fourneau College."

Arthur fired the Mauser at Leonard. The Frenchman fell to the ground. His forehead was covered with blood.

"Josine, you're just a treacherous tart like your mother."

Arthur fired three times at Joséphine. Her blouse was covered with red stains. She slumped lifelessly to the floor.

Another gunshot was suddenly fired. Arthur felt a sharp pain in his right hand and dropped the Mauser. He saw Leonard standing with a revolver. Joséphine Balsamo lifted herself up from the floor and picked up the Mauser. Aguirre also rose up and laughed.

"You all should be dead!" shouted Gordon.

"Have you forgotten the special ammo that you and Bailey made for Gunsight Eyes?" replied Joséphine.

"The fake blood capsules…"

"Yes, Arthur. Aguirre found an ample supply. We knew all about your relationship to the Mute Shootist."

"How?"

"You may thank the late great Corbucci for that. Satanas told me about your conversation concerning my late associate's literary efforts. His *Il Grande massacro is* a sensationalized account of your son's death in 1876. It even mentions the mutilation of your grandson."

"But why did you let me attend the convention if you knew I wanted to avenge my grandson's death."

"Your arrival here was planned from the beginning. I lured you to this auction."

"But I received a letter from Djanko."

"A letter that Djanko was prompted to write by the Swedish co-owner of Washburn-Peterson Armaments, a firm indebted to me for their lucrative African deal-. If it is any consolation, Djanko was totally unaware that he was being used as a pawn. He really thought that he was helping you take revenge for your grandson's death."

"How could Djanko trust that Swede so implicitly?"

"The Swede is one of Djanko's bastards. In fact, he's the spitting image of his father except his hair is blonde. Illegitimate children can't always be trusted by their parents. This is a painful fact that you are about to learn, Father."

"Stop it with those lies! Bielowsky told me the truth!"

"Bielowsky made that supposed revelation as part of a deal that we made. His old friendship for you is outweighed by his need to please Queen Antinea. He needed to procure at least one of Malaki's statues to keep her content. I sold him one of the seven idols before the auction, and then he competed unsuccessfully for the other six. Part of the price of that one idol was the telling of a lie to you."

"Is Leonard then really your uncle?"

"No, that portion of Bielowsky's story was true. However, don't harbor any doubt about my parentage. My mother told me that you were my father on her deathbed. Sabine's father was someone else."

"Why have Bielowsky pretend that you aren't my daughter?"

"To cause you to suffer, Father. I want you to suffer."

"Why do you hate me so?"

"You incarcerated me at the Fourneau College! A purgatory for the unwanted daughters of the wealthy! You can't imagine the depravities that I had to endure there in order to survive!"

Joséphine removed the phony ammo from the Mauser. She then inserted a real bullet into the gun before giving it to Aguirre.

"Do what you do best," she advised.

Aguirre pressed the barrel of the Mauser against Arthur Gordon's forehead.

"Give my regards to your grandson when you see him in Hell."

Dear Mr. Djanko,

Mr. Peterson has graciously agreed to deliver you this letter. As you must have heard by now, my beloved father has tragically perished. My father was overjoyed to see me when he arrived at the auction. Together we both plotted to avenge the death of my nephew. Unknown to us, Aguirre had discovered my father's relationship to the Mute Shootist. He was betrayed by an old friend, Count Bielowsky, who was acting on the instructions of Queen Antinea of Ahaggar. The price of the Count's treachery was an ivory idol. When the auction concluded, my father and I were alone with Aguirre in my office. My nephew's Mauser was lying on my desk. Aguirre put out a revolver. I grabbed the Mauser, but I was too late. Aguirre shot my fath

Peterson explained why the letter ended abruptly to Djanko.

"She was so overcome with grief that she just couldn't finish writing it, Dad. She loved her father with her whole soul."

"Did Aguirre die a painful death at least?"

"She shot off both his thumbs, and then drilled him through the head."

227

"What a woman! It's too bad, son, that you don't have a sister like her. Where's this Ahaggar?"

"It is located in the Hoggar Mountains of North Africa."

"You remember my saying that if any harm came to Arthur, I would slaughter those responsible. I am packing my machine gun and taking a trip to North Africa."

Afterword

This series is essentially a war between two women, Irina Putine and Joséphine Balsamo. Irina is derived from *La Residencia*, a 1969 Spanish film directed by Narciso Ibañez Serrador. The film's English titles are *The House That Screamed*, *The Finishing School*, and *The Boarding School*. The movie was essentially a reworking of Alfred Hitchcock's *Psycho* (1958) transplanted to a late nineteenth century boarding school in France. The strict girls' school atmosphere was heavily influenced by a 1958 German film, *Mädchen in Uniform (Girls in Uniform)*. The 1958 film starred Lilli Palmer as a benign school teacher hoping to mitigate the oppressive policies of a Prussian school for girls during the 1890's. In *La Residencia*, Palmer was cast in a role that was sort of the evil twin to her earlier German teacher. Palmer portrayed Madame Fourneau, the despotic ruler of her own boarding school.

The most memorable character from *La Residencia* is Irene (played superbly by Mary Maude). In the course of the film, Irene evolves from being the female equivalent of Flashman from *Tom Brown's School Days* to a rebel against conformity. The credits do not give a spelling for Irene's surname, but the characters in the film pronounce it as "Too-pan." Possibly Irene's last name is spelt "Tupin" The name Irene Tupin is suspiciously similar to Arsène Lupin (pronounced either "Loo-pan" or "Loo-pon"), the famous thief created by Maurice Leblanc. Therefore, I decided to make Irina the sister of Arsène.

The archenemy of Arsène Lupin was Joséphine Balsamo, Countess Cagliostro. She only appeared in two books, *La Comtesse de Cagliostro* (1924) and *La Cagliostro se venge* (1935). Both of these novels have been collected together in new English translations as *Arsène Lupin vs. Countess Cagliostro* (Black Coat Press, 2010). Joséphine first battled Lupin in 1894, but the final culmination of their duel actually happened in the 1920s. In fact, Joséphine was actually deceased in *La Cagliostro se venge*, but her vengeance extended beyond the grave. The same Joséphine Balsamo collection also includes Maurice Leblanc's "The Queen's Necklace," as well as a pastiche, "The Death of Countess Cagliostro" by Jean-Marc and Randy Lofficier. If you read that new story, you will understand the reason why I had to include a reference to an 1884 trip to the Cascabel family in Normandy in "Consequences of a Funeral." "The Death of Countess Cagliostro" also features a cameo by my own Marga Sandorf.

Joséphine was the great-great-granddaughter of Joseph Balsamo, Count Cagliostro. Joseph Balsamo actually existed, but his role in history was greatly exaggerated by novelists like Alexandre Dumas.

The name Cagliostro became associated with vampires in Mexican horror films. *The Bloody Vampire* (1962) and *The Invasion of the Vampires* (1963) postulate a feud between the Cagliostro clan and the vampiric Frankenhausen family. In "All Predators Great and Small," I made the Frankenhausens minions of Bram Stoker's Dracula. In order to do this, I drew upon the speculative theories of my friend Chuck Loridans, who is the basis for the fictional Charles Maurice Loridan. My story also contains allusions to the films *Son of Dracula* (1943) and *Captain Kronos–Vampire Hunter* (1974). Peter Tremayne wrote a trilogy of novels in which Dracula was portrayed as the acolyte of an ancient dragon god: *Dracula Unborn* (1977, also known as *Bloodright*), *The Revenge of Dracula* (1978) and *Dracula, My Love* (1980). I have modified this concept to fit into H. P. Lovecraft's Cthulhu Mythos by drawing upon the tales of Robert E. Howard, Robert Bloch, Zealia Bishop and Lin Carter. Slidith was a monstrous god aroused by blood rituals in Carter's novels about Thongor of Lemuria. In Tremayne's Dracula novels, the dragon god was called Draco. I have combined Carter's and Tremayne's deities into Slidith, the Draconic Adder. An earlier attempt to tie vampires into the Mythos was Henry Kuttner's "The Secret of Karlitz." Pontius Pilate was portrayed as a vampire in "The Dragons of Mons Fractus," a Mythos tale by Richard L. Tierney.

Although many films have created the impression that sunlight was fatal to Dracula, the vampire lord was able to function in the day in Stoker's novels. Sunlight just stripped Dracula of his special powers. Tremayne's prequels were inconsistent with Dracula's ability to walk in daylight. In *The Revenge of Dracula*, there was an aborted ritual that was intended to increase Dracula's powers. In "All Predators Great and Small," I cite this botched ceremony to reconcile Tremayne with Stoker.

Gorcha the Vourdalak is the vampire from Alexis (Aleksey) Tolstoy's "The Family of the Vourdalak." Boris Karloff played this character in *Black Sabbath* (1963).

Another fictional vampire cited in "All Predators Great and Small" was Count Szandor from Paul Féval's The *Vampire Countess* (1856). Féval was also the creator of the Black Coats, a European crime syndicate featured in seven novels. This series was translated into English by Brian Stableford for Black Coat Press. The All-Father and the Marchef are major characters in the Black Coat novels. Féval had the All-Father hide sometimes under the alias of Cavalier Mora. I spelt Mora backwards (Arom) since the name was too similar to Moriarty, Moran and Moreau. Vaguely connected to the Black Coat series is Féval's *John Devil* (1861). Henri de Belcamp was a major character from that novel. He was a consummate liar. Henri's usage of the Serge Dolgorouki alias in "All Predators Great and Small" is meant to be a deception.

In the original English translation of Leblanc's *La Comtesse de Cagliostro*, *The Memoirs of Arsène Lupin* (1925), Serge Dolgorouki's name was inscribed on the back of an 1816 portrait of the first Joséphine Balsamo. The current French text and the new Black Coat Press translation mention the portrait, but omit the exact wording of the inscription on the back. Therefore, Serge Dolgorouki fails to appear in *Arsène Lupin vs. Countess Cagliostro.*

Claude Dupont-Verdier (alias Satanas) is from Louis Feuillade's 1915 silent film serial, *The Vampires.* In the serial, the Vampires are a non-supernatural gang of criminals led by Satanas. His chief underling is a woman called Irma Vep (anagram of "vampire"). Dupont-Verdier's ship originated from William Hope Hodgson's "The Haunted *Jarvee.*"

Certain genealogical references are influenced by Philip José Farmer's *Doc Savage: His Apocalyptic Life* (1973). For example, that book asserted that Carl Peterson (from H. C. "Sapper" McNeile's Bulldog Drummond novels) and Dr. Caber (from Lord Dunsany's Joseph Jorkens series) were the grandsons of Professor Moriarty, the nemesis of Sir Arthur Conan Doyle's Sherlock Holmes. Carl Peterson was very similar to Claud Darrell from Agatha Christie's *The Big Four* (1927).

I have made my own additions to the Professor's list of relatives. Noel Moriarty germinated from the reference to the Professor's younger brother in Doyle's The *Valley of Fear.* My depiction of Noel Moriarty is based on Andrew Lumley (alias Julius Pavia) from John Buchan's *The Power House* (1916). Dominick Damien Moriarty is supposed to be Dominick Medina from Buchan's *The Three Hostages* (1924). Dr. Noel and Madame Zephyrine are from Robert Louis Stevenson's "The Suicide Club." Their offspring, Suzanne Noel, is from *La Residencia.* For the theory that Dr. Noel was the father of Professor Moriarty and his younger brother, see my essay, "The Secret History of Captain Nemo," in *Rick Lai's Secret Histories: Criminal Masterminds* (Altus Press, 2009). The rationale for the existence of Trickie Moriarty can be found in "Professor Moriarty's Other Daughter" in the same volume.

I have incorporated many characters and concepts from the mysteries of L. T. Meade and Robert Eustace. Madame Koluchy, Norman Head and Anna Beringer are from *The Brotherhood of the Seven Kings* (1899). Madame Sara appears in *The Sorceress of the Strand* (1903). Syivia Pence is intended to be Madame Sylvia from "Finger Tips" in *The Oracle of Maddox Street* (1904). Dr. Paul Cato is from *The Sanctuary Club* (1900). Cato's friend, Arthur Spratt, is a testimonial to the cantankerous Lancelot Spratt from Richard Gordon's "Doctor in the House" series.

A. J. Raffles, the gentleman burglar was created by E. W. Hornung, Conan Doyle's brother-in-law. The death of Raffles in the Boer War was depicted in Hornung's "The Knees of the Gods." Jacques Saillard was a painter from a Raffles story, "An Old Flame." The male pseudonym masked the identity of an unnamed manipulative woman. I conflated Saillard with the scheming Isadora Klein from Doyle's "The Adventure of the Three Gables."

In "The Fate of Faustina" and "The Last Laugh," Raffles tangled with Count Corbucci of the Camorra. There was also a famous director of "Spaghetti Westerns" named Sergio Corbucci. Among his innovative Westerns are *Minne-*

sota Clay (1964), *Ringo and His Golden Pistol* (1966), *Django* (1966), The *Mercenary* (1968), *The Great Silence* (1968), and *Compañeros* (1970). I have made an in-joke where Count Corbucci is an author of Westerns that parallel Sergio Corbucci's films. Other Westerns (not directed by Corbucci) alluded to in my collection include *A Fistful of Dollars* (1964), *For a Few Dollars More* (1965), *A Pistol for Ringo* (1965), *The Return of Ringo* (1965), *The Good, The Bad and the Ugly* (1966), *Taste for Killing* (1966), *Yankee* (1966), *The Big Gundown* (1966), *Arizona Colt* (1966, also known as *The Man from Nowhere*), *Vengeance is Mine* (1967), *10,000 Dollars Blood Money* (1967), *A Stranger in Town* (1967), *Day of Anger* (1967), *Face to Face* (1967), *Run, Man, Run* (1968), *Death Sentence* (1968), *Today It's Me...Tomorrow You!* (1968), *If You Meet Sartana...Pray for Your Death* (1968), *Cemetery Without Crosses* (1969), *Sabata* (1969), *Adios, Sabata* (1971), *The Return of Sabata* (1971), *They Called Him Cemetery* (1971) , *The Price of Death* (1971), *Black Killer* (1971), *The Legend of Frenchie King* (1971), *Hannie Caulder* (1971), *The Grand Duel* (1972), *The Fighting Fists of Shanghai Joe* (1972) and *Django Strikes Again* (1987). There are also veiled tributes to two Western novels, Roy Chanslor's *The Ballad of Cat Ballou* (1956) and Louis L'Amour's *The Man Called Noon* (1970). I made some in-jokes about the pseudonyms of Italian directors of Westerns. Some early Westerns directed by Sergio Corbucci and Sergio Leone were released under the respective aliases of Stanley Corbett and Bob Robertson.

The American publisher of Count Corbucci's novels, Pickman and Sons, was an elaboration stemming from "Hell Come Sundown," a supernatural Western by Nancy Collins. The story features *Pickman's Illustrated Serials*. It is probable that this periodical was published by relatives of the artist from H. P. Lovecraft's "Pickman's Model."

Gaston Morrell and Jacques Lefèvre are from the horror film *Bluebeard* (1944). Other horror films tied into my fictional universe are *The Raven* (1936), *The Pit and the Pendulum* (1961), *Dark Intruder* (1965) and *Chamber of Horrors* (1966). The character Eva Relli paid homage to E. Varelli, the enigmatic architect from Dario Argento's *Inferno* (1980).

Fantomas is one of the most influential villains in French literature. His original creators were Pierre Souvestre and Marcel Allain. The aliases of Juan North and Gurn are from the Fantomas series. The alternate identity of the Pallid Mask was not from the original French novels. Instead, it was derived from *The King in Yellow* (1895) by Robert W. Chambers. Boris Yvain, the sculptor suspected of being Bluebeard III, is from the same book. The Royal Palace Hotel, Dr. Biron, the Beltham family and *The Old Fellow* are from the Fantomas novels.

A variety of supporting players and fictional items came from multiple sources. Other master criminals from fiction appearing in these stories include Dr. Antonio Nikola from Guy Boothby's novels, Henry Lakington from

McNeile's Bulldog *Drummond* (1920), Oliver Haddo from Somerset Maugham's *The Magician* (1908), and Horace Dorrington from Arthur Morrison's *The Dorrington Deed Box* (1897). Many characters from Doyle's Sherlock Holmes stories surfaced such as Colonel Moran and Parker (the Garrotter) from "The Adventure of the Empty House, Henry Peters from "The Disappearance of Lady Francis Carfax," John Clay from "The Adventure of the Red- Headed League," Baron Gruner, Shinwell Johnson (Porky Shinwell) and Kitty Winter (Kaitlin de Winter) from "The Adventure of the Illustrious Client," and Mary Holder from "The Adventure of the Beryl Coronet." Louis Caratal is the victim of an unnamed crime syndicate in Doyle's "The Lost Special." Helen Lipsius is meant to be the mysterious Helen who worked for Dr. Lipsius in Arthur Machen's *The Three Imposters* (1895). Jacob Dix is from Fergus Hume's *Hagar of the Pawnshop* (1898). Eric Malbodius was influenced by Dr. Mabuse, an evildoer created by writer Norbert Jacques and later immortalized in film by Fritz Lang. The stolen jewels in "Unseen Stratagems" are from Max Pemberton's "The Ripening Rubies." The Northumberland Hotel Conference of 1895 is from David McDaniel's *The Dagger Affair* (1965). Emanuel Medjora's diphtheria is from Rodrigues Ottolengui's *A Modern Wizard* (1894). Leonard Wolfe is from R. Austin Freeman's "The Aluminium Dagger." Cesarine and Colonel Clay are from Grant Allen's *An African Millionaire* (1897). The identity of Moreau the vivisectionist will be obvious to any reader of *The Island of Doctor Moreau* (1896) by H. G. Wells. The film *La Residencia* briefly mentioned an Avignon inhabitant named Moreau. In the same movie, Madame Fourneau also identified a well-known botanist, whose name sounded like Marguerite Chavain, as a graduate of the boarding school.

French literature was plundered for other characters and places. Anatole Cerral is meant to be the father of the surgeon from Maurice Renard's *The Hands of Orlac* (1920). The Ville-d'Avray asylum was visited by Arsène Lupin in "The Lady with the Hatchet" from Leblanc's *The Eight Stokes of the Clock* (1923). Madame Vabre's boarding house and the Institution Bachelard are from Emile Zola's *Pot Luck* (1882). Madame Delhomme, the bordello owner, is from the same author's *Earth* (1887). Victor Chupin, Arthur Gordon and the Chalusse family are from *The Count's Millions* (1870) and *Baron Trigault's Vengeance* (1870) by Emile Gaboriau. Chupin had earlier appeared as a member of the Mascarot blackmail ring in *Caught in the Net* (1869) and *The Champdoce Mystery* (1869). Van Klopen the fashion designer can be found in the same novels. Although Marga Sandorf is my own creation, her Hungarian uncle is the protagonist of Jules Verne's *Mathias Sandorf* (1885). Other Verne characters were cited. Professor Schultze of Stahlstadt is from *The Begum's Fortune* (1879), while the man aptly named Killer appeared in *The Barsac Mission* (1919). Some English translations of *The Begum's Fortune* alter Schultze's surname to Schultz. Prompted by Jean-Marc and Randy Lofficier's "The Death of Countess Cagliostro," I also included the protagonists of Verne's *César Cascabel* (1890, also published as *Caesar Cascabel*). Ballmeyer and Stangerson's *Dissociation of Matter Through Electricity* come from Gaston Leroux's *The Mystery of the Yellow Room* (1907). Fritz Kramm is from the Doctor Cornelius stories (1912-13) by Gustave Le Rouge. The story of Countess Yalta can be found in Fortune du Boisgobey's *The Lost Casket* (1880, also known as *The Severed Hand*). Count Bielowsky is from Pierre Benoit's *Atlantida* (1919). Justin Ganimard is a recurring character in the Arsène Lupin series.

Benoit's novel dealt with a colony of Atlantis in the Hoggar mountains. While revising "The Last Test" for Adolphe de Castro, H. P. Lovecraft transformed this Hoggar colony into the residence of Surama, an Atlantean sorcerer. Lovecraft also created a sanctuary for felines in "The Cats of Ulthar."

Even though Thuggee has a basis in historical reality, the version presented in my stories is drawn from fictional presentations. Achmet Genghis Khan and the Warrender alias were lifted from Sir Arthur Conan Doyle's "Uncle Jeremy's Household." The name Sharita came from Gardner Fox's *Woman of Kali* (1954). Thuggee really has nothing to do with Nagas, the snake creatures of Asian myth. However, Emilio Salgari's Sandokan novels postulated such a connection. Adana is the Snake Mother from A. Merritt's *The Face in the Abyss* (1931). Sithra and Ixcatl are from Richard L. Tierney's "The Dragons of Mons Fractus." They also appear in *Against the Prince of Hell* (1983), a novel co-written by Tierney with David C. Smith.

Kung Fu movies from Hong Kong influenced "The Last Vendetta." These films include *The Flying Guillotine* (1975), *The Master of the Flying Guillotine* (1975), *The Flying Guillotine 2* (1978), *The 36th Chamber of Shaolin* (1978) and *Flag of Iron* (1980). Steel-Skin Kung Fu (cited in "Corridors of Deceit") is from *Shaolin Martial Arts* (1974).

The various Japanese characters mentioned in "Unseen Stratagems" are from film, television and manga. The unnamed woman in a white kimono from "The Last Vendetta" resulted from seeing the film version of Lady Snowblood, another manga character. The legend concerning the actual Yagyu family of Japan (cited in the same story) comes from the film *The Yagyu Conspiracy* (1978). A variant history of the Yagyu family involving supernatural demons was depicted in *Samurai Reincarnation* (1981). This alternate history is alluded to in "Kingdom of the Blind." Both Yagyu films were directed by Kinji Fukasaku amd starred Sonny Chiba. Hattori Hanzo III and Tarao Hanzo are characters played by Chiba in *Shadow Warriors*, a Japanese TV series from the 1980s. The sword makers Koutatsu and Senzo are from the film *Zatoichi's Cane-Sword* (1967).

Associating Japanese characters with Countess Cagliostro and other Leblanc characters is not an original idea. There is a Japanese character, Lupin III, depicted as the grandson of Arsène Lupin. In a famous animated Lupin III film, *The Castle of Cagliostro* (1979), a golden ram was revealed to be the family crest of the Cagliostro family. The same film had a fictional Duchy of Cagliostro that resembled the Duchy of Strackenz from George MacDonald Fraser's *Royal Flash* (1970).

A 1978 episode of the animated *Lupin III* TV series, "The Case of the Risible Dirigible," had a family named Gabriel owning a jewel called "Dracula's Tear." This gem is the basis for Akivasha's Tear (named after a vampire created by Robert E. Howard in "The Hour of the Dragon"). Other borrowings from Howard include the references to Vathelos ("Black Colossus") and Agnes de la Fere ("The Sword Woman").

The reference in "Consequences of a Funeral" to Durnais, a lawyer, was sparked by Cole Porter's musical, *Can-Can*.

In *Doc Ardan: City of Gold and Lepers* (Black Coat Press, 2004), Jean-Marc and Randy Lofficier adapted a 1928 French pulp novel by Guy d'Armen into a thinly disguised exploit of Sax Rohmer's Fu Manchu. The Asian mastermind of this novel adopted the alias of Natas ("Satan" spelt backwards). In "The Last Vendetta," I also portrayed Natas in a Rohmer-like manner. For example, Kegan Van Roon is from Rohmer's *The Return of Dr. Fu Manchu* (1916). Van Roon's publisher, Golden Goblin Press, is from Robert E. Howard's "The Black Stone" and "The Thing on the Roof."

Many fictional painters surfaced in my stories. Joseph Bridau is from Balzac's Human Comedy series. Hallward was the artist in Oscar Wilde's *The Picture of Dorian Gray* (1890). Coswell was the name signed on Josette's portrait from *Dark Shadows*, the classic soap opera of the 1960's and 1970's. The unicorn symbol on Irina's umbrella was prompted by a reference to such a horned horse on *Dark Shadows*.

Sisters of the Shadows is a sequel of sorts to my Revenant stories collected in *Shadows of the Opera* (Black Coat Press, 2013). In the Revenant tales, the symbol "V" was cut into various criminals by the Revenant. The letter was said to stand for "*voleur*," the French term for thief. The feminine form of "*voleur*" is "*voleuse*," which is used in the climax of "The Lady of the Black Gloves." The death of Théophraste Lupin (mentioned in "The Diary of Desolation" and "The Lady in the Black Gloves") will eventually be told in detail in the Revenant series.

Six stories in this collection appeared earlier in the *Tales of the Shadowmen* anthologies edited by Jean-Marc and Randy Lofficier for Black Coat Press:

1) "The Last Vendetta" (Vol. 1, 2005)
2) "Dr. Cerral's Patient" (Vol. 2, 2006)
3) "The Lady in the Black Gloves" (Vol. 3, 2007)
4) "Corridors of Deceit" (Vol. 4, 2008)
5) "All Predators Great and Small (Vol. 5. 2009)
6) "Incident in the Boer War" (Vol. 6, 2010).

"Urania's Babysitter" was first published in *Farmerphile* #12 (April 2008), a fanzine devoted to the works of Philip José Farmer, the author of such important works as *Escape from Loki* (1991). The name of two characters in "Urania's Babysitter," Urania's half-sister and governess, were modified slightly in the new version.

All of the old stories have undergone revisions to varying degrees. The major events of each tale weren't changed, but some alterations were done to insure continuity. For example, "The Last Vendetta" originally had Joséphine Balsamo living in America from 1894 to 1900. Since I now have her active in Europe during 1896-97, I had to make necessary adjustments to the text. There was also the matter of Joséphine's sister and Marga Sandorf. Neither had existed when I wrote the original version of "The Last Vendetta." "All Predators Great and Small" was revised in the respective passages surrounding Dracula's origins and Frankenhausen's earlier destruction.

"The Lady in the Black Gloves" has Victoire Chupin describing to her daughter the 1880 death of Joséphine Balasmo's mother (alias "Gloria Scot"). This event was depicted in "The Necklace of the Crime Empress" from *Shadows of the Opera*.

There will be at least one more volume of stories about Irina, Joséphine, Sabine, Blythe and Marga.

Cast of Characters

Character (In Alphabetical Order) - Source

Absalom, Sabine (see Sabine, Balsamo)
Adana - Abraham Merritt
Aguilar - Giuseppe Mangione and Warren Garfield
Aguirre - Sergio Corbucci, Mario Armendola, Bruno Corbucci and Victoriano Petrillini
Akivasha - Robert E. Howard
All-Father (see Arom, Cavalier)
Alucard, Countess (see Von Frankenhausen, Eugenia)
Antinea - Pierre Benoit
Arom, Cavalier - Paul Féval
Baian, Dr. - Shotaro Ikenami
Bailey, Leeman ("Lee") - David Haft, Burt Kennedy, Ian Quicke and Bob Richards
Ballmeyer - Gaston Leroux
Balsamo, José Alejandro - Miguel Morayta
Balsamo, Joseph - Alexandre Dumas (based on history)
Balsamo, Joséphine (I) - Maurice Leblanc
Balsamo, Joséphine (II) - Maurice Leblanc
Balsamo, Joséphine (III) -Maurice Leblanc
Balsamo, Lorenza - Alexandre Dumas
Balsamo, Sabine - Rick Lai
Balsamo, Sara (see Sara, Madame)
Balsamo, Sharita - Rick Lai
Belcamp, Henri de - Paul Féval
Beltham, General - Pierre Souvestre and Marcel Allain
Beltham, Lady - Pierre Souvestre and Marcel Allain
Bennet, Manny - Dario Argento, Claude Desailly and Robert Hossein
Beringer, Anna - L. T. Meade and Robert Eustace
Bielowsky, Count - Pierre Benoit
Biron, Dr.- Pierre Souvestre and Marcel Allain
Black Coats - Paul Féval
Black Indian - Renato Izzo and Gianfranco Parolini
Black Sashes - Rick Lai
Black Skirts - Rick Lai
Blake, Jillian - Philip José Farmer
Bookkeeper - Cheh Chang and Kuang Ni
Bridau, Joseph - Honoré de Balzac

Brotherhood of the Seven Kings - L. T. Meade and Robert Eustace
Brown, Angel-Face - Alfonso Balcázar and Duccio Tessari
Bugoff, Lily - Philip José Farmer
Burnwell, Sir George - Arthur Conan Doyle
Butcher of Baltimore - Stephen Kandel and Ray Russell
Caber, Claud - H. C. McNeile and Agatha Christie
Caber, James - Lord Dunsany
Caber, Urania - Philip José Farmer
Cagliostro, Count (see Balsamo, Joseph)
Cagliostro, Countess (see Balsamo, Joséphine (I thru III))
Caine, Corben - Dario Argento, Claude Desailly and Robert Hossein
Caoutchouc, Cesarine - Allen, Grant
Caratal, Louis - Arthur Conan Doyle
Carineaux, Duc of - Pierre Gendron, Arnold Phillips and Werner H. Furst
Cascabel, César - Jules Verne
Cash, Death-Sentence - Mario Lanfranchi
Cato, Paul - L. T. Meade and Robert Eustace
Cerral, Anatole - Based on Maurice Renard
Chalusse, Hermine - Emile Gaboriau
Champdoce family - Emile Gaboriau
Chavain, Marguerite - Narciso Ibañez Serrador and Juan Tébar
Chupin, Irene (see Tupin, Irene)
Chupin, Polyte - Emile Gaboriau
Chupin, Victoire - Maurice Leblanc
Chupin, Victor - Emile Gaboriau
Clay, Colonel - Allen, Grant
Clay, John - Arthur Conan Doyle
Clayton, Gruesome - Philip José Farmer
Connal, Corporal- E. W. Hornung
Corbett, Stanley (see Corbucci, Salvatore)
Corbucci, Catarina (see Koluchy, Catrarina)
Corbucci, Carolina - Rick Lai
Corbucci, Salvatore - E. W. Hornung
Coswell - Sam Hall, Gordon Russell and Violet Welles
Coyatier, Jean-Francois -Paul Féval
Coyatier, Orianne - Rick Lai
Daigoro - Kazuo Koike and Goseki Kojima
d'Andresy, Clarisse - Maurice Leblanc
d'Andresy, Henriette - Maurice Leblanc
d'Andresy, Maurice - Based on Maurice Leblanc
d'Andresy, Raoul (see Lupin, Arsène)
Daphne, Sister - Rick Lai
D'Arcourt, Etienne Cressy Raimond - Gardner Fox

de la Fere, Agnes - Robert E. Howard
Delhomme, Madame - Emile Zola
Dickson, Patrick - Carlo Alberto Alfieri, Mario Caiano and Fabrizio Trifone Trecca
Dix, Jacob - Fergus Hume
Djanko, Ignacz - Sergio Corbucci, Bruno Corbucci and Franco Rosetti
Dolgorouki, Serge (see Belcamp, Henri de)
Dorrington, Horace - Arthur Morrison
Dracula, Szandra (see Von Frankenhausen, Eugenia)
Dracula, Vlad - Bram Stoker and Peter Tremayne
Dreux-Soubise, Count de - Maurice Leblanc
Dreux-Soubise, Countess de - Maurice Leblanc
Dupin, C. Auguste - Edgar Allan Poe
Dupont-Verdier, Claude Gabriel - Louis Feuillade
Durnais, Maître -Cole Porter
Durward family- Brian Clemens
Einem, Hildegarde - Miguel Morayta
Faber, Lord - Max Pemberton
Faustina - E. W. Hornung
Fenix, Countess de (see Balsamo, Joséphine (III))
Forest, John - Ernesto Gastaldi, Luciano Martino and Sergio Martino
Fourneau, Berenice - Rick Lai
Fourneau, Louis ("Luis") - Narciso Ibañez Serrador and Juan Tébar
Fourneau, Philippe - Rick Lai
Fourneau, Natalie - Narciso Ibañez Serrador and Juan Tébar
Gabriel family - Yutaka Kaneko
Ganimard, Justin - Maurice Leblanc
Gentlemen of the Night - Paul Féval
Gonzales, Jefferson - Adriano Bolzoni and Franco Rossetti
Gorcha the Voudarlark - Alexis Tolstoy
Gordon, Arthur - Emile Gaboriau
Gordon, John - Sergio Corbucci, Mario Armendola, Bruno Corbucci and Victoriano Petrillini
Gordon, Wilkie - Emil Gaboriau
Gosart, Clio (see Balsamo, Joséphine (III))
Great Old Ones - H. P. Lovecraft
Great Vampire (see Dracula, Vlad)
Grévin, Mathilde - Narciso Ibañez Serrador and Juan Tébar
Grévin, Teresa - Narciso Ibañez Serrador and Juan Tébar
Grost - Brian Clemens
Gruner, Baron - Arthur Conan Doyle
Gunsight Eyes - Renato Izzo and Gianfranco Parolini
Gurn, Dirk (see North, Juan)

Haddo, Oliver - Somerset Maugham
Hallward, Basil - Oscar Wilde
Hattori Hanzo III - Sonny Chiba
Head, Norman - L. T. Meade and Robert Eustace
Holder, Alexander - Arthur Conan Doyle
Holder, John - Arthur Conan Doyle
Holder, Mary - Arthur Conan Doyle
Hong Chen - Guy d'Armen
Huan Tsung Chao - Sax Rohmer
Indian - Luciano Vincenzoni and Sergio Leone
Ixcatl - Richard L. Tierney and David C. Snith
Juana, Maricruz (Mijanou) - Sergio Corbucci, Bruno Corbucci, Franco Rosetti and Franco Fogagnolo
Karlitz, Baron - Henry Kuttner
Khan, Achmet Genghis - Arthur Conan Doyle
Killer, Harry - Jules Verne
King, Louise - Eduardo Manzanos Brochero
Klein, Isadora - Arthur Conan Doyle
Klein, Otto - Based on Arthur Conan Doyle
Koluchy, Catarina - L. T. Meade and Robert Eustace
Koutatsu - Ryôzô Kasahara, Kan Shimosawa
Kramm, Fritz - Gustave Le Rouge
Lakington, Henry - H. C. McNeile
Lanky Gunman -Victor Auz and Tonnio Valeri
Lecoq - Emile Gaboriau
Leferve, Jacques - Pierre Gendron, Arnold Phillips and Werner H. Furst
LeFrank, Xaviera (see Xavier, Francine)
Legacy - Rick Lai
Leonard- Maurice Leblanc
Lipsius, Helen - Arthur Machen
Loridan, Charles Maurice - Rick Lai
Lupin, Arsène - Maurice Leblanc
Lupin, Théophraste - Maurice Leblanc
Mackenzie, Inspector - E. W. Hornung
Malaki, Professor - Barre Lyndon
Malbodius, Eric Heinz - Based on Norbert Jacques
Manders, Harry - E. W. Hornung
Marchef (see Coyatier, Jean-Francois)
Mascarot, Baptiste - Emile Gaboriau
Mauberge, Eric (see Malbodius, Eric Heinz)
Medina, Dominick - John Buchan
Medina, Sebastian - Richard Matheson
Medjora, Emanuel - Rodriguez Ottolengui

Moran, Frank - Dario Argento and Tonino Cervi
Moran, Sebastian - Arthur Conan Doyle
Moreau, Dr. - H. G. Wells
Moreau, Rochelle - Based on Narciso Ibañez Serrador and Juan Tébar
Moriarty, Catarina (see Koluchy, Catarina)
Moriarty, Dominick Damien (see Medina, Dominick)
Moriarty, James -Arthur Conan Doyle
Moriarty, Noel - Arthur Conan Doyle and John Buchan
Moriarty, Trickie- Based on Laurie King
Morrell, Gaston - Pierre Gendron, Arnold Phillips and Werner H. Furst
Mute Shootist - Sergio Corbucci, Mario Armendola, Bruno Corbucci and
Victoriano Petrillini
Natas - Guy d'Armen
Neptune Society - Based on Henry Sharp and John W. Bloch
Nevermore, Milady - Based on Alexandre Dumas and Edgar Allan Poe
Nightingale Hierarchy - Based on David McDaniel
Nikola, Antonio - Guy Boothby
Nine Fingers - Renato Izzo and Gianfranco Parolini
Noel, Dr. - Robert Louis Stevenson
Noel, Suzanne - Narciso Ibañez Serrador and Juan Tébar
North, Juan - Pierre Souvestre and Marcel Allain
North, Maude - Pierre Souvestre and Marcel Allain
Order of the Serpent Heart - H. Rider Haggard
Pallid Mask (see North, Juan)
Parker, Estascy
Parker, Larry - Arthur Conan Doyle
Parker, Purity - Rick Lai
Pavia, Julius (see Moriarty, Noel)
Pegler, Coleen - Louis L'Amour
Peisser, Anna - Miguel Morayta
Peisser, Ricardo - Miguel Morayta
Pence, Sylvia - Lt. Meade and Robert Eustace
Peters, Henry (I) - Arthur Conan Doyle
Peters, Henry (II) (see Lakington, Henry)
Peterson the Swede - Sergio Corbucci
Pickman Family- H. P. Lovecraft and Nancy Collins
Pienaar, Hendrika (see North, Maude)
Prinn, Ludvig - Robert Bloch
Putine, Irina (see Tupin, Irene)
Queen of the Outlaws - Roy Chanslor
Raffles, Arthur J.- E. W. Hornung
Ramirez - Luciano Vincenzoni and Sergio Leone
Red Hand - Gustave Le Rouge

Red Scarf Gang - Sergio Corbucci, Bruno Corbucci and Franco Rosetti
Relli, Eva - Based on Dario Argento and Daria Nicolodi
Reloj, Gordo - Ernesto Gastaldi, Lewis Ciannelli, Michele Lupo and Luciano Martino
Reloj, Pilar - Giuseppe Mangione and Warren Garfield
Robertson, Bob - Sergio Leone
Rogers, Wilmot - Dario Argento, Claude Desailly and Robert Hossein
Roget, Marie - Poe, Edgar Allan
Rojo Brothers - Víctor Andrés Catena, Jaimie Comas Gil and Sergio Leone
Routh, Gabrielle - Based on John Buchan
Saillard, Jacques - E. W. Hornung
Salazar, Isadora (see Klein, Isadora)
Saladin -Paul Féval
Sanchez, Manuel- Sergio Sollima and Sergio Donati
Sandorf, Aristide Olowsky - Franco Reggiani and Nello Rossati
Sandorf, Count - Jules Verne
Sandorf, Marga - Rick Lai
Santillana, General - Pompeo De Angelis and Sergio Sollima
Sara, Madame - L. T. Meade and Robert Eustace
Sartana, Ace - Renato Izzo and Gianfranco Parolini
Satanas (see Dupont-Verdier, Claude Gabriel)
Saxon, Adam - Ernesto Gastaldi
Schultze, Professor - Jules Verne
Scot, Gloria (see Balsamo, Joséphine (II))
Senzo - Ryôzô Kasahara, Kan Shimosawa
Set - Robert E. Howard
Sharita - Gardner Fox
Shinwell, Porky - Arthur Conan Doyle
Silver, Jake (see Sartana, Ace)
Sisters of the Night - Bram Stoker
Sithra - Richard L.Tierney and David C. Smith
Skimmel, Colonel - Sergio Sollima and Sergio Donati
Skimmel, Heidi - Rick Lai
Slidith -Lin Carter
Snowblood, Lady - Kazuo Uemura and Kazuo Koike
Spode, Dorcas - Based on P. G. Wodehouse
Spratt, Arthur - Based on Richard Gordon
Stedor, Martin - Based on Ladislas Fodor
Stefano - E. W. Hornung
Stepphun, Lothaire (see Lupin, Théophraste)
Strangerson, Professor - Gaston Leroux
Sumeru Yuki - Based on Sax Rohmer
Surama - H. P. Lovecraft and Adolphe de Castro

Szandor, Count -Paul Féval
Tarao Hanzo - Sonny Chiba
Ten Killers of the Underworld - Cheh Chang and Kuang Ni
Thompson, Captain - William Hope Hodgson
Trevor, Rosette -Based on Guy Boothby
Tupin, Irene - Narciso Ibañez Serrador and Juan Tébar
Tupin, Victoire (see Chupin, Victoire)
Vadarasse, Cornelia - Jules Verne
Valencia, Raquel- Based on Walter Gibson
Undertaker (see Djanko, Ignacz)
Unnamed Japanese Woman (see Snowblood, Lady)
Vabre, Madame - Emile Zola
Valgeneuse, Felina de - Based on Frédéric Soulié and Alexandre Dumas
Van Klopen - Emile Gaboriau
Van Roon, Keegan - Sax Rohmer
Vathelos - Robert E. Howard
Vep, Irma - Louis Feuillade
Vollin, Roger - Based on David Boehm
Von Frankenhausen, Eugenia - Miguel Morayta
Von Frankenhausen, Kurt- Based on Miguel Morayta
Von Frankenhausen, Siegfried - Miguel Morayta
Von Herder, Julius - Arthur Conan Doyle
Von Schulenberg, Baron -Sergio Sollima and Sergio Donati
Von Schulenberg, Fritz - Rick Lai
Von Schulenberg, Ivonne - Rick Lai
Von Schulenberg, Sigi - Rick Lai
Warrender, Sarah (see Sara, Madame)
Washburn, John - Sergio Corbucci
Washburn, Kate - Rick Lai
Washburn, Mr. (John's brother) - Luciano Vincenzoni
Webb, Hamish - Luigi Angelo and Carlo Croccolo
White Priest - Kung Fu folklore
Winter, Kaitlin de (see Winter, Kitty)
Winter, Kitty - Arthur Conan Doyle
Wolfe, Leonard - Freeeman, R. Austin
Xavier, Francine - Based on Robert E. Howard
Yalta, Countess - Fortune du Boisgobey
Yankee Whistler - Alberto Silvestri and Tinto Brass
Yiggurath - H. P. Lovecraft, Zealia Bishop and Robert Bloch
Yvain, Boris - Robert W. Chambers
Zatoichi- Kan Shimozawa
Zephyrine, Madame - Robert Louis Stevenson

SF & FANTASY

Alphonse Allais. *The Adventures of Captain Cap*
Henri Allorge. *The Great Cataclysm*
Guy d'Armen. *Doc Ardan: The City of Gold and Lepers*
G.-J. Arnaud. *The Ice Company*
Charles Asselineau. *The Double Life*
Cyprien Bérard. *The Vampire Lord Ruthwen*
Aloysius Bertrand. *Gaspard de la Nuit*
Richard Bessière. *The Gardens of the Apocalypse*
Albert Bleunard. *Ever Smaller*
Félix Bodin. *The Novel of the Future*
Louis Boussenard. *Monsieur Synthesis*
Alphonse Brown. *City of Glass; The Conquest of the Air*
Emile Calvet. *In a Thousand Years*
André Caroff. *The Terror of Madame Atomos; Miss Atomos; The Return of Madame Atomos; The Mistake of Madame Atomos; The Monsters of Madame Atomos; The Revenge of Madame Atomos; The Resurrection of Madame Atomos*
Félicien Champsaur. *The Human Arrow; Ouha, King of the Apes; Pharaoh's Wife*
Didier de Chousy. *Ignis*
Jules Claretie. *Obsession*
Michel Corday. *The Eternal Flame*
Captain Danrit. *Undersea Odyssey*
C. I. Defontenay. *Star (Psi Cassiopeia)*
Charles Derennes. *The People of the Pole*
Georges Dodds (anthologist). *The Missing Link*
Harry Dickson. *The Heir of Dracula*
Jules Dornay. *Lord Ruthven Begins*
Alfred Driou. *The Adventures of a Parisian Aeronaut*
Sâr Dubnotal *vs. Jack the Ripper*
Alexandre Dumas. *The Return of Lord Ruthven*
Renée Dunan. *Baal*
J.-C. Dunyach. *The Night Orchid; The Thieves of Silence*
Henri Duvernois. *The Man Who Found Himself*
Achille Eyraud. *Voyage to Venus*
Henri Falk. *The Age of Lead*
Paul Féval. *Anne of the Isles; Knightshade; Revenants; Vampire City; The Vampire Countess; The Wandering Jew's Daughter*
Paul Féval, *fils. Felifax, the Tiger-Man*
Charles de Fieux. *Lamékis*
Arnould Galopin. *Doctor Omega; Doctor Omega and the Shadowmen* (anthology)
Judith Gautier. *Isoline and the Serpent-Flower*
Léon Gozlan. *The Vampire of the Val-de-Grâce*
G.L. Gick. *Harry Dickson and the Werewolf of Rutherford Grange*
Edmond Haraucourt. *Illusions of Immortality*
Nathalie Henneberg. *The Green Gods*
V. Hugo, P. Foucher & P. Meurice. *The Hunchback of Notre-Dame*
Romain d'Huissier. *Hexagon: Dark Matter*

Michel Jeury. *Chronolysis*
Gustave Kahn. *The Tale of Gold and Silence*
Gérard Klein. *The Mote in Time's Eye*
Fernand Kolney. *Love in 5000 Years*
Paul Lacroix. *Danse Macabre*
Louis-Guillaume de La Follie. *The Unpretentious Philosopher*
Jean de La Hire. *Enter the Nyctalope; The Nyctalope on Mars; The Nyctalope vs. Lucifer; The Nyctalope Steps In; Night of the Nyctalope; The Return of the Nyctalope; The Fiery Wheel*
Etienne-Léon de Lamothe-Langon. *The Virgin Vampire*
André Laurie. *Spiridon*
Gabriel de Lautrec. *The Vengeance of the Oval Portrait*
Alain le Drimeur. *The Future City*
Georges Le Faure & Henri de Graffigny. *The Extraordinary Adventures of a Russian Scientist Across the Solar System* (2 vols.)
Gustave Le Rouge. *The Vampires of Mars; The Dominion of the World* (w/Gustave Guitton) (4 vols.)
Jules Lermina. *Mysteryville; Panic in Paris; To-Ho and the Gold Destroyers; The Secret of Zippelius*
André Lichtenberger. *The Centaurs; The Children of the Crab*
Jean-Marc & Randy Lofficier. *Edgar Allan Poe on Mars; The Katrina Protocol; Pacifica; Robonocchio; The Return of the Nyctalope; Tales of the Shadowmen 1-9*
Xavier Mauméjean. *The League of Heroes*
Joseph Méry. *The Tower of Destiny*
Hippolyte Mettais. *The Year 5865*
Louise Michel. *The Human Microbes; The New World*
Tony Moilin. *Paris in the Year 2000*
José Moselli. *Illa's End*
John-Antoine Nau. *Enemy Force*
Marie Nizet. *Captain Vampire*
C. Nodier, A. Beraud & Toussaint-Merle. *Frankenstein*
Henri de Parville. *An Inhabitant of the Planet Mars*
Gaston de Pawlowski. *Journey to the Land of the 4th Dimension*
Georges Pellerin. *The World in 2000 Years*
Ernest Pérochon. *The Frenetic People*
Pierre Pelot. *The Child Who Walked on the Sky*
J. Polidori, C. Nodier, E. Scribe. *Lord Ruthven the Vampire*
P.-A. Ponson du Terrail. *The Vampire and the Devil's Son; The Immortal Woman*
Edgar Quinet. *Ahasuerus*
Henri de Régnier. *A Surfeit of Mirrors*
Maurice Renard. *The Blue Peril; Doctor Lerne; The Doctored Man; A Man Among the Microbes; The Master of Light*
Jules Rengade. *Voyage Beneath the Waves*
Jean Richepin. *The Wing; The Crazy Corner*
Albert Robida. *The Adventures of Saturnin Farandoul; The Clock of the Centuries; Chalet in the Sky; The Electric Life*

J.-H. Rosny Aîné. *Helgvor of the Blue River; The Givreuse Enigma; The Mysterious Force; The Navigators of Space; Vamireh; The World of the Variants; The Young Vampire*

Marcel Rouff. *Journey to the Inverted World*

Han Ryner. *The Superhumans*

Brian Stableford. *The New Faust at the Tragicomique;The Empire of the Necromancers (The Shadow of Frankenstein; Frankenstein and the Vampire Countess; Frankenstein in London); Sherlock Holmes & The Vampires of Eternity; The Stones of Camelot; The Wayward Muse.* (anthologist) *The Germans on Venus; News from the Moon; The Supreme Progress; The World Above the World; Nemoville; Investigations of the Future*

Jacques Spitz. *The Eye of Purgatory*

Kurt Steiner. *Ortog*

Eugène Thébault. *Radio-Terror*

C.-F. Tiphaigne de La Roche. *Amilec*

Théo Varlet. *The Golden Rock. The Xenobiotic Invasion; The Castaways of Eros; Timeslip Troopers* (w/André Blandin); *The Martian Epic* (w/Octave Joncquel)

Paul Vibert. *The Mysterious Fluid*

Villiers de l'Isle-Adam. *The Scaffold; The Vampire Soul*

Philippe Ward. *Artahe*

Philippe Ward & Sylvie Miller. *The Song of Montségur*

MYSTERIES & THRILLERS

M. Allain & P. Souvestre. *The Daughter of Fantômas*

A. Anicet-Bourgeois, Lucien Dabril. *Rocambole*

A. Bernède. *Belphegor; Judex* (w/Louis Feuillade); *The Return of Judex* (w/Louis Feuillade); *The Shadow of Judex*

A. Bisson & G. Livet. *Nick Carter vs. Fantômas*

V. Darlay & H. de Gorsse. *Arsène Lupin vs. Sherlock Holmes: The Stage Play*

Séamas Duffy. *Sherlock Holmes in Paris*

Paul Féval. *Gentlemen of the Night; John Devil; The Black Coats ('Salem Street; The Invisible Weapon; The Parisian Jungle; The Companions of the Treasure; Heart of Steel; The Cadet Gang; The Sword-Swallower)*

Emile Gaboriau. *Monsieur Lecoq*

Goron & Emile Gautier. *Spawn of the Penitentiary*

Rick Lai. *Shadows of the Opera: Retribution in Blood; Sisters of the Shadow: The Curse of Cagliostro*

Steve Leadley. *Sherlock Holmes: The Circle of Blood*

Maurice Leblanc. *Arsène Lupin vs. Countess Cagliostro; Arsène Lupin vs. Sherlock Holmes (The Blonde Phantom; The Hollow Needle); The Many Faces of Arsène Lupin*

Gaston Leroux. *Chéri-Bibi; The Phantom of the Opera; Rouletabille & the Mystery of the Yellow Room; Rouletabille at Krupp's*

Richard Marsh. *The Complete Adventures of Judith Lee*

William Patrick Maynard. *The Terror of Fu Manchu; The Destiny of Fu Manchu*

Frank J. Morlock. *Sherlock Holmes: The Grand Horizontals; Sherlock Holmes vs Jack the Ripper*

Antonin Reschal. *The Adventures of Miss Boston*

P. de Wattyne & Y. Walter. *Sherlock Holmes vs. Fantômas*

David White. *Fantômas in America*
Pierre Yrondy. *The Adventures of Thérèse Arnaud*

SCREENPLAYS

Mike Baron. *The Iron Triangle*
Emma Bull & Will Shetterly. *Nightspeeder; War for the Oaks*
Gerry Conway & Roy Thomas. *Doc Dynamo*
Steve Englehart. *Majorca*
James Hudnall. *The Devastator*
Jean-Marc & Randy Lofficier. *Royal Flush*
J.-M. & R. Lofficier & Marc Agapit. *Despair*
J.-M. & R. Lofficier & Joël Houssin. *City*
Andrew Paquette. *Peripheral Vision*
Robert L. Robinson, Jr. *Judex*
R. Thomas, J. Hendler & L. Sprague de Camp. *Rivers of Time*

NON-FICTION

Stephen R. Bissette. *Blur 1-5. Green Mountain Cinema 1; Teen Angels*
Win Scott Eckert. *Crossovers* (2 vols.)
Jean-Marc & Randy Lofficier. *Shadowmen* (2 vols.)
Randy Lofficier. *Over Here*

ART BOOKS

Jean-Pierre Normand. *Science Fiction Illustrations*
Raven Okeefe. *Raven's L'il Critters; Rave's Faves*
Randy Lofficier & Raven Okeefe. *If Your Possum Go Daylight...*
Daniele Serra. *Illusions*

HEXAGON COMICS

Franco Frescura & Luciano Bernasconi. *Wampus*
Franco Frescura & Giorgio Trevisan. *CLASH*
L. Bernasconi, J.-M. Lofficier & Juan Roncagliolo Berger. *Phenix*
Claude Legrand, J.-M. Lofficier & L. Bernasconi. *Kabur*
Franco Oneta. *Zembla*
L. Buffolente, Lofficier & J.-J. Dzialowski. *Strangers: Homicron*
Danilo Grossi. *Strangers: Jaydee*
Claude Legrand & Luciano Bernasconi. *Strangers: Starlock*